TO WHOM MUCH IS GIVEN

A novel

BY

MAURICE M. GRAY, JR.

WRITE THE VISION

NOTE: Sale of this book without a front cover may be unauthorized. If this book was purchased without a cover, it may have been reported to the publisher as "unsold or destroyed." Neither the author nor the publisher may have received payment for the sale of this book.

This novel is a work of fiction. Any resemblance to real people, living or dead, actual events, establishments, organizations and/or locales is intended to give the fiction a sense of reality and authenticity. Other names, characters, places and incidents are products of the author's imagination.

Published by Write The Vision
Box 13083 Wilmington, DE 19850
(302) 765-8709
E-mail: writevision2000@yahoo.com
Web site: www.writethevision.biz
Library Of Congress Control Number: 2006902420

Gray, Maurice M, Jr.
    To Whom Much Is Given by Maurice M. Gray, Jr.- 4th ed

ISBN: 0-9700514-6-8

Fifth Printing- February 2015

Acknowledgements

We do nothing in this world by ourselves; everybody needs a helping hand at some point, and I am grateful for the many people who have extended theirs to me. Thank you all for everything you've done, are doing and continue to do that blesses my life so richly. If I missed anyone, charge it to my head and not my heart.

God- For EVERYTHING.

My father Maurice M. Gray, Sr., for understanding why I just gotta write.

My sister Regina Gray, for proofreading this book a few chapters at a time, and for threatening to lock me in my room until I finished.

My Uncle Joe and Aunt Jackie and all my cousins for relentlessly promoting my books- thanks y'all!

My other proofreaders Linda Beed (also a threatener!), Natalie Mangham, Nichole Christopoulos (your time is coming!) and Terrance Johnson, thanks for your feedback and your honesty.

My pastor, Rev. Silvester Scott Beaman and the Bethel African Methodist Episcopal Church family, for supporting me unconditionally and for bragging about me to anyone who will listen.

Patricia Haley-Glass, for teaching me how to publish my own works and for introducing me to so many of the authors I know now (Jacquelin Thomas, Victoria Christopher Murray, Marni Williams and Terrance Johnson just to name a few).

My first "road dawgs," the Writers Group: Jamellah Ellis, Kevin Johnson and Gloria Thomas Anderson. The signings and workshops we did together were wonderful! Keep on writing for Him.

My brothers of Kappa Alpha Psi Fraternity, Inc., who always encourage me to achieve even greater things with each new accomplishment

Bernard and Linda Beed, thank you for your hospitality during my first visit to Seattle. Linda, thank you for ruthlessly editing any manuscript I push at you (wow, who taught you how to do that?)

My fellow authors Sharon Ewell Foster, Kendra Norman-Bellamy and Pat G'orge-Walker for your godly support and good humor from the start. Jeanette Hill, you're more than just a playwright. Get to novelizing already!

Elissa Gabrielle and my fellow contributors to The Soul Of A Man anthology. Soul Brothers, I've enjoyed getting to know you all. Let's continue to be about our Father's business as we do The Soul Of A Man II.

Wanda B. Campbell and my fellow contributors to the Home Again anthology. We have a winner! I'm glad Wanda talked me into it.

Isaiah David Paul and K.L. Belvin, thanks for putting in such hard work on Soldiers Of The Cross. Let's keep it moving

Dedication

I dedicate this book to those who have gone on before me.

Rev. Theodore A. Gray- Pop-Pop, you always thought I could do no wrong. Thank you for spoiling me rotten as a child, and for bragging about my slightest accomplishments. I wish you were here to share my joy, but I know you're bragging about your grandson the author to anyone in Heaven who will listen!

Mrs. Cecil S. Gray- Mom-Mom, I always thought that if you'd had the opportunity to go to college, you would've been somebody's CEO. You encouraged me in anything I set my mind to- if I said I wanted to start a flea circus, you'd have given me money to buy the fleas! Thank you for encouraging all of us grandchildren to be entrepreneurs.

Miss Elva Green- Grandmother, you were bedridden for as long as I knew you, but you always seemed so alive when we visited. Thank you for always being cheerful despite your circumstance, and for teaching me that there's more to life than just your physical condition.

Mrs. Joan K. Gray (6/18/36-8/8/05) - Mom, thank you for instilling within me a deep appreciation for the written word. You taught me from an early age to love reading, which led me to love writing as well. I'll miss you until we meet again.

Prologue

Roscoe Hemingway flopped onto his couch. After three hours of moving his things from his van into the small Newark, DE apartment and sixteen hours of driving before that, he was exhausted.

He pulled out a rumpled snapshot, focusing two years worth of unrequited rage on the image.

Once I learn how to get around this state, it won't take but a minute to find her and teach her a lesson.

He started to get up, but exhaustion anchored him to the couch. He slept like a baby, dreaming dreams of long-delayed vengeance.

1

Max Carson's life changed forever in the cookie aisle of the College Square Pathmark.

His arm was at full extension in its quest to snag a bag of Chips Ahoy when the woman of his dreams appeared. The cookies were forgotten as his mind filled with her beauty; five foot three, caramel-skinned, healthy figure, hair falling to her shoulders and eyes as mysterious as the passage of time.

I've seen those eyes somewhere before, Max thought.

Just then, she removed her glasses to clean them, and forced all doubt from Max's mind.

That's HER!

At the opposite end of the aisle, Donna Randall felt eyes all over her. A quick peripheral glance confirmed her hypothesis.

Uh oh. That guy is seriously interested. Where's Yolanda when I need her?

Max added the cookies to his basket. Needing an excuse to linger, he studied the selection of Fig Newtons, angling his body to keep her in his line of sight.

"You're staring at them cookies awful hard, Max. They put a naked picture on the package?"

Max nearly jumped at the approach of his best friend and shopping partner for the day. Fred had a wide smile at the glazed look on Max's face.

"Never mind player. I see what's got your attention!"

Max snapped out of his stupor and grabbed a box of Apple Newtons, using the movement to mask his whisper.

"Fred, that's HER."

Fred matched Max's low tone of voice. "HER?" Who is HER? Beyonce? Halle Berry?"

Max rolled his eyes. "The woman from my dream."

Fred reached high on the shelf for a bag of oatmeal cookies, turning his head slightly to check Donna out. You're right- she's *fine*! And she's got a friend."

Max glanced sideways and saw a second woman join the first. This woman was taller, nearly matching Max's five foot eight with Afro-Hispanic features. Her skin was cinnamon, and her body more voluptuous, but to Max, this second woman was a stick figure drawing next to a Van Gogh.

"Yolanda, don't look now, but we're being watched. The two guys at the end, near the Keebler section."

Yolanda pretended to study a selection of shortbread cookies and checked them out. Neither man realized that their attempts at stealthy surveillance failed miserably.

"Oh, you mean Lost and Lonely down there?"

Donna held the shopping list between her and Yolanda, effectively covering her laughter. "You'd think they never saw cookies before."

Yolanda pretended to check something off the list. "That tall light-skinned guy's limber. It takes skills to grab something off a high shelf and pretend like you're not checking somebody out at the same time."

The roommates grabbed their carts and moved on before their barely contained laughter burst out of its own volition. Max and Fred admired their retreat.

"They look single. Shall we engage in hot pursuit, player?"

Max rolled his eyes, knowing that Fred was more of a player then Max would ever be.

"You said that woman looks like the one you dreamed about. Why not step to her?"

Max sighed in frustration. "Fred, she doesn't look like her. That IS her!"

Fred put his hands up in mock surrender. "I just wanted to

know what you wanna do. I'll help you out if you want- her girl is FOINE!"

"That'd be kind of obvious. The next aisle over is feminine hygiene." Fred laughed. "Not exactly prime macking ground."

They kept their eyes peeled for the women as they shopped, not realizing that Donna and Yolanda did the exact same thing, only more subtly. They wound up in separate checkout lines, sneaking looks at one another. Donna and Yolanda laughed to see Max and Fred's visible frustration at being trapped behind an elderly couple with a good seventy-five items in their cart.

Max's hopes of possibly approaching Donna in the parking lot were dashed when the elderly couple reached the cashier. After the woman transferred items from the cart at the speed of a wounded turtle, they decided to pay by check. Max fumed as the woman took forever to find the checkbook and hand it to her husband, and simmered some more as the gentleman took even longer to fill out the check. Even the cashier seemed to move in slow motion.

Ten agonizing minutes later, Max and Fred hauled their groceries towards Fred's Saab. Realizing that his dream woman was long gone, Max let an expletive slip before he caught himself.

"Ooh, I'm gonna tell your pastor!"

The look of faked shock on Fred's face made Max laugh and calm down.

Fred smiled and shook his head. "You must be hot for that woman to make *you* cuss."

Laughing, Max and Fred loaded their groceries and climbed into the car. Max relaxed into the passenger seat, and without thinking about it, fell into silent prayer.

"Lord, thank you for showing me she's real (and I'm sorry for cursing just now). I don't know why You sent me the dream first, but thank You for revealing her to me now. If I meet her Lord, please give me the right words to say. Amen."

Newark's not that big. Shoot, the whole state of Delaware isn't that big. God willing, I'll run into her again soon.

Donna and Yolanda drove home, laughing hysterically.

"Yolanda, did you see the looks on their faces when that old guy pulled out his checkbook? I thought they were gonna kick his butt!"

Yolanda wiped tears and gasped for breath. "Yeah, they just knew they were gonna get a chance to pick us up in the parking lot!"

She obeyed a Stop sign, and turned to look at Donna. "You think they both wanted to mack or was one just going to help his friend out?"

"It was the dark-skinned guy's idea." Donna smiled. "He really wanted to talk to me."

They stopped again, this time for a red light. Yolanda took the opportunity to look at Donna again. "Como lo sabes?"

Donna looked at her out of the corner of her eye, making Yolanda smile.

"Oops, I'm sorry. I keep forgetting you don't speak Spanish. I said,

"How do you know that?"

Donna smiled. "Trade secret."

The light turned and Yolanda stepped on the gas. "Oh, right. You have an edge."

From their earliest childhood in Baltimore, Donna and Yolanda were inseparable. Early on, Yolanda realized that Donna had the ability to feel what people around her felt. She soon figured out that this gift sometimes caused Donna to have mood swings, and she made it a point to stand by Donna on her worst days.

"Hey, do you know if either of them is married?"

Donna laughed. "I'm not that good. I could tell that the dark-skinned guy was serious about wanting to talk to me. It's easier for me to discern more intense emotions, and the darker guy really felt it." "Takes his macking seriously, does he?" They laughed all the way home.

"No!"

Merry Lucas sat straight up in bed, sweating as if she'd run a marathon. Heart pounding, she swallowed to clear her suddenly dry mouth, and took deep breaths to calm herself as she struggled to remember where she was. This time it took thirty seconds to realize that she was home in bed, and that home this year was a townhouse in Newark, Delaware.

It was just a dream. Dreams can't hurt me.

Merry cursed to herself and slid out of bed, heading for the bathroom. *I can't get one good night's sleep, and then I can never remember what I dreamed that scared me so bad.*

Splashing cold water on her face didn't help; Merry was exhausted but feared sleep, and the combination both irritated and frightened her. Her manila complexion was at least half a shade paler now, and worry lines traced well-worn paths across her forehead.

Three in the morning. There's no way I'm going back to sleep now. I might as well work.

Merry donned a pair of thin black gloves and headed for her living room. Her VCR was state of the art. Dual cassette decks allowed her to edit and duplicate videotapes at high speed without the inconvenience of a second VCR and a lot of irritating connecting wires.

A red light indicated that her copy was finished. Merry rewound it and hit Play. A crystal-clear image materialized, Merry and a muscular black man in her queen-sized bed.

Perfect. You can see his face clear as day.

She rewound both tapes, removed them from the VCR and put the copy in a clear plastic case. She slid it into a business-sized envelope addressed to the law firm of Parker, Grant, Yorkins and Hayden. She marked it "Hayden: PRIVATE."

Attorney Spencer Aurelius Hayden III, I bet you'll think twice about cheating on your wife after you see this.

Merry booted up her computer and typed a note to enclose with the tape. The note explained how Hayden should make the initial three thousand dollar payment, and which TV stations, newspapers, friends and associates would also receive copies the first time he failed to pay one thousand dollars a month payment afterwards.

Hayden was Merry's latest victim, one of over a hundred men spanning ten states over five years. Merry's original home state Delaware was her latest stop, and she intended to stay until the well ran dry, and maybe even "retire" here.

I didn't want to move back. I loved Atlanta, but that Hemingway moron got too close. I can't believe I left because of him.

The "stars" of Merry's tapes were all very rich and very married men who paid well for her not to "out" them. Most of them suspected Merry of being their blackmailer, but couldn't prove it. Merry wore gloves when handling tapes, and none of them knew her real name, address or how many copies of their tapes existed. They sent payments to a variety of PO boxes in post offices across

Delaware, and one in Pennsylvania. Merry had mastered the art of having mail forwarded when she moved from state to state. She'd lost a few in transition, but for the most part, her cash flow was fine.

Merry laughed as she sealed the envelope. *If men could control their hormones, I'd probably be broke and homeless.*

"It was like dropping through a rainbow; I saw every color imaginable swirling around me, and I fell forever. One minute I was falling and the next, I was standing beside a big pond. I've never liked the so-called great outdoors; a Cub Scout camping trip when I was eight convinced me that a soft bed in an air-conditioned room beats sharing a sleeping bag with bugs and snakes. But despite my active dislike for being outdoors, I liked this place. Squirrels chattered, birds chirped and the smell of pine needles was sweeter than anything I've ever known.

That's when she showed up, and she was FINE! She was maybe five inches shorter than me, caramel skin, and hair past her shoulders. She had those subtle cheekbones, not high like a Native American, but somewhere in between. Her nose was somewhere between black person broad and European dainty, and her lips were at that same halfway point. Her eyes were dark, piercing, warm, and inviting all at the same time. It was as if she was created just for me. She walked toward me, and I could see that this wasn't some artificially thin super model type. This was a real woman, with real proportions.

A firecracker went off in the distance and the scene changed. Just like that, the woman and I were lying beside that crystal clear water kissing. And then I woke up."

Max closed his notebook. This was his third time reading his account of the recurring dream since Fred dropped him off, and he knew he'd keep reading it until it made sense.

I've had that dream five times this month and I'm still no closer to knowing why.

He returned the small notebook to his cluttered night table. *Glad I started keeping this here. It's amazing how fast I forget what I dreamed about, and this one I really want to remember.*

Max thought about putting the rest of his groceries away, but knelt beside his bed instead.

"Lord, thank you for waking me up this morning, and for carrying me through today. I need Your help, Lord; I just don't understand why this dream comes to me over and over, and especially why You chose to have me meet that woman now. I don't know why I've been dreaming about her or why I can't stop thinking about her. Lord, I want to see her again, but not my will, but Your will be done. In Jesus' name I pray, Amen."

Waves of mild nausea infiltrated Donna's rest. Swiftly racing visions amid color-filled darkness filled her mind. None of the images stayed still long enough to fully register on Donna's brain.

"Donna?"

"Hmmf?"

Donna automatically put her right hand on her abdomen. Disoriented, she squinted towards the door of her room where her roommate stood. The haggard look on Donna's face immediately elicited pity.

"Pobrecita. Why does it always hit you so much harder than anyone else?"

"Because if cramps were fair, men would have them. Leave me alone."

Yolanda held up her hands defensively. "Hey, I just wanted to confirm it's your turn to drive to church tomorrow. Chill out!"

Donna tried unsuccessfully to soften her expression. "Sorry."

"No problem. Hasta luego."

Used to her roommate's mood swings, Yolanda returned to her own room, chuckling as she left.

Keep laughing 'Landa. You're next.

Donna grudgingly got out of bed and headed for the bathroom. She found the bottle of Pamprin, and as she swallowed two pills, her reflection in the mirror startled her. Donna's luxurious black hair was unruly, her eyes were puffy and red from lack of good sleep and she looked pale. Suddenly dizzy, she returned to bed and pulled the blanket close around her, assuming a fetal position. *God, please take this pain away!*

Without warning, she found herself encircled by tall trees. A crystal-clear pool of water lay about fifteen feet away, and he was also there. "He" was a tall black man, but she couldn't see him clearly, as if she weren't wearing her glasses.

Donna took a step towards the mystery man, slipping on the damp grass as she moved. She felt a sudden headache and then nothing. The first setting returned and she now found herself lying beside the water, kissing the blurry man like her life depended on it. The dream faded, but before it ended, the scene shifted again. The blurry man held out his hand and offered to remove her pain. She took his hand, and just like that, her cramps vanished. Donna smiled as she shifted into comfortable sleep.

Unable to sleep, Max got up and began to practice kata. He'd learned several sequences of the complicated dance-like movements from the Tae Kwon Do lessons he'd had as a teenager. Kata was now his preferred form of exercise.

Twenty minutes later, he paused on the way to the shower to look at himself in the mirror. Max was every bit as dark-skinned as his "dream woman" was light, and his five foot eight inches were just enough to get him out of the "short" category by most women's standards.

Nobody will ever mistake me for a body builder, but I'm starting to get some definition.

As Max reached for his bathrobe, an abdominal spasm doubled him over. It felt like someone grabbed his stomach from the inside and squeezed. Max dropped the robe and grabbed the closet door to keep from falling.

The pain stopped as suddenly as it started. Naked and feeling vulnerable, Max crouched where he was for long minutes, taking increasingly deeper breaths to reassure himself that he could now do so without pain. He finally rose cautiously and went to shower, wondering what happened.

Donna awoke Sunday morning refreshed; her body's discomfort had subsided to the point where she felt human again. As she showered, her mind rolled back to the day she discovered her gift. She and Yolanda went to a classmate's twelfth birthday party, giddy with excitement because they knew the incredibly fine Raymond Baines would be there. However, the excitement faded when Raymond was overheard deriding Donna as cute, but weird. Donna was disconsolate, and soon, nearly everyone else at the party was upset too, for no discernable reason. Yolanda got her friend out of there to calm her down, and once Donna was removed from the scene, the other kids snapped back to normal. It didn't take Yolanda long to figure out that Donna was the cause, and she took this discovery in stride.

The second part of Donna's gift manifested two weeks later. Donna told Yolanda of a dream where she and her family left Baltimore on a plane and went someplace sunny, filled with excitement and laughter. Within three days of that dream, Donna's parents surprised her and her two younger brothers with a trip to Walt Disney World in Orlando, Florida.

Things haven't been the same since. The dreams in particular scare me; I mean, what if I dream about something life-changing?

Max found himself fully alert at six A.M. He'd awakened several times during the night for no good reason, and at the first hint of sunlight, gave up on sleep altogether.

This is ridiculous. I'm twenty-five years old, have a job I like, friends to hang with and a good church home. Why am I tripping about this woman? It's not like I don't know any others.

His mind wandered back to a Monday night not quite a month ago. He'd gone to the Bear Public Library to return books and pick up a few more. He'd been there ten minutes when a woman caught his eye. She was just his type; nearly his height and skin color, winning smile and the ability to look drop-dead gorgeous in a casual outfit (jeans, a Support Black Colleges T-shirt and a Negro Leagues baseball cap). They struck up a conversation, and Max left the library half an hour later with three books and Jenisse's phone number.

Wish it had worked out, but she had issues. She told me she wasn't ready for a relationship, but the truth is, she was already in one, and wasn't convinced I was worth rocking the boat for. Next time I go for character instead of looks.

Max went into the kitchen to find some breakfast, still thinking things over.

That dream has me thinking girlfriend again. No wonder I'm all wired up. I haven't had a dream to come true in ten years; why now?

Out of the corner of his eye, Max saw his Bible sitting on the table where he'd left it yesterday. He had been in the middle of flipping through the book of Isaiah when Fred called him for the shopping trip.

"Fear thou not, for I am with thee. Be not dismayed, for I am thy God. I will strengthen thee; yea, I will help thee; yea I will uphold thee with the right hand of My righteousness." Isaiah 41:10

Encouraged, Max flipped forward to Isaiah 53 and read some more.

Merry settled onto her couch with the Sunday paper and the harvest from yesterday's trip to her various PO Boxes. Fifteen minutes and seven thousand dollars richer, Merry plotted her next moves.

William didn't take me seriously. What a shame- I'm sure his wife will take the copy of the tape I send her quite seriously.

As she pondered the object lesson she planned to dish out, her eyes fell on one final payment, three thousand dollars from Jericho Walker. Walker was the last one she'd gotten in Atlanta before moving to Delaware. He was the accountant turned politician Merry met in line at the bank where ironically, she was depositing money from her previous victims.

Walker might be an egotistical jackass, but he's no fool. If this tape got out, his political career would end before it even started. Not to mention his marriage.

Merry sighed. *There has got to be an easier way to make a living.*

She picked up the paper for a leisurely read. Before she could search for the comics, a headline jumped out at her.

BEAR RESIDENT WINS POWERBALL'.

Merry scanned the story and sucked in her breath as she saw who just won twenty-eight million dollars; after taxes.

It was Karl Hurzen.

Her father.

2

Max stared at his computer and tried to focus. After five minutes of writing the same sentence, he decided to let his article and his eyes rest for a few minutes.

Monday, Max thought. *This week's edition is just out and now we have to start all over again for next week. City Voice, the newspaper that won't die.*

Across the room, Fred hurried to his computer, pulled out some notes and started writing. *Must have finally caught that guy for the interview. Good. We need that human-interest piece to fill out the next issue.*

Max stretched and sat back down at his desk to finish writing. After that, he had three articles to proofread and the weekly editorial meeting to dread.

We're not busy enough getting the next issue off the ground without wasting an hour rehashing stuff we resolved last meeting. Guess I can't complain too much though. I went from editorial assistant to reporter to assistant editor in less than two years thank God, and like it or not, that means more responsibility. My career is going well. Now all I have to do is stop dreaming about strange women and I'll be good to go.

Max laughed and kept on writing.

Merry steeled herself for the ordeal ahead.

Dealing with him won't be any tougher than dealing with any other man.

She dialed before she could lose her nerve, and was surprised that she had to force herself to breathe normally.

"Hello."

The voice on the other end of the phone was arrogant and accustomed to being obeyed.

You got up early on a Monday for this. Don't wimp out now.

"Hello Karl."

Karl Hurzen's tone lightened immediately. "Merry! It's been awhile, hasn't it?"

"Yes it has, Karl; I had nothing to say to you."

Karl heard the sandpaper edge to his daughter's voice and dropped all pretenses of civility. "Karl, is it? What ever happened to *Dad*, or even *Father*?"

Merry's voice dropped below freezing. "If you'd been any kind of a father to me, I might be able to call you that instead of something more colorful."

Sounds just like her mother, Karl thought. *Wish I'd been able to beat that sarcasm out of her the way I did Lorraine.*

"Now that we've established that this isn't a social call, what do you want? And make it fast. Taylor and I have a belated honeymoon trip to prepare for. We never got to take one when we first got married, you know."

Merry took a deep breath, ignoring her hatred of Karl's current wife for the time being. *Stay focused.*

"It's burned me for years that we had nothing remotely resembling a normal family. You beat my mother like a slave, and when you got through with her, it was my turn. I wanted- -I *deserved* a father, not a man who stopped even pretending he loved me once his precious son was born."

Merry fought back tears; Karl suppressed laughter. "Your point?"

"My point is you owe me, Karl. All those years of abuse and neglect come at a cost. I know you're incapable of showing me any genuine affection, so I'll have to settle for what you can provide."

"And that is- - -?"

"Money. If you can't love me, then pay me. Five million dollars."

There was silence for a moment, and then Karl roared with laughter. While Merry clutched the phone in disbelief, Karl acted as though he was watching his favorite comedians on TV while his wife manipulated his most ticklish areas.

Merry finally found her voice and unleashed a skillful barrage of profanity, using language that would make the devil cringe. "You owe me, and I intend to collect, by whatever means necessary."

Karl struggled to speak through his laughter. "I knew it! This isn't about how I treated you; this is about the money I won. I never thought I'd say this Merry, but you've lost your mind! Why in the world would I just give you five million dollars? I wouldn't give

Bryan that much money, and I *like* Bryan!"

Karl's calculated cruelty rocked Merry to the core of her soul, but she vowed not to show it.

"If my bratty little brother asked you to, you'd cut off your own leg, yet you choose to ignore your firstborn child. Clearly this call was a waste of time. It *won't* happen again."

Karl laughed some more. "You should try out for Showtime At The Apollo. It's clear to me you have a gift for telling jokes."

Still laughing, he hung up. Shaking with rage, Merry continued cursing Karl in absentia.

On top of everything else, she thought, *I didn't even get to slam the phone down in his ear.*

Karl tried his best, but could not contain his mirth. His sides ached as he lay in bed and shook with laughter.

"What's so funny?"

Through tears, Karl saw his wife of two years enter their bedroom. Taylor Tyler-Hurzen was young, blonde like Karl and her body could easily earn her a guest appearance on any beach movie. Unlike Merry's mother, Taylor knew when to shut her mouth. She also knew what Karl wanted and when, and never failed to provide it. In this instance, "it" was a steaming cup of coffee with cream and two sugars.

"Tell me the joke so I can laugh too."

Karl gasped for air and smiled at Taylor to compose himself. "That was your college roommate on the phone. She wanted five million dollars as compensation for me having been a lousy excuse for a father."

Taylor laughed so hard she had to put the coffee down. "That *is* funny. Next thing you know she'll be dragging you on talk shows to have it out."

Karl guffawed loudly. "Poor daughters of interracial marriages who need to get a life, today on Springer!"

Still laughing, Taylor sat on the bed beside Karl. "You know sweetie, she *is* your daughter. You should send her- - -something."

Karl looked up. "You sound like you have "something" in mind already."

Taylor smiled wickedly and shared her idea. Karl laughed even harder and immediately implemented her plan.

Donna sneezed for about the four hundredth time in the past half hour. Cleaning the high shelves in her bedroom yielded more than dust bunnies; Donna thought these were more like bears.

I'm so short of things to do that cleaning is actually a viable option. I'm glad that new temp assignment starts on Wednesday; if I don't get out of here soon, I'll either die of boredom or dust inhalation.

Donna reached for the books she'd brought down in order to clean, and her Paul Lawrence Dunbar High School senior yearbook drew her attention. She paged through it, reminiscing until one picture stopped her cold.

Clarence Perry. Skinny, smart and the best friend I ever had besides Yolanda.

Donna smiled at the memories his picture evoked. From her first day at Dunbar, Donna's beauty provoked competition for her affections among the jocks and other trophy-girlfriend seekers, but her heart was already set. She approached Clarence on the first day of school and struck up a conversation.

They became friends immediately, and when he finally summoned up the nerve to ask her for a date, she surprised everyone except Yolanda by not only agreeing to the date, but to become his girlfriend as well.

Clarence was great. Being able to feel other people's emotions made it easy for me to ignore those guys who were sniffing around, because I knew all they wanted was sex. Clarence was different. He had normal hormones, but unlike the rest of them, he focused on getting to know me as a person and not in the Biblical sense.

Donna and Clarence dated all through high school, mainly because he was emotionally safe for her. He was levelheaded enough not to cause her many mood swings, and understanding enough to let her be herself.

Too bad it couldn't last. But, he got his scholarship to UCLA and I went to University Of Delaware. We knew a long distance relationship wouldn't work, especially when he couldn't get rid of that inferiority complex.

Donna reluctantly tore herself away from the yearbook, replacing it and the other books on the clean shelves. *I miss how special he made me feel. I wish I could meet a man like that now.*

A brief image of the shadowy man from her dream appeared in her mind, but a sneezing fit diverted her attention. Blowing her nose, she kept dusting, shoving aside thoughts of men known and unknown for the time being.

Merry stretched and yawned as she got up from the couch. *Time to get the mail. Like there will be anything there but bills. I hate Wednesdays.*

She opened the door just as the mailman was about to put the mail in her box. Smiling, she accepted it from him and went back inside.

That was convenient. Let's see, junk, junk, phone bill, more junk- - -.

The last envelope was a personal letter; her address was handwritten, and there was no return address. Curious, she dropped the rest of the mail onto her dining room table unsorted and opened it first.

The mystery envelope contained a brief, handwritten note. Merry scanned the page and her blood went cold.

Merry,
Here's that money you asked for. I took out for taxes- hope you don't mind.

Sincerely,
Your Loving Father

P.S. Do keep in touch.

Merry threw the letter towards the table. It fell to the floor instead, releasing its contents: a crisp, new five-dollar bill.

Stunned at Karl's blatant cruelty, Merry cursed him out loud again. When her profane tirade ended, she paced around the room, still furious.

Karl is a dead man. I'll dance on his grave when I'm through with him.

Max pulled up in front of Calvary United African Christian Church and to his surprise, found a parking spot close to the door. He got out quickly, checking his watch to see if he was on time for his appointment.

I don't want to keep Pastor waiting. I'm sure he's got a lot to do besides talk to me about whatever's on his mind.

Max went through the sanctuary, out the side door and into the hallway containing the meeting rooms. As he rounded a corner, he heard muffled conversations and movement of chairs from a room directly in front of him. The door opened, and just like that his dream woman was coming towards him.

Max froze for a millisecond, even as his brain screamed at him to say something before she could leave. "Uh, hello."

She smiled radiantly, and Max nearly melted. "Hi."

Max felt as though English was his second language. He forced his words past a suddenly thick tongue. "Is, uh, is Pastor Nathan inside?"

Donna struggled slightly with her own words. "Yes, he just finished with New Members Class."

Some of Max's nervousness faded as he sensed his opening. "Oh, that's why I've never met you before. I'm Max Carson."

She smiled again and extended her hand. "Donna Randall."

As their palms met, Max was overpowered by a vision. He and Donna were in the midst of a large social gathering of some kind. He wore a black suit and Donna wore a festive white gown; the implication was clear.

Donna was stunned silent for a different reason. She was back in her dream, in those same woods beside that same clear body of water kissing the same man whose face she couldn't quite make out, and it felt like Paradise.

"Hey there, Brother Max. I see you've met my star pupil."

Both of them jumped slightly as their joint focus returned to the here and now. Pastor Travis Nathan suppressed a laugh as he sized up the situation.

"Sister Donna and the other new members will receive the Right Hand Of Fellowship at the eleven o'clock service tomorrow, but it looks like you're way ahead of me."

Both of them immediately turned a shade of red neither of them thought they could attain. Pastor Nathan looked pleased and decided to test Max further.

"Brother Max, this is Donna's friend, Yolanda Mason. Sister Yolanda, this is Max Carson. He's one of my "good members."

The pastor gestured to a woman Max hadn't even noticed was there. Yolanda stood near Donna with an amused look on her face. Max suppressed his surprise and greeted Yolanda without a trace of nervousness

I was right, the pastor thought. I believe Max knows what he wants, and it's not a date with Yolanda.

"You're right on time for our appointment, Brother Max. Everyone else has gone, so we can meet in here instead of going to my office. Is that okay with you?"

Max was determined to muster up some shred of dignity. "Sounds good to me. Ladies, it was nice to have met you. See you in church tomorrow?"

Yolanda spoke for a suddenly speechless Donna. "Sure, see you tomorrow. Nice to have met you too."

The two women walked out in silence. Max watched them until they turned the corner.

Pastor Nathan smiled. "Looks to me like we have more to discuss then just establishing a church newsletter."

Max chuckled. "That's an understatement."

"Okay Donna, you want to explain to me what that was back there?" Donna kept her eyes studiously on the road. "What?"

Yolanda rolled her eyes. "Don't *even* try to front. I'm talking about you and that man we saw in church doing your best Romeo and Juliet impression."

Donna blushed again as she realized how it must have looked from Yolanda's perspective.

"Oh please! He introduced himself, I said hello back and we shook hands. That's all."

Yolanda smiled. "Uh huh. Then why were your tongues dragging on the carpet?"

"They were *not*!"

Both of them cracked up.

"Okay 'Landa, maybe we did have a moment."

"More like an hour!"

Donna glared daggers at her friend and quickly looked back at the road.

They rode in silence for a while. As they neared their apartment building, Yolanda broke their silence.

"What was it about him that stunned you like that? I'm curious."

Donna smiled; she knew Yolanda wasn't going to let the topic rest until she got an answer that satisfied her.

"It was the weirdest thing. When our hands touched, I, well, I *saw* something."

Yolanda snapped her head around. "You mean- - -?"

"Yeah 'Landa, a vision. It was clear as day, just like all the others."

"What was it this time? What did you see?"

Donna described the vision in vivid detail. "It's part of a dream I had recently. I'm still trying to sort out what it all means."

Yolanda cocked her head and regarded Yolanda curiously. "Well, I can't say much about the trees and the water and all, but one thing is obvious to me."

"What?"

"Max has to be that man in your dream."

Merry couldn't figure out the best way to kill her father.

She thought through a dozen scenarios, each of which would hasten his admission into Gracelawn Internment Center. However, each of these methods would also ensure Merry a very long stay in the Baylor Women's Correctional Institute, and possibly the notoriety of becoming one of the few women in Delaware history to receive the death penalty.

I can't walk up and shoot him, and I can't set his house on fire. It has to be less suspicious.

Merry woke up screaming for the seventh time in as many days, and with little hope of getting back to sleep, chose to get up and do some work. However, work failed to distract her this time. Nothing could, not after her father had humiliated her yet again.

I should have known better than to call. The only way I'll ever see that money is if he dies and I inherit. And there are too many people ahead of me in the will: Taylor, bratty Bryan and dear old Mom. I guess I'll just have to make sure Karl dies and there's no competition when it comes time for his estate to be settled. When that happens, I can afford to live in the style to which I'd love to become accustomed.

Merry laughed, turned on her TV and VCR and set to work again.

3

Max awakened an hour earlier than usual, tingling with anticipation at the thought of going to worship.

I know I'm going to see Donna in church today. Maybe I'll even get to ask her out.

Max chuckled to himself as he showered, hoping God wouldn't be upset with him for being so happy about going to church because of a woman.

"Yolanda, if you aren't out here in ten minutes, you're getting left!"

A muffled voice came through a closed bedroom door. "I'll be ready in a few minutes, Madame Impatience!"

Donna brushed lint off her red dress and sat down with her Bible to wait for Yolanda. She was finishing I Corinthians 13 when Yolanda emerged from her bedroom, nearly tripping herself as she pulled on her other blue shoe.

"They gonna shoot us if we're a little late?"

Donna closed her Bible. "No, but we might end up sitting in the hallway. You know how fast it fills, and we're supposed to sit with the other new members."

"Okay, you're right. Let's go."

As the sermon ended and the pastor gave the invitation to those who wanted to accept Jesus into their lives, join the church or just be prayed for, Max sat up eagerly in his seat.

Sooner than Max expected, the altar emptied and Pastor Nathan nodded towards the first row to his left. Ten men and women came to the front of the church and lined up in front of the altar, facing towards the congregation.

Max scanned the row and craned his neck to catch a glimpse of Donna. A tall, attractive woman in blue caught his eye first.

That's her girlfriend, which means Donna can't be far.

He looked until a vision in red caught his eye. Max's heart leaped to see Donna at the far end of the row.

I get to save the best for last.

"Having confessed Jesus as your Savior, you are already part of the body of Christ. Now in the name of the Father, the Son and the Holy Spirit, I offer you the Right Hand Of Fellowship. Welcome to this body; to Calvary United African Christian Church."

The congregation applauded loudly as Pastor Nathan shook hands down the line, followed by the associate ministers. After them came the officers of the church and then the remainder of the congregation.

Max stood stiffly, wiped his suddenly sweaty hands on his handkerchief and got in line. He checked himself automatically; dark green suit, gold tie and matching handkerchief and newly shined shoes.

Don't say or do anything stupid. All you have to do is greet everybody the same.

As Donna felt a unique and familiar presence as she greeted passersby.

It's Clarence No, not quite. This man is like I remember Clarence, but he's different somehow. And nervous. Who is he? Where is he?

The line's pace reminded Max of turtles and snails and slugs. Butterflies the size of bats fluttered in his stomach as he eventually reached the first person in line.

Okay Max, get it together. Act like you've actually seen an attractive woman before.

Max greeted each new member in turn, introducing himself and welcoming them into fellowship. *You've done this a thousand times in the past. Just relax and do it again.*

I can't believe this, Donna thought. *Max is the one who set me off. Maybe Yolanda was right after all. He's getting closer. I'd better breathe; I'd lose cool points if I passed out before he got to me.*

Sooner than Max expected, he reached the end of the greeting line. The sight of Donna close up paralyzed him for a second.
She's more beautiful than when I saw her yesterday. Those eyes- - -.

He's still fine. Okay Donna, get it together. One of us has to speak sooner or later.
"Good morning. Nice to see you again."
Donna's voice and extended hand snapped Max out of his trance. He smiled as he extended his hand in return, only to see Donna shift gears and open her arms for a hug, which Max delivered awkwardly.
"Good to see you again too. Welcome to Calvary."
Abruptly they both realized that while they had released their hug in a timely fashion, they were still holding hands and locking eyes after about thirty seconds. Blushing, they released their grips and Max returned to his seat, oblivious to the barely concealed smiles on the faces of those seated closest to the front.
The warmth of Donna's hand stayed on Max's for the rest of the service.

After all of the greeters had filed past, the new members returned to their seats. All of them smiled at the hearty Calvary greeting they'd received, but Donna felt especially warm.
Mom keeps telling me that church is where you meet good men, but I never really believed it until now. Max looks good, but he feels good too. He feels like trust itself. And he's definitely interested.
Yolanda leaned over and whispered. "We made the right choice joining here. It really feels like we're welcome."
Donna sat back and smiled. "Amen."

As the service ended, Max grabbed his Bible and slipped out of his pew, keeping Donna and Yolanda in sight. He'd decided that if he could get to Donna, he would pull her aside and talk to her.

Lord, help me out. She's with her girlfriend and it might take a minor miracle to get to talk to her alone. But, if I have to ask her out in front of her friend, so be it. I'm not going to miss this chance.

Max noticed that the two women had stopped moving and took advantage of the opportunity to close some of the distance between them.

Yesterday told me something, and today confirmed it. For all I know that could be my future wife over there. At the least, I'm not leaving here without asking for her number.

"Yolanda, do you see anyone here who we know?" She looked around. "No, why?"

Donna glanced around the sanctuary. "Well, I have this feeling. You know how it is; you think somebody's familiar, but they're not. Guess I was just dreaming."

"Dreams sometimes come true. Mine just did."

Donna gasped at the deep, familiar voice behind her, and turned to see a welcome sight. He stood six-foot-four, lean but somewhat muscular in build, wearing a gray Armani suit and a big smile.

"Clarence!"

All thoughts of Max vanished as Donna's first love pulled her into a big hug. Passersby smiled at the intensity of their reunion; all but one.

Who is that, Max thought, barely restraining a curse. *Where did he come from?*

Max had gotten to within five feet of where Donna and Yolanda stood when without warning, a tall light-skinned man with unnaturally wavy hair and an expensive suit swept Donna off the floor like he owned her.

Looks like he knows her real well. So much for prophecy.

Unfortunately, he had to pass Donna, Yolanda and the tall man to get out of the church and now he didn't want to catch Donna's eye.

What good would that do me? They'd just see how pitiful I look now that I've missed my chance.

He tried to slip past unnoticed. Yolanda saw him and waved, but Max pretended not to notice.

Donna was overjoyed to see her first love, all grown up and very glad to see her again. She felt a brief wave of disappointment, couldn't pinpoint the source and quickly forgot about it. Yolanda greeted Clarence and quickly found a pressing need to talk to the pastor's wife, who was beside her husband, shaking hands with worshippers as they left.

"How've you been? It's been years! What, you forgot how to call a sister when you came home for visits?"

Clarence laughed. "Yeah, it's been awhile. And believe me, I didn't forget about you."

Donna blushed at the intensity of his feelings. It's just how he felt about me back in the day, she thought, only more because he hasn't seen me in awhile.

"Oh man, there's so much I want to tell you, I don't even know where to start. And I don't want to hold you up. I'm sure you've got things to do."

He smiled mischievously, and Donna socked him playfully on the arm. "I haven't seen you in all this time and you think I have something better to do than catch up?"

Clarence laughed. "Okay, okay, I was hoping that was the case. Are you free for dinner?"

"Sure! I have to drop Yolanda off at our apartment, and then we can meet."

"Sounds good to me. How about three o'clock? I'm staying at the Hotel DuPont, and their restaurant is fantastic."

Donna smiled. "Works for me. I'll see you then.

Roscoe Hemingway sat on his couch, reveling in his unexpected triumph.

It was so simple, he thought as he downed the rest of his Budweiser. *I spent two years tearing up the Dirty South looking for her, and I find the skank in this little-behind state by accident.*

Hemingway was driving back to Atlanta from visiting his brother in New York. During a rest stop at the Marriott Travel Plaza in Delaware, he saw a familiar face.

She must feel pretty secure here. It was easier than it should have been to follow her home and then to find out who she really is. "Crystal Lawrence" my butt; she even gave me a fake name!

Hemingway returned home with renewed purpose. Within a week, he'd packed his things and left his run-down ranch home in Atlanta for a small apartment in Newark, Delaware. The desire for revenge fueled him through the sixteen-hour drive.

All right Crystal or Merry or whoever you are now, your butt is mine. Well, it was once before anyway- what's the difference now?

Hemingway laughed and reached for a third beer.

"Hold up, Max. You mean you got aced out?"

Max shifted the phone to his left ear, adjusting the flame under a small pot of water as he talked.

"Yeah Fred, like a pro. I was set to make a move, but before I could get to her, she was hugged up with some lanky, high yellow, process hair having two million dollar suit wearing- - ."

"Careful Max. I resemble that remark."

Max laughed despite his bad mood. "Okay, your cousin stepped to her before I could, and it looked to me like they've known each other a long time."

"That's rough, man."

"Tell me 'bout it."

They fell silent for a moment, as Fred considered his next words.

"Didn't you tell me that other girl called you? The one from the library you said was so fine?"

"I did have a message when I got in from work Friday. It was kinda late to call her back, so I figured I'd do it Saturday. You know why I didn't get around to it."

"Nothing stopping you now. Shoot, it's better than you sitting around the house making light-skinned voodoo dolls. You might get me by mistake!"

Max cracked up as he put macaroni into the boiling water to cook. "Good point."

"Clarence, I'm dying of curiosity. What brought you here?"

Clarence picked up his menu. "Officially, work. My company, WestTech, is starting an East Coast division here in Wilmington, and I'm on the team that's setting it up. We'll be here all month."

Donna smiled. "That's great! They must think a lot of you."

"I hope so. This could mean big promotions all around if we pull it off."

He took Donna's hand. "That was the official reason why I'm here. You're the *real* reason."

Donna blushed deeply and started to say something, but couldn't get the words out.

"When your folks told me where you and Yolanda lived, I couldn't wait to get here. I've missed you Donna. I've really missed you."

Donna took a sip from her water glass. The love Clarence felt for her radiated from him like summer heat off the sidewalk, and she reveled in it.

"I've missed you too, Clarence. In fact, I was thinking about you just the other day, and wondering where you were and what you were doing with yourself.'

Clarence smiled. "Well, now you know."

Max dried the last of his dishes, putting them in the drainer beside his sink. Out of chores, he sat down with the TV remote and a huge attitude problem.

Dude just comes out of nowhere and beats my time, and I can't say nothing because I only ever spoke to the woman once, like two minutes ago. Not like I had a claim on her or anything.

I guess it just wasn't meant to be.

As she and Clarence talked, Donna opened her unique perceptions, wanting to know all she could about the man she'd never stopped loving.

Something's different about him, and I want to know what.

"Yolanda and I stayed here when we graduated. University of Delaware has a good Job Placement center, so we figured we'd be able to find work. Yolanda got her teaching job pretty quickly, but I'm still temping to pay rent while I'm looking for a real job. But enough about me- how was UCLA?" Clarence smiled. "The best thing that ever happened to me. I'd never been that far from home before in my life, and I didn't realize how bad I needed to get away until then. I was forced to make new friends, adjust to unfamiliar situations, the works."

"Did it take you long?"

"The first week was rough, but before I knew it, I was enjoying myself. That's why I stayed in California when WestTech offered me the job."

As they talked and ate, Donna felt the fondness he held for his undergraduate days. *He really changed while he was out there. He feels more confident now, less nervous than I remember. He's almost arrogant.*

Just then, a vision of Max appeared in her mind, startling her so badly she dropped her fork. Donna managed to keep her attention on Clarence, but she was shaken.

Max jerked awake, startled. He'd been napping in front of the TV when a vivid image of Donna shocked him out of slumber.

First I dream about her and now I daydream about her after I know she's taken. This is getting ridiculous.

The phone rang. Grateful for the distraction, Max picked up without checking the Caller ID.

"Hello?"

"Hi, Max. This is Jenisse."

"Yolanda, am I doing the right thing?"

Yolanda looked up from the pages of Victoria Christopher Murray's Temptation, the Christian novel she'd just bought.

"What do you mean? Is this about Clarence" Donna sat next to her friend on the couch.

"His coming back to find me after all these years is so romantic! And it's good to see him again, especially looking that good!"

Yolanda laughed. "He's definitely upgraded his appearance since the last time I saw him."

"He even remembered the nickname he gave me back then."

"Oh, you mean "Deevee?" Your middle name is Victoria; how tough is *that* to remember?"

"Shut up. Anyway, it felt good spending time with him today but- - -."

"- - -but you're not quite sure he's the one."

"Yeah, I guess that's it. He's changed since high school of course. Maybe it's just going to take me awhile to adjust to how he is now as opposed to what he was like back then. We do have all month, after all."

Yolanda shifted on the couch and looked Donna in the eye. "Oh, I saw your friend on the way out of church today, what's his name, Max? He seemed upset about something."

Yolanda went back to her reading. Donna said nothing, but sat there, thinking.

"Max, this was a great idea! Thanks for bringing me."

Max smiled, stopping at a hastily erected table to pay the ten-dollar fee for each of them.

"No problem. I haven't been bowling in ages, and when that sister in church gave me the flyer, I thought you'd enjoy this."

She likes it! Good, I was hoping I hadn't played myself by asking her here for our second date.

Relieved, Max flashed back three weeks to that Sunday night when he and Jenisse talked. He was about to call her and ask her out when she beat him to the punch. She reassured him that she was now quite available, and he gladly accepted. Their movie outing encouraged Max to ask her for a second date, and Jenisse's reaction told Max that this one would go well too.

As he and Jenisse selected bowling balls, various members of the AKA sorority (the sponsors of the bowling party) ensured that everything was going smoothly.

Jenisse hefted her ball, testing the weight. "Perfect. You know, I almost pledged AKA in college, but the chapter was suspended before I had a chance. Oh well, their loss."

Max laughed politely, checking his own ball. He looked up to see the AKA from his church approaching their lane.

"Excuse me, but we've got more people here than we expected. Would you mind if we put another couple on this lane with you?"

Max looked at Jenisse, who smiled. "I don't mind if you don't."

Max mentally sighed with relief and turned back to the AKA. "Okay. We haven't started yet- send them on over."

She scurried off to find the other couple. Max looked Jenisse up and down as she made her practice roll. Jenisse was a beautiful

Tootsie Roll color, stood close to five foot six and had legs that reminded Max of a track star.

I'm glad she called after the whole Donna thing didn't work. This might become something.

"Evening folks. Room for two more?"

Max smiled at the confident "impress-your-date" baritone rumbling from behind him. "Sure brother, come on- - -in?"

His eyes widened at the sight of the tall light-skinned guy from church with Donna.

Merry sealed the envelope and set it aside for later delivery.

That takes care of Jacob. Now I can figure out what to do about dear old Dad and his not-so-dear wife. I know that heifer put him up to sending me that note- it has Taylor written all over it. When I get through, both of them will wish they'd never even thought about crossing me.

She put New Jack City, one of her all-time favorite movies, into the VCR to relax with as she plotted.

Clarence picked up his ball, set himself and sent it rocketing down the alley, scattering pins forcefully in its wake. "Strike!"

Donna cheered, and Max and Jenisse applauded politely. Jenisse patted Max's arm. "Your turn, Max. Make it good- they're pulling away from us."

Max tried to smile pleasantly. He took his ball from the rack and studied the pins, trying hard not to let his eyes wander to Donna yet again, even as he felt hers on him.

Bad enough I looked like a deer in the headlights when I saw Donna, but I keep staring at her. Can I be any more disrespectful to Jenisse?

He made his approach and released. The ball slipped out of his hand, and only took down one pin. Smiling sheepishly, he held his nose playfully as he stepped back to wait for his ball.

"Can you tell it's been a few months since the last time I bowled?"

Jenisse smiled. "More like a few *years*. If you were any more rusty, I'd have to oil you."

Clarence and Donna laughed, and in that moment, Max and Donna's eyes met. Their shared gaze lasted a moment longer than either of them wanted.

The thump of Max's ball coming up on the automatic return startled them both. Max grabbed it and quickly made his second roll without thinking about it. This time the ball left Max's hand in a graceful curve, heading for the gutter before spinning back towards the middle and picking up the spare.

"All right Max! That's what I'm talking about!"

Jenisse kissed him on the cheek, and Max smiled as Clarence congratulated him.

"Look out Donna- I think we got ourselves a game."

Donna avoided Max's gaze as she picked up her ball. His feelings drenched her, and she had no umbrella capable of shielding herself from this downpour.

There's no reasonable excuse why either Max or I could ask to move to a different lane. He's really attracted to me, and Lord knows I'm feeling something for him too. Why, I don't know. He's obviously trying to forget me, and I need to stop disrespecting Clarence and do the same.

Donna knocked down six pins, and sighed as she waited for her ball to return.

I'm here with Clarence, and I'm trying to sort out my feelings for him. Drooling over another woman's date isn't the best way to do that. I should be happy Clarence is back in my life and focus on him. I wish Max wasn't so- - nice.

"Honestly Max, it seemed like you were a million miles away most of the night!"

Max sighed. "Sorry Jenisse. I had a rough week at work, and I guess I brought some of it home with me."

Max pulled up in front of Jenisse's building and put the car in park, leaving the engine running. She smiled coyly.

"Well I suppose I'll have to do more to keep your attention on me."

Jenisse leaned over and kissed Max on the lips. He responded automatically, and Jenisse deepened the kiss. She pressed closer, angling her body for maximum effect.

Without warning, Max lay with Donna beside the clear water again, kissing her as if their lives depended on it. The kiss grew in intensity until both of them stopped suddenly.

The vision ended, and Max snapped back to reality. Jenisse smiled. "Wow! Felt like I had your attention that time." *Max suppressed a grin. If only you knew- - -.*

She smiled seductively. "Want to come inside and finish this-conversation?"

Every bone in Max's body screamed yes, but he managed to half-whisper a reply. "No. I can't."

Jenisse smiled. "I remember what you told me, about abstaining and all. I wouldn't make you break your resolve."

Max cleared his throat. "I- -think we better call it a night."

Jenisse winked at him. "Your choice. Call me. Soon."

She got out and headed for the door of her building, using the cadence of her walk to show Max exactly what he just turned down. As soon as she got safely inside, Max rolled down all his windows and let the March wind lash his face as he drove home, relieved, excited and frustrated all at once.

He's nervous. This could be it.

Donna and Clarence were at the Golden Dove Diner on DuPont Highway, the only restaurant they both liked open after midnight.

"Donna, you know my month is almost up. Now that the work is done, I have to go see my parents in Baltimore, and then fly back to LA next weekend. I just want you to know that being with you these past three weeks means more to me than I can say."

Donna smiled. "I'm glad you came. I've really had a good time too."

Clarence shifted in his seat. I've enjoyed it too, and frankly, I don't want it to end."

He's going to propose! What do I say? How do I handle it? Do I want to marry him?

Clarence took her hands in his and leaned in even closer. "Donna, will you- -?"

4

"How was your weekend?"

Max looked up from the story he was editing. "Don't ask. I had a date from hell."

Fred laughed. "You took your girl to that AKA bowling thing. What happened? She drop a ball on your foot?"

Max described the bowling date in detail. By the end of the story, Fred was chuckling and shaking his head.

"Man, you both need to break up with them wrong people you're with and hook up. Matter of fact, you should hook your boy Clarence up with Jenisse so nobody won't be mad!"

Max laughed. "Might have to try that. Okay, I'm almost afraid to ask, but how was *your* weekend?"

"More like *who* was my weekend." Fred smiled. "This time it was Lenne."

Max regarded Fred curiously. "Thought you two weren't a couple."

"We're not. She didn't feel like going hunting and I was lying low, so we spent the weekend together at my place."

Max shook his head. "Only you could have a woman whom you cheat on constantly and who does the same to you and call it a relationship."

"Hey we got it like that." Fred laughed "Sometimes one of us will be busy when the other calls, but when we're both free, it's *on*. Best relationship I never had."

Fred returned to his own desk and the work awaiting him there. Max continued editing the story he was assigned, but Donna ruled his thoughts.

This is getting ridiculous. We're running into each other at church, the supermarket, you name it. I can't even go bowling without running into her! If she weren't still seeing the Jolly Lean Giant, I'd have to make a move just for peace of mind.

Images of their first face-to-face meeting bubbled to the surface of his mind. He remembered the chance meeting at the church, and the spiritual fireworks when their hands touched. It was like joy was a physical thing, and the two of them were briefly able to grasp it. And that vision- -.

Enough of this! Donna's fine, but she's taken. End of story. Moving on. Next! Yeah, right. If I say it enough times, maybe I'll believe it.

Maybe I should consider that job offer downstate, with the Dover Post. If nothing else, I wouldn't have to listen to Fred's sexcapades all the time.

"He did *what*?"

Donna smiled. "Dag 'Landa, tell the whole building. I'm sure they'd like to hear this too."

"Okay, I'll calm down. But tell me again what happened."

"We went to that AKA bowling party, and *why* did they put us on the same lane with Max and his date? We were staring at each other all night. I felt bad for Clarence and Max's date Jenisse. They couldn't figure out why we were both so tense."

Yolanda frowned. "I know all that. Get to the question!"

Donna laughed. "Okay, okay. We went to dinner afterwards. He told me that he had to go back to Los Angeles soon, and he asked me to move there with him."

Yolanda's eyes blazed. "This is the man who says he didn't forget you for all those years and the best he could do was ask you to play house?"

Donna laughed again at the venom in her friend's voice. "Guess so. Actually he did me a favor."

"How so?"

Donna sighed. "I was wondering if he was the one, and that clinched it. You *know* how I feel about living together. If you're too cheap to buy a cow, you *won't* get free milk here!"

Yolanda gave her a high five. "Amen!"

They laughed for a full minute. "How'd you handle it?"

"We went to dinner again Saturday night and I told him how I felt."

Yolanda hugged Donna tightly. "It's never easy to fire a good one, is it?"

Donna laughed and held her friend. "No it isn't, but our moms always told us not to settle for less. Sooner or later our shining black (or maybe Hispanic for you) princes will come, and all this will be worth it."

Yolanda put on an air of artificial brightness. "Have you seen Max lately?"

"Shut up, 'Landa."

"Max, you done with the piece on teenage crime?"

Max rolled his eyes and turned to face his immediate superior. "Almost, George. I just need to proofread it one more time."

Max activated the spellchecker function and then followed that scan with a visual check. Finding no errors, he saved the file and e-mailed it to George for final edits.

That should hold him for a while. He needs to relax and remember that the Voice is a weekly newspaper, not a daily.

Max looked out the window, resting his eyes. *I keep this up and I'll need bifocals before I'm thirty.*

Max closed the story file and opened a new blank document, for personal use. After a quick glance around to ensure that no one was watching, he pulled a rumpled sheet of notebook paper from his pocket and transcribed his thoughts on recent events to electronic form.

Finished, he printed one copy, erased the file and quickly went to retrieve it before anyone else could.

"This yours, Max?"

Max's heart sank. Fred hovered over the printer, holding Max's printout.

"Could be."

"I hope so. We don't need two folks here printing out weird stuff like this."

Max snatched the page from Fred's hand. "Very funny."

Fred lowered his voice. "You're still worried about all this, aren't you?"

Max hesitated slightly, debating whether or not to try to explain it all. *Fred might think I lost my mind. Then again, he's been my best friend since I started here. If I can't tell him, who can I tell?*

"Yeah, I am. It keeps getting weirder."

"Well, it's almost noon. Let's go to lunch and I can decide if you've lost your mind or not."

Max feigned an annoyed look. "Thanks a lot, Fred. You're a real pal."

They took the elevator to the first floor cafeteria, bought food and settled into a back table.

"Let me get this straight. You dreamed about Donna for about a month before you actually met her. Then, when you were with Jenisse and she was with Clarence, you kept staring at each other. And then later on, you were kissing Jenisse but you had a daydream like it was Donna. Do I have it all right?"

Max smiled sheepishly. "Yeah, that's the gist of it. It was part of that dream about Donna, the part where we were lying beside some clear water, kissing."

"Oh yeah, I remember that. Sounds like straight up romance novel stuff."

Max laughed. "The thing is, I responded to Jenisse like I was kissing Donna, and she liked it. She invited me inside."

Fred nearly jumped up from the table. "What? Player, *please* tell me you went in."

Max shook his head. "Wouldn't have been right, Fred. You know I don't believe in premarital sex, and even if I did, I would have been using Jenisse as a substitute for Donna."

"And your point is- - -?"

Max laughed. "Man, shut up! That only would have caused more drama. It's gonna be hard enough to tell Jenisse that it's not working out between us."

Fred smiled. "Doesn't mean you couldn't get it and *then* tell her."

Max laughed again. "That's your style Fred, not mine."

Fred looked Max in the eye. "Okay, so you're gonna fire Jenisse. Donna's still taken. Isn't she?"

"I don't know." Max shrugged. "But I'm definitely going to find out."

"What you gonna do, hire a private investigator? Grill her friend for information?"

Max smiled. "She and her friend just joined my church. I'll see them there Sundays."

"Uh huh. You better hope she ain't a CME member. You know, only shows up on Christmas, Mother's Day and Easter."

Max smiled. "Guess *you'd* know if she was."

"Ooh, that's cold."

"*I know you're in there, Frank! You better open this door!*"

Fred and Lenne paused in mid-kiss. She looked at him like he had something in his nose.

"*Frank?*" Player, PLEASE! *That's the best you could do?*"

Fred smiled sheepishly as the woman outside continued generating noise pollution beneath Fred's window. She punctuated her last statement by profanely calling Fred out of his name. Fred started to get up, but Lenne stopped him.

"Chill out, 'Frank.' I got this. What's this heifer's name?" Fred thought for a moment. "Nela. Nela- - -Sanders."

"Hmm. I think I know her."

Lenne stalked downstairs, barefooted and determined. Fred enjoyed the sassy roll of her hips in her tight jeans as she went.

She ain't but five foot nothing, Fred thought, but she carries herself a lot taller.

Nela's voice carried upstairs, echoing loudly through Fred's window. "What you want, Le-nay? I ain't got nothing to say to you. My business is with Frank."

Lenne cut Nela off with a "talk to the hand" gesture. "Your 'business' is with me."

Fred heard female voices conversing in hushed tones, followed by the slamming of a car door and the screeching of tires as a car hastily left the parking lot. Lenne came back inside humming a tune and sat back down on the bed. Fred looked at her in astonishment.

"What happened?"

Lenne chuckled. "We had a woman-to-hoochie talk. I politely informed her that you were spoken for, now and at any other time she'd care to come here acting ghetto."

Fred's eyes widened. "And she listened?"

Lenne smiled impishly. "I also told her if she didn't take her drama elsewhere, not only would I beat her behind in front of this entire apartment complex, but I would call her boyfriend so that he could do the same when she went home."

Fred roared with laughter. "Boyfriend? I thought she'd quit him. I like how you handled that, playa."

Lenne beamed proudly. "Thanks. Now, where were we?"

Fred finished his story with a wide grin. Max laughed himself to tears.

"Fred, you're the only brother I know who could tell me a story like that and not be lying."

"Hey, I got it like that. Listen, here's why I told you that. The way I'm living, Lenne is right for me. The way you're living, Donna is right for you. Now I'd be a fool if I didn't keep Lenne, and you'll be a bigger one if you don't go for yours with Donna. Don't worry about who she's dating, because it's clear to me you two got something special."

They got up from the table and took their trays to the dish line. "I think I *will* go for it. Thanks for the advice."

Fred smiled. "That's what friends are for."

Donna grabbed the next customer letter in her stack and scanned it to see what action to take.

Clarence wasn't supposed to come back from the West Coast to ask me to shack up. He was supposed to propose!

Well, if it wasn't meant to be, it wasn't. I'm back to Square One. No good men in sight, another long dry spell on the horizon.

Just then Max's face came to her. The daydream lasted all of a second, but it seemed much longer.

This is getting out of hand. Why am I still dreaming about a man who's probably forgotten my name by now? Max'll probably end up marrying that woman he was bowling with and I'll be sitting around alone and mad because I never gave him a chance.

Maybe Yolanda's right. Maybe I should go out somewhere with her this weekend.

She finished that letter and reached for another, lost in thought.

An eternity later, five o'clock came and Max joined the throng of people flowing towards the elevator. As he entered the parking garage, he heard two women mumbling. Metal hit metal and one of the women uttered a short curse.

Max looked up, and saw two women crouching beside a nearby car. A short heavyset dark-skinned woman held her hand in pain; a tire iron lying beside her foot testified to her lack of success in helping her equally short friend with a flat tire.

They're struggling. I better lend a hand.

He walked over slowly, and not wanting to alarm the women, stopped a short distance away. "Do you need help?"

The heavyset woman grimaced and sucked her right index finger. "Sure do. Her tire's flat and neither one of us can work this tire iron. I just broke my nail!"

The second woman looked up, and when she saw her rescuer, she smiled broadly. "Max!"

He did a double take. "Donna! I didn't know you worked around here."

She smiled, fighting the urge to throw herself into his arms in response to his feelings for her. "I just started yesterday. Finders sent a bunch of us here to do Customer Service Correspondence. We're answering letters for the next month or so. This is Tina."

She took her finger out of her mouth to shake his hand. "Charmed. Especially if you know how to change a tire."

Max smiled and took off his suit jacket. "I can handle it."

Ten minutes later, Max had changed Donna's tire and put the ruined one in her trunk. Donna handed Max a cloth from her trunk to wipe his hands.

"Max, thanks a lot. You don't know how much I appreciate this."

Max laughed. "Glad I could help."

He slowly replaced Donna's tire iron in her trunk, and handed her back the cloth, wishing Tina would leave so he could make a move.

Aw forget it, he thought. *If I try to push the issue now, I'll come off like a stalker.*

"Nice seeing you again, Donna. It was good meeting you Tina, but I should be going."

They said their goodbyes. Max reluctantly returned to his car and slid behind the wheel. He drove home without remembering how he got there.

"Mm-MMM! I love me a dark chocolate man. Where you know him from, Donna?"

"He goes to my church."

Tina laughed. "If it's some more there like him, I might have to start going again!"

Donna thanked Tina for her help and they went their separate ways. *She really blocked my action, but I'm glad she hung around. For all she knew, Max was a stalker. I like that kind of helpfulness in a sister.*

And I really like the fact that Max is still interested.

Despite Max's best efforts to concentrate on his work, his thoughts stayed on Donna; where she might live, what she might like to do for fun, how she might respond if they ever had a real conversation, and if she were still dating that tall guy.

Since learning that Donna worked in the cluster of four buildings that shared the same parking garage, he'd kept an eye out for her to no avail. Jenisse was now a distant memory; after calling to break up with her, he stopped answering her calls, focusing his thoughts on Donna.

Fred did his best to keep his friend from obsessing, with limited success.

By Friday, all of Fred's tactics were exhausted and he decided to return to basics.

"Doing anything tonight?"

Max smiled. "Sure am. I'm going to sit on my butt and watch the Sixers game on TV. If I'm not tired after that, I'll watch a movie or something and then go to bed."

"See, that's your problem." Fred grimaced. "You don't go nowhere to see any real women, so you got to invent women!"

"Fred, I'm twenty-five. My idea of a good time is different than when I was in college."

"I just turned thirty and I can still hang. Can you?"

Max laughed. "Fred, you ain't gonna shame me into hanging out with you. The only women I want to see are the Sixers dance team during time-outs."

Fred rolled his eyes. "Pitiful. How you think you're gonna meet any woman, much less your dream woman if you don't go nowhere but work and church? What, you think she's just gonna come to your apartment? "Knock, knock, knock. Hi, I'm looking for Max Carson. OhmiGod, it's you! I've been looking all over for you! Take me, I'm yours!"

Max cracked up. "Fred, you *know* you ain't right."

"That mean you're going?"

"Aw come on, Donna! It'll be fun! We haven't gone out in ages."

Donna smiled wryly. "And there's a reason why. Remember the Plateau?"

"You keep bringing that up, don't you?" Yolanda sighed. "Just because we had one bad night at a club--."

"'Landa, we almost got trampled to death when that idiot yelled "Fire!" That's more than just a "bad night.""

"Okay, so it was a disaster. That doesn't mean this place will be too. It beats sitting around here by ourselves."

Donna laughed. "Like either of us is gonna meet somebody in a club. Unless you're looking to marry a man with three gold teeth, a Jheri curl and no job, you're out of luck!"

"So I suppose you just want to sit here fighting over the remote for the tenth straight Friday."

Donna rolled her eyes. "'Landa, I have no problem going out. We could go see a movie or go bowling or do something human. Why a club?"

Yolanda looked exasperated. "Sometimes I swear you're seventy-three instead of twenty-three. I want to be around people, get my party on for a change."

"Can't you do that by yourself?"

"You know it wouldn't be any fun without you to help me bust on the unworthy men. And I wouldn't feel safe clubbing alone, not these days."

It took another half hour of cajoling and convincing, but Donna finally agreed to accompany Yolanda to the Diamonds High, recently built in the heart of downtown Wilmington. As they chose outfits, Donna grumbled insincerely about testing the limits of friendship.

I hate clubs, but I can't let 'Landa go alone. I owe her too much to let her take that kind of risk.

Merry finished cleaning her living room and sat down to rest. *Nice haul today. Another four thousand I didn't expect until next week. Apparently these guys are really worried. If this keeps up, I might be able to coast for awhile.*

She got up and went into her bedroom, pausing in front of her closet to look over her wardrobe. *I need to go out. The victims have been pitiful lately; I need somebody who knows what he's doing.*

Well, tonight's Ladies Night at Diamonds, which means I can get in free before eleven. Maybe I'll get lucky.

5

"Refresh my memory, Fred. This is supposed to be fun *how*?"

Ladies Night at Diamonds High (nestled in the heart of downtown Wilmington) was in full swing; the strobe lights flashed, the music blared and the patrons danced as if their lives depended on it. Max and Fred stood near the bar, scouting for an empty table.

It was nearly eleven o'clock, but the dance floor was already three quarters full. Fred surveyed the scene, swaying with the music. A slight smile crossed his lips as his eyes caressed the room.

Fred's getting off on just being here, Max thought. *He is truly in his world.*

Although the lights gave Max a headache and the music was so loud a deaf man could hear it, he had to admit the beat was compelling. The DJ was playing some older songs at the moment. Everybody Dance Now was the current choice, and Max found himself wishing he were dancing.

Fred had to almost yell to be heard over the ruckus. "Let's slide over this way and see what's happening."

Max nodded and followed Fred through the thick crowd towards the opposite end of the bar. Behind them, male heads turned as a unit to behold the vision of loveliness entering the club. Her red pantsuit clung to her pale skin, defining the sleek contours of her body. Her shoulder length hair was swept atop her head so that everyone could behold her beauty. Merry styled and profiled for all she was worth, and enjoyed the attention. A few of the bolder men called out to her as she passed, but she ignored calls of "Hey, baby!" and "OOO-WEE!" and kept on walking.

"Wow. It's jumping in here already."

Donna couldn't reply. As she and Yolanda entered the club, Donna was swept up in an emotional maelstrom; adrenaline-fueled joy, raw anger, naked desire, drunken confusion, subtle deception and a dozen other feelings assaulted her from every side. Not trusting herself to feel any of those conflicting emotions, Donna wrapped herself in a stony indifference to shield herself.

"You okay, Donna?"

No I'm not okay. I just willingly stepped through the gates of hell!

"I'm fine, 'Landa." Donna lied. "Just a headache."

At the far end of the bar, Max stood beside Fred, visibly uncomfortable.

This isn't my scene anymore. I don't think it ever was, to be honest. Fred's into it though. He'll probably pick up his woman du jour inside of an hour and be gone. I hope he does- then I can get out of here too.

Oh well, at least I saw the Sixers play.

Questioning her decision to come here with each step, Donna fought a pitched battle with the noise and all the feelings in the room. She was losing when Yolanda tapped her on the shoulder.

"See anybody we know?"

Donna followed Yolanda's gaze and cracked up. Max and his friend from the store were together by the bar; Tall Light Guy seemed to be checking out every woman within his visual range while Max looked aggressively disinterested. The sight of Max sent strengthened Donna enough to resist the negative atmosphere around her. Donna wanted to go over to him, but she couldn't leave Yolanda alone in this mob.

The only reason I came, she thought, *was to be bodyguard/companion. Maybe if she gets up to dance--.*

"Oh yeah, them."

She cupped her hands and did a fair imitation of an intercom. "Attention Pathmark shoppers, pick-up on Aisle Six!"

Yolanda laughed. "Yeah, it's our supermarket buddies, and they still look hungry. I bet they want more than cookies this time!"

Sweating from the stuffy heat, they squeezed their way to bar (ignoring various leers and come-ons in the process) and ordered

Cokes. As they turned towards a vacant table, a tall woman in red elbowed her way past them heading the opposite direction. As Donna recoiled from her, the woman bumped Yolanda hard enough to splash soda on her blouse.

"Aay! Excuse you! Hay una problema?"

Yolanda turned and started after the woman, but Donna stopped her with a hand on her arm.

"'Landa, you *don't* want to do this. Not now, and not with her."

Yolanda took a deep breath. "Yeah, you're right. I don't have enough in my checking account this month for rent and bail money; not to mention her medical bills."

Yolanda sat down, muttering under her breath in a patois of English and Spanish about people who could use a good butt-kicking. Deep in thought, Donna barely listened.

When the woman in red brushed past, Donna felt an angry coldness; it cut through the tidal wave of emotions already present and drilled itself directly into Donna's heart.

This is the kind of woman who would just as soon shoot you as ignore you. Apparently she had better things to do; she wasn't the one to walk away from a fight. Or lose one.

At the bar, Merry sat quietly, still ignoring the unworthy men all around her, vying for her attention. *Forget that Spanish heifer*, she thought. *I'm here to find somebody worth taking home, not to waste time on a behind whipping.*

Glancing down the opposite end of the bar, a pair of men making their way through the crowd drew her attention.

Donna strained to sense Max's presence, but couldn't tell if he was still in the club or if he'd given up and gone home.

Guess he left. I'm not surprised; he didn't look like he was enjoying this any more than I am.

She thought back to the disappointment she felt from Clarence on the night she rejected his offer.

I hurt him deeply, but I had no choice. First love is nice, but we're not compatible anymore. Clarence isn't the one for me.

I wonder who is?

"Oh yes! Max, look down the other end of the bar."

Max glanced sideways and spotted the woman in question instantly. *Has to be that tall woman in the red pantsuit. She has "Fred's Type" written all over her.*

"In red? Real light skinned?"

Fred smiled. "That's her. I just made good eye contact. If I get it again, I'm in there."

Just then, the woman looked Fred's way and smiled seductively before turning to talk to the bartender.

"*Seey*a."

Fred made his way through the crowd, arriving at the woman's side simultaneously with her drink. Ever the smooth operator, Fred paid for it and ordered one of his own before striking up a conversation.

Max rolled his eyes. *I've seen this a hundred times before. They'll drink, they'll dance and after awhile, they'll leave together. And he wonders why I insist we drive separately.*

Max got up and made his way towards the exit. *No need for me to hang around any longer,* Max thought. *Wish I could get my money's worth though. It'd be nice to dance once before I leave, but any woman I meet here will think I want more than just a dance.*

On cue, the crowd parted slightly. Amid the collection of drunks enhancing their level of inebriation and obnoxious men striking out with various women, Max saw two women sitting at a table in the far corner. His heart leaped with recognition.

That's Donna! And it looks like just her girlfriend with her. No tall yellow men in sight. I might not like the setting, but I'm not letting her get away from me again. Lord, be with me.

"Hey Donna- there's your man."

Donna glanced where Yolanda indicated and saw a brown-skinned man with a glistening Jheri curl trying to look like he wasn't sizing them up.

"I'm gonna get you, 'Landa. Look at him working up his nerve. He'll probably be over here in a minute."

Yolanda smiled. "And I bet *you're* the one he wants."

"Don't put that on me!"

Max made his way across the dance floor, evading drunks and wildly flailing dancers alike. Halfway to his goal, he looked up and his heart stopped. A colorfully dressed man with a Jheri curl was headed straight for Donna's table.

Lord, Max prayed, don't let him ask Donna to dance. Or if he does, let her say no!

The man reached the table, hesitated between the two woman and then asked Yolanda to dance. *Okay friend,* Max thought, *dance with that guy. I need a chance to talk to Donna alone.*

Inexplicably, Yolanda got up with Jheri, leaving Donna alone to giggle at her friend's questionable choice of dance partners.

Perfect, Max thought as he closed the remaining distance to the table. *Now all I have to do is not say anything stupid.*

"Donna? I thought that was you. How you doing?"

Didn't take me long to blow that one.

Donna looked up in surprise. "Max! Didn't know you were here."

Max smiled. "I didn't plan to be, but it just sort of happened. Mind if I sit down?"

"No, go right ahead."

As Max took a seat, Donna was puzzled. *I didn't know he was still here. Then again, I'm surprised I can feel anything in a place like this.*

Max sat self-consciously. *Her friend will probably dance just one song with that loser. I don't have a whole lot of time for conversation.*

Donna smiled. "If you didn't plan to be here, what happened?" *Real good Donna. Just throw yourself at him.*

Max smiled in relief. *She just gave me an opening.* "He did."

Donna looked where Max pointed, and saw Fred and Merry looking as if they'd been dance partners for years.

"That's your friend?"

"Yeah, that's Fred. Only a best friend could have convinced me that this is more fun than staying home watching movies."

Donna laughed. "Sounds familiar. My friend Yolanda- the one dancing with Jheri Curl over there- is the one who dragged me here. Frankly, I prefer your idea of a Friday night to this chaos."

Max was hard-pressed not to ask her out on the spot. *She doesn't like this scene any more than I do,* he thought. *I have a shot.*

"By the way, if you value Fred's friendship, you might want to warn him about the company he keeps."

Donna described the near fight between Yolanda and Merry, and Max laughed.

"Sounds like Fred's kind of woman."

Just then the DJ switched songs, keeping it back in the day with Cheryl Lynn's "To Be Real." Donna perked up at the first few notes.

"Oh, I love this song!"

Max smiled. "So do I. Would you like to dance?"

"Thought you'd never ask."

They found a spot on the dance floor not far from Yolanda and her greasy-haired admirer. Donna suppressed a laugh as Yolanda shot a "why did I dance with this clown?" look her way.

Looks like 'Landa has her hands full with that one. I'm glad he didn't ask me.

After a few minutes, the song changed to something slower, clearing half of the dance floor. Max was about to sit down as well and was surprise when Donna stepped forward and put her hands on his shoulders. Fighting back surprise, he placed his hands gently on her back and sighed as they began to sway in time with the music.

He also prayed for the divine suppression of any unfortunate physical reactions.

Max knew Atlantic Starr's Always quite well, and without realizing it, he began to sing the words softly in Donna's ear. She looked up briefly, smiled to see that his eyes were closed and laid her head back on his chest.

Holding Donna was like nothing Max had ever experienced. It felt natural for them to be there, suspended it time, the two of them basking in a timeworn melody. Max felt energized, as if opposite charges of electricity flowed between them and held them together.

All too soon, the song ended. Donna looked up, smiled and indicated by letting go of Max's shoulders that she was through dancing. Disappointed, but happy for the one slow dance she'd granted him, he took her hand and led her back to the table.

Max walked on air, but Donna, while enraptured by the experience, was disgusted with herself.

What was that? Why did I just slow-dance with a man I just met? Where did my pride go between the table and the dance floor? I'm practically throwing myself at Max tonight!

As they arrived at the table, Yolanda informed her coiffure-challenged dance partner that she wasn't interested in any further interaction, tonight or ever. Undaunted, he bid her farewell and set off in search of a new woman to harass.

Donna smiled. "Short dance, 'Landa."

"I had no choice I was starting to get high off the smell of activator."

They laughed. "Yolanda, you remember Max?"

"Yes, from church. How are you?"

"Can't complain."

They all sat for a time, watching the dance floor. The song had changed to "I'll Make Love To You" by Boyz II Men. How appropriate, Max thought. That's Fred's theme song on any given night.

"There's your new best friend, Yolanda. And that's Max's friend Fred she's dancing with."

Yolanda sucked her teeth in disgust. "He better keep one hand on his wallet. I don't trust that heffa."

Donna laughed. "You're just mad because I wouldn't let you kick her butt."

When the song ended, Fred and Merry left the dance floor together and headed for the exit. As they passed the table, Donna felt intense desire crackling between Fred and Merry. It flowed from them and washed over her. It made her light-headed, and also somewhat excited.

"Well 'Landa, unless you want to wait for Jheri to come back, I've had enough fun tonight."

Yolanda reached for her purse. "Me too. Let's go."

Max stood and helped Donna to her feet. "My sentiments exactly. Let me walk you two out."

They carefully picked their way through the thick of the crowd. Waves of conflicting stimuli attacked Donna again; desire and anger, excitement and disappointment, lust and misplaced hope, mostly overlaid by an alcoholic haze. Their cumulative effect made Donna sicker with every step. She unconsciously pressed closer to Max, who automatically took Donna's hand, assuming she was trying not to get separated from them in the crowd. His touch was electric, and from it, Donna gained the strength to weather the emotional storm.

"You okay, Donna? You look pale."

Donna tried to smile. "I'm fine, Max. Why they have the music so loud I don't know. It's giving me a headache."

Yolanda put a hand on Donna's other arm to help guide her through the crowd. In that instant, Donna accidentally transmitted what she felt to her best friend. Yolanda blanched, and quickened her pace, wanting to get Donna out of there.

Donna felt better as soon as they separated from the crowd. She was parked a block from the club, and they arrived at her car without incident. They thanked him for walking with them, and an exchange of goodbyes later, Yolanda slid behind the wheel of Donna's car. Max watched them drive safely away.

I never thought I'd run into Donna at a club. Thank God Yolanda was as persuasive as Fred or else this would have been another wasted evening. I should've gotten the number, but I didn't feel right asking for it out here. Oh well, there will be another opportunity.

A horn blared, and Max braked just in time to avoid running a red light. Once out of Wilmington and safely back on I-95 South heading back towards Newark, his thoughts ran back to the events of the evening.

That was too much to be coincidence. I doubt Yolanda really wanted to dance with that guy. And, Jheri seemed like he wanted Donna, but asked Yolanda. Why would he switch up? Would God answer a selfish prayer like that?

6

"Look out!"

Everything was a blur. Hemingway couldn't react before Mark Ronald Ellis thrust him backwards. As Hemingway hit the ground, a hail of bullets hit Ellis, who jerked spastically several times and dropped like a stone, his shirt blossoming with red.

"NO!"

Return fire from Hemingway's platoon cut the sniper to pieces, but Hemingway saw nothing but his best friend, dying in a foreign country where neither of them had ever wanted to be.

"Hang on, M.R. Hang on man. The medic's coming."

Ellis's breathing was labored, and the intense effort it took for him to speak told Hemingway everything he needed to know about M.R.'s condition. "I'm- - -done."

"Don't say that, man! You gotta live so you can get home to Val."

Ellis shook his head. "Tell Val- -what happened. Take care- -for me. Tell Val- - I love her."

With a groan, Ellis died, the first casualty of his platoon. The others bowed their heads; they knew he wouldn't be the last.

"NO! NOOOOOO!"

Hemingway sat up straight in bed, drenched in sweat. Crying uncontrollably, he held himself with both arms and rocked back and forth like a small child.

"Not my fault, man. You didn't have to take my bullets. Not my fault."

When the dreams got rough, Val understood and helped me deal. Now she's gone too.

Hemingway repeated this phrase like a mantra, sobbing like a baby until sleep finally overtook him.

Max unlocked the door to his apartment, still pondering what happened in the club.

Tonight's blessing notwithstanding, I need to stay out of clubs from now on. There's far too much temptation there.

After forty-five sleepless minutes, he got up to pray.

"Lord, I'm confused. I guess You already know that, but I am. I don't quite understand what happened tonight, but something did and it scared the mess out of me. Please God, help me to understand.

He knelt there for twenty minutes, communing with God.

Donna went directly from the car to her bed, vowing never to go to a club again as long as she lived. Away from the overpowering emotions in the club, Donna felt much better, and fell into a fitful sleep.

She tossed and turned, murmuring incoherently in response to her dream. She wasn't in the small apartment she saw, but she could see everything happening inside.

A thin middle-aged black man with a developing potbelly sat on the floor, drinking a beer and laughing over a folded document. Donna couldn't see it clearly, but it looked like a travel brochure. As she strained to focus her nearsighted vision, the woman in red from the club snatched the brochure and laughed as she tore it to pieces. The man was furious and lunged at her.

As Donna looked on in shocked amazement, she felt a tug, like she was attached to a rope and someone pulled. The room dissolved; she fell through blackness and then she found herself outside in a forest. *The* forest!

Without warning, a man appeared to Donna's right. As the scene shifted, her vision became blurry. *Not now*, Donna thought. *I want to see this guy!*

Her vision didn't improve enough to recognize him. He held out his hand to Donna and said something she couldn't quite make out. She felt compelled to speak to him.

"You look familiar. Who are you?"

She woke up suddenly. *What was that all about? First I'm in a crappy apartment and then I'm in that paradise. I don't get it.*

On impulse, she got up and found a pen and some paper.

I want to remember this. If I keep dreaming this weird, I might need to get professional help.

Max woke up with a start for the second time that night. The first time, he'd awakened still kneeling beside his bed. After stretching to get the kinks out of his neck, he crawled into bed and fell asleep, immediately sliding into a dream. There was darkness and then there was light and he was in the woods again. Same trees, same water, same everything. Just as he wondered when Donna would show up, she was there. She started to speak, but she vanished before he could answer. Max woke up quickly.

Man! I can't even talk to her in my own dreams!

He laughed at how that sounded, grabbed his notebook from the nightstand, scribbled something and went back to sleep. He didn't remember any more dreams.

Around ten A.M., Fred and Merry awoke in his Newark apartment. For the first time in years, Fred wanted the woman beside him to stay longer and hoped she felt the same way. He didn't know why.

Debris from their sexual explosion was strewn across his bedroom. Clothes lay everywhere, and more condom wrappers than Fred remembered using littered the room. He smiled and nudged his companion.

"Get up, Merry. If we stay in bed, we might kill each other."

Merry laughed. "What better way to go?"

Both of them showered and dressed slowly.

What's wrong with me, Merry thought as she buttoned last night's pantsuit. *I got what I needed; I should be long gone by now. Why am I trying to hang around?*

Why don't I want her to leave? Fred searched for a clean shirt. *I know how to get rid of a woman, but what do I do to keep one around?*

He cleared his throat nervously. "Listen, um, you want to go somewhere for brunch? There's a good place not far from here."

Merry smiled. "Sounds good. Tell you what. I live about ten

minutes away. Let me get some fresh clothes and I'll meet you there. Where is it?"

Fred told her the restaurant he had in mind and then walked her to her car, watching as she drove off.

Max, you may be right. You can find someone worth hanging onto these days.

Merry entered her townhouse and went straight to her bedroom, smiling all the way. She exchanged the tight red pantsuit for a looser fitting turquoise blouse and black pants.

Normally I'd leave a guy hanging at this point, but there's something different about Fred. I need to spend more time with him and find out what it is. If nothing else, I haven't been with anyone as good as him in years.

She picked up her purse and keys and left to meet Fred, still wondering why she'd given Fred her real name.

Max reclined comfortably on his couch, and finished reading Nobody's Perfect by Patricia Haley. He'd recently discovered a wealth of African-American written Christian fiction, and in response, spent what seemed like a small fortune stocking his bookshelves with their works. Destiny's Cry by Derek Jackson was the one he'd finished before discovering this one.

Besides Haley, books by Jacquelin Thomas and Terrance Johnson now lined his shelves, and he'd just learned of three other Christian fiction authors, Pat G'orge-Walker, Sharon Ewell Foster and Kendra Norman-Bellamy. *More books to buy when I get paid.*

He replaced the book on his shelf and closed his eyes, smiling to himself as he thought about Donna.

Sooner or later I'm gonna get a chance to talk to her again, and when I do, I'm going for the phone number no matter what. It's past time to find out if I have a chance with her.

A sudden thought occurred to him, and wanting to reread the account of his recurring dream, he went to get his notebook. He was surprised to see a new entry.

I don't remember writing anything new. What's this?"

He scanned the page and his heart skipped a beat. "Authority is a gift. I Corinthians 12. Matthew 10:1."

Intrigued, he reached for his Bible and started to read.

Donna sat up in bed, reading her hastily written account of last night's dream.

That one's easy to figure out, she thought. *That man I dreamed of was probably Max, just like Yolanda said.*

Just then there was a knock on the door. "You awake?" "Sure, come on in."

Yolanda entered the room, wearing an oversized University Of Delaware T-shirt and shorts. She sat on the edge of Donna's bed.

"Listen I just, well, I wanted to apologize. I never should have dragged you to that club. I didn't realize how- - -unhealthy it was for you to be in a place like that."

Donna smiled. "Don't worry about it. How could you have known? I'd never had the opportunity to share that with you before."

"When you showed me that- -that chaos you felt- - -how do you cope with that?"

"I can't avoid crowds for the rest of my life, so over the years, I've learned to block it out as best I can. It's just tougher to do that in a club where everybody's acting all crazy."

Yolanda shook her head. "I see why saved folks don't need to be in places like that. What you showed me was like pure spiritual warfare."

Donna nodded. "Yeah, it is. I never thought about it that way, but you nailed it."

Yolanda went to take a shower. Donna got back under the covers for a bit more sleep before starting her day.

Actually, I'm glad she dragged me to that club. It was nice spending time with Max, despite the surroundings. I hope I see him tomorrow in church, and I hope he asks me out, because I'm sure ready to go.

Merry was watching TV when her phone rang. *Who would call me at seven o'clock on a Saturday?*

"Hello?"

"Hi Merry. It's Fred."

Merry's entire mood brightened. "Good to hear from you."

Fred drew a deep breath, hoping Merry wouldn't notice. "Any plans for tonight?"

"Actually I was just heading out the door."

Merry could almost hear Fred's face falling over the phone as he exhaled disappointedly. "Oh."

Merry smiled. "To your place."

She felt his smile return. "I'll be here."

Fifteen minutes later, Merry smiled as she approached Fred's apartment.

I'm glad he called. I definitely wanted to see him again.

The door opened, and Merry burst out laughing. Fred stood there clad only in a plush towel and a big smile.

"I figured why waste time?"

Max sat at his computer scanning revisions to his latest story. Try as he might though, the words on the screen kept fading into images of Donna. He saw her smile, her warm eyes and even smelled the subtle perfume she had on when she greeted him in church yesterday.

You act like you've never seen a woman before. Sitting here doing nothing; can't even work thinking about her.

"Quit dreaming about your woman and get some work done!"

Max jumped slightly in his chair. Fred had sneaked up behind him while he was zoned out.

"Fred, don't you have anything to do besides scaring me?"

Fred grinned. "Obviously not. And don't get mad at me because I'm right. You must be thinking about Donna; you're drooling so hard you almost shorted out your computer."

"You know Fred, we're still looking for somebody to cover that frog jumping contest in Lewes."

Fred laughed. "Aw, it's like that now? That's all right. I'll leave so you can get back to daydreaming about your woman and pretending like you're working."

He returned to his seat, leaving Max alone with his thoughts. Before Max realized, he was in silent prayer.

God, I don't know what's going on here. It makes no sense at all, but it feels right. I mean, for all I know she's not thinking about me like that and still has that boyfriend. Should I chase this dream or am I making another huge dating mistake? It could be too soon after that Jenisse situation. Lord, just let me know what to do and I'll handle it. Better yet, You handle it for me. That way I'll know it's being done right! In Jesus' name I pray, Amen.

Max resumed his work with renewed vigor.

Fred kept working on his story on the recent Night Out Against Drugs Rally in Wilmington.

Max is GONE. I'd tell him to turn in his player's card, but he never had one! Oh well, a good woman can do that for you. I'm busting on him and here I am still thinking about some weekend pickup.

He thought back to Saturday, when Merry surprised him by keeping their date at the restaurant. He half expected her to ditch him once they had their clothes on, like he had done to women in the past.

Actually, I wanted to see if I could get her out of my system. All I needed was to see her order a greasy sausage and egg platter and that would've done it.

Merry surprised him by ordering the same breakfast he usually got at Demeter's- an egg white omelet and their assorted fruit platter with freshly squeezed orange juice on the side. Amazed, they talked most of the morning, which made Fred decide to call her again that night. They didn't part company again until late the next afternoon.

I don't know what to do now. I figured after we hooked up one more time, I'd be over her. I'm not used to wanting to see a weekend pick-up again after the weekend is over. Wonder if I should call her again?

Naah, she's a playa. She knows the rules- leave weekend stuff on the weekend and move on. If I called her tonight, she probably wouldn't remember my name.

Or maybe she would.

Max worked steadily, trying not to let thoughts of Donna break his concentration.

I didn't get a chance to talk to her after church yesterday. I guess I could have, but there were a lot of people around.

As noon arrived, Max found himself engrossed in the story he was editing. *I don't want to stop while I'm on a roll. I'll go to lunch later.*

At one o'clock, Donna turned her computer off, grabbed her purse and her lunch and headed for the elevator.

The scent of lilacs greeted her as she stepped outside. A black and gold monarch butterfly pirouetted past Donna's nose, landing on a nearby flower for a moment before continuing its daily dance of life and death. Squirrels conversed excitedly in the nearby trees, and off in the distance, ducks splashed in their private man-made pond.

The park was there when developers bought the land to create the New Castle Business Center, and they decided to leave a large part of it intact, as an oasis of natural beauty in the middle of developed land.

Maybe I'll come out here for lunch more often. Staying inside all day every day gets dreary.

Max finished eating in ten minutes, anxious to enjoy the small park as long as he could. He couldn't stop smiling as he walked slowly, taking in each sight and sound.

This is really beautiful. I should've started coming out here to eat a long time ago.

He rounded the corner and almost ran smack into Donna.

Having finished her lunch, Donna pulled a paperback book from her purse and settled back. She relaxed, allowing her unique perceptions to float unchecked so she could fully enjoy her surroundings. While animals didn't have many emotions Donna could discern, she could feel pure pleasure emanating from the squirrels and ducks as they enjoyed their surroundings.

Max was breathless. He absorbed every aspect of Donna's appearance: caramel skin, flowing black hair, piercing eyes and an absolutely gorgeous outfit (pink blouse and tan skirt). Max was hard pressed not to stare at her legs. He quickly popped a peppermint to forestall any chance of bad breath.

She sat on one of the benches with a copy of Nobody's Perfect and laughed to herself as she read.

Good thing she's into the book. I'd hate for her to catch me standing here staring like a dork. She might think I was a stalker or something.

Absorbed in the book and her surroundings, Donna's ability to feel other people's emotions was muted. However, she still sensed Max's approach without having to look up.

Somebody's close. I hope it's a man because they're attracted to me.

Donna giggled to herself. *Bet it's that jerk from the third floor. Time to prepare the polite brush-off lines.*

God, thank You for giving me this chance to talk to her. Help me to just be myself.

Max took a deep breath and stepped forward.

Whoever it is, they're really nervous. I can't feel anything else from them because of it. It must be a man, deciding whether or not to try and talk to me. Hope he makes up his mind soon.

"Hello Donna."

Startled by the familiar deep voice, Donna nearly dropped her book. As she recognized Max, her eyes brightened and her neutral expression dissolved into a smile.

"Max! Good to see you again. Sit down for awhile?"

"Sure."

Suddenly self-conscious, she moved her purse to make room for Max, all brush-off lines completely forgotten. He sat down a moderate distance from her, nervously basking in the subtle fragrance of her perfume and trying not to get lost in her eyes. He looked down at her book and smiled.

"I read that. It's really good."

Donna returned his smile. "I like it so far."

They conversed briefly about books and suggested a few titles to one another.

Donna looked around and smiled. "It's so beautiful out here. Makes me wish we had more than an hour for lunch."

Max sighed. "Yeah, me too. It's a shame we can't work out here. Then again, we'd never get anything done."

Donna giggled musically, causing a tremor of joy to whisper through Max.

"You're probably right. My manager would fire us all for dreaming on the job."

Max laughed. "I can see a few drawbacks in that."

"You know, I know you work in one of these buildings, but I never asked which one."

"Oh, uh, I work for City Voice. I'm an assistant editor, which basically means the other assistants and I do all the work and the editor-in-chief gets all the credit."

Donna laughed again. "That sounds a whole lot more interesting than Customer Service Correspondence."

"It is to me. I haven't been bored since I started."

Donna looked at her watch. "Quarter of two. I better start back- it takes a little while to get back to the buildings from here."

They got up and walked slowly back through the garden, chatting as they went. Each of them noticed that the other seemed to be in no particular hurry.

If Donna's not really into this conversation, she's the best actress I've ever seen. This is my best chance, and I refuse to blow it.

"You okay, Max? You're moving slow- don't tell me you're not in a big hurry to get back to work."

"Actually, I'm not. If I had a choice, I'd rather stay out here with you." Despite getting exactly the response she wanted, Donna blushed. "You would?"

"I would. But since staying out here would get us both fired, can I call you sometime so we can continue this?"

"Sure."

Donna restrained her joy as she dug a pen out of her purse. She wrote her name on a scrap of paper she found inside and gave it to Max. Max took it and deftly extracted a business card from his wallet in the same motion. "Thanks."

They simultaneously looked at their watches, and, noticing how they'd mirrored each other, laughed and continued back towards their buildings, arriving at exactly two o'clock.

"It was nice talking to you, Max."

Max barely restrained himself from breaking into a holy dance. "Thanks, I enjoyed talking to you too. Talk to you later."

Donna smiled and headed back to work. Max watched her until she disappeared inside her building before going on his way.

That night, Merry removed the cleaning tape from her VCR, dusted the whole unit and turned the system off.

I haven't made any new tapes since dear old Attorney Hayden, she thought. *I haven't really needed to- I've got enough money saved and enough coming in to coast for a few months, and I just haven't felt like going through all that with any new guys.*

Thoughts of the mechanical liaisons she'd had with most of her "costars" flashed through her head, and left her cold. Fred came to mind, and she couldn't stop smiling.

Why am I still thinking about him? That was a weekend thing, and I'm sure he's not still thinking about me. He's no doubt moved on, and so should I.

Then again, good men don't grow on trees. He's actually interesting to talk to and great in bed. I shouldn't throw him away so soon.

Besides, I'm sick of my life being nothing but business. I deserve some pleasure too.

Resolved, she picked up the phone and dialed a number she'd committed to memory.

"Hello, Fred?"

Donna hung up the phone, almost in a trance. Yolanda looked up from the test papers she was grading and smiled.

"Let me guess. Mr. Wonderful called already."

Donna laughed. "Yes, that was Max."

Yolanda smiled. "You just gave him the digits today and he's asking you out tonight. The brother works fast."

"You don't hear me complaining."

They talked for another hour before Donna ended the conversation to allow Yolanda to finish grading her fifth graders' tests. Donna went to bed, but didn't want to go to sleep without praying first.

"God, I thank You. Thank You for every blessing You give me; food, clothing, shelter, health, family, friends and so much more. And God, thank you for allowing me to get to know Max. You could have sent him to any woman of God, but You sent him to me, and I am grateful. Lord, let our friendship grow, and anything else that might come from it. In Jesus name I pray, Amen."

She crawled into bed and fell asleep almost instantly, still smiling.

Fred and Merry lay in bed, talking softly. It was a relaxed time for both of them, a rare thing in their lives. During a lapse in their conversation, Fred looked over at Merry. She lay on her back with her eyes closed, completely at peace.

I made a huge mistake trying to let her go after last weekend. We have something here, and I want to keep exploring it to find out how far we can go.

Wish I'd met her sooner. I'm thirty now, and getting new women all the time is hard work. It just might be time to think about settling down.

Merry felt content for the first time in years. *I'm enjoying just being with him. I wonder if Fred feels the same way?*

"You're getting quiet on me, Merry. What's on your mind?"

She smiled luxuriously. "I'm thinking about how I wish we could spend more time together like this."

"We could. I could quit the Voice, you could quit whatever it is you do and we could take our savings and run off to the Bahamas. We could spend the rest of our lives having sex and listening to reggae."

Merry laughed and squeezed his arm playfully. "You are *crazy*! And cute too. Come here."

They didn't talk any more for the rest of the evening.

"Hey Fred! Wake up!"

"Hmm? Oh, yeah. Sorry Max."

Max playfully smacked the back of Fred's head. "Did you or did you not ask me to proofread your story? What's wrong, the roaches keeping you awake?"

"Yeah, I raised their rent and throwing wild parties is how they get back at me. That and they have turf wars with the rats every other day."

Max laughed. "Seriously though, what's wrong? You sleeping okay?"

"I was until I met Merry. She came over last night and we didn't get to sleep until about four this morning."

Max raised one eyebrow. "Mary? Which one's that?"

"The one I met at the club last Friday, remember? And it's not Mary, it's Merry like "Merry Christmas."

Max's eyes widened. "It's a week later and you remember her name? Wow, when's the wedding?"

Fred rolled his eyes. "Very funny."

"I'm serious. She must have turned you *out* if you're still seeing her."

Fred smiled. "It's like that sometimes. One of these days you'll start having sex again and you'll understand."

"Yup. After I get married, we can catch up on years of conversations."

They both laughed, recalling countless conversations about sex. Fred couldn't see the value of abstinence any more than Max could understand the allure of being a player. Max was no virgin, but he'd practiced abstinence for the past three years and made sure to tell Fred why he intended to keep it up until marriage. Max started to reopen that conversation, but the look in Fred's eyes stopped him.

"You're getting serious about her!"

Fred smiled. "Max, there are some girls you just get it from once and others you keep around for emergencies. Merry's the kind who makes you throw away your phone book."

He walked away, leaving a stunned and speechless Max to edit his story. He returned to his desk, still smiling.

I still don't get this. Merry's fine and all, and she's good to talk to, but I've been with women I could talk to before. This is different somehow.

We match either deep down. I guess if we keep hanging out, we'll find out exactly why sooner or later.

Something about her just feels right.

Still shaken by his latest round of nightmares, Roscoe Hemingway paced his apartment, revenge filling his mind.

She lied to me from jump. She used me and thought she could just leave me hanging.

Hemingway flashed back two years. He was married then, and had a thriving career as an architect with a substantial income. He'd married Mark Ronald Ellis' widow Valerie a year after returning from Vietnam in one piece, more out of a sense of duty and guilt than out of love. Twenty-seven years later, he felt confined.

Hemingway met "Crystal Lawrence" through his best friend and neighbor Dr. Thomas Chamberlain. Doc introduced them at a party, and when Hemingway realized that this fine young light-skinned sister wanted him, he couldn't sneak off to Crystal's place fast enough. She made him feel twenty years younger.

He quickly learned that messing with Crystal was the worst mistake of his life. Within a week, Valerie received an explicit videotape of her husband's transgression. Given the excuse she needed to end their failing marriage, she wasted no time. Hemingway came home from work the day after she got the tape to find his things packed and on the lawn. Valerie stood at the door holding a gun; she informed him that if he didn't grab his stuff and hit the road inside of half an hour, she would shoot.

Hemingway was gone in twenty minutes.

He handed over a substantial portion of their property in the settlement, and a hefty alimony check each month. Fearing negative publicity, many of his clients backed off. If not for the few who stuck with him, a few investments and his military pension, Hemingway might have gone broke.

Everything I've found out since I followed her here says her name is really Merry Lucas. That heifer never loved me; she was just after my money and when I didn't give her any, she played me. I can't change what happened, but I can make sure she never does it again. I should have known better then to deal with her.

Something about her just didn't feel right.

7

Max paced his apartment in his bathrobe. The clock seemed to have stopped at five o'clock, two hours before he was to pick Donna up.

This is crazy. I'm acting like a high school kid about to go on his first date.

Having showered ten minutes ago, Max sat on his couch to relax. Unable to remain still, he returned to his bedroom to review his wardrobe.

It's just dinner and a movie. No need to break out a tuxedo, but I can't look raggedy either.

He went through his closet for about the two hundredth time since four o'clock, and chose yet another outfit. After laying the clothes on his bed, he glanced at his watch. Only ten minutes had passed.

I bet Donna isn't going through all these changes.

"Yolanda, help!"

Yolanda stopped in her roommate's doorway and shook her head at the sight before her. Donna stood in front her bed in her underwear, rooting through a huge pile of freshly laundered clothes. It looked like her closet exploded.

"I don't know what to wear!"

Yolanda smiled. "What you got on would get his attention."

"Funny. You gonna help me or not?"

Yolanda laughed and joined Donna at the clothes pile. Fifteen minutes later, they had Donna dressed.

"Now was that so hard?"

Donna glared at her friend. "Get back to me in six months when you have your next date and see if you laugh then."

Donna couldn't quite duck Yolanda's pillow to the face.

Fred smiled as he hung up the *phone.*

Merry isn't sick of me yet. I keep thinking it's all a dream and I'll wake up in bed with something nasty and ugly.

Fred laughed, got off the couch and went to prepare for his date.

Max pulled into the parking lot of Donna's apartment complex exactly at seven o'clock. He found her building and got out, sucking mightily on a peppermint drop to ward off any sudden attacks of halitosis. He reached back into the car for the flowers he bought her, and with a deep breath, he headed towards Donna's place.

"Donna, what time did he say he'd pick you up?" "He said he'd be here now actually. He- - -." Donna stopped in mid-sentence.

"Donna?"

"What? Oh, sorry. Max just got here and he's nervous. It distracted me."

A moment later, their door buzzer sounded. Yolanda looked at Donna and shook her head. "I will never get used to you doing that as long as I live."

Donna smiled. "Neither will I."

Having withstood his initial nervousness, Max opened the door as it released, and made his way to Donna's second floor apartment.

This is it, he thought. No turning back. Be with me Jesus.

Holding the flowers down and to one side, he knocked on the door before he could lose his nerve. Yolanda answered, looking relaxed in a baggy blue University Of Delaware sweatshirt and gray sweatpants. As she caught sight of Max, she smiled as if privy to some private joke.

"Donna! Your date's here!"

Yolanda stepped aside and invited Max in. Donna came out of her bedroom and stopped short. She and Max smiled at the sight of one another; without meaning to, they had coordinated their outfits. Max had on black jeans, a red turtleneck sweater and a red and black vest. Donna had on a black blouse, black jeans and a red jacket over it.

"You look great"

Max and Donna spoke simultaneously, and that made them laugh as well.

Yolanda chuckled. "Never has the phrase "Great minds think alike" been more appropriate."

Max smiled and gave Donna the flowers. "Donna, these are for you."

Donna's eyes widened in surprise as she saw the multicolored carnations peeking out at her from within green wrapping paper.

"Max, they're beautiful! Thank you!"

Her smile illuminated the room as she cradled the flowers in her arms. Yolanda also smiled, and gave Max a thumbs-up.

After Donna put the flowers in water, they bid Yolanda farewell and headed for Max's car. He surprised Donna by opening the passenger door for her and making sure she was settled before closing it behind her. As Max slid in behind the wheel, he caught a glimpse of Donna's face and the happiness he saw there made him feel downright giddy; it was all he could do not to burst out laughing or shouting for joy.

Merry blinked in surprise as she opened the door. Fred was dressed to kill in a silver-gray suit and a blue and white patterned tie.

"Fred! I- -wow!"

"Didn't expect me to show up like this, huh?"

Merry smiled. "Definitely not looking so smooth. What's the occasion?"

"You."

He produced a single white rose from behind his back and handed it to Merry; she was so stunned she couldn't speak or move for a second.

"Fred, thank you. This is the sweetest thing anyone's ever done for me."

She turned to go inside, beckoning Fred to follow her. He smiled broadly and sat on the couch. "Let me know when you're ready to go."

Merry turned to face him. "Go where?"

Fred smiled. "Well, you *did* say you were tired of just sitting around the house all the time, and I have to admit, so am I."

Merry looked amused. "Give me twenty minutes. You're too smooth for me right this minute."

Fred laughed. "Take your time. Where we're going ain't going nowhere."

Yolanda put her mystery novel down, giving up on trying to read through her distraction. Directly above her, the sound of an overworked mattress groaning in agony kept her from focusing.

This has to be the twentieth time this week. Those two need to take up a hobby before they break through the ceiling.

Yolanda laughed at the thought of her upstairs neighbors, newlyweds Kyle and Sherrie Owens, landing naked in Donna and Yolanda's living room.

Talk about your unexpected visits. That'd be the most action this apartment has ever seen!

The squeaking ended, giving way to a tentative silence.

Must be halftime. Once they get going, I've never known them to pass out before midnight.

Now thoroughly unable to concentrate on her book, Yolanda got up and went to the kitchen. She wasn't really hungry; just bored and mildly excited. When nothing in the refrigerator appealed to her, she wandered back to the living room and absently toyed with the TV remote.

I'm happy for you Donna, but why I can't I find a decent man too? This sitting home alone on any given occasion is getting old fast.

As Yolanda channel surfed, her mind rolled back to the last few significant men in her life. She knew her relationship with Harold wouldn't survive their University of Delaware graduation because he lived in Illinois and neither of them was up to a long distance relationship. After Harold came a long dry spell, followed by Isaac, who was less mature than her fifth grade students. Isaac made the dry spell seemed like pure joy.

Above her, the mattress groaned anew as the upstairs neighbors got a second wind.

Just need to be patient. My man is out there somewhere, and I just need to be patient and let God bring him to me.

Max pulled into the Bennigan's parking lot and found a space almost immediately. As he held the car door for Donna, she smiled as she sensed attention and attraction from other men in the parking lot.

I hope those men are here alone. If they're with dates and staring at me, they're in for some trouble tonight.

Having noticed a few of the stares himself, Max took Donna's hand as they crossed the Bennigan's parking lot. Neither he nor Donna noticed the two men who stared intently as they entered the restaurant.

"Okay Merry, you can look now. We're here."

Looking stunning in a blue evening gown, Merry opened her tightly closed eyes and blinked in surprise to see Fred inserting his key into the door of his apartment.

"This is your place!"

Fred smiled. "Not tonight. Tonight this is Chez Frederique's, and you are in for an evening of wining and dining."

She took his arm and allowed him to escort her inside. Strutting pompously, he led her into the dining area and ushered her to a seat at the table. Merry chuckled; Fred's exaggerated steps and actions created an atmosphere of fake pretentiousness and serious romance all at the same time. "Would Madame like to see ze Kool Aid list?" Merry laughed until she cried.

Donna settled into her seat and smiled. *Since Max came to pick me up on time, he complimented my outfit, gave me flowers, opened doors, held my hand and pulled my chair out when we sat down. My last three dates combined didn't do that!*

After the waitress came to take their drink orders (Coke for Max, iced tea for Donna), they picked up their conversation where they left off from the car.

Merry was all smiles as Fred served her a home cooked meal of baked chicken, green beans and brown rice.

He worked really hard on this. This is more than just a sex thing. If it was, he just would have taken me to bed again and that would have been that. I doubt that I would have minded, but this is a nice change.

Fred brought his own plate to the table. Smiling, she winked at him and they started eating.

When the waitress came to take Max and Donna's orders, they were laughing so hard they had to signal her to come back in a few minutes.

"You had to wear those too?"

Max gasped for air. "Yup! I had some serious bobos. Mom wouldn't even get the ones that remotely looked like they could be cool; she got me those orange or purple boys out the big bin in the supermarket!"

Donna wiped away a few tears. "Only a black mom would buy you some sneakers from the same place she just went grocery shopping!

"And then she'd get mad if I didn't want them! My mom was like "I paid $5.00 for those and you're gonna *wear* them!"

They ordered when the waitress returned and then kept on talking, shifting smoothly from subject to subject with none of the awkward pauses that both of them had encountered in the past. Donna felt joy building inside her as they shared different insights, and found that more often than not, they were in total agreement.

When their food came, Donna was really impressed that Max took her hands and blessed the food without hesitation. *This is beautiful, she thought. He feels so- -so right. I feel like I've known him forever.*

"Fred, everything was great. Thanks again for bringing me over."

Fred smiled broadly. "Glad you liked it. I haven't cooked for anyone in a long time now. Nice to know I haven't lost the touch."

"Oh, so I was your guinea pig?"

Fred laughed. "Basically, yes."

They both laughed and cleared the table, scraping the dishes carefully before putting them in the dishwasher. Fred turned it on, and then he and Merry went into the living room, settling down on the couch.

Merry sighed luxuriously and settled into Fred's arms. "This is cozy. I could stay like this forever."

"So could I."

"What if we just stayed here like this until we couldn't stand it anymore?"

Fred smiled. "If we did that, we could be here for years!"

"Donna, we have a choice, and either option is fine by me. We still have time to catch the movie if we leave now, or we can linger over dessert and keep talking each other to death."

"Right this minute I'd rather linger." Donna smiled. "We can see the movie next time."

"What? You mean you actually want to go out with me again?"

He pretended to write something on his napkin, mumbling to himself in the process. "Make sue to use the line about the orange and purple bobos- it works."

Donna nearly fell out of her chair laughing. "You are crazy!"

Fred and Merry held each other until leg cramps and bladder pressure made them separate. They got up slowly, flexing their cramped muscles. Fred stretched his legs as he watched Merry walk slowly to the bathroom, gazing contentedly until the door shut behind her.

This is wild. I never thought I could be with a woman and just want to sit and hold her.

Merry returned to the couch and Fred's lap. "Miss me?"

"You just don't know."

She laughed and they got comfortable again.

It was nearly midnight when Max paid the check. He and Donna held hands as they crossed the parking lot, now empty except for Max's car and those belonging to restaurant employees. The night was warmer than usual for mid-March, but cool nonetheless.

Too bad we drove, Max thought. *This would be a perfect night for a walk.*

The sight of Max's front driver's side tire slashed to ribbons shattered his pleasant thoughts. Donna went pale.

Furious and alarmed at the same time, Max tried to lighten the moment.

"Donna, what is it with you? You're rough on tires."

Donna chuckled, but couldn't shake a chilly sense of danger. As Max removed the spare tire from his trunk, Donna transmitted her fear to Max, giving him a renewed sense of urgency. It seemed to Donna like the predatory evil she felt would suddenly manifest itself in some huge, dark shapeless mass.

"Okay, I'm done."

Relieved, Donna reached for the passenger side door. Just then, a movement to their left caught her attention.

Two men, each about Max's height stood there, smiling expectantly.

One held a gun.

8

One thought reverberated through Max's mind as he stared down the barrel of the first .357 Magnum he'd ever seen in real life.

That thing is HUGE!

Stunned to silence, he edged in front of Donna to protect her as best he could.

The hero thing might work on TV, but in real life it gets folks killed. We'll just give them what they want and get out of this alive.

The twin thugs regarded their prey calmly. "This here is called a 'jack. Namely, if y'all don't hand over what we want, you're getting jacked up!"

Seeing fear in their prey's eyes, the robbers laughed and exchanged a high five. Max noted that they were the same height and build, and that they were similarly dressed in black jeans, black long sleeved shirts and black ski masks. One was black and one was white, but Max and Donna couldn't see any other identifying factors.

"I'm counting five, and then somebody's getting shot!"

Max slowly reached for his wallet. Behind him, Donna just as slowly surrendered her purse to Max, not wanting to panic the gunman into shooting.

Dear Lord, Donna prayed, *what now? I don't know what I can do, but there has to be something. I can tell that these men aren't going to let us live. And they won't kill me right away.*

"Trust in the Lord with all thine heart, and lean not unto thine own understanding." (Proverbs 3:5)

Donna blinked in astonishment that such a timely Word would pop into her head. *Pastor Nathan did focus on Proverbs 3 for a sermon not long ago, and it's definitely appropriate here.*

"Throw that stuff on the ground in front of us."

Max complied, somewhat testily. The white man laughed at the expression on Max's face.

"Yo bro, I think my man here's upset!"

The black man cracked up. "He *should* be! We're robbing his butt in front of his woman."

The white man drew a Bowie knife from the sheath on his hip and placed the tip of the blade near Donna's throat. "Don't you mean *our* woman?"

It was all Max could do not to rush them. *Can't do that,* Max thought as he fought the wave of adrenaline surging through his system. *They'd shoot me dead and then they'd have Donna at their mercy. God, what do I do? How do I do it?*

"Then Jesus summoned His twelve disciples and gave them authority over unclean spirits to cast them out- - -." Matthew 10:1

Max almost jumped as scripture popped unbidden into his mind.

Take charge. You have the same authority.

Along with this word of instruction came a second scripture, the verse from Proverbs that Donna had just received as well.

This doesn't make sense, but it feels right. God, are You giving this to me?

"Fear thou not, for I am with thee. Be not dismayed, for I am thy God. I will strengthen thee; yea, I will help thee; yea I will uphold thee with the right hand of My righteousness." Isaiah 41:10 *Okay God. I'll trust You.*

"That's enough. You have our money and you can have my car keys too. Let us go."

The two thugs looked at each other and laughed. Behind Max, Donna closed her eyes, shut out the world around her and prayed silently for calmness.

"For God did not give us a spirit of fear, she thought, *"but of power and of love and of sound mind."* II Timothy 1:7

Calmness and tranquility filled Donna's spirit. She smiled as she received the word from Isaiah that Max just got, and released the calmness that overflowed her being, enfolding them all in a blanket of peace. Oblivious to and unaffected by Donna's efforts, Max continued to talk, submerging his will in God's and letting Him direct the situation.

"I will even drive you anywhere you want to go. But in the name of Jesus, *you will not lay hands on us.*"

To Max's surprise and their own, Max straightened up and stood taller. The thugs stepped back, fear welling up inside them. "S-sure."

"*Take your hands off of God's anointed!*"

To Donna's surprise, the white man immediately took the blade from her throat and tossed it aside, stepping away from her in the process.

Max turned to the other man. "*Demon, your weapon will not harm us. Cast it aside.*"

Where did that come from?

The black man put his gun down on the asphalt and sat meekly, offering no resistance. Max subtly gestured to Donna to leave while she could. She started to back away, cognizant that God was in control of the situation.

Just then a car roared past the parking lot, doing at least ninety MPH. The sudden commotion startled Max and broke his concentration. The black man realized that Max had lost his advantage and jumped up to throw a punch. Max ducked, blocked a second punch and drove an underhand left into his opponent's stomach. Before the gunman could catch his breath, Max drove a hard right into his mouth, sending him sprawling to the asphalt.

Where's Donna? Max looked around wildly. *I hope she got away; these guys might jack me up out here and if they do, she's dead.*

A scraping sound from behind alerted Max; instinctively he ducked, pivoted on his left foot and lashed out hard with the right, punctuating the move with a loud martial arts scream. The perfectly timed kick caught the white man squarely in the face, sending him flying one direction and his knife the other; it clattered off Max's car as its owner slumped to the ground unconscious.

As Max regained his footing, the black man clambered to his feet and launched himself at Max, determined to wrestle him to the ground. Max dug in his heels, but despite his best efforts, the other man forced him backwards. *If I could just-*.

WHANG!

Max jumped, startled at the harsh musical sound of metal on flesh as his assailant collapsed forward into his arms. Behind him, Max saw Donna wielding his tire iron, breathing hard and grinning ear to ear.

"So Max, what do you have planned for our *second* date?"

Merry awakened with a start. The sudden movement woke Fred; he looked at Merry and was alarmed to see her crying.

"Merry, what's wrong?"

She couldn't speak right away. In her dream, two shadowy figures threw a world-class temper tantrum, shrieking like frustrated children at their unexpected defeat in the restaurant parking lot. She hoped that waking up would end it, but she felt as though the shadows followed her up out of sleep.

Fred sat up and pulled her into a gentle embrace. "It's all right, Merry. I'm here. Nothing's gonna hurt you."

Merry's sobs degenerated into hiccupping gasps; she lay her head on Fred's chest and went limp. "E-every night, Fred. I can't sleep well because I'm afraid to dream. There are things in my dreams, surrounding me, threatening to get me."

Fred wasn't sure how to react. "What do these- - -things look like?"

Merry's teary gasps slowed into intermittent sniffles.

"Nothing. It's pitch black, so I never see them. I just feel them all around me and I know they're dangerous. I feel like one of them stays close, like it really wants to torture me. I can't take any more!"

Fred kissed her on the forehead and held her, hoping he'd say the right thing. "Don't even worry about it, Merry. Nothing's going to get you while I'm here."

She smiled weakly and leaned in, enjoying the warmth of Fred's arms. He held her close, talking in soothing tones and stroking her hair until she fell asleep.

"Here it is. My 'bachelor pad.' "

It was nearly three A.M. when Max unlocked his apartment door and stepped aside to let Donna in first. She blinked in surprise, impressed at the sight before her. There was a small couch with a tan slipcover, a small easy chair also covered in tan and matching carpeting. Family pictures were strategically arrayed atop the television, and there were a few paintings on the wall, all by African-American artists featuring African-American subjects.

Donna smiled. "What is this? No dirty clothes, no empty six packs, no pizza boxes, no old Playboys. You sure you're single?"

Max laughed. "I'm too much of a neat freak to live like that. Besides, I threw out the beer cans and skin magazines this morning."

"Congratulations, you just wrecked my stereotype about single guys' apartments. I feel like I should go home and vacuum."

Still laughing, they collapsed onto the couch. They'd spent the last few hours at the police station pressing charges and talking to reporters. Max replayed their conversation with the police in his head.

"You mean we beat up professionals?"

Detective Garrett smiled. "Yup. These clowns are wanted for murder, rape, robbery here, in Pennsylvania and in New Jersey."

Max nodded. "Guess I'm not surprised. They seemed to have their routine down pat."

The detective paused in the middle of filling out paperwork to stare at Max and Donna. "If you don't mind me asking, how exactly did you guys get away?"

Max tried hard to look innocent. "Huh?"

"You said one guy put a knife to her throat, and the other guy had a Magnum pointed at your head. Yet and still, the two of you beat the cow flop out of *both* of them. How'd that happen?"

Max didn't want to explain what happened for fear the detective would think he was on crack.

"All I knew was they were going to kill us. They must have gotten overconfident because they moved their weapons off of us. When they did, we rushed them."

Detective Garrett frowned. "You guys are either great fighters or totally nuts."

Max smiled. "God was with us."

"I'll say. There are men and women on this police force who wouldn't have gotten out of that in one piece."

The detective gave them forms to sign and then reached into the desk drawer. "By the way, those guys had a price on their heads. Here."

Max and Donna were stunned to see a voucher for five thousand dollars.

"Max, I'm really glad you invited me over. We have to talk."

Max snapped back to the present. "Definitely. But first, are you okay?"

Donna smiled. "I feel fine, Max. I should be asking you that."

He rubbed his throbbing right hand and winced. "Good point."

Donna took a deep breath. "Max, what I want to know is how did you do what you did? You- -ordered them to drop their weapons and they just did it. Your voice even sounded different, like thunder or something."

Max got up from the couch and paced, stopping in front of Donna. He took a deep breath. "Donna, that wasn't me. I wasn't sure at the time, but now I think I know what happened."

He grabbed his Bible off the coffee table and tuned to Philippians 2.

"Therefore God also highly exalted Him and gave Him the name that is above every name, so that at the name of Jesus, every knee should bend in heaven and on earth and under the earth, and every tongue should confess that Jesus Christ is Lord, to the glory of God the Father."

Max closed the Bible. "I was praying hard, asking God what to do. The first thing that came to mind was the word "authority." I recently read about how Jesus gave His disciples authority over evil spirits and how even the devil and his demons have to bow before Him, and I just knew that demons influenced those men to rob and kill us."

Donna's eyes widened. "And you just told them to back off in Jesus' name."

"And it worked! Until I let myself get distracted anyway. I forgot that God is in control and not me, and it almost got us killed."

Max shuddered involuntarily as Donna spoke. "Have you ever done anything like this before?"

"You know, I think I have. When I was a teenager."

Max's thoughts rolled back to age thirteen, his first day at Gunning Bedford Junior High School. Within minutes of Max's arrival, Cameron Bailey backed Max up against his newly assigned locker and requested a donation of lunch money. With no leverage to use his new Tae Kwon Do lessons, Max had two choices: surrender the money or get his butt kicked. Max prayed not to get beaten up and was about to hand over his money when he felt led to try and talk Cameron out of it. To both of their utter surprise, Cameron let Max go, and with the exception of a stray insult here and there, left Max alone.

Donna looked thoughtful. "It sounds to me like a less dangerous version of what happened tonight."

Max laughed nervously. "That's it. I didn't know about spiritual warfare back then, but I knew enough to pray when I was in trouble. God answered that prayer and let whatever thieving demon that was using Cameron know that He is in charge."

"Incredible. Until I read Frank Peretti's books, I never really thought of spiritual warfare, but now- - -."

Max nodded. "This is new to me too. I mean, I never thought about authority back in the day. I just wanted to keep my lunch money! And now this."

Donna moved closer and put her hand on Max's. "You did what you had to do. You let God control the situation and He used you in a way neither of us expected. Max, in all the confusion I didn't get to say this, but thank you. From the bottom of my heart, thank you for saving my life."

They hugged like long separated lovers. In that moment, they felt a powerful bonding pull, and could not let go.

An eternity later, they released the hug and Donna slid back to her original position on the couch. Max sat quietly, still transfixed by the power of what they had experienced.

"Wow."

Donna smiled. She couldn't adequately verbalize what she had felt, and clearly neither could Max.

"That was- - -."

Max tried to fill in the blanks. "---powerful. Uplifting."

"Yes, that's it. Uplifting and reassuring as well."

Max stretched and headed for the kitchen. "I'm making tea. You want some?"

Donna smiled. "Sure."

She laughed as he started making the tea. "What's so funny?"

"You shattered yet another stereotype. I thought all you single guys drank coffee."

"Live and learn. All us bachelors don't live life in the fast lane."

"Oh really? And how are you living?"

Max laughed. "More like life in the parking lot."

"I don't know- that last parking lot was pretty lively!"

They both laughed as Max brought in two cups of tea, cream, sugar and slices of lemon. He set everything down on the coffee table in front of Donna.

"Donna, you really impress me."

"Why's that?"

"Two reasons. One, you came back to help me. The only reason I fought was so you could get away."

Donna laughed. "I was about to run, but that guy jumped on you. The tire iron was there, and before I knew it, it was in my hand and upside his head!"

Max laughed even harder. "You wore him *out*! Remind me never to make you mad!"

Donna pretended to glare at him. "Okay wise guy. Was that the second thing- my swing?"

Max looked her in the eye. "No. We were just delivered from a dangerous situation by divine intervention. You saw God's hand on me, and you're accepting it like everyday stuff."

Donna sipped her tea, frowned and added sugar. "I'd have to be pretty dense not to believe what I saw happen right in front of me. Besides, you feel trustworthy."

A moment of dawning comprehension hit Max, and a question he never would have thought to ask normally came to him.

"When you say that I feel trustworthy, do you mean that literally?" Donna smiled. *He's ready to hear this. Thank You, God.*

"Literally. Max, God uses me too. I can feel what people around me feel, and sometimes I can make people around me feel what I'm feeling as well."

Max's eyes widened with comprehension. "Did you do something to affect Ebony and Ivory out there?"

Donna smiled and shook her head yes.

"That might be another reason why they backed down so easily. God double-teamed them through us."

"I was hoping to make them so relaxed that we could get away. In fact, I was getting set to drag you away from them- I thought you might be affected too."

"Believe me, I was anything *but* calm!"

They laughed. Other questions came to mind, and they had to resist the impulse to ask them all simultaneously.

"Donna, could you have made those guys feel anything you wanted? Pain for example?"

"Only if I was already feeling some myself. Maybe I could've made them feel someone else's, but I'm not sure."

A thought occurred to Max, along with a memory of the unexplained agony he'd felt the night after he'd first seen Donna. *Could she have- - -?*

"Max, where did you learn to fight like that? One minute you were fighting like anyone else, and the next you turned into Bruce Lee!"

Max laughed and brushed his musings aside. "I studied Tae Kwon Do starting when I was twelve. I stayed with it long enough to earn my black belt, and I still do the exercises to stay in shape. How about you?"

Donna laughed. "I have two younger brothers. Roland and Richard used to irritate me until I snapped, and then I'd grab Richard's Wiffle Bat and go off on them."

"If I'd known you were so tough, I would have stood back let you handle my light work."

"What, and give up the chance to show off for your date?"

They high-fived each other, stinging Max's sore right hand in the process. Just then a thought occurred to both of them, and they spoke at the same time.

"Max, did you- - -?"

"Donna, have you- - -?"

They burst out laughing again, and it took them a few minutes to calm down.

"Go ahead Donna."

"What I was going to say might sound weird, but no stranger than what happened tonight."

She took a deep breath and collected her thoughts.

"Have you had any strange dreams lately?"

Merry awakened during the night, and smiled to find herself nestled in Fred's arms. Despite the fact that it was still pitch black, she felt no fear.

I could stay like this forever. She snuggled up to Fred like a child clutching a teddy bear and went back to sleep, still smiling.

"Why am I not surprised you're asking me this? For the past month, I've had the same dream. I was outside, which is strange because I hate the woods. There were these really tall trees all around me- - -."

"There was a lake. A crystal-clear lake, or maybe a pond."

Max blinked in surprise at Donna's timely interjection. "Yeah, a pond. It was so clear you could see down to the bottom- - -."

"- - -and count the goldfish at the same time."

They gaped at each other in surprise, electrified by this revelation. "You had it too."

Donna nodded. "About two or three weeks ago. It was on a Saturday morning. I remember I woke up and I wasn't feeling well, so it took me awhile to get back to sleep. When I drifted off, I had that dream."

Max looked stunned. "The same day I last had it. Were there any other people in your dream? In mine, I saw- - someone."

Donna described the shadowy black man in her dream, and as she did, a thought occurred to her.

Max took a deep breath. "In mine, I saw a woman standing in the clearing. She was a light-skinned black woman, about five foot three or four, hair past her shoulders, dark brown eyes. Sound familiar?"

Donna felt her stomach flutter. "Yes."

"It was you, Donna. I saw you in my dream, clear as day. And that Saturday you just mentioned? I saw you and Yolanda in the Pathmark that same day as we both had the dream! And I met you in church a week later."

Donna was visibly shaken, but kept her composure. A thought nagged at her, demanding her immediate attention.

"Max, can I use your bathroom?"

"Sure. Past the kitchen, first door on the left."

She took a glasses case and a small contact lens container from her purse and rose from the couch.

Max couldn't resist calling after her. "This is a man's apartment- don't forget to leave the seat up!"

Donna laughed as she closed the door behind her. She emerged a few minutes later, wearing glasses; small hazel colored frames that suited her face well.

"No Poindexter jokes, if you don't mind."

Max smiled. "Sure, no problem. By the way, who are you?" Max laughed and ducked the pillow Donna threw at him.

"Hey, you didn't say I couldn't make Clark Kent jokes! Seriously though, I don't usually do that. I got my glasses in third grade, and if I hear one more four eyes joke, I'll scream!"

Donna smiled. "I wanted to get my contacts out before they started irritating me. Besides, I want to check something."

She removed her glasses and stared at Max as hard as she could through her blurred vision. Satisfied with what she saw, she put them back on, relieved at the restoration of her vision.

"It's you."

Max didn't have to ask her what that meant.

"In my dreams, I see things like I don't have my contacts in. You're the blurry man."

Max shook his head in amazement. "This is too much to be coincidence. It has to mean something."

He studied Donna's face. "You know, I like you better without your glasses. You have beautiful eyes."

Donna blushed. "Thank you."

Fred and Merry walked hand in hand, enjoying each other's company. They strolled through a park or a zoo on a sunny spring day- Fred couldn't remember the last time he felt so much at peace.

He woke up suddenly, and realized that he still held Merry close. She watched him with a bemused expression on her face, and when she realized that he was awake, she kissed him the rest of the way conscious.

"Last time I slept with a woman who stared at me like that, she was deciding whether or not to set me and the bed on fire!"

"Last time I watched a man sleep, I was waiting to hear if he'd mumble another woman's name again."

Fred hugged her again and Merry relaxed completely, submerging herself in the hug for maximum pleasure.

"Looks like we've both traded up."

They held each other awhile longer before they finally got up. After a leisurely shower and breakfast, they went their separate ways, happier than either of them had been in a long time. Neither of them noticed the blue van parked about a block away nor the man behind the wheel who observed them.

"Six fifteen? Donna, we talked all night!"

Donna smiled as she looked at her watch. After discussing prophetic dreams, the conversation turned to more normal first date fare, such as their jobs and their families.

Donna stood and stretched. Max sat and watched.

"Max, I had a great time, but I need to go home. Yolanda worries about me."

"The mark of a good friend. I'm glad you had such a good time. A lot of women in your situation would never want to see me again!"

Donna smiled. "And they would be crazy. I have to admit though, I haven't had a date quite like this one."

Max laughed. "Yeah, you won't hear stuff like this on Love Connection."

"Now I know we've been up too long. We're getting silly."

"We passed silly three hours ago. I think we've moved on to demented."

They laughed for about the five thousandth time.

Max looked out the window, and an idea hit him. "Donna, since you stayed this long, can you spare me a few more minutes? There's something I'd like to show you."

"Sure. What?"

"This."

He took her gently by the hand and led her out onto the balcony. "Watch."

Still holding hands, Max and Donna fell silent and observed the morning sun. All of their usual concerns seemed insignificant compared to the glory of God before them. Neither of them spoke or moved until the sun completed its transformation from a red ball off in the distance into a blinding yellow mass hanging high in the sky.

Donna turned to Max, tears of joy forming as the beauty of the moment filled her. "Max, thank you. That was beautiful."

"Thank God. He did the work. All I had to do was find someone equally beautiful to share it with."

They locked eyes, both all too aware that further words were unnecessary. Their kiss was soft and tender, and lasted longer than either of them intended. Donna felt like she was soaring on wings of light, and electricity surged through her veins. Max felt as if he possessed Donna's gift and could touch her feelings; he could barely distinguish his joy from hers.

When they could no longer sustain the kiss, their lips parted, but they held each other in a strong hug, not wanting to lose their closeness. An indiscernible time later, they finally let go.

"Max, I really don't want to leave, but Yolanda will call the police if she wakes up and I'm not back."

Max forced a smile. "Yeah, next thing I know they'd be kicking my door down and getting ready to do a Rodney King on me for kidnapping you!"

"You could take them."

They laughed yet again, and as Max picked up his car keys, he heard the familiar sound of his morning paper hitting the door. There was a picture of them on the front page, along with a story of how such an unassuming couple managed to subdue the brutal "Movie Muggers" and then gave thanks to God for their deliverance.

"Nice. I'll have to get one of these later to show Yolanda."

Max laughed. "Funny, I always thought Fred would be the one to have a date make the front page."

The ride back to Donna's apartment was quick, even with a stop at the closest Wawa so that Donna could get her own newspaper. Max took no chances: he parked in front of Donna's building and walked her to her door.

"Max, thank you. The whole night was unforgettable. It's the best time I've had in years, and definitely the most exciting."

"Yeah, we should get carjacked more often." They kissed again.

"Donna, thanks for understanding, not to mention for saving my behind! Not many women could handle what happened tonight. I really appreciate that. And you."

And again.

"Get some rest, you look tired."

"You too, Max. Call me around seven tonight. We should both be recovered by then."

"Sounds good to me. "Well, good ni- - -, er morning."

She unlocked her door and went inside, leaving Max with a pleasant smile as his last glimpse of her. Max stood there momentarily and then snapped out of his trance and returned to his car, pleasant memories of a great date floating through his mind. As he started his car, a thought hit him.

*What **can** we do for a second date?*

9

"All hail the conquering hero! All hail Sir Max of Roundhouse!"

Max stopped short at the sight of Fred and two other men bowing before him.

"We live to serve you, o mighty warrior!" Max laughed. Fred was in rare form this time.

"You guys are sick!"

Max reached his desk and burst out laughing again. Someone (most likely Fred) took the picture of him and Donna from Saturday's newspaper, blew it up to poster size and taped it to his computer monitor. Beneath the picture was a headline lifted from a past issue – *Heavyweight Champion To Wed: "Iron" Mike Tyson And New Love Spotted At Restaurant.*

Still laughing, Max removed the picture and turned on his computer. As it booted up, his phone rang.

"City Voice, Max Carson speaking."

"Hi."

The angelic soprano coming over the line made Max feel like everything was right with the world.

"Hi Donna."

"Our computers are down for about an hour, so I thought I'd call while I was waiting."

Max smiled. "I'm glad you did. I was going to call you at home later and tell you how badly they're clowning me here."

He described the warm welcome Fred arranged, and Donna cracked up.

"Nobody here's that creative. However, I have taken eight million questions. Folks want to know when I met you and was I scared when those guys stepped to us and how did we get out of it and all that. And I don't even know half these folks!"

Max laughed. "The high price of fame, Donna. Guess we'll just have to learn to deal with it."

Merry relaxed with the morning newspaper, trying not to think about her father for a few minutes.

She read a follow-up story about the "Movie Muggers" and their extensive history of mayhem across New Jersey, Pennsylvania and Delaware.

That man risked his life for his date. I didn't think there was a man alive who would put himself in that kind of danger for a woman.

I wonder if Fred would go that far for me?

Fred sat at his desk, wondering what to do. Teasing Max distracted him for awhile, but now he was alone with only a little work to do at the moment and his thoughts. He hadn't talked to Merry since she left his apartment last Sunday afternoon, and he wasn't sure if he wanted to.

Trying to have a one-on-one relationship is one thing, but her having those attacks or whatever is scary. Maybe we should take a break from each other for a few days.

"This is great! Who drew this?"

Max laughed. "Fred must be bored. This is his fifth joke on me in five days."

He and Donna had lunch on "their" bench again. Donna held a drawing Max had brought her.

"It was taped to my computer screen. I can't believe Fred came in early just to rag on me."

The surprisingly well-rendered drawing depicted Max as a superhero, complete with yellow tights and a flowing red cape. In the middle of the overly muscular chest was an insignia with the letters "MM" - for "Mighty Max."

Donna could barely stop laughing. "I thought you told me everything, Max. When did Fred learn your secret identity?"

Max chuckled. "He saw me changing clothes in the supply

room. See, I don't even need these glasses- they're part of my disguise!"

Donna laughed even harder. "Your secret's safe with me."

Max smiled mischievously. "I tried to get Fred to draw one of you in a Wonder Woman outfit, but he refused."

"Smart man."

Jason's Lyric was Merry's all-time favorite movie, but this time she barely paid attention for thoughts of Fred.

Why hasn't he called? And why does it bother me that he hasn't?

A frown crossed her face. *Listen to me, acting like we're a couple or something. Like it or not, I don't have any papers on Fred.*

Merry paused the movie and went to the bathroom, still deep in thought.

Her memories of the date Fred arranged a week ago produced another smile.

He didn't have to dress up and cook for me. That tells me all I need to know; he cares about me, and I know good and well I care for him.

After washing and drying her hands, Merry went straight to the phone.

"Max, how's the popcorn coming?"

"Almost ready."

He gathered butter, salt, bowls and napkins and brought them all to the living room just as the popper stopped. Max transferred the popcorn to a large bowl and brought that into the living room as well.

"Donna, tell me again why this is such a great idea."

Donna laughed. "I told you why, and you agreed with me. Our friends need to get to know each other."

"That's what I'm worried about." Max smiled. "In case you haven't figured it out yet, Fred doesn't know how to act around available women. I don't want to have to soothe Fred's wounded ego after Yolanda kicks his butt!"

Donna laughed. "Max, where did you put the tape you brought?"

"On the arm of the couch."

Donna reached for the videotape, which eluded her grasp and

slid under the TV. She went down on all fours to retrieve it, belatedly recognizing her undignified position.

"Max?"

"Yeah?"

"Are you looking at my butt?"

"Should I be?"

"Max!"

"Seriously though, if I said no, would you believe me?"

"No!"

"Okay then, I am. Nice view too."

"When I get out from under here, I am gonna *smack* you!" They both laughed.

Actually, I wasn't looking until you mentioned it, Max thought. *A man can only take so much.*

Donna put the tape on top of the TV just as Yolanda came through the door, more tapes in hand. To Donna's amusement, she greeted Max first, refusing his handshake and offering a hug instead.

"I know I barely know you, but anyone who makes Donna this happy is someone I know I'll like."

Donna blushed. "Dag 'Landa, you make me sound like an ogre or something."

"Well, I call them like I see them."

She adroitly evaded Donna's playful swipe. "What, you put him to work already? Don't scare him away!"

Max smiled. "Believe me Yolanda, after our first date, it'd take a whole lot more than this to run me off."

"What did you get 'Landa?"

"The Five Heartbeats and Forget Paris, just like you suggested."

Donna smiled "Good. Max brought Jurassic Park in case we need a change of pace."

Max picked up the second tape. "Fred actually suggested Forget Paris. Any time he picks a movie where nobody gets shot or eaten alive, I figure it must be good."

Donna laughed. "Sounds like a ringing endorsement to me."

The doorbell sounded, and Donna buzzed Fred in. He appeared in the doorway a moment later, two liter bottles of Coke and Diet Coke in hand. Max took them and put them on the table with the popcorn and other snacks before making introductions.

"Fred Bennett, this is Donna Randall." They shook hands cordially.

"And this is her roommate Yolanda Mason."

Fred's entire demeanor transformed. His eyes thirstily drank in every curve and contour, leaving no doubt as to the tenor of his thoughts.

"Nice to meet you, Fred.

Yolanda let the tone of her voice convey her disgust at being mentally groped. Fred either didn't notice or didn't care; he took her hand and kissed it formally.

"Very nice to meet you, Yolanda. Any friend of Max and Donna's is surely someone I would enjoy getting to know better."

"Chill out, Romeo. Not interested."

As he and Max sat down on the couch, Fred was relieved. His flirtation was force of habit.

"Don't have a seizure; I was just being polite."

Yolanda's eyes narrowed. "Oh, so you slobber all over everyone Max introduces you to then. Tell me, doesn't that make the guys nervous?"

Amused by Yolanda's rapier wit, Fred chuckled, and Max with him.

"Fred, behave. Dag Negro, can't take you nowhere."

Donna rolled her eyes at the possibility that Max was right after all. "You too, Yolanda. We're here to relax and get to know each other, not to try out for the Olympic Playing The Dozens team."

Yolanda put up her hands as if in surrender. "Lo siento. I'll cool it."

Fred perked up. "'Lo siento?' Por que hablaste in Espanol?" ("I'm sorry?" Why did you say that in Spanish?)

"Sorry. Every now and then I'll forget and slip into Spanish, like I do when I'm with my family."

"Eres puertoriqueno?

Max groaned silently at Fred's utter lack of tact, but Yolanda was unfazed. "No, mejicano. Mexican and African-American to be exact."

Fred nodded. "Cool. None of us are pure anything anymore. Shoot, one of my grandmothers was white."

Yolanda smiled. "I'm in touch with both sides of my heritage. Are you down with both sides of yours?"

"Not really, but every spring I have the uncontrollable urge to get a tan."

Donna and Yolanda laughed and Max groaned at Fred's standard joke.

Yolanda regarded Fred curiously. "One of my mother's favorite sayings is, "El alma no tiene color."

Fred smiled. "'The soul has no color.' Your mom is deep. Hey, y'all must have some interesting family reunions. 'Como te llamas?' "Me llamo Laquita Maria Shanika Guadalupe--."

Max shot Fred a warning glare, which he ignored. Yolanda remained unperturbed.

"Funny. You know, I was just about to ask if you remembered that rapper, Vanilla Ice. I think Vanilla Swirl would be a good name for you."

Donna's eyes widened. *No she did not just bust on him*, Donna thought. She started to say something to Yolanda, but stopped when she felt a wave of something.

She and Fred are having fun. They're enjoying this.

Fred rose to the challenge. "Oh, I *know* you ain't trying to bust with that big-old forehead. Oh wait, that's more like a eight-head!"

Yolanda didn't hesitate. "Don't go there Fred, not when you're so light that when you go outside at night, moths circle you."

"Your feet so big you don't leave footprints, you make potholes."

"Your head's so big you don't have dreams, you see movies."

Max and Donna laughed hysterically.

Fred launched his next verbal assault. "Aw, okay. That's why your lips so big you put on lipstick with a paint roller."

Yolanda smiled, and Donna felt a burst of confidence surge through her.

She's moving in for the kill, Donna thought.

"Fred, you're so ugly if I took you to the zoo, the *gorillas* would pay to see *you*!"

Fred started to reply, but burst out laughing instead. Max, Donna and Yolanda joined him, and it seemed like they'd never stop laughing.

"Dag Laquita Maria, why you have to go there?"

Yolanda wiped a few tears and tried to stop laughing. "Hey, you started it. And I won, didn't I?"

Max gasped for breath. "You sure did."

Fred rolled his eyes, knowing that Max would never let him live this defeat down. The four of them soon settled down with Forget Paris. Max was still chuckling as the movie started.

I've seen Fred play the dozens a hundred times, but usually not with someone he just met. And until today, I never saw anybody who could shut him down.

Hemingway sat alone in his apartment, pondering a variety of revenge scenarios.

That heifer ruined my marriage and my career. And then she thought she could ditch me with a dye job and a move to this tiny rat hole of a state. Not likely.

He fingered the high-powered binoculars lying on the couch beside him, the same instrument he'd used to spy on Merry and Fred a week earlier.

That guy must be her new toy. Well, he'll learn the truth about her soon enough.

Just then an idea came to him, and he hurried to the makeshift workshop in his second bedroom to see if he had what he needed to pull it off.

Fred whistled cheerfully as he entered his apartment.

I thought Max's girl and her friend were gonna waste my Saturday night, he *thought, but Yolanda was funny! And Donna's nice. Max struck gold with that one.*

A flash of red registered on his peripheral vision, and he realized that there was a message on his answering machine. *Uh oh, which one is this?*

"Hi Fred, it's Merry. Just called to see how you're doing. Give me a call when you get a chance."

A burst of warmth shot through Fred as he heard the familiar musical voice. *Good,* he thought. I *was thinking maybe I messed up by not calling her all week. Won't make that mistake again.*

Ain't this nothing. I been a player forever, and now when I think I might settle down, I pick another player!

He picked up the phone and punched in Merry's number, smiling at the fact that he knew it by heart.

"Merry, please! I'm trying to apologize! What else can I do?"

Merry cursed Lorraine Lucas so hard she nearly melted the phone.

"You can do what you always did when Karl decided that I was his personal punching bag- *nothing!*"

"Merry, I- -."

Merry cut her off with more profanity. "You've done enough to ruin my life, now just stay out of it! Have some more vodka and leave me alone!" She slammed the phone down, not wanting to hear any more of her mother's feeble excuses.

How dare she try to apologize now! Where was this desire to do right by me when Karl was on a rampage? Why didn't she do something when he went off besides drink herself blind?

Merry stalked into her dining room and looked in the full-length mirror, disdaining the image before her. She stood a full five foot nine inches tall and was more slender than she wanted to be. She'd dyed her hair from its natural reddish-brown to jet-black a few months ago, but it hadn't helped her outlook.

Why didn't they think before they got married? When they divorced, he was still white and she was still black, but I'm the one stuck in the middle. And they had to give me the worst features of each race. Big nose, big lips, too much height, a small chest and a big butt. Wish I could reverse those last two.

Just then the phone rang, breaking into Merry's thoughts. *If that's my so-called mother calling back- - -.*

"Hello?"

"Hi Merry. It's Fred."

Merry perked up and started to speak, but couldn't.

"Hey, what's wrong? You sound upset."

Inexplicably, Merry burst into tears. Until meeting Fred, she hadn't cried since she was a teenager, but now she sobbed uncontrollably for the second time in as many weeks. Her sadness cut Fred to the bone.

Oh no! She's having another fit.

"Merry, you want me to come over?"

Her first instinct was to say no, but she really wanted to see him. Choked up with emotion, she managed to whisper a yes before hanging up.

She sounded bad. Hope I can help.

He grabbed his keys and hustled to his car.

"Still think it was a bad idea?"

Max looked up from the bowl he was washing and laughed. "I did at first. You saw how Fred acted."

Donna laughed. "Yeah, but 'Landa put him in check *real* quick."

"Okay, so it worked out. Tell you what. Next time we can invite your friend from the club so Fred can have a date too!"

He dodged the potholder Donna threw at him.

"Yeah, right! Like he's still seeing her."

Max smiled. "Actually he *is* still seeing her. We were talking about her a few nights ago."

Fred pulled up in front of Merry's townhouse. Preoccupied with her mental state, he didn't see the blue van parked half a block away. As before, the occupant sat behind the wheel, using high-powered binoculars to check things out.

She has company. Maybe she ordered out.

He switched on his binoculars' night vision function and took a closer look.

That's the same dude from last week! Don't tell me she has a boyfriend!

As he watched, Merry came to the door and threw her arms around the new arrival before escorting him inside.

That looked serious. Maybe I'll do that brother a favor and tell him what he's up against before he becomes a porn star against his will.

Merry had calmed down, but Fred's strong embrace shattered the dam and released another flood of tears. Fred guided her to the couch.

"Nobody's gonna hurt you, Merry. I'm here. I'll take care of you."

She blew her nose and tried to talk. Fred held her close, rocking her in his arms like a child as the pain and frustration of a lifetime burst free.

"Fred, my mother called."

He suppressed surprise, and simply held her while he listened. She told him she despised her father for beating her and favoring her little brother, and that she hated her mother for staying as long as she did. She alternated between being happy when her mother finally took her and left Karl and angry that Bryan was in no danger from their father because of his gender.

"It's okay, Merry. You were a kid. There was nothing you could do about it."

Merry trembled, unconsciously curling up in Fred's arms.

"Y-yeah, I guess you're right. But she keeps calling me and saying she's sorry. That reminds me of how she used to be, afterwards. Karl would get mad and knock her around. When she was too drunk to be a good punching bag, I was next. He'd beat me bloody and she'd let him. After he was done, she'd come in my room talking about how sorry she was. If she was sorry, she would have pulled him *off* me!"

Fred's embrace gave her the strength to keep talking.

"She says she's stopped drinking and started going to church again. She wants me to forgive her. For years she let that man beat me half to death. I can't forgive *that!*"

Fred fought back tears at the revelation of the brutality that marred Merry's youth, and how in some ways, her relationship with her mother mirrored his own with his.

"It's all right, Merry. I won't let anyone else hurt you. Ever."

He held Merry for another half-hour while she rested. She woke up from her catnap half an hour later, feeling refreshed and hungry. Fred warmed up some leftover chicken stir-fry, and they ate together in silence. She looked up at him from time to time, and his reassuring smiles made her glad to be alive.

After eating, they watched TV together until Merry fell asleep again, on Fred's shoulder this time. Smiling, he carried her upstairs to bed and tucked her in, as if she were a small child. She woke up briefly and smiled, mumbling, "Don't go" as she dropped back off to sleep. Tired from their long evening, he kicked off his shoes and stretched out on the bed next to her, fully dressed. They slept that way all night.

"That's it, Donna. All cleaned up."

Donna smiled, and Max felt the warmth of it clear down to his toes.

"Thanks for helping clean up. You didn't have to, you know. There wasn't that much to do."

Max smiled. Yolanda went to bed almost immediately after Fred left, and Max knew it was to give him and Donna time alone.

"It didn't seem right to leave it all for you."

She reached up and hugged him. He melted into the embrace, and didn't want to ever let go.

"See you Sunday, Max?"

He smiled. "I hope so; it's your turn to drive to church. Oh, I've got something for you."

He pulled an envelope out of his pocket and presented it to Donna. Her eyes widened at the thick wad of bills inside, totaling $2500.00.

"It's your share of the reward money. I just cashed the voucher in today." Donna smiled. "I'd almost forgotten about this. Thanks Max!"

"Almost forgot?' If I'd known that, I could've kept this!"

She laughed, and they hugged one last time before Max headed for his car.

I never thought I'd be this happy ending an outing with no goodnight kiss, he thought. Then again, those hugs were better than a thousand kisses.

Darn, I must be in love.

10

Merry woke up in Fred's arms, totally refreshed. For the first time in years, her sleep wasn't disturbed by night terrors.

"Morning Merry. How you feeling?"

She smiled. "Much better. Fred, thank you for coming over. I'm sorry I dragged you out like that."

"Don't even worry about it. You needed a friend and I needed to be here with you."

Merry looked shocked. "You did?"

"Yup. I called because, well I was feeling a little down earlier yesterday, and talking to you always makes me feel better."

"Flatterer."

While Merry showered, Fred went downstairs. *Normally I would have dumped her after the first love marathon. Now I'm in her kitchen cooking her breakfast. Max would laugh his butt off.*

Just then Merry came downstairs, wearing a pink summery blouse and white pants. Fred couldn't stop staring; Merry looked absolutely radiant.

"Like what you see?"

Fred smiled. "Beats what you looked like snotting and sniffing last night."

Merry laughed and swatted him with a potholder. "All right now. Don't make me hurt you before I can thank you properly for last night."

She threw her arms around his neck and kissed him half to death. To Fred's surprise, his knees buckled and he had to sit down.

"You're welcome."

They laughed and sat down to breakfast.

Max and Donna held hands as they entered the sanctuary, Yolanda right behind them. Normally Max wasn't into public displays of affection, but with Donna it felt right.

Max smiled when some of the older church members perked up at the sight of him and Donna together.

It feels good to be here with her like this. Until I met her, I didn't realize how much I needed this special closeness we've found. It feels like I've always known her.

And I don't want to be without her.

Just then, Pastor Nathan announced Luke 12 as the scripture for the day. Max and Donna's attention snapped out of their pleasant thoughts of one another as they prepared for the Word.

"Fred, I meant to ask you earlier. What was it that had you feeling so down last night that you wanted to see me?"

I was hoping she'd forget to ask. "You'll think I'm being funny if I tell you."

Merry wiped her mouth daintily with a napkin.

"Fred, I told you all my business last night. The least you can do is tell me a little of yours."

Fred sighed. "Okay, but don't say I didn't warn you."

He took a sip of orange juice and continued. "My mom called. She doesn't call often, but when she does, it puts me in a mood."

Merry looked surprised. "You don't get along with your parents?"

"My dad and I get along okay. He's one of those never-let-'em-see-you-sweat kind of guys. We don't talk about much but sports and women."

Merry nodded. "At least you talk."

"True. Now my mom, that's a whole 'nother story."

In a voice surprisingly devoid of emotion, Fred told Merry what he'd told no one, not even Max. The memory still blazed brightly despite all the years that had passed. When Fred was eleven, his father announced that he was divorcing Fred's mother.

Merry looked astounded. "What for?"

Fred's voice was hollow. "Mom's an alcoholic. She would go out with her friends, get tore up from the floor up and wind up in some strange man's bed. It happened twice before my dad found out."

Fred grew silent as the memories threatened to overwhelm him. When he came home from school that day, the utter lack of emotion on Joe Bennett's face scared Fred silly. When Lena Bennett came home from work, Joe didn't scream, cry, curse or even think about hitting her. Instead, he told her in a quiet voice that he knew what she'd done and to pack her stuff and get out. She left without a word, which to Fred's eleven-year-old mind was confirmation of guilt.

"If I've spoken to her five times since then, it's a miracle."

Merry sighed. "I can't blame you. She's your mother. You were looking to her for stability and she betrayed your trust."

They washed the breakfast dishes in silence, lost in thought over the revelations of the past two days.

No wonder I fell for her so fast. Both of us are still trying to get over having trifling parents and the stuff that comes with it. We're a lot alike, and I must have seen it in her.

As service ended, Max and Donna prepared to leave.

This is all happening so fast. First I start having those dreams again, and then I meet Donna, we go out and I find out we both have spiritual gifts. Before I can blink, we're seriously dating. God, what next?

Just then Max looked up. He saw a tall dark-skinned woman approaching and froze.

"I wish you were with me last night. I was hanging out with my boy Max and he had me over his new girlfriend's house to meet her and her roommate."

Merry's eyebrows went up. "Is she nice? The girlfriend I mean. "

"Yeah, she's real nice; just Max's type. And her roommate was funny. She and I actually got in a busting contest and she did pretty good."

Merry smiled. "Did she win?"

Fred laughed. "I said she was good, not great."

They laughed and settled back into the couch. Merry felt lighter now that she knew where Fred was, and Fred felt better for having told Merry, even though he didn't understand why he felt led to do so.

Without turning around, Donna knew that a woman Max found attractive was near. The sudden surge of surprise tinged with desire she felt from Max was a dead giveaway. Donna's contentment shattered; jealously flared white hot inside her as she turned to glare at Max. The object of his desire stood next to him, smiling seductively. I know her, Donna thought. But from where?

"Hello Max. Long time no see."

Max felt like a deer paralyzed by a set of headlight beams. *What in the world is she doing here?*

"Uh, hey Jenisse, how you doing?"

"I'm okay. Surprised to see me?"

Max fought to keep his voice from rising to a higher octave. "Frankly, yes. I thought you went to Mount Zion Christian Assembly."

Jenisse smiled. "I do, but my friend Chloe invited me here today. I'm glad she did; I really enjoyed the service."

Max suddenly realized that not only was Donna still standing there, but she was growing angrier by the second.

Hope it's not too late for damage control.

"Donna, you remember Jenisse? Jenisse Anderson, my girlfriend Donna Randall."

Jenisse raised her eyebrows in surprise. "Yes, from bowling. Nice to see you again."

"Likewise. Max, if you'll excuse me for a moment- - -?"

Without waiting for a reply, Donna slowly crossed the room to where the pastor's wife Annie and the rest of the Women's Day committee stood, leaving Max and Jenisse alone.

"Well, this answers the question of why you haven't returned any of my calls. That and the picture I saw of you two in the paper, grinning like you won the prize."

Max sighed. "Question? I told you last time we talked that it wasn't working out between us. You didn't want to accept that."

Jenisse took a deep breath, keeping her voice low. "It seemed to be working out pretty well in your car that night."

Max dropped his voice even more. "Don't *even* go there. I did *not* appreciate you pulling that kind of stunt after I told you my stance on abstinence."

Jenisse looked suitably chastened. "So what we had means nothing to you."

"Jenisse, what *did* we have? We went out twice, and it seemed like we disagreed about everything, including our views on premarital sex. That's why I told you it wasn't working out. I'd be a liar to say I don't find you attractive, but we're on different pages. We don't have what it takes to make a relationship last."

"And you and Donna do."

Max looked Jenisse in the eye. "Yes. Neither of us was looking, but we just found each other. It's what you wait your whole life for."

Max felt the warmth of confidence as he talked about the woman he was rapidly falling in love with to the woman he thought he wanted to be with a few short weeks ago. Jenisse stared at Max, unnerving him with the intensity of her gaze.

"You know Max, if any other man said that to me, I'd slap the mess out of him. But you- you're too straight up to play games. I like that."

As she picked up her purse to leave, Donna walked slowly back to Max's side, sliding purposefully up to him and leaning in for a shoulder hug. Max hadn't meant to flaunt Donna in Jenisse's face, but he pulled her close. Jenisse smiled, letting Donna know that her victory gesture had not gone unnoticed.

"Nice seeing you again, Max. Maybe we'll run across each other sometime."

Jenisse leaned closer to talk directly into Donna's ear.

"You've got a good one, girl. Don't let anybody take him from you."

She turned and walked slowly away, swaying her hips as she found her friend Chloe and they made their exit, leaving a stunned Max and a perturbed Donna in their wake. Assorted onlookers (Yolanda included) pretended they hadn't been eavesdropping as they moved aside to let Jenisse pass.

"You can suck your tongue back in, Max. She's gone now."

Max started to defend himself, but the rage in Donna's eyes froze the words on his tongue. Catching the prevailing mood, Yolanda whispered a goodbye and slunk off to catch a ride with a friend, leaving Max and Donna to walk to his car together. Max could feel her anger building like lava within a volcano. When he opened the passenger door for her, she got in, and instead of letting him close the door behind her, yanked it out of his hand and slammed it shut, barely missing Max's fingers.

God, Mount Donna is about to erupt. Help!

With a goodbye kiss at the door, Fred left Merry's apartment to spend the rest of his Sunday relaxing. His mood turned sour fast when he noticed that his driver's side front tire was flat.

"How did that happen? The car's been sitting still all night."

Angry, Fred opened his trunk and retrieved his spare tire to replace the ruined one. As he worked,

Hemingway sat down the block, committing Fred's face to memory through his binoculars.

You're mine. Let the games begin.

Max and Donna drove three blocks in arctic silence before Max decided to try to defuse the situation. "Donna, talk to me. Why are you angry?"

Max could feel her rage about to explode, and he braced for impact.

"Well now, let's see. A tall, attractive, well-built woman you used to date like yesterday comes on to you in my face, and, in the process of drooling all over her, you forget I'm even there. When you finally *do* remember you're spoken for and manage to spit that out to her, she then all but tells me she's gonna try to get you back. And then when she leaves, you stare at her *butt* for ten minutes *in front of the entire congregation!*"

At least she's not holding anything back.

"Donna, it's not like that."

She whirled to face him, eyes blazing with a level of anger Max didn't know Donna could summon. He almost flinched behind the wheel.

"Oh, so I'm a liar and a fool? You're gonna tell me you weren't looking at her butt?"

As Donna struggled to regain control, Max fought back fear at the force of her outburst.

"Yes Donna, I was looking at her, and I apologize. It was really crude and insensitive of me to do that, and I apologize. I shouldn't have gone there. That was disrespectful of me, both to her and to you."

He turned into the parking lot of Donna's building. Donna felt her rage begin to ebb. "Apology accepted."

"As for drooling all over her, no. She and I aren't compatible, and I told her so. She's attractive, but you're the one I want to spend all my time with. You and nobody else."

Donna chose her next words carefully. "Max, will you come in? We need to talk."

He noticed that her anger had vanished as quickly as it came. Without saying a work, he parked, let Donna out of the car and warily followed her inside.

Merry stood quietly, looking out the window at Fred changing his tire.

This is what it's supposed to be like. It's early spring on a Sunday; I'm supposed to be watching my man work on the car or mow the lawn or even just watch sports on TV. I'm tired of watching my back all the time. I shouldn't have to live like this.

Just then, Fred looked up and saw Merry at the window. He blew her a kiss and returned to working on his tire.

Merry waved cheerily in return, as a feeling of peace and joy filled her. *I could get used to this.*

"Make yourself comfortable, Max. I need to change."

Donna vanished into her bedroom, leaving Max alone to ponder what just happened. *I never thought Donna could be so volatile. She had every right to get mad, but darn, I thought she was gonna throw a punch!*

Donna emerged from her bedroom, looking relaxed in a light blue sweat suit. She'd exchanged her contact lenses for her glasses, and her calm expression for a slightly sheepish one. Max quickly stood as she approached.

"Donna, I'm sorry about what happened. I was so busy panicking over Jenisse showing up that I didn't think of how you might feel."

Donna sighed. "I'm sorry too, Max. I overreacted."

"Hey, you had the right to be mad."

"To be annoyed maybe, but not to explode."

They sat on the couch. She took a deep breath and looked Max in the eye.

"Max, if our relationship is ever going to go anywhere- and I want it to- I have to tell you this. My gift can be a burden sometimes."

Max looked at her curiously. "How do you mean?"

"If I don't concentrate on keeping a mental wall between myself and people around me, I start feeling all of their emotions piling on. It's like in football. What do they call it when somebody drops the ball?"

Max suppressed a chuckle. "A fumble."

"Right. When somebody has a fumble and everybody tries to jump on it, sooner or later one guy gets the ball and he keeps it. When I get hit with a bunch of feelings all at once, it's hard to handle. I have to grab one and hold onto it until I can regain control. And sometimes I grab the wrong ball."

Max wanted to laugh at Donna using a football analogy when he knew she hated the sport. However, the seriousness of her tone kept him somber.

I could end this right now. Surely there's a less moody woman out there for me.

Even as the thought crossed his mind, he banished it. *There's something special about Donna. I feel like I've known her all my life, and I can't imagine not being with her.*

Without saying another word, he reached out and pulled Donna into a hug. Donna returned his embrace enthusiastically, exhaled in relief. She was worried that Max would want to dump her for someone less high-maintenance, and feeling his brief indecision didn't help. But, when the full force of his feelings for her pushed all else aside, Donna felt tears of joy welling up.

"Donna, if you can put up with your gift and me at the same time, I can deal with your mood changes."

She smiled and leaned her head on his shoulder. "So I suppose we're stuck with each other?"

"Darn right. You still owe me fifty cents for that newspaper!"

She pretended to smack him playfully in the back of the head, but hugged him tighter instead as they burst out laughing.

Fred wiped his hands on a rag, threw it and his tire iron into his trunk and waved to Merry before getting into his Saab and heading home.

Of all the jacked-up stunts! If I get my hands on the guy who stuck that screwdriver in my tire I'll make him eat it. I'll kick his butt so hard his kids won't be able to sit down.

Exhausted, Fred turned into the parking lot of his building, dumped the offending instrument into the trunk with his tire iron and headed inside for a long-awaited communion with his couch and TV. He failed to notice the headlights of the van that had followed him from Merry's house to his building.

11

"Explosion!"

Max jerked awake from a nightmare. His heart hammered in his chest, and he was bathed in cold sweat. As he tried to calm down, he grabbed the notebook from his night table and wrote furiously.

Three minutes later, he finished writing and was surprised at the level of detail he remembered. Feeling much calmer, he put the notebook and pen down and turned his light back off.

Enough of this. I have to get up in just three hours.

Donna had trouble focusing on her work. The dreaded Monday Malaise hung heavily over her department; it was all Donna could do not to be drawn into their mental tiredness.

For protection, Donna wrapped herself in a stony indifference. *It's bad enough I had that nightmare without having to deal with all these Monday morning depressives.*

Oh well, at least I paid off my student loan. No more "When will you be sending a payment?" calls, ever. Thank God for that reward money, even though I spent it all on that loan. Hmm, wonder if there's anyone else Max and I could beat up for a few thousand more?

Donna laughed and returned to her work, looking forward to lunch with Max.

Max sat on a park bench, rereading his account of last night's dream.

This is weird stuff. Maybe Donna can help me make sense out of it.

Just as he closed the notebook, he caught sight of Donna coming down the path and his heart leaped with joy.

-Donna felt Max before she saw him. She felt his unmistakable presence and the happiness he felt, and her own mood lightened considerably.

Max stood as she approached, and greeted her with a warm hug and a quick kiss. Passersby smiled in approval, with the exception of one tall light-skinned black man, who glared daggers at Max as he passed them.

"What's up with Mellow Yellow over there?"

"Max!"

They both laughed. "Seriously though, what's his problem? He glared at me like I cut him off in traffic or something."

Donna smiled. "Actually, you did cut him off, to his way of thinking. He works on the floor above mine, and he's hit on me every day since I started. I've been politely turning down his dinner invitations for a month now."

"Why? Does he pick his nose in public or something?"

Donna laughed. "No, but he is seriously obsessed with sex, and I don't need my gift to know that!"

Chuckling, they ate their bag lunches, making harmless small talk for the first half hour. Finally, Donna put her soda down and looked thoughtfully into Max's eyes.

"Something's bothering you, Max. What is it?"

He took a deep breath. "Two things I want to talk to you about actually." "Go ahead."

He cleared his throat nervously. "Donna, how would you feel about, well, meeting my parents?"

Donna felt a burst of warmth wash over her. She wanted to shout for joy, but restrained herself. "I'd love to."

Max smiled sheepishly. "I didn't want to put you on the spot, but I talked to the folks last night. When they realized that I was still seeing you, they decided they wanted to meet you, like yesterday."

Donna smiled. "Well, we can't disappoint them, can we?"

"If we did, they'd track us down wherever we hid. I'll call them tonight and find out when they want us to come."

"Sounds good. I'm looking forward to it already."

Max took another deep breath; Donna could feel that there was something more than nervousness driving his mood.

"Max, what else is bothering you?"

Max forced a smile. "I should've known I couldn't fool you. There is something else actually. I had a nightmare last night. I can't figure out what it means, and I was hoping you could help me with it." "You know I'll try. What was it?" Max handed Donna his notebook.

"Night was falling. From a distance, I saw this huge explosion. It rocked the entire area I was in. I'm not sure where I was, but I don't think it was Delaware, and I felt compelled to investigate.

It was the most horrible thing I had ever seen. There was smoke and dust all around the wreckage of this building (I think was a hotel). There were bodies and pieces of bodies all around. There were survivors, and the ones who were still conscious cried uncontrollably. I was crying too- the loss of life was appalling. I wanted to help- -I tried to help, but there was nothing I could do.

One of the survivors stared at me with this haunted look on his face and kept saying that I "should have done something to stop him from killing us." I tried to ask the man who the "him" was that he referred to, but the survivor wouldn't tell me. All he did was keep telling me I could have prevented this if I'd been there. I woke up in the middle of a dying man's accusations."

Donna read Max's account of the dream twice through without stopping. She then turned to Max and pulled him into a reassuring hug. He clung to her for long moments, needing her closeness to help dispel the haunting images of the nightmare.

He studied Donna; intense concentration framed her face, tinged with worry.

"There's something you haven't told me yet, isn't there?" Donna smiled grimly. "Yes Max, there is."

She described a disturbing dream of her own. "Max, I had that dream twice in the past two weeks. Both of us have had the same kind of dream recently and I don't think that's a coincidence."

Max nodded in agreement. "Not likely. I think we should sit down together and figure out what the dreams mean."

Donna looked thoughtful. "Good idea. I'll write down everything I can remember about my dream so we can have it all to look at when we get together."

They returned to their buildings a minute or so late; with a fast hug, they returned to their jobs to ponder this conversation and what it meant for their future.

Merry unlocked her door and walked into her house, humming a cheery tune. It had been a long week, and she was glad to see Friday.

She stopped short as she cleared her doorway. All of her Ebony and Essence magazines were scattered around the room. She'd turned the TV off when she left the house to run errands, but now it was on, mocking her. Her videotape collection was also strewn across the floor; she nearly slipped on her copy of Boyz In The Hood as she moved around.

Someone broke in. I'd better be ready in case they're still here.

Merry put down her grocery bags, slipped her pepper spray from her purse and did a room-to-room search, eyes darting all around for signs of an intruder. Satisfied that downstairs was secure, she slipped upstairs, still alert.

Something caught her attention immediately as she entered her bedroom. Someone taped a photograph of Merry in the center of a poster sized piece of paper and in true third grade fashion, wrote the b-word in huge block letters across the photo and stuck it to her wall- with a hunting knife.

Merry smoldered with rage as she examined the unwanted artwork. The photo was unfamiliar; Merry faced away from the camera, indicating that someone took the picture without her knowledge.

She ripped the offending item off her wall and then noticed the oversized note sitting on her pillow. She kept one hand on her pepper spray and grabbed it with the other.

"This is where you do your best work, so I figured I'd leave this here for you. You thought moving from the *Dirty South* would hide you, but I found you and now you're going to pay. I'm going to ruin your life the way you did mine. Watch your back B; next time you won't get a warning."

The note was unsigned. Merry exchanged her pepper spray for the loaded Colt .45 semiautomatic pistol she kept in her nightstand drawer. Fully armed, she checked the rest of upstairs and then rechecked downstairs before she was satisfied.

Somebody went to great lengths to scare me, and that Dirty South reference makes me think I know who.

Still fuming, Merry picked up the phone.

Donna wrote furiously as she tried to remember the details of her recurring nightmare. It was surprisingly fresh in her mind even though her last time dreaming it was two days ago.

"I saw that skinny, crazy-looking black man again. He scares me to death and I don't know why. This time he put something together, and he stood back marveling over how good it looked. He turned and invited somebody I couldn't see to check it out, and all of a sudden that girl Yolanda almost fought in the club appeared. She kicked the thing over and disappeared again, leaving the man screaming and cursing in her wake.

Right before I woke up, the man was muttering about some foolproof plan of his and how he was gonna get that B-word back. While he was rambling, she appeared again, snatched some papers (they looked like blueprints) out of his hand and tore them up, throwing the pieces in his face. He ran after her, but she stayed out of his reach, taunting him about how much faster she was than he.

And then I woke up."

Max and I really need to get together on this.

She dialed, smiling at the prospect of spending more time with Max even as the eerie similarity of her dream and Max's unnerved her.

And I still have that dinner with Max's parents.

Merry did a double take. "Somebody broke into your place too?"

Fred arrived within ten minutes of her call, and was shocked at the condition of her townhouse.

"A couple days ago while I was at work. They didn't take anything, but they wrecked the place. Took me all day to clean up."

Merry remained silent as Fred helped her put her place back in order, fearful that she and Fred had one more thing in common now; the same obsessive man targeting them.

Max sat in his apartment and prayed for guidance.

"God, I need your help. It's obvious that we're onto something important with these dreams. I don't know what else to try to help us figure this out. Touch our minds Lord; help us to know what it is You're trying to reveal to us. In Christ's name I pray and for His sake, Amen."

An idea came to Max and he went to find his Bible.

Sometime after eleven PM, Fred returned home. He pulled into his parking lot, stepped out of his car and headed for the door, deep in thought.

First somebody flattened my tire and then somebody trashed my apartment. And then a couple days later, somebody trashed Merry's place too.

Wonder if it's all connected?

Without warning, the back of Fred's head exploded with pain. As Fred staggered from the impact, someone dragged him into the darkest part of the lot and punched him so hard his parents probably felt it. The blow split Fred's lip and sent him crashing into the big green dumpster. Fred bounced off the cold metal and fell forward into a flurry of punches worthy of a heavyweight boxer. He never had a chance to defend himself.

Mercifully, the beating lasted less than a minute, and ended with a kick to the stomach. Fred doubled over and tried not to vomit as he hit the asphalt.

"Tell Merry to watch her back or this becomes your regular Friday night thing."

Surprised to hear Merry's name, Fred passed out. His assailant stood over him for a moment, flipped a broken Budweiser bottle into the dumpster and vanished into the night just as Fred's neighbor came out to dump some trash.

"Blessed is that servant whom his master will find at work when he arrives. Truly I tell you he will put that one in charge of all his possessions. But if that slave says to himself, "My master is delayed in coming" and if he begins to beat the other slaves, men and women, and to eat and get drunk, the master of the slave will come on a day when he does not expect him and at an hour he does not know; and will cut him in pieces- - -."

Max fell asleep in the middle of Luke 12:43-48. His Bible still lay on his chest when the phone rang. It took three rings before Max was coherent enough to answer. "Hello?"

"Hey Maxth. Fred."

Max looked at his clock, noting that it was after one A.M.

"Fred? You sound kinda funny."

"Thath 'cause th' guy who mugged me almoth broke m' jaw."

Max sat straight up, knocking his Bible to the floor. "WHAT?"

"I'm at Chrithtiana. Emergency room. C'n you gimme a ride home?"

Max jumped out of bed and reached for the closest pair of jeans. "Be there as soon as I can."

"- - -*and put him with the unfaithful. That servant who knew what his master wanted but did not prepare himself or do what was wanted will receive a severe beating. But the one who did not know and did what deserved a beating will receive a light beating. From everyone to whom much has been given, much shall be required; and from the one to whom much has been entrusted, even more will be demanded.*" Luke 12:43-48

Across town, Donna woke from a sound sleep. She'd gone to sleep reading that verse and woke up with it and Max on her mind.

Strange. I could swear that Max is upset about something, but I'm not close enough to catch his feelings.

Donna retrieved her Bible from under the covers where it had fallen and returned it to her nightstand.

1:05. Maybe he's having another nightmare and I'm picking up on that.

Resolved, Donna picked up the phone. She was surprised to get Max's answering machine.

Max ran into the emergency room and looked around until he saw Fred. He was appalled at the sight; Fred's left eye was puffy and turning black, he held an ice pack on the right side of his swollen jaw and the back of his head was bandaged.

"Dag, what happened to you?"

Fred tried to smile- his fattened lips almost made Max laugh despite the circumstances.

"Got caught in a turf war in m' house. Th' rats held me down and th' roaches kicked my butt."

Max chuckled as he helped Fred to his car and pulled slowly out of the parking lot.

"Okay Fred, tell me what really happened."

Fred leaned back in the seat, eyes closed. "Thomebody jumped me in the parking lot of my apartment; hit me upthide the head with a bottle and beat me down. Never thaw him."

"He take your wallet?"

Fred reclined the seat as far as it would go. Max could tell it took an effort for Fred to speak. "Nope."

He repeated the mugger's parting words.

"Merry? You think she has something to do with this?"

Fred took a deep breath. "Sure gonna ask when I thee her."

Back at his apartment, Hemingway celebrated a job well done.

I dropped that punk like a bad habit. Young boys are soft these days. When I was that age, I coulda whipped a grizzly bear's butt and been ready to take on another one.

Hemingway smiled as he envisioned the look on Merry's face when she found out what the "mysterious mugger" said to Fred. *That oughtta take the shine off their relationship. Hmmm, once she'd had a day or so to think things over, maybe she should get the next visit.*

Laughing, he drained the rest of his beer and grabbed another.

Max unlocked the door to his apartment, dead tired.

Fred's taken care of, he thought. I'll check on him from work tomorrow-today actually.

He headed back to bed, but a flashing red light in the darkness caught his eye. Answering machine, he thought. *Who would call me this late?*

"Hi Max, it's Donna. I just- -well, I had this feeling that you were upset about something and that I should call you. Guess nothing's wrong. Give me a call when you get a chance."

Whoa, that's eerie. The time on that message was 1:10 A.M. I had just left to go get Fred. She must have picked up on me being shocked to hear about Fred getting jacked up.

Wonder if she's still up?

Fred carefully rearranged himself on the couch. He'd rested all day, but still felt the lingering effects of last night's beating.

Creep almost knocked a tooth out. If I ever get my hands on him- - -.

Fred reached for his glass and drained its contents. The apple juice was cold and refreshing, and most importantly, easy to take. He was hungry, but his swollen jaw made eating unpleasant. Fortunately for Fred, the juice was satisfying.

Almost out. Maybe Max can bring me some when he gets off work.

Just then the phone rang. Fred stretched painfully to get it. "H'lo?"

"Fred? What's wrong?"

The concern in Merry's voice warmed Fred's heart. "Mouth's kinda thore."

"Do you need anything? Do you want me to come over?"

Fred smiled, remembering the times he'd rushed over to be with Merry and feeling good that she felt the same desire to help him.

"Yeh. C'n you bring me thome apple juice? I'm almoth out."

Twenty minutes later, Merry arrived, grocery bag in hand. She waved off the money he offered, and produced not only the requested juice, but also four packages of instant pudding.

"You need to eat something, and this is good when your mouth is sore."

Merry had all four wisdom teeth pulled six years ago, during her junior year at Rutgers. Nelson Young, her first and only real boyfriend, fed her juice and pudding and waited on her hand and foot until her mouth healed.

Surprised at how natural it felt for her to nurse Fred the way Nelson had her, she made him lie back down with a fresh glass of apple juice and then prepared one package each of chocolate and vanilla pudding. The phone rang while she was cooking.

"Hey Fred, how's it going?"

Fred smiled. *Good to have friends.*

"Hey Max. I'm hangin' in there."

"Good. I'm leaving here in another hour or so. You need anything?"

Fred smiled even wider. "Nah. Merry's here. Brought me thome juice and pudding so I wouldn't thtarve to death."

Max laughed. "Okay then, I'll hang up and let you enjoy being babied."

"Fred, it's just about ready. Give it a few minutes to cool off and we're ready to go."

Fred was ravenous by the time the pudding was ready to eat, and she fed him two bowls of each before he was full. Despite having questions for Merry, Fred was glad she came.

He took some Aleve with the last of his apple juice. "Thanks Merry. I feel a lot better."

Merry smiled. "You sound better too. Must mean you're going to live." She took Fred's bowl and glass and put them in the dishwasher. "You never told me what happened to your mouth. Did you have some teeth pulled?"

He sat up and took the ice pack from his jaw. "I wish. Sit down, and I'll tell you."

Fred described the attack to Merry, who turned pale. She was horrified that he was attacked in front of his own building, and even more shocked at the mugger's parting words.

"Merry, the way this went down bothers me."

Merry tried not to show how agitated she was. "In what way?"

"The doctor found glass and alcohol in my hair. From the smell of things, he hit me with a beer bottle." Merry turned pale.

"And then after he kicked my butt, he didn't take my wallet or my car or anything. All he did was tell me what he told me. That's how thugs send a message- they beat the snot out of someone close to you as a warning."

Fred leaned forward slightly.

"Merry, I think you know who sent you that message."

"So right around the time I called you, you were headed out the door?"

Max nodded. "Sure was. Fred called around one in the morning, and I ran right out to pick him up."

"You could've called me back when you got in."

"Nah, I figured I'd let you sleep."

Donna smiled. "How's Fred doing now?"

"Resting. I just called over there, and he's doing fine. Yolanda's buddy from the club is there taking care of him."

"I'm glad. Getting mugged like that- it's awful!"

Max shifted the phone to his other ear, one eye on the story he was editing. "Fred's pretty mad. I'd hate to see what would happen if he ever finds the guy who jumped him."

Merry took Fred's hand and rubbed it gently.

"Fred, I'm so sorry. I think I know who did this. The note I found at my place makes me think it's Roscoe Hemingway. He's an old boyfriend and a *huge* mistake."

Fred blinked. "Bad enough I got my butt kicked, but by a Roscoe? Man!"

Merry giggled in spite of herself. "I'm afraid so. I was with him briefly two years ago, but I should have left him alone. He didn't take it well when I dumped him; I almost had to hit him with a baseball bat to get him out of my apartment. I thought I left his tired behind in Atlanta, but the "Dirty South" reference in the note- it's him."

Fred puffed up. "Where's he live at? I want to have a word with that brother."

Merry rubbed Fred's shoulders. "I had a restraining order put on him in Atlanta. Since he seems to live here now, I'll tell the local police about it. Stalking is a big deal now- they'll lock his behind up in a heartbeat."

Fred calmed down a little. "And I thought *I* had a crazy ex! Compared to that loser, Nela banging on my door hollering at one in the morning was nothing."

Merry laughed, and ran her fingers down Fred's chest, gently probing the bruises on his ribcage. After applying some first aid cream, she gently removed his sweatpants and ran her fingers over his rear end.

"What are you doing?"

Merry smiled. "Checking for footprints."

Fred's eyes widened, and he laughed so hard tears flowed.

Max cleared his throat. "Donna, there's something else I wanted to share with you. Right before I went to sleep, I was reading in Luke. I was in chapter twelve, and I saw something there that really hit home."

Donna's eyes widened. "I was reading from that same chapter! Wh-what verses?"

Suddenly filled with awe, Max pulled out the small New Testament he kept in his desk and started reading from last night's verses. Donna started reading with him halfway through, and Max knew without a doubt that, the night before, they had read the same verses at the same time.

"To whom much is given, much is required. I can't get past that portion of it."

Donna swallowed hard. "Me neither. When you consider what

we can do, we've definitely been given a lot. But how do we know what's required?"

Max smiled and shifted the phone to his other ear. "I think it's time we got some expert advice."

"Thanks for squeezing us in tonight, Pastor. We appreciate the last-minute appointment."

Pastor Nathan smiled. "Not a problem, Max. I have time before the Trustee meeting. What can I do for you? Judging by the looks on your faces, either I need to schedule premarital counseling or someone's been called to preach!"

Max and Donna laughed politely. "None of the above, Pastor. At least not yet."

Donna shot Max a glare; he skillfully ignored her as he continued, and Pastor Nathan pretended not to notice. "I'll try to keep it brief, but this is complicated."

Max told Pastor Nathan about their dreams, the mugging and their gifts, with Donna chiming in as necessary. Pastor Nathan remained silent until they finished.

"Now I understand how you two escaped those two murderers. God was with you both in a mighty way."

He stared at Max for a moment, so long that Max began to feel uncomfortable.

"Philippians 2 talks about the authority of Christ, to the point where the mere mention of His name is enough to make the devil submit and put his demons to flight. We as His people have the authority to drive out evil spirits, but most of us don't realize it. Those who do, sometimes don't have the faith to use their authority."

Max blushed slightly. "Pastor, there was no other choice but to trust God. Those men were going to kill us, and there was no way we could stop them from without God. I was scared enough to let go, and God moved on our behalf."

Donna spoke up. "Pastor, it was incredible! Max didn't even sound like himself. He just ordered those thugs to let us alone, and they did it, no questions asked. They were scared of Max!"

Pastor Nathan looked thoughtful. "Not of Max, but who he represents."

They talked for another forty-five minutes before Pastor

Nathan had to go to his meeting. He gave them relevant scriptures to read and prayed with them before sending them home.

"We did the right thing in asking Pastor's advice, Donna. I can tell."

Donna smiled as she braked for a Stop sign. "I think so too, Max. Pastor barely blinked when we told him the whole deal, and he gave us what we need to study this some more."

Max thought for a moment. "Discernment is your gift. It makes perfect sense to me. You do understand more than us normal folk."

Donna laughed. "Oh, you're normal? So everybody has dreams that eventually come true then."

Max cracked up. "Good point. Anyway, what we can do does line up with the gifts of the Holy Spirit. I never thought about them like this, but it makes perfect sense now."

"Well, now that we're better equipped with knowledge, what now?"

Max took a deep breath. "We keep going forward and take it as it comes."

12

"What's on your mind, Merry? You look, well, distant."

She and Fred held each other under the covers, enjoying the "afterglow" as the early morning sun peeked through the open curtains. Merry reached for the first aid cream and gently smoothed it on Fred's fading chest bruises.

"I was thinking about Sunday mornings when I was little, right after my brother was born. We'd get dressed up and go to St Luke United Methodist Church. Half the congregation was black and half was white- my family fit right in!"

Fred laughed. "Dr. Martin Luther King, Jr. would've loved that church."

"My parents would go into the service, and all the children would go downstairs for Children's Church."

"Is that like Sunday School?"

"Pretty much. Rev. Hanson didn't want all the children sitting in church bored, so he set us up downstairs with one of the assistant ministers. Rev. Bob was really funny; we all liked him a lot."

Fred sighed wistfully. "Yeah, I remember my mom taking me to church every Sunday too. We didn't have no Children's Church though. All of us had to sit there in the same service. And you know Baptists like to hang around!"

Merry laughed. "Had to pack a lunch and stay for the day, huh?"

"Sure did. Service started at eleven a.m. and if we were out by two thirty, something was wrong. New Gethsemane Baptist Church didn't believe in short services. And even if they did, my granddad's preaching would've made that impossible! He could get down, but he wasn't brief."

"I have to admit, those were fun days." Merry sighed. "But once you've crossed a certain point in your life, you can't go back."

"I don't know about that." Fred squeezed her gently. "I never intended giving up being a player and look at me now."

Merry smiled. "That's because when I'm through with you, you don't have enough strength for anyone else!"

"Oh, we're just too full of ourselves, aren't we?" Merry laughed and swatted him with a pillow.

Two hours later, Merry left Fred's apartment and drove with no particular destination in mind. She rolled the windows down, enjoying the first real spring weather of the year.

That was close. I thought Fred would find out more than I needed him to know. Somehow I don't think he'd understand the real reason why a man would come after me that way. It has to be Hemingway. He's the only one I ever dealt with who's crazy enough to follow me here. If I get my hands on him, the beating I gave him before I left Atlanta will seem like a love tap.

Merry wiped away a tear. *Fred deserves better. He shouldn't be lying around sore because my life is hopelessly screwed up.*

As she drove aimlessly, she felt the desire to turn into an area of Newark she usually avoided, where the University Of Delaware encroached on a sprawling residential area.

Might as well look around. I haven't been through here in awhile.

Sitting at a stoplight, Merry heard noises, like a parade or a concert. She looked towards the source of the sounds and saw something she hadn't paid attention to in years; a church.

Max, Donna and Yolanda sat in their usual seats, halfway towards the front on the left side of the church.

This is how I always wanted it to be, Donna thought. *I'm with a man who doesn't hurt me emotionally and who understands me. Never thought I'd have that again after Clarence.*

Donna flinched at a familiar presence. Max looked over at her, mouthing words of concern. She waved him off; there was nothing he could do to help her. *Somebody set me off. I wonder who?*

A horn blared behind Merry, alerting her that the light was now green.

Stop.

Merry barely registered the thought before she inexplicably slowed down and pulled into a parking space at the curb. Merry had planned to drive into

Wilmington, to Brandywine Park to walk around the zoo, but the small church compelled her.

As she climbed the stairs, she suddenly felt self-conscious about her attire. She had on light blue summery pants and a sleeveless pink blouse- hardly traditional church finery. Nevertheless, she approached the open door, ignored the thought that maybe she was wasting her time and went inside.

"If we have any visitors among us this morning, will you please stand so we may recognize you?"

Five people stood at Pastor Nathan's urging, and as usual, everybody craned their necks to see them. Donna didn't bother; she preferred to hear what they had to say, and if any voices stood out to her, she'd look then.

Around the third person, Donna felt another sense of familiarity and felt compelled to look. As she started to turn, someone spoke and turned her world upside down.

"My name is Clarence Perry, from Los Angeles. I attend Calvary UAC out there, and I'm here visiting my aunt, Jada Swanson."

Donna went pale. Yolanda put her hand to her mouth.

Fellowship Christian Church was about the size of Merry's living room and a bit of her kitchen, but from outside, it sounded like the small edifice housed a congregation of hundreds instead of dozens. Merry stood in the hallway, just outside the open door to the sanctuary and took in the still familiar sights; rows of oak pews with red padding, a stained glass window depicting Jesus and the disciples and a large golden cross hanging above the altar.

Merry's attention was riveted to a second stained glass image depicting Jesus on the Cross. She saw Him hanging there, His thorn-crowned head bowed in pain, nails through His hands and feet.

Tearing her eyes away from the gruesome image, Merry looked to the pulpit. The young preacher was at the apex of his sermon, eyes flashing as he preached the Word.

"Don't you *worry* about all the stuff you did; God still loves you! The dying thief on the cross next to Jesus did wrong *all* his days, but he knew to look to Jesus for salvation. He didn't ask to be a disciple, or even to have his life spared; he just asked to be in God's presence! *"When thou comest into thy kingdom, remember me!"*

"Jesus didn't send the man to New Members class or make him memorize the Bible or try to force him to speak in tongues to be saved. Jesus just took time out from His own suffering, turned to that thief and said, *"Verily I say unto you, today thou shalt be with me in Paradise."* It's *not* too late to receive Him. As long as you're living, it's never, never, *never* too late to let Him in!"

Merry stood there, transfixed by the power of the preached Word, unable to leave even though she wanted to with every fiber of her being.

How could he know what I'm thinking and feeling?

Amid thunderous applause and shouts of agreement, the preacher stepped away from the pulpit and wiped his brow with a handkerchief.

"Salvation is offered unto you this day. Yesterday is gone and tomorrow is not promised to anyone. John 3:16 says, *"For God so loved the world that He gave His only begotten Son, that whosoever believeth in Him should not perish, but have everlasting life."* And the next verse says, *"For God sent not His Son into the world to condemn the world, but that the world through Him might be saved."* Take the gift freely offered, His gift of love. Give me your hand, but give

Jesus your heart."

He motioned to the choir to sing. The pianist played softly as the minister urged the unsaved to give their lives to Jesus Christ.

Merry felt like someone attached wires to the front of her clothes and pulled her towards the altar. She resisted the urge to move forward, and stood there on the verge of tears and not understanding why.

The choir box was filled to capacity. Five men and ten women, all fairly young, stood up with open hymnbooks. A tall dark-skinned man took one of the two microphones. As the pianist played a soft, haunting melody, the man began to sing softly in a high, clear tenor voice. Enraptured, Merry listened intently.

"Shackled by a heavy burden
'Neath a load of guilt and shame
Then the hand of Jesus touched me/And now I am no longer the same.
He touched me/Oh Jesus touched me
And oh the joy that floods my sou-oul/Something happened/And now I know He touched me and made me-e whole.

As the choir sang "He touched me" over and over, Merry stood in the doorway, tears running down her cheeks.

"Merry."

No one spoke, yet Merry heard a voice, clear, insistent and urgent. Merry blinked in astonishment as the words came into her heart moreso than her ears.

"Now, Merry. Give me your life and I'll make you brand new."

Merry was surprised to find herself wondering if what she heard from the preacher and now from the choir was true.

Maybe I'm not hopelessly screwed up. Maybe I can be happy living a normal life.

She started forward, hesitated, started again and stopped.

Donna absorbed the rest of the service without really hearing anything. *Oh God,* she thought, *why is he here now?*

Beside her, Max could tell that she was agitated and now he knew why.

Clarence. That eight-foot-seven brother she was with before me. Hope he doesn't think he's getting her back.

Service ended much too soon for Donna and everyone got up to leave.

"Brother Max, can I talk to you for a second?"

Great. Just when I need to stay close so Clarence doesn't get any ideas.

"Sure Pastor. What's on your mind?"

As the two men spoke in low voices about the upcoming Men's Prayer Breakfast, Donna and Yolanda waited for him, knowing what was about to happen.

"Can you handle this Donna, or should I stay close?"

Donna smiled. "Thanks for offering, but I can handle this. Actually there's nothing to handle. Max is all the man I need."

"Uh huh. Then why your knees shaking?"

They both giggled. Before Donna could answer, a tall light-skinned man pushed through the crowd and headed directly for her. Donna faced the opposite direction, but sensed his approach as clearly as if she had eyes in the back of her head. She closed her eyes and took a deep, cleansing breath.

"Yolanda, is he coming this way?"

"Yes."

"Is he still fine?"

"Very."

"Lord help me."

"Sister, you need somebody to walk with you?"

Startled, Merry looked around to see a heavyset cinnamon-skinned woman with genuine concern in her eyes offering to take her hand.

"It's okay if you're scared. We all done made this walk before."

Her voice was gentle with just a hint of a Southern accent (noticeable in her pronunciation of words like "maide" and "befoah"). Merry started to reach out in response, but a burst of panic welled up in her. She heard a second voice, harsher and more urgent than the other one.

"No! You'll have to give up everything you love! Get out now, before it's too late!"

Nearly hysterical, Merry turned and ran from the sanctuary, not stopping until she reached her car. She pulled away from the curb, glad to put distance between herself and the church that almost brainwashed her.

Hearing voices- I must be losing my mind. If I am, getting religious won't solve that or any of my problems.

Eager for a distraction, she turned on the radio.

"At the name of Jesus, every knee shall bow and every tongue shall confess that Jesus Christ is Lord. When He calls your name, don't ignore Him, but receive Him and be blessed with eternal life. Remember, it wasn't the nails that held Him on the Cross; it was His love."

The voice was a soothing Caucasian tenor, reminiscent of the famous children's TV show host Mr. Rogers. To Merry however, his words were harsher than sandpaper. Repulsed by what she was hearing and wondering how her radio got on a religious station in the first place, Merry quickly changed it, searching for the "Cool Jazz" station.

"You may want to change this station, but you can't change the Truth."

Merry nearly rear-ended the car in front of her, not realizing that the light had turned red.

I changed that station! How did it get back to that minister?

A horn blared behind her, alerting Merry to the green light ahead of her. Waving apologetically, Merry drove home, keeping a wary eye on the radio the whole way and completely unaware of the tug-of-war being waged in the spirit realm for her soul.

"Donna!"

She turned and gasped in surprise despite having sensed his presence. It was barely a month since she'd rejected his offer to move to Los Angeles with him.

"Clarence!"

She gave him a warm hug, which was entirely too long for Max's taste. He kept them in his peripheral vision and frowned as he continued his conversation with Pastor Nathan.

"How've you been?"

Clarence smiled. "Can't complain. And before you ask, they sent me here to evaluate the new division's progress. I'll be here until next week."

He and Yolanda exchanged pleasantries; Yolanda suddenly discovered a pressing need to talk to the pastor's wife, who happened to be across the sanctuary.

Thanks a lot 'Landa. I really did need you to back me up.

As Clarence and Donna continued their conversation, Max heard less and less of what his pastor said.

"Brother Max, is something wrong? You seem distracted."

"Huh? Oh, sorry Pastor. My mind drifted for a second."

Pastor Nathan chuckled. "My guess is that it drifted straight over to where that tall handsome brother is talking to Donna."

Max forced a smile. "Good guess. He's her last boyfriend before me."

"And you're afraid that she still might have feelings for him."

Max smiled sheepishly. "The thought had occurred to me."

Out of earshot, but not liking the level of familiarity this man had with Donna, Max took a deep breath.

That guy's got to go. I've given her plenty of time to catch up, but he's getting too comfortable.

Max excused himself from the pastor and walked slowly and

deliberately towards Donna and Clarence. Pastor Nathan, Mrs. Nathan, Yolanda and others looked on from where they were, utterly fascinated but trying not to appear overly nosy.

Clarence reached inside his suit coat. "Deevee, I was wrong. I didn't realize how much you mean to me until I flew back to LA alone. I never should've asked you to move in with me. I should have asked you to marry me."

Donna took a deep breath. *I was hoping he wouldn't go there, but I knew he would.*

"Clarence, I'm flattered. I probably would have strongly considered it not too long ago. But that's not possible now."

Just then Max arrived at Donna's side. "Sorry I took so long. Pastor wanted to talk to me."

Perfect timing Max. Just like you wanted it.

She put her arm around Max, sending a burst of warmth through him and a ripple of jealousy/disappointment through Clarence. Donna felt both with equal clarity.

"Clarence, this is my boyfriend Max Carson. Max, you remember Clarence?"

The two men shook hands, perhaps more firmly than they normally would have. "Good to see you again Clarence."

Clarence nodded. "Likewise."

Having made his appearance, Max decided that it was now time to make his exit. "I'll go get the car. Take it easy, Clarence."

"You too."

Max strolled off, Yolanda close on his heels.

"Well Donna, I guess I'm a bit too late."

Clarence took his hand out of his pocket and Donna was relieved to see it empty. She put a hand on his arm. "I'm sorry you had to find out like this. If Max hadn't been talking to the pastor, I could've- - -.

"---saved me some embarrassment? Donna, I could never be embarrassed to be in love with you. But I'm glad you found somebody. I mean, you always had such high standards."

They laughed and hugged one last time. "Clarence, believe me when I say this. There *is* someone out there for you. If I could find somebody, anybody can!"

Clarence smiled wistfully. "I'm sure. Well, I need to get going."

Donna wrote her phone number on a piece of the worship bulletin and handed it to Clarence. "Call me before you leave town? We still have a lot of catching up to do."

Clarence took the number, disappointment radiating from him. "Do I get invited to the wedding?"

Donna blushed slightly. "Whenever I do get married, you'll be among the first to know."

They made small talk for another minute or so and then Clarence left. She stared after him briefly, thinking about what might have been and then headed out to the car to meet Max and Yolanda.

Fred lounged on his couch absently flipping channels. He was about to turn it off when he heard the knock on his door.

Who is this? Merry just left and Max always calls before he comes over.

Fred grudgingly got up and opened the door. To his surprise, Merry flung herself into his arms and held on for dear life.

"Oh my God, are you all right? What happened?"

Merry was crying again, which angered her like nothing else in the world, but right at that moment, nothing was more important than security. Fred's arms were a shelter in the storm she called her life.

"Just hold me, Fred. Please. And don't let go."

Still puzzled, he held her close as he shut the door with his free hand.

"Max, we need to talk."

Having dropped Yolanda off, Max and Donna were on their way to his parents' house for dinner.

"Yeah, we do. And I need to apologize."

Donna's eyes widened in surprise. "For what?

"For acting like you couldn't be trusted. I could have waited for you to finish your conversation before I came over."

Donna smiled. "Max, I'm glad you did. You saw when I got fidgety in church. That was because I felt him nearby and it threw me off. Clarence and I go way back."

"Old boyfriend?"

"My only boyfriend until you. We dated in high school and again- - recently."

Max chose not to revisit their awkward experience at the bowling alley.

"Max, until I met you, Clarence was the only man who really understood me. He didn't know about my gift, but he was safe for me emotionally, if you understand what I mean. He didn't pressure me for sex like all the other guys either did or wanted to do. His being such a sweet guy made it easier for me to feel, well, normal."

Max seemed lost in thought. "Clarence was your first love."

"And my best friend next to Yolanda. We dated all through high school, went to the prom, the works. We broke up when it was time for college. He got a full scholarship to UCLA and I got one to University Of Delaware." Max reached put his hand on top of hers. "Any regrets?"

She smiled and rubbed his arm. "None. Max, you have nothing to worry about. We broke up this time because both of us have changed. We're just not on the same page anymore. Not the way you and I are."

Donna smiled as Max's relief cascaded over her like a waterfall. *He really was worried about Clarence*, she thought. *I kind of like that.*

Merry lay in Fred's bed, eyes closed tightly, but awake nonetheless. She was still perplexed by what had happened earlier in the day, and the more she thought about it, the tighter she held Fred as he lay beside her.

Why in the world did I think I needed to get religious all of a sudden? I guess finding out that somebody broke in my house has me more upset than I thought.

It's too late for me anyway. God wouldn't want me now.

13

Max turned off I-495 at the Wilmington exit, hung a right, and within two minutes, turned into the development called Dunleith. He pulled up in front of a modest two level home.

"Ready?"

Donna took a deep breath. "Let's do this."

Max smiled at the nervousness he heard in Donna's voice, produced a well-worn key and let them inside. As Donna crossed the threshold, a feeling of comfort, love and security overwhelmed her. It felt the same as when she visited her parents' house.

"We're here!"

Footsteps sounded in the hallway ahead of them. As Max closed the door behind them, a round-faced dark-skinned woman with graying curly hair appeared from around the corner and reached up to smother Max in the kind of all-encompassing hug that only a mother can deliver.

"Ohhh, it's good to have my child home again!"

Max smiled sheepishly and held his mother close. After having risked death with Donna recently, being home felt wonderful.

"Feels good to me too. It's been too long."

Mrs. Carson assumed a look of mock disapproval as she looked up into her son's eyes. "I'll say it has. The last time you came, you didn't have *this* pretty young lady with you."

He smiled. "Mom, this is Donna Randall. Donna, my mother, Corrine Carson."

She hugged Donna as warmly as she had Max. "As much as my son talks about you, you can call me Mom if you choose."

Donna smiled. "I'd like that."

They followed Mrs. Carson into the living room. An older version of Max sat in an armchair, reading the newspaper and trying not to show how eager he was to greet his son. As they entered the room, he put the paper aside and rose to greet them. Donna smiled; Max Carson, Sr. wasn't as heavy or muscular, but at six foot four, he was the same height and the same dark brown shade as her own father.

"Long time no see, son."

They hugged, slapping each other heartily on the back in the process.

Donna was touched to see the two men displaying their affection so openly.

"Donna, this is my dad, Max, Sr. Dad, this is- -."

Max, Sr. smiled. "No need to tell me who *this* is. We've heard plenty of good things about Miss Donna already."

She smiled as he hugged her, more gently then he had his son. "Good to meet you Mr. Carson. I've heard a lot about you too."

He smiled. "Of course we *did* have to read about you in the paper before we got to meet you, but- - -."

"Dad!"

Fred usually enjoyed watching Merry sleep, but this time her fitful slumber frightened him. She tossed, turned and whimpered, even when Fred pulled her close to comfort her.

I like her a lot, but I'm not sure if I can deal with these fits. And it seems like every time we get together, we wind up in bed. I never thought that would bother me.

The tension drained out of Merry, and she relaxed in Fred's embrace. She woke up, smiled, leaned up and kissed him. She then reclined in his arms, ignoring the still, silent voice that had spoken to her earlier in church and that was trying to get her attention now.

"Fred, thank you. You were there for me again when I needed you. My own family never did that. It, well, it means a lot to me."

Fred's face flushed, catching him by surprise. *I don't blush! What's up with this?*

"You're welcome. I'm glad I could help. Usually all I can do when somebody's crying is to make them feel worse."

Merry laughed, and they lay back again, holding each other and enjoying their closeness.

"Thanks for having us over, Mrs.- -uh, I mean Mom. Everything was great."

Mrs. Carson was all smiles. "You're welcome, "daughter." Don't let my boy make a stranger out of you either. Come over and see us any time you want."

With farewell hugs exchanged and leftover food packed for Max and Donna to take with them, they got back into Max's car and headed back to Newark.

"I really like your parents, Max. Now I see why you're such a wonderful human being- you had no choice!"

Max laughed. "Yeah, let's hear it for good genes. Well, they sure liked you, "daughter." Mom didn't give you her famous evil eye once, and Dad was more talkative then I've seen him in years."

Donna blushed. "Well, I'm glad I made a good first impression."

She looked pensive. "Max, do you realize that this is the first time since we met where we spent all day together and didn't talk about spiritual gifts or dreams?"

"You're right. Normal people don't get this deep this fast." He smiled as he pulled into her parking lot. "Of course you *could* argue that we're not normal- -."

Donna laughed and invited him upstairs. Max gratefully accepted; he really wanted to continue their conversation. Yolanda greeted them warmly and then returned to her room to finish watching Touched By An Angel.

"Okay Max, let's keep playing Normal Couple. Work with me though. I've only had one relationship my entire life before I met you. What do people talk about when they're at the "just met parents" stage?"

"Who you asking?" Max smiled. "My last relationship attempt ended right before we met, and that was far from normal."

"Would that be Miss Jenisse, by any chance?"

Max blushed. "Yeah, that was her."

Donna laughed. "Oh yeah, Miss Thing herself. She really wasn't your type, was she?"

Max cracked up. "Gimme a break! Everybody makes mistakes, you know. Hey, maybe we should hook her up with Clarence!"

Donna laughed and pretended to slap him. "What tipped you off that she wasn't the one?"

"You sure you want to hear this?"

Donna gave him a fake glare. "You think you can shock me after *our* first date? Give it up, Max. Inquiring mind wants to know."

He laughed. "Okay, here goes."

Donna listened as Max described his many disagreements with Jenisse, including her blatant desire to entice him into bed after both of their dates against his wishes.

"Darn Max, what did you do to her? She couldn't keep her hands off you!"

Max blushed again. "I think it was the challenge. Once she found out that I'm abstaining from sex until marriage, she figured she was fine enough to change my mind."

Donna felt a surge of gladness sweep through her heart at Max's casual revelation.

"Well, I'm glad she didn't get to you, but I have to question her logic. As hard as it is to find a man who won't put his hands all over you, she should have been glad you weren't trying."

"I'm not a virgin, and I told her so. I had three girlfriends during my four years of college, and in each of those cases, we did whatever we thought we were grown enough to do. I didn't get it until after I graduated. While I was in school, I didn't go to church except for when I was home for the summer and my folks made me."

Donna laughed. "I feel you on the church thing. To me, Sundays were better spent sleeping in, especially if Yolanda and I had been out partying on Saturday night."

Max chuckled. "I rededicated my life to Christ after I graduated and started going to Calvary. I realized that I couldn't go back and undo the past, but I *could* keep myself pure from that point on. I expect other guys to laugh about that, but I thought women would understand. Jenisse claims to be a Christian, but she clearly doesn't agree with me when it comes to abstinence."

Donna looked Max in the eye. "I do."

"Thank God."

"What are you thinking about?"

Fred smiled. Normally he hated it when a woman started getting deep on him, particularly in bed. However, coming from Merry, the question seemed perfectly natural.

"You. Being with you these past few weeks is, well, it's like magic or something."

Merry smiled and started gently rubbing Fred's back. "Magic?"

"Yeah, magic. I can't believe we met by chance and that we hit it off so well."

She kneaded his shoulders. "I agree. Just when I thought there was nobody special out there, you stepped up to the bar and bought me a drink."

Fred laughed. "I bet guys want to buy you drinks all the time."

"Yes, but wanting isn't always having."

They kissed again, and held each other close under the sheets. Neither of them wanted to let the other go, and smiled when they realized this was the case.

"Fred, if I didn't know better, I'd think you were falling in love with me."

He smiled and kissed her again. "Nothing's impossible."

They chose to change the subject and to enjoy some nonverbal communication for awhile. Afterwards, they held each other, enjoying their closeness.

"Have I told you in the past ten minutes what a blessing you are?"

Donna smiled and squeezed Max's hands. "No, but I'd love to hear it again."

"Okay Donna. I'm really glad we met, and blessed because we got together."

Max stopped talking abruptly, and looked into Donna's eyes, sending a powerful surge of warmth through her. She shivered at the intensity of his emotions, unable to speak for a moment.

"Wow! What was that for?"

Max smiled, sending another delicious surge through her. "I hope I never have to find out what it's like without you in my life."

She brushed her fingers across his face. "If prayer means anything, you won't."

Their lips brushed lightly, but their spirits connected powerfully. Max held Donna in a warm embrace; they held each other, rocking gently as if dancing. Max had no idea what he was going to say until the words dropped into his spirit, and he knew it was the right time to say them.

"I love you, Donna."

Donna wasn't surprised; she felt the sincerity behind Max's words, and it matched her own feelings. "I love you too, Max."

They continued to hold each other, communing silently and basking in the love God had granted them.

Having stopped at the supermarket on the way home from Fred's place, Merry felt wonderful.

That was nice, she thought as she unlocked her front door. *It feels good to be able to trust Fred like that. I was beginning to think I couldn't trust anyone but myself.*

Merry put her bag down, closed the door behind her and reached for the light switch.

"Don't bother."

Before she could react, someone reached out of the darkness and grabbed her from behind.

14

"How's fear taste, ho? You're gonna pay for what you did to me."

A man's powerful arm locked around Merry's neck, and the stench of beer attacked her nostrils. As the unknown assailant groped at Merry's clothes and mumbled the B word over and over, she fought down panic and remembered the self-defense lessons she'd taken shortly before leaving Atlanta.

She stomped hard with her right foot, driving her heel into his instep. When he let go, Merry turned and smashed her purse into his nose. He cursed loudly and stumbled backwards into the door. Before he could recover, Merry pulled her pepper spray from her purse and blasted him in the face. He hit the floor, covered his eyes with his hands and writhed in agony.

"Bill me."

She flipped the light switch and was not the least bit surprised to see Roscoe Hemingway.

As "Crystal Lawrence," Merry attended a party at the Atlanta home of one Dr. Thomas Chamberlain, a recent conquest. He was so eager to introduce her to Hemingway that Merry knew Chamberlain's intent instantly; he wanted to "share the wealth." Ironically enough, sharing the wealth was what Merry had in mind too, although her intent was more literal.

Merry correctly figured that Hemingway and Chamberlain were on the same playing field economically, and wasted no time getting next to him. However, it was more than Merry bargained for. Before the sweat from their highly unsatisfying encounter evaporated, Hemingway offered to leave his wife for her. Angry that Hemingway couldn't take their encounter for what it was and disappointed by his appalling lack of stamina, Merry rejected him angrily.

I'll never forget what he did next, Merry thought.

Hemingway swelled with anger and slapped Merry across the face. As Merry's eyes widened with rage, Hemingway sputtered weak apologies. Merry grabbed a miniature souvenir baseball bat (the first thing she could reach) and attacked. The first swing missed, the second hit him squarely on the "funny bone" of his left arm and the third connected with his stomach and knocked the wind out of him.

"Crystal, stop! I'm sorry! I- -I lost my head for a second."

Merry/Crystal stopped swinging. She held the bat like a samurai warrior and glared coldly at him.

*"You might lose more than that. Get out now. If I ever see you again, rest assured that I will **kill** you."*

Hemingway dressed as fast as his numb arm allowed and ran out of her apartment. Merry kept the bat ready, hoping he'd do something stupid so she could hit him again.

He hit the wrong woman. I had to teach him a lesson.

Mrs. Valerie Ellis Hemingway received a videotape of their tryst two days later. A day after that, Hemingway was freshly separated from his wife and out for revenge on Crystal Lawrence.

A low moan snapped Merry back to the here and now. She looked down at Hemingway, who lay in a fetal position on her floor.

I should have killed him two years ago, but that would have caused problems. What do I do with him now? I could call the police, or I could call Fred for advice. Or I could kill him now.

She looked down at him in disgust. *I definitely need a new line of work.*

Merry picked up the phone, but hung up before dialing Fred's number.

No, this is my problem and I'll solve it. Besides, Fred would kill him.

Hemingway's eyes burned from the noxious spray and his stomach lurched from side to side. Through blurred vision, he saw someone move and heard soft footsteps going up the stairs and then returning. Hemingway wrenched one eyelid open with his right hand and immediately wished he hadn't.

Merry/Crystal stood over him and aimed a gun at his head.

She chambered a bullet with a loud click.

"Remember what I said last time I saw you?"

Hemingway coughed and sputtered as the police yanked him to his feet, handcuffed him and dumped him in the back seat of the squad car.

"Thank you for coming so quickly Officer. I really appreciate it."

Officer Carter smiled. "No problem, ma'am. I'm just glad you were alert or it might have been you needing medical attention."

Merry watched as the police car drove off.

Hemingway's lucky my gun isn't registered, she thought. *Otherwise I would've shot him in "self-defense" instead of hiding it.*

Fred's Monday was painful. First, the main contact for the story he was writing continued not to return his calls. Someone else then called about a mistake in a story from the previous edition, and now his computer was acting up.

I can take a hint. It's time to go to lunch.

It was 11:45, fifteen minutes earlier than usual, but Fred needed a break and Max was willing to join him.

"Okay Fred, what's wrong? You haven't busted on me in any way, shape or form all day. Something's up."

Fred smiled. "Yup. Mark your calendar, because I'm about to ask you for advice about women."

Max pretended to faint. "A sure sign of the Apocalypse. What's on your mind?"

"Okay, I usually don't keep a woman this long, but I don't think this is normal. Merry's great most of the time, but sometimes she'll be all broke up for no reason. She'll jack up a box of tissues and she can't calm down for like half an hour. She'll wake up in the middle of the night scared and can't go back to sleep unless I hold her. What am I supposed to do with that?"

Max studied Fred carefully. "You really care about her."

"We wouldn't be having this conversation if I didn't!"

Max smiled. "Fred, all I can say is, hang in there. Remember, you're not used to having a committed relationship. It takes time and effort. If you really care about her, you can't bail out the first time something bothers you. You're going to find out things about her- and her things about you- that aren't pleasant. If your relationship is gonna go anywhere, you need to talk to her about this."

Fred thought for a moment. "Makes sense. Thanks Max. I'll just have to hang in there and see if this keeps up. Maybe I should offer to take her to the doctor and see if there's some medical problem behind it."

Max smiled slyly. "You might want to abstain from sex for a minute too.

Get to know her as a person instead of just in bed."

Fred laughed. "Yeah, right! She'd love me for that!"

They talked and finished their lunches, discussing how much space Merry and Donna now occupied in their lives.

"You know, we had it good before they came along. Now they own us!"

Max laughed and raised his Cherry Coke as if in salute. "Here's to willing slavery!"

They clanked soda cans and drank a toast.

Merry had a long week. On Tuesday Hemingway made bail and was free pending trial. She had her locks changed, but this latest news made her keep her gun within easy reach at all times.

On Wednesday she and Fred got together at his place. Neither mentioned her emotional outbursts, but there was tension in the air that damped their usual enthusiasm. They wound up apologizing and cutting the evening short. She chose to go home rather than stay over, and her sleep that night was fitful and filled with nightmares.

Merry made the rounds of her various P.O. boxes on Thursday and collected two thousand dollars from her current victims. She couldn't help but wonder how Fred would react if he learned her true occupation.

I have to quit this. If they keep sending the money I'd be a fool not to keep it, but I don't enjoy this anymore. I need to find a better way to make a living.

Fred came to her house to cook on Friday, hoping to rekindle the fire they'd felt before this week. Merry did her best, but they ended up falling short of expectations once again.

"Merry, uh, well, can I ask you something?"

"Sure."

They lay in bed following an evening together that they'd probably grade as a seventy-eight out of one hundred.

"Did I, well, do something to irritate you?"

Merry's eyes widened. "No! What made you ask that?"

"Well, you know. It hasn't been as good for us lately. I was wondering if you were mad at me or something."

Merry moved closer to Fred and held him tightly. "No, not at all! It's just that, well, these nightmares I've been having are taking their toll on me. I haven't slept well in weeks."

Fred rubbed her back. "Oh. Does this happen a lot?"

Merry stroked his arm. "I go through stretches like this. It's usually only a few days though. This is the longest I've ever had this go on."

"Do you think going to the doctor might help? Maybe it's something like migraines, and they can give you something that will help."

Merry felt a surge of warmth sweep through her. He really cares, she thought. *That wasn't pity last weekend; he really cares about me!*

"It could be. I never thought about it that way before. Maybe I *should* go see my doctor about it."

Fred squeezed her hands gently. "If you want, I could go with you."

Merry smiled. "Thanks. I'll keep that in mind."

She rolled over and kissed him. "I feel a lot better all of a sudden."

Fred smiled broadly. "Me too."

This time, they agreed, was one hundred.

Karl Hurzen smiled as he put the phone down. He'd just had a pleasant hour-long conversation with Bryan, who was enjoying college life as only a nineteen-year-old can.

Just initiated into Lambda Beta. I always knew the boy would do well, despite everything against him. Nice to see tradition still counts for something. My dad was an LB, I was an LB and now Bryan is an LB as well.

Karl sighed, wishing he'd been able to send Bryan to his alma mater Yale instead of the University Of Delaware. He wrote a check for five hundred dollars, enclosed a short handwritten note of congratulations and put it in an envelope to mail to Bryan's dorm address.

Of course he'll be moving into the frat house soon, but not right away.

He sighed as he put a stamp on the envelope and put it with his other outgoing mail. *I could've done so much more for him if my parents hadn't been so unreasonable and inflexible.*

Karl involuntarily flashed back to his own college days. He knew from a young age that as the oldest son, he would go to Yale like his father before him, get a degree in something useful and eventually take over his dad's vast communications empire.

I hated Econ more than all my other courses put together, but I needed it for my major. No degree, no inheritance.

When Karl realized he was in equal danger of failing Econ and of going an entire semester without getting laid, he reluctantly signed up for help. He hoped to be assigned an attractive female tutor and thereby kill two birds with one stone. He got Lorraine Lucas.

I never saw her coming. I was hoping for gorgeous and available, but never thought any girl could master Econ that thoroughly, never mind a black girl.

Karl sighed, remembering how quickly and completely he'd fallen for Lorraine, and how thoroughly his parents (his father in particular) hated their relationship.

We had such big dreams for our life together. Why'd she have to screw it up?

As if sensing Karl's sudden melancholy, Taylor swept into the room and sidled up to him, massaging his shoulders as only she could. Smiling, Karl turned to her, put aside thoughts of the past and focused on here and now.

"That's it! I can't think about this anymore today. I need a break!"

Donna laughed as Max threw his hands in the air in mock exasperation. They'd attended the eight A.M. service this particular Sunday morning and after almost a full week of avoiding all talk of dreams, they spent the past three hours comparing notes.

"I know the feeling, Max. We've been focusing so hard on trying to figure this out that my brain's starting to hurt."

Max leaned over and gently massaged Donna's temples. "Does that help?"

She laughed. "Yeah, I feel smarter already. Actually though, we do need to take a break, and I have an idea."

"You can sit down. It won't take me long to change and then we can go."

Merry settled onto Fred's couch to wait. After spending most of the weekend in bed, they'd decided to take advantage of the warm April weather by spending the day outside. The lesson their childhoods had taught them hung unspoken in the air; "Enjoy your happiness while you can; it won't last."

"All set."

Fred came out of his bedroom wearing a black and white Georgetown University T-shirt and matching shorts, which emphasized his muscular legs.

Merry smiled when she saw him. "Careful now. We might not get out of here with you dressed like that!"

Fred faked a shocked expression. "You're starting to sound like me!"

They stepped out into the sunshine, laughing and holding hands.

Max had been to the Brandywine Zoo many times as a child, but being there with Donna seemed like the first time all over again. He felt as giddy as a high school boy on his first date. They held hands, walking slowly from one end of the small park to the other, enjoying each other's company. They stopped to see llamas, ducks, monkeys, weasels, otters, a pair of Andean condors and a peacock that seemed accustomed to being the center of attention. When Donna raised her camera, he stopped and spread his colorful tail feathers wide as if posing. Donna laughed so hard she almost couldn't take the picture.

"Reminds me of Fred."

Max assumed a fake mean look. "Hey, leave Fred alone. He's not here to defend himself."

Donna smiled and pointed. "Guess again."

Max looked up and was surprised to see Fred and Merry coming towards them, holding hands.

"I'll be darned. I guess miracles do happen. Hey, Fred!"

Fred and Merry made their way over to Max and Donna, both smiling radiantly. Merry wore summery white pants with a light blue blouse, which looked good with Fred's outfit. *Check them out. They're even color coordinated!*

As they drew nearer, Donna felt a familiar sensation from Merry, just below the surface of her joy. It was cold anger, just as strong now as when Donna encountered her at the club, and it had the same numbing effect.

She must really like Fred, Donna thought. *I thought she couldn't be this cheerful unless she was killing a small animal.*

"Max! Didn't know you were coming out here today."

"Neither did I. Donna suggested it on the spur of the moment and I figured, why not?"

The two men exchanged their customary brotherly handclasp-hug, which amused Donna greatly. *Why can't men just hug and get it over with*, she thought.

Fred turned to Merry, still smiling broadly. "Merry, this is my friend Max. Max, this is Merry."

They shook hands. "Good to finally meet you. You're all Fred ever talks about. I feel like I know you already."

Max returned Merry's smile. "Fred does the same thing with you. This is Donna."

Donna avoided shaking hands with Merry, or even getting too close. Merry reciprocated without knowing exactly why. "We've met."

Merry knew she'd crossed paths with this woman somewhere before, but couldn't place it. She sensed Donna's dislike and returned it in kind. "That we have."

Puzzled by Donna's uncharacteristic coldness, Max tried to lighten the moment. "Hey Fred, check out your relative over there."

He aimed Donna's camera at the peacock, who stopped and fanned his tail feathers out on cue. Fred and Merry both cracked up.

"That's what happened to Uncle Stanley! I told him not to date that voodoo woman! Serves him right for cheating on her."

They all laughed this time, even Donna. With a parting handclasp-hug between the men, the two couples separated. Donna felt better as the distance between her and Merry increased.

Max watched Fred and Merry fade into the crowd.

"I don't think I've ever seen Fred this way with any woman. He *must* be in love to take her to the zoo."

"He did look rather domesticated."

Max looked at Donna strangely. "You okay? It's Merry, isn't it? You don't like her."

Donna took a deep breath. "It's more that I don't like what I feel from her. Remember when you saw 'Landa and me in the club?"

Max smiled. "I'll never forget that!"

"That was my first time being around Merry, but I didn't know her name then. She and Yolanda almost fought."

"Yeah, I remember you telling me that."

"Well, the closer I got to Merry, the more I could feel about her, and she scares me. Max, that woman is *dangerous*. She'll eat Fred alive if he's not careful."

Max stopped walking and stared at Donna. "You make her sound like the Antichrist. Maybe she has an attitude problem, but nobody's perfect."

Donna sighed in annoyance. "Max, you can't understand how she feels to me. Deep down where it counts, that woman is completely cold-hearted. I've never felt anything like that in my life, and I hope I don't ever feel it again."

"And I hope for Fred's sake you're wrong this time."

Donna glared icicles at Max. "I think I've had enough zoo for today."

They walked towards the parking lot, their buoyant mood deflated by the unexpected encounter.

"So, what did you think of Max?"

Merry smiled and rolled down her window. "Can't say much for his taste in women, but I can see why you like him. You need some classy people in your life."

Fred laughed. "First he dogged me about that peacock and now you too? Where's the love?"

They both laughed as he pulled up in front of her townhouse. "Here we are. Last stop."

Merry rubbed his arm. "Coming in?"

As they went inside, Merry looked around warily for signs of intrusion, hoping that Fred wouldn't notice. Satisfied that all was well, she took off her sandals and sat down on the couch, massaging her feet.

"Here, let me."

Fred slid onto the couch beside her and lifted her feet into his lap. He began to rub them gently, jokingly holding his nose against imaginary odor.

"Seriously though, I think Max is a nice guy. I'm glad you have a friend like him. I was beginning to think you were as lonely as I was before I met you."

Fred started working on her left instep. "You mean you've been in Delaware all this time and you don't have any girlfriends? Nobody to hang with?"

She shook her head. "Just you. By the way, thank you for taking me to the zoo today. I had fun."

"Me too. I haven't done that in years. My mom used to take me to the zoo all the time when I was a kid."

Merry sighed. "Mine too. My parents would take my little brother and me, and we'd make a day of it. That was before things got ugly."

She felt a wave of melancholy coming on, and slid her feet out of Fred's grasp before it could hit her. "I'm all sweaty. I need a shower."

Merry tossed a seductive wink over her shoulder. "Wash my back?"

Fred smiled and followed her upstairs. Two houses down, Hemingway stood in the shadow of some trees, watching the house through binoculars and smiling.

He's still her boyfriend. That means it's time to take this to another level.

He got back into his car and took off, patting the small box and envelope on the front seat beside him as he thought on how best to implement his plan.

Max sat back on the couch, yawning as he reached for the TV remote. *Today was nice until we ran into Fred and Merry. I'd love to know why Donna started tripping like that.*

He channel-surfed, and eventually settled on the Philadelphia/Indiana basketball game. Philadelphia was so far out of first place they needed binoculars to even see Indiana.

I hope Donna's wrong about Merry. Fred needs to settle down, and he looked so happy with her. If she's not the real thing, he's in for a world of hurt.

And who would be able to tell better than Donna?

I need to call her and apologize.

The phone rang; Max jumped at the sudden sound before picking it up on the second ring. "Hello?"

"Hi Max."

He smiled broadly. "Donna, I was just about to call you. And if you say, 'I know,' I'm going to have to hurt you."

She laughed. "No, I'm not that good. I just called to apologize for being snappish earlier."

"Apology accepted, but only if you accept mine. I had no call acting like you don't know what you're talking about. I just, well, I wanted you to be wrong about Merry because she's good for Fred."

Donna sensed the sincerity behind Max's words and exhaled in relief. "He's really happy with her, and in her own way, she feels the same for him. I didn't say this earlier, but I hope I'm wrong about her. Fred's not happy chasing women any more. He needs one woman in his life and maybe Merry's it."

Max smiled and shook his head in amazement. "You are something else, Donna! It took me two years of knowing him to realize that, and you figure it out after being around him twice."

Donna laughed. "I'm getting good at this, remember?"

Roscoe Hemingway laughed as he drove, pleased with the scenario he'd set into motion.

This'll fix her. The ho and her new man ain't never gonna forget this night.

He cackled uncontrollably and sped off into the night.

At two A.M., Fred and Merry awoke to an unfamiliar sound. As always, Merry came fully awake in an instant, with an animal's awareness of her surroundings and any potential danger in them.

"What was that?"

The question barely cleared Merry's lips before something hit the ground outside with a loud clang.

Fred jumped out of bed and pulled his pants on. "I don't know. Maybe a dog knocked your garbage can over."

Merry reached for her robe. "No, it was louder than that."

"Well, whatever it is, I better check it out."

He was dressed and out of the room before Merry could protest.

WHOOMP!

Merry jumped at the muffled explosion right below her window. *Fred!*

Worry became fierce resolve. As smoke rose past her window, Merry quickly pulled on a T-shirt and sweatpants, and got her gun from the night table drawer.

Fred might've run across a prowler, she thought as she slapped in a clip, *and I'm not going to let anyone hurt him if I can help it.*

Just as she reached her back door, it flung open. Fred reentered, rubbing his eyes and coughing painfully. He was surrounded by an obnoxious odor.

"Either somebody set off a stink bomb in your garbage or you've got a skunk out there the size of an SUV."

Merry lowered the gun and guided Fred back to the bedroom, where she sat him on the bed.

"Are you okay? You didn't come back right away, and then the explosion- -I was worried about you."

Fred smiled and stifled a cough, indicating the gun in her hand. "So I see."

Blushing, Merry unloaded the gun and replaced it in the drawer.

"You can't be too careful these days. I was stalked once, when I lived down South. You never know what kind of sick people might come after you these days."

Fred chuckled. "If they break in here, they got a surprise coming. Dirty Merry."

Merry laughed at Fred's perfect Clint Eastwood impression.

"You should talk. What did you do, roll in the wreckage? You smell awful!"

Fred coughed again. "Funny. I got to the door right when the thing blew up. I'm lucky I didn't get hit by any garbage or pieces of the can. Whatever they used though, it's *nasty*. I need a shower real bad."

Merry smiled and held her nose. "You sure do. Come on, I'll help you with those hard-to-reach areas."

Fred rubbed his eyes. "Shouldn't you call the cops or something?"

"Why, do you want an audience?"

Fred looked at Merry in amazement and burst out laughing. Merry joined him, and it took them five minutes to calm down.

"Seriously though, it was probably one of the neighbor kids playing a joke. I'll clean up in the morning."

Fred smiled. "*We'll* clean up in the morning."

She started undressing Fred as she guided him towards the bathroom.

Obviously you didn't learn your lesson last time. Well Hemingway, if I catch you anywhere near my house, you'll get more than just pepper spray.

15

Thump.

A strange noise woke Merry from a sound sleep. She sat up, listening.

THUMP.

Somebody's in here. She slipped her gun from the drawer and slid out of bed to investigate. *Nice and quiet,* she thought. *Don't let them hear you coming.*

As Merry paused at the top of the stairs to adjust her vision, a shadow loomed in front of her. Merry screamed and pulled the trigger by reflex. The shot echoed loudly, but it couldn't mask a man's death-scream or the rhythmic thudding of his body as it tumbled down the stairs.

Great. Now I have to explain this to the police.

Every instinct in her body screamed for her to call 911, but she felt compelled to first find out who she killed. Her hand hit the light switch before she realized it.

"Oh. My. God."

Fred lay in a pool of blood at the bottom of the stairs. Merry tried to scream, but her voice failed. As the light faded from Fred's eyes, he fixed whispered a last word, which chilled her soul.

"Why?"

"NOOOOOOOO!"

Merry jerked awake and sat up in bed, heart thudding heavily in her chest. Tears flowed freely, mixing with her perspiration to sting her eyes with a salty brew. She stumbled into the bathroom. Washing her eyes with cold water felt better than anything had in a long time.

I'm glad Fred's not here. I don't think I could explain this nightmare to him.

She toweled her face off and returned to bed.

This isn't a game anymore. Hemingway beat Fred like a dog and showed me how easily he could have killed him.

I can't let that happen. I have to take Hemingway down first.

White static had long ago replaced the tape Fred was watching, but he didn't notice.

This can't be true. There has to be some other explanation.

When Fred returned from Merry's apartment, a manila envelope sat on his doorstep like a stray dog. Fred took it inside, but held off opening it; he barely had time to change clothes and go to work. When he returned home, the first thing he did was open the envelope. He played the videocassette he found inside first, and it shocked him beyond belief. The tape showed Merry and some guy in bed together, and the note he discovered in the bottom of the envelope was equally stunning.

"Congratulations! I had to pay through the nose for what you're getting free. Believe me, I'm not the only one. You might want to go see a doctor just to be sure everything's cool down there.

From One Victim To Another"

Fred's chest tightened. *No way*, he thought. *This can't be right.*

Merry can't be a prostitute.

Merry felt like someone shoved sandpaper into her ears and scoured her brain. She was exhausted, but she viewed sleep the way a rabbit views a fox.

I've felt like this before. I wish I could forget, but I can't, no matter how hard I try.

Merry's mind rolled back to the end of her time in Atlanta. After she rejected Hemingway, he focused on making her life miserable. He used a variety of juvenile tricks, including egging her car and letting the air out of her tires to get Merry outside where he could attack her. Merry instead bought pepper spray and a gun. She never set foot outside without the spray within easy reach, the gun in her purse and neighbors outside as witnesses.

When the tricks didn't work, Hemingway escalated things. Five harassing phone calls in five nights and a dead squirrel tied to the hood of her car earned him a restraining order and caused Merry to take self-defense lessons. Sleep was the enemy; Merry lay half-awake most nights with her gun loaded and on her nightstand until she couldn't take it anymore.

Two months after her night with Hemingway, Merry loaded her car and drove out of Georgia at midnight. As much as she loved living in Atlanta, moving on was a huge relief.

I had to uproot my entire life because of that psycho. I'm not running any more. He started this down there, but I'm going to finish it here.

Max and Donna lounged on his couch, thoroughly exhausted. For the second straight week they went to the eight A.M. service and came straight from church to his place to talk. After two more hours of pondering their dreams, they were still no closer to solving the mystery.

This is going nowhere. What if we can't figure this out and somebody dies?

Donna squeezed Max's shoulder gently. "Don't worry Max, we'll figure this out sooner or later. Don't lose faith."

Max smiled. After two months together, it still amazed him how Donna could read his moods so effortlessly. "I know Donna, but this is *frustrating*! I feel like we're so close, but we're missing just one or two pieces of this puzzle."

They now attended Bible Study faithfully on Wednesday nights. Ironically, the first lesson they got was on I Corinthians 12 and dealt with spiritual gifts.

Pastor Nathan welcomed their presence, going so far as to tease them as he concluded his teaching.

"Brother Carson, Sister Randall, make sure you attend next week. We'll be moving on to the 13th chapter, commonly referred to as the love chapter."

Both of them blushed furiously; in the past two months, they'd spent more time turning red then they'd done their entire lives.

Donna rolled her neck to relieve tension. "That study really backed up what Pastor told us in counseling. Now that we know what we're dealing with, maybe we can understand of what these dreams are trying to tell us."

Max smiled. "We'll see."

Hemingway smiled as he connected the last two wires. That oughtta do it. Now all I have to do is set this where it will do some good.

He smiled as he pictured Merry walking into her house, turning on the lights and blowing herself to kingdom come before she realized what was happening.

It didn't have to be like this. I wasn't lying; I would've left Val for you.

Hemingway remembered the rage he felt at Merry's disappearance like it was yesterday. He'd broken into her apartment at two AM with murder on his mind, only to find the place deserted. Merry vanished without a trace, and Hemingway couldn't exact revenge if he couldn't find her.

I found you now though, he thought. *Enjoy yourself "Crystal" or whoever you are. Your time's about to be up.*

Eyes weary from reading and reading I Corinthians 12, Max put a Take 6 CD on his player and they settled back on the couch to relax. Neither of them said a word. Max smiled and held Donna close as the music played. Neither of them realized how tired they were until sleep swallowed them simultaneously.

Unlike Max and Donna's first shared experience, this dream was explicit and brutal. Donna again saw the skinny, wild-eyed black man with the cold smile. He was in a workshop; his hands virtually flew over a combination of wires, circuits and various chemical compounds until he had an explosive device primed for use. He hastily packed a bag and laughed as he went out looking for his target.

Donna stirred in her sleep as the dream shifted, this time to something neither she nor Max had seen before. Merry was inside a house and she also packed hastily. Clothes, shoes and other essentials flew into her two small bags. As thoroughly as she packed, it seemed odd that she left a travel brochure for Virginia Beach and her hotel confirmation slip for the Holiday Inn in Portsmouth, VA sitting on the kitchen table.

As had the black man before her, Merry started driving. Despite the fact that he was obviously following her, she drove with a hunter's confidence instead of the prey's fear. Max and Donna watched both of them navigate Interstate 95 South. Merry pulled away, leaving the black man cursing in her wake. He continued as if he knew where she was going.

Merry's car pulled up at the aforementioned hotel and vanished. The black man's van followed soon after and stayed there. Late the next day, the black man made his move. Max groaned in his sleep as he anticipated the emergence of the dream fragment that had been his alone up until now. Now wearing a blue jumpsuit and carrying a battered brown toolbox, the man slipped into Room 717, attached the bomb, set a timer and left quickly.

Max and Donna looked on in horror as the Portsmouth, VA Holiday Inn exploded. Max again saw the horrific panorama of death and destruction, and the same accusing survivor.

They woke up together with a start. Both of them were crying, and they knew instinctively that they'd shared this dream. Badly shaken, they managed to get pens and paper to write down everything before important details could fade.

With the dream recorded, Max looked at Donna and reached out his hands to her. Without a word, she smiled and took his hands. Max praised God for His excellent greatness and thanked Him for the gifts He had blessed them both with. He asked for clarity of mind and strength of spirit so that they could discern the meaning of their shared dreams.

Donna took up the prayer, thanking God for His goodness and His mercy in sparing their lives. She petitioned God for a spirit of obedience so that they would do God's will and remain on one accord, touching and agreeing, ready willing and able to do what they had to.

After about fifteen minutes, they came out of prayer. They were awed at having been in the presence of the Holy Spirit and a bit fearful of the task ahead of them, but also determined to carry out the task God had given them.

Donna blinked. "Wow, that was incredible. But what now?"

Max exhaled. "Looks to me like we're going to Virginia Beach."

Fred sat at his desk, oblivious to his surroundings.

It feels right, but what do I know anyway? I mean, I haven't known her very long and she did always change the subject whenever I asked her what she does for a living. And when you think about it, you can't afford a townhouse like that working the makeup counter at Macy's.

He pulled a small jewelry box from his desk drawer. He'd found it in the box of his late grandmother's things he'd barely touched since her passing; until recently, he thought he'd never have a use for that ring.

Maybe I still will. She said she wants me to come over tonight so she can explain that tape. Maybe that jealous ex of hers has something to do with it. She thinks he's the one jumped me that time, and he did get arrested for breaking in her place. If he's crazy enough to do that, he's crazy enough to send me that tape.

Oh well. I'll find out for sure tonight.

"George, can I talk to you for a minute?"

"Sure Max, come on in."

Max wiped sweat from his palms as he entered the managing editor's office and closed the door behind him.

He's not gonna like this, Max thought as he sat down. Well, I never call out sick. That should count for something.

"So, what's on your mind?"

Max took a deep breath. "I need the rest of the week off."

George raised his eyebrows. "Come again?"

Max fought down a host of smart remarks and continued as he had rehearsed it at home.

"Something's come up, just last night actually, and I need time to resolve some personal things. I might even have to go out of town to get things squared away."

George nodded sympathetically, just as Max had hoped. "Family problems?"

"You could say that."

Five minutes later, George had moved four of Max's scheduled vacation days forward by three months. Max thanked George for understanding and returned to his desk, hoping to finish as much work as possible so as to make it easier on the other assistant editors whom he knew would assume his workload.

I didn't lie. If Donna and I don't get there in time, a whole lot of families will have problems- as in dealing with grief over the loss of their loved ones.

Donna hung up the phone, relieved at how well her conversation had gone. *It took my whole break, but I got through to*

Finders. *This tells me God has His hand on this situation. Normally they'd take me off the assignment and take their time finding me another. Instead, they're holding my spot until next Monday.*

Donna opened her folder and pulled out another letter to work on, wondering how well the "family problems" story was working for Max.

I hate that we have to lie about this, but telling the truth would have folks questioning our sanity. We wouldn't be able to get to Virginia Beach because they'd have us locked up in the asylum.

Wonder how we're gonna break this to our friends? And our parents?

"Hey Max! You get called out by the boss or something? I seen you coming out his office."

Max smiled. *Fred's in the right job*, he thought. *Nothing* gets past him.

"No, I'm not in trouble. I just had to rearrange my vacation days."

Fred frowned. "I thought you got the ones you wanted."

"I did, but something came up. Come to the cafeteria with me a minute and I'll tell you."

They settled at a back corner table with sodas and Max filled Fred in.

"All right, player! I knew you had it in you, but I didn't think it'd come out this soon!"

Max chuckled. *I knew Fred would react like this.* "Fred, this isn't a vacation trip, It's sort of a business trip."

"Uh huh. And I'm sure you'll be taking care of business as soon as you get her there!"

"Man, get your mind out the gutter! This is something we have to do. I can't explain it just now, but *please* don't go telling everybody where I'm going or who I'm going with. They'll think the exact same thing you're thinking."

Fred feigned ignorance. "And just what might that be?"

"You think I'm sneaking Donna off on a romantic getaway so we can have sex."

"Really? Gee, that never occurred to me. People do that?"

Max playfully smacked Fred on the back of his head. Fred laughed so hard he had to stop drinking his Diet Dr. Pepper or risk snorting it through his nose.

"I don't care why you think we're going to Virginia Beach as long as nobody else gets the chance to think it to. You got me?"

Fred smiled. "Chill out, player. You want to sneak off and answer that booty call, be my guest. You've covered for me enough times."

Max sighed in annoyance. He had hoped Fred wouldn't think the worst of him.

Then again, Max thought, *why shouldn't he? I'm telling him nothing except that I'm going out of town with my girlfriend. What else would he think?*

Their short break over, they headed for the elevator. Fred chuckled all the way there and back to his desk about Max finally earning his player's card while Max thought of the preparations to be made. He and Donna knew they needed to be on the road within fifty-two hours and there was a lot to do before then.

I wonder if I should warn him about Merry. We don't know what she might be into, and Fred did get beaten up once already.

Max prayed for wisdom as he returned to his desk.

That lowlife Hemingway went too far this time, Merry thought. *I should've shot him when I had the chance, but I had to be nice.*

She sighed as she thought back to last night. Fred called her nearly in tears and asked her why somebody gave him a videotape of her having sex and claimed it was prostitution. She nearly cried herself at the despair in Fred's voice.

That psycho won't give up. I could call the cops and have them enforce the restraining order, but then they might start asking questions about that tape. If I knew where he lived, I could just go over there and take him out, or have someone else do it.

Hmmm. Karl said he was taking Taylor on a trip soon. Maybe I should try to kill two birds with one stone.

Resolved, she picked up the phone to get a little information.

"How'd it go, Max?"

Max and Donna sat on "their" bench eating lunch. It was an absolutely beautiful April day; seventy-five degrees, no breeze to speak of and the flowers were coming into full bloom; daffodils to one side and lilacs behind them.

"Pretty good. My boss didn't question me much; all he did was sympathize about my family problems and move my vacation days to this week. I had a short week planned in August, but there wasn't anything in particular I was going to do with it."

"Who's going to cover your work?"

Max smiled. "Fred's taking most of it. One of the assistant editors will help him, but Fred's getting the chance to show what he can do with editorial responsibility."

Donna applauded vigorously. "See that? Another good thing's coming out of that this. Fred might finally get promoted."

Max smiled. "I hope so. He trained me and I became an assistant editor first. He never complained, but if it were me, I'd be a bit upset."

"Fred's a good guy. He wouldn't let that bother him."

Max wadded up his empty lunch bag and tossed it into a nearby trashcan. "How did it go with Finders?"

"Family problems worked with them too. My coordinator didn't even ask any questions; she just put me down as absent excused until next Monday."

Max smiled. "Good, you'll have a job to come back to. I was hoping I wouldn't have to rent out your spot on the bench." Donna swatted at him playfully.

Merry finished packing her overnight bag. *If I pull this one off, it'll be one for the record books.*

She chuckled at how simple it had been to call travel agencies until she found the one Karl used. She then pretended to be Taylor and "confirmed" their travel plans with ease.

Everyone at Rutgers always said Taylor and I sounded alike on the phone. I guess they were right.

A memory came to Merry unbidden. She'd sworn never to let the name and face of Nelson Young cross her mind again, but suddenly he was there, like someone put a videotape in and then tied her to a chair so she couldn't turn it off.

Nelson was the star point guard on the Rutgers basketball team, a straight-A student and a true gentleman. Nearly every woman on campus (including a few professors) wanted him, but one look at Merry in an otherwise boring Biology lab and he was smitten. Merry wanted nothing to do with him at first. She thought he was too good to be true, but Nelson gently pursued her until she realized that he was what he appeared to be.

He took her to fancy restaurants and fast food joints, operas and dollar movies and treated her as if the sun didn't rise until she got up in the morning. When he realized that Merry was a virgin, he suggested they not have sex until marriage so their first time would be special. When Merry disclosed the abuse in her past, Nelson reassured her that he loved her and would never raise a hand to her. Despite herself, Merry fell deeply in love.

Nelson proposed at the end of their junior year. As a sure-fire NBA lottery pick, he planned to graduate on time and then enter the NBA draft, and he wanted Merry to be sure he wouldn't leave her behind. Merry was happy and at the same time fearful that this wouldn't last. Nothing in her childhood prepared her for unconditional love, but she held onto it, believing that this was her reward for years of unwarranted beatings from Karl.

During their final semester at Rutgers, Merry entered the dorm room she shared with Taylor, her best friend since they were assigned a room together as freshmen. Taylor had agreed to serve as Merry's maid of honor, and Merry returned to campus early from a weekend of wedding planning to give Taylor an update. She left a perfectly normal Sunday afternoon out in the hallway and took a left turn into hell.

Taylor spent so much time undressed that Merry learned to call and warn her when friends were accompanying her back to the room so Taylor could cover up. It wasn't a surprise that Taylor was naked, but it *was* surprising to find a naked Nelson with her.

They stammered out excuses, but Merry heard nothing. She saw red, and determined to do as much physical damage to her former best friend as possible before someone stopped her. She performed her self-assigned task with a level of skill and focus she never knew she had.

When Nelson tried to hold her back, Merry drew on reserves of strength she didn't realize she had and threw him clear across the room before giving Taylor the beating of her life. It took Nelson, the RA and three of Merry's floor mates to restrain her, and then only after she had pummeled Taylor unconscious.

Nelson managed to pull on a pair of pants before the room filled with witnesses, but Taylor was naked through the entire incident. They had to cover her up to take her to the infirmary, where she was treated for a broken arm, several cracked ribs, a broken nose and assorted cuts and bruises. Taylor didn't press charges, but the university expelled Merry a semester shy of graduation.

Merry never finished her degree anywhere else.

Identifying the bodies will be one of the shining moments of my life, Merry thought. *The other will be seeing Hemingway's face when he realizes I used him again- right before I shoot him.*

This has to be done, just in case.

Max sat on his couch, writing in the small notebook he'd bought earlier. He wanted to record all he could while he had the chance.

"*Donna and I have really been trying to solve two puzzles at once. One is our dreams of course, but the second is the most intriguing. We've had these gifts all our lives, but until recently, God chose not to let us understand the full meaning of them. I know I never gave much thought to it, and I'm pretty sure Donna never did either. But, now that we've been studying the Word, it's clearer. I Corinthians 12 talks about the gifts of the Holy Spirit, and we are definitely gifted.*

Our abilities have been there throughout our lives; God let us have them just when we needed them. Gifts like these are precious beyond price, and we thank God for using us the way He surely has. Luke 12:48 says, "- -to whom much has been given, much will be required." We have a responsibility to use these gifts and not hide from them. In doing so, we acknowledge the fact that doing what God is calling us to do might cost us our lives. Make no mistakes; I don't want to die. Not yet anyway, not when Donna and I have just found each other. But if that's God's will, who am I to argue?

If God does indeed call for us while we're away, hopefully this journal will help our families and friends understand why we had to do this.

Praise His holy name.

16

Merry's face was grim as she finished packing.

If Hemingway holds true to form, he's waiting for me. He won't break in anymore unless he's wearing a gas mask, but he'll sit out there for a month if he has to.

Merry carefully packed the gun and ammunition in the bottom of the bag. She hesitated and then removed the ten thousand dollars cash she kept in a locked box beneath her bed for emergencies. She divided the money between her bag and her pocketbook, being careful not to let it cause any tempting bulges.

Okay Hemingway, show me what you got.

Fred rang Merry's doorbell promptly at seven P.M. As he waited, his hand strayed to the pocket of his olive green suit jacket, stroking the jewelry box inside as if reassuring himself that it was still there. As he waited for her to answer, he mentally rehearsed what he wanted to say until it sounded right, as he had the whole drive over.

This is crazy, but what about this whole thing isn't? I've known her two months and I'm about to break Player Rule #1: never even think about marriage.

When three minutes had elapsed with no answer, Fred started to worry. *She said she'd be here. Why isn't she answering?*

He tried the door, and was surprised to find it unlocked. Fred entered casually as if he belonged, just in case some nosy neighbor was watching.

"Merry? You here? It's Fred!"

His only answer was an ominous silence. The air seemed still, as if weighed down with some dark secret.

"I'm not a burglar, so don't shoot me!"

Fred smiled, remembering how fierce Merry looked on that night when he first saw her armed. A sudden thought occurred to him, and he raced upstairs. Something moved at the edge of Fred's vision as he entered the bedroom. He turned to see Merry's night table drawer open and sliding off its tracks. He reached to put it back, and it dawned on him that the drawer was empty.

"Aw, no."

He rushed to check the room. Some of her clothes were missing from her closet. Her underwear drawer was empty, and her favorite sneakers were missing from the shoe rack.

Fred's stomach dropped. Clearly, Merry left in a hurry with no indication of where she went or why.

He stood there stunned until a drop of water hitting his hand snapped him out of his trance. Startled, Fred realized that for only the third time since he was fourteen, he was crying.

"Yolanda, you seen my luggage set?"

"It's in my closet. I'll get it."

Yolanda came into Donna's room carrying her roommate's two maroon suitcases, garment bag and overnight bag. Donna finished folding a week's worth of underwear. On the bed in front of her, a pile of light colored shorts, jeans and blouses awaited her attention.

"Girl, how long you planning to stay there?"

Donna sighed. "I told you we don't know how long we'll be there. This is dangerous enough without worrying about running out of underwear too."

Yolanda laughed. "Okay then, why you packing this?"

She indicated a dress, red with black highlights. "Que es ese, amigita? You already packed something for church."

Donna smiled and took it back, placing it gently in her garment bag. "I don't know why I grabbed this. Something just told me I need it."

"Uh huh. Must be one of those formal emergencies."

Donna laughed. "Shut up and hand me those pumps."

Fred sat at his desk looking at the small jewelry box in his hand and hoped against hope that last night was some sort of misunderstanding.

She wouldn't just up and leave. If she wanted to break up, she'd just tell me. She wouldn't play me like that.

Unless she was guilty of something and couldn't tell me.

Suddenly feeling self-conscious, he put the box back in his pocket and called up a story file, pretending to work.

And Max isn't here to talk to. He's home packing today and about to take off on the mystery trip.

Pushing aside his customary desire not to let anyone know anything was wrong, Fred reached for the phone

Max zipped his black garment bag and put it on his bed. It contained a charcoal gray suit, a dark red silk shirt and a black and gray swirl patterned tie along with a more subdued white shirt and blue tie for church wear.

Don't know why I think I need this outfit, he thought, *but I'm learning to trust.*

Just then the phone rang. Putting aside the clothes he was packing, he grabbed the cordless phone.

"Hello?"

"Max! All packed for the love marathon yet?"

Max sighed. "Fred, how many times do I have to tell you? This is *not* a romantic getaway!"

Fred laughed. "Tell me another one. You ain't never got to lie to me about going away to get some."

Max nearly choked on his laughter. "Fred, you ain't right. I gotta finish packing now. When we get back, I promise I'll explain everything."

"You better. We got a pool going here, and we need information to pay the winner."

"Goodbye Fred. And be careful- I won't be here if you get jacked up again."

"Make sure you get some- I got twenty bucks riding on that!"

Max laughed and hung up.

Fred is a trip. Then again, we are best friends and I'm blatantly holding out on him. He'll probably be real mad when I tell him the whole story. Well, I'll worry about that when we get back. If we get back.

Fred hung up, disappointed.

Max was in a good mood. Can't get deep on him now. We can talk about it when he gets back.

Merry maneuvered her car in and out of traffic as she checked her rear view mirror. She'd glimpsed an old blue van when she got on South College Avenue, and it stayed with her as South College became 896 and as she exited onto Interstate 95 South.

I lost him about twenty miles ago. Hemingway thinks he's slick, but I've seen that rusty hoopty parked near my house way too often recently, and always right around the time something happened.

She accelerated to eighty-five MPH and maintained that speed.

This ought to let him know I'm not going to roll over and play dead for him. He's going to have to work to even get close to me, and when he does, he's got a big surprise coming.

At three thirty P.M., exactly a day and a half since they received their "assignment" to travel, Max rang Donna's door buzzer. Yolanda let him in and waited as he came upstairs.

"Hi Max, come on in. Donna's bringing her stuff out now."

The three of them quickly transferred Donna's bags from her bedroom to the trunk of Max's car.

Yolanda hesitated as Max closed the trunk. "Can we say a prayer before you guys go?"

The three of them joined hands in the parking lot and bowed their heads. Yolanda surprised herself by leading.

"God, uh, I just want to, uh, give thanks to You for waking us up this morning and for giving us a bright sunny spring day. Please- -watch over my friends as they travel, God- -protect them on the highway and in a strange state as they go to do whatever it is You have for them to do. In Jesus name I pray, Amen."

Max and Donna echoed Yolanda's Amen. Each of them hugged Yolanda and thanked her for her eloquent prayer. Max unlocked the passenger side for Donna and closed the door behind her before sliding in behind the wheel.

"You sure you guys can't just call the police to handle this?"

Donna frowned. "'Fraid not. Frankly I like that option better, but we don't have enough hard evidence to convince them there's danger. By the time we got any, it would be too late."

"Yeah, this is how we have to do it. Don't worry, Yolanda. I'll bring her home safe."

He started the car and pulled safely out of the parking lot. Yolanda watched until they were out of sight.

Vaya con Dios. And be careful. Tengo mucho miedo. I'm real scared for both of you.

Max and Donna rode in silence for ten minutes.

"She's really worried about us, Max."

"Fred is too, but he'd never admit it. He called while I was packing and joked around, but I could tell he was worried."

Donna looked uncomfortable. "I explained as much as I could to Yolanda before you came. She's known all about my gift since we were kids. I felt like I owed her an explanation."

Max nodded his approval. "It's okay. I really should've told Fred, but I couldn't. He's not a Christian. He wouldn't believe me right away, and I didn't have the time to explain things to him."

Donna thought for a moment. "You don't have to worry about Yolanda. She won't gossip."

"Good. I'd rather be the one to break this to my parents when the time comes. Besides, it's good that somebody else knows why we went if- - -"

The sentence trailed off as Max realized both he and Donna were thinking the same ending for it: "- -if we don't come back."

The blue van swerved in and out of traffic, trying to make up lost time. Inside, Hemingway cursed softly under his breath for having underestimated Merry yet again.

That heifer can drive! And she moved fast- I didn't even get to deliver my little surprise package before she skipped town. Guess that little surprise I left for her man made things too hot for her, he thought. *Bet she's glad to leave town!*

Like it's gonna matter when I get through with her.

He accelerated to eighty, hoping not to get pulled over.

I'm not supposed to leave the state. I'm still waiting to stand trial for breaking in her house. And if the cops pull me over with a bomb in my car, I am done.

He cursed some more, he slowed back down to sixty-five.

Two and a half hours into the trip, Max and Donna got back into the car. As they pulled back onto I-95 from the Maryland rest stop, Donna felt fresh stirrings of panic.

Why am I doing this? We've been going out for two months and all of a sudden we're running off into potential danger, and when we get there, we have to share a hotel room. That might be the real danger.

She tried unsuccessfully to push her panic aside and finally drifted into a fitful slumber.

Max only half concentrated on the road as Baltimore and Washington, DC signs gave way to signs indicating how soon they would enter Virginia.

We're not ready for this. Despite what it feels like, we haven't known each other all that long and here we are on some kind of mission we don't fully understand. There's a little fact behind this, but most of what we have to go on is dreams and visions. This is crazy!

And it's real embarrassing that we're so broke we have to share the room.

Half asleep, Donna snapped suddenly to awareness. She suddenly realized that Max's tension was hitting her like a sledgehammer, and that she was unwittingly adding her own to it and sending it back to Max doubled.

I'm making us both more nervous! I need to stop this now before we completely panic.

Closing her eyes, she prayed a short prayer and focused her entire being on calmness. Peace. Sweet peace. Understanding.

A scripture popped into her mind. *"Trust in the Lord with all thine heart, and lean not unto thine own understanding. In all thy ways acknowledge Him, and He shall direct thy paths."*

Proverbs 3:5 again. This is what came to me when we were carjacked. Well, it's definitely appropriate now.

As Donna meditated on the Word, her fears lessened. Her calmness projected outward, and soon Max's worries were dispelled as well.

I've gotta calm down. I have to be strong for Donna. I know she's nervous about all this. God, he prayed, *help me. Guide me through this, because I can't make it on my own.*

Max took a deep breath and was pleased to feel the tension ebb from his body. Thank You God, he thought. I needed that.

Donna stirred next to him, and he smiled to see her coming out of her slumber.

"You're awful quiet over there, Donna. How you doing?"

"Are we there yet?"

Max laughed at the childlike tone she adopted. "Another two and a half hours tops. You hungry?"

Donna nodded, and fifteen minutes down the road, Max pulled into the next rest stop. They got out of the car stiffly, stretching to loosen their cramped muscles.

"Let's see. We have a choice. Roy Rogers, Bob's Big Boy or S'barro's. Or, we can go a few more miles and hit Cracker Barrel."

Donna smiled. "Real food."

"Cracker Barrel it is."

As Max and Donna got back into his car, a blue van pulled back onto I-95 South. The driver blew impatiently at oncoming traffic as he merged without looking or yielding.

"Tell me Donna, what would your parents have said if you told them all this before we left?"

Donna laughed. "After Dad finished having a stroke, they'd have had me committed!"

Max cracked up. "Yeah, I guess I wouldn't be too comfortable with my daughter doing something like this. And I know my folks would've thought I was out to corrupt you."

She giggled. "Well, it's not like my folks know nothing about you. Mom thinks she's slick, but every time we talk, she grills me about you like she works for the CIA. Every now and then I toss her a crumb to keep her happy."

"My folks are the same way. My mother calls at least twice a week just to harass me about not having brought you back yet. It's so bad now they ask how you are before they ask about me!"

The waitress brought their food. Max said a brief grace and they dug in.

"Well Max, you know what has to happen now. We have to do the dreaded "meet the parents" thing once this is settled. Mine this time."

Max pretended to faint. "Can I get Pastor Nathan to pray over me first?"

Donna laughed. "My parents aren't bad, but I have to warn you about my brothers. They'll start grilling you as soon as you hit the door. I lost more potential boyfriends that way."

"Hey, we handled those carjackers didn't we? Your brothers can't be tougher than that."

After a half-hour break, they got back on the road. Donna fell asleep shortly after they entered Virginia, leaving Max alone with his thoughts.

I'm still not a hundred percent sure about this, but God, I know You're with us. Please show us what to do once we get there, and put a hedge of protection around us to keep us from danger. And Lord, despite my jokes earlier, I do want to get through this and meet Donna's family.

They might be my in-laws someday.

An hour after Merry checked in, Hemingway pulled into the Portsmouth Holiday Inn parking lot, cursing under his breath.

You better be there. I don't feel like searching every hotel within a ten-mile radius.

He went to the front desk and struck up a conversation with the clerk.

Satisfied that his prey was there, he checked in.

Okay "Crystal," let the games begin.

"Wake up Donna. We're here."

Max pulled into a space two rows from the front door. He helped Donna out of the car and they unloaded the luggage.

Wish we'd been called to Budget Inn. Maybe then we could've afforded separate rooms. We're in agreement about no sex until marriage, but this is a major challenge.

They checked in without incident, and at nine fifteen P.M. the elevator deposited them near their room. Donna used the electronic key card to release the lock and then held the door as Max carried their luggage inside.

As requested, two double beds sat side by side, separated by a night table containing a small clock radio, a lamp and a telephone. The bathroom sat on their left and two small but roomy bureaus on the right. A twenty-inch TV sat against one wall, facing the beds.

Max hauled the bags to the bed closest to the window and then flopped down next to them, exhausted. He stretched out to relax his cramped muscles and offered Donna first use of the shower.

Donna laughed. "If I didn't know you were such a gentleman, I'd think you were trying to tell me something."

Max passed her bags over. "I am. I'm telling you to hurry up before I change my mind!"

Donna laughed and vanished into the bathroom. Max lay where he was, feeling incredibly comfortable. The sound of running water hypnotized him; his aching muscles adhered to the mattress and he was out cold before he realized it.

A strange sound woke Max up suddenly. Mildly disoriented, he sat up and looked around the room. Donna stood beside her bed, wearing only a plush white hotel towel. She dug through one of her bags; the sound he'd heard was her unzipping it. When she realized that Max was awake, she blushed furiously.

"I'm sorry. I didn't mean to wake you."

Max's voice stuck dry in his larynx. He cleared his throat and tried unsuccessfully not to stare. "Uh huh."

Donna clamped her left hand across her towel, even though it was securely fastened. "I, uh, I must have packed my hair dryer in the wrong bag."

Max struggled to maintain control of his voice. "Uh, yeah. Hey, white's a good color for you. You should wear it more often."

Glaring fire at him, she found what she was looking for. Keeping a firm grip on her towel, she crept back into the bathroom. Now wide-awake, Max sat up in bed.

No makeup, just out of the shower, hair all wet and she still looks incredible, Max thought.

Jesus keep me near the Cross.

Half an hour later, both of them were showered and in their beds. Donna was already dozing under her covers. Max quietly turned off the light and the TV, and with a whispered "good night" to Donna, burrowed underneath his own crisply starched bedspread. Donna murmured an incoherent response in her sleep and turned over, breathing softly and rhythmically.

In his newly rented room, Hemingway tried in vain to sleep, vengeful thoughts keeping him up. He finally gave up and turned on the TV, searching for an interesting movie or for SportsCenter on ESPN.

"Crystal," *I hope you get a good night's rest, he thought. It will be your last.*

He patted the travel bag on the floor beside his bed. "Old Faithful" here oughtta teach you a good lesson about jerking people around.

Hemingway looked at the travel brochure and hotel confirmation notice he'd lifted from Merry's kitchen table.

For someone who lies as well as she does, she's awful careless with her stuff. Made it real easy to find her. I might have to go to jail behind this, but it'll be worth it to frag that ho once and for all.

Donna awakened suddenly.

One thirty-seven A.M. showed in red against the darkness. A sound Donna couldn't place had awakened her, and the shadow moving stealthily past her bed told her that she wasn't the only one awake.

"Max? You up?"

With no answer to her soft question, she instinctively turned on the lamp. Max turned towards her, startled. He wore nothing but boxer shorts and an embarrassed half-smile.

"I- -uh, well, I got hot and took off my T-shirt and, uh, well, you were asleep and I had to- -I figured I could- -."

Sensing his embarrassment, Donna couldn't contain her laughter. Max blushed as deeply as Donna had earlier, and turned away from her, trying to cover up with his hands as best he could.

"Now you know how I felt earlier coming out of the shower!"

Max laughed too, and pulled a pair of blue sweat pants out of his suitcase. "Kind of like locking the barn after the horse got out, huh?"

Donna smiled wickedly. "Don't flatter yourself."

Max pulled the pants up and snapped his head around to face her again. His openmouthed surprised stare quickly dissolved into laughter, and she joined him.

"See, people think you're all quiet and nice. I *know* better now!"

"Hey, I owed you one for that crack you made about me in that towel! Now we're even."

Their laughter subsided. Max sat on the side of his bed facing Donna and they started talking on a wide variety of topics. They discussed movies and then politics, deliberately avoiding all talk about why they came to Virginia. They were starting on current events when Donna finally looked at the clock.

"Max, it's after three A.M.! We need to get some sleep. Only God knows what'll happen tomorrow."

She took a last lingering look at Max. He hadn't put on a shirt, and his dark skin in the shadows of the room created a mysterious and attractive effect. As Max leaned over to turn off the lamp, he glanced over at Donna. Her deep brown eyes hypnotized him, questioned him, answered him and invited him all at the same time. Before he realized it, he crossed the short gap between their beds and kissed Donna as if their lives depended on it. Max and Donna felt a powerful urge to surrender to gravity and then to whatever might happen next. *Stop!*

A sudden jolt of guilty panic hit them, and they quickly stopped. Max let go of Donna, facing away from her again for modesty's sake. Neither of them spoke right away; they took deep, cleansing breaths and prayed mightily for the return of self-control.

"I'm scared, Max. Of what could happen."

He took deep breaths. "So am I."

"I don't mean just about stopping the bombing."

"Neither do I."

They sat on Donna's bed, her head on his bare shoulder. They said nothing; their closeness was all the communication they needed.

Merry woke up in her modest hotel room, refreshed and for the first time in the past twelve hours, smiling.

Let's see him find me here.

Merry had checked into the Portsmouth Holiday Inn, but instead of settling in, she sneaked down the fire stairs and out the back door at the first opportunity. A half hour's drive brought her to Virginia Beach, where she had her choice of a seemingly endless array of hotels.

Larger chains like Holiday Inn, Tropicana Resorts, Hilton, Ramada and Best Western mingled with smaller entities such as the Sand Castle Motel, Beach Cabana Motel, New Castle Motel and Dunes. It seemed to Merry as if virtually every hotel and motel in the world, large and small, had set up shop on this one strip of land.

From each of these temporary safe havens, a weary traveler could literally step out of their door and onto the beach. Merry chose Budget Inn, where she checked in as Jennifer Bannon, the only of her aliases for which she had an actual driver's license (courtesy of a former lover).

A sudden thought occurred to Merry. She'd been in such a hurry to stay a step ahead of Hemingway that she'd completely forgotten about Fred.

I stood him up. He doesn't know where I am any more than Hemingway does, and he still thinks I'm a prostitute.

Her pleasant mood ruined, she got back under the covers to get more rest, fighting a sudden wave of sadness.

Max and Donna awakened when the alarm went off at nine A.M. They'd spent the past six hours in Donna's bed; despite their lack of sleep, they both got up at once. While Donna was in the bathroom, Max slipped down to the gift shop in the lobby. When he came back, he turned on CNN to watch the news.

"Max, could you turn it down a bit? We have to talk."

Donna came out of the bathroom fully dressed this time, in a pink blouse and baggy white shorts. Max turned the TV off, and she sat beside him on his bed.

"Max, do you- -you know, regret last night?"

"No, not at all. You?"

"No. It may sound funny, but not making love with you was wonderful!"

Max laughed. "I agree. We were moving way too fast. We should wait until- - -.

"- - -until it's right."

Donna finished Max's sentence, letting him off the conversational hook even as they both contemplated the implications of what he stared to say. He grabbed his shaving kit and the bag from the hotel gift shop and excused himself into the bathroom, thankful that they were still on one accord about their relationship.

This has been anything but a normal relationship, he thought. *Regular couples don't do stuff like this. Heck, soap opera couples don't even do all this! I sure wasn't ready to share a room, and I know she wasn't either.*

At least we have a plan. We know that whatever happens, it will be today or tomorrow. Since the dream took place towards the evening, we'll play tourist and wait for further direction.

Donna sat on her bed, deep in thought. She couldn't stop thinking about how close she and Max came to defiling this bed scant hours ago, and how glad she was that they'd stopped before it was too late.

We're not ready for this kind of closeness. Lord, help us to not give in to temptation. We're here to do your will, not to serve our own pleasures. Show us how to keep from repeating last night's mistakes. In Jesus' name I pray, Amen.

"Ready to hit the beach?"

Donna took one look at Max and burst out laughing. Wanting to defuse the situation, Max bought an outfit from the gift shop designed to tickle Donna's funny bone instead of her libido. He wore a pair of wildly colored plaid shorts and a white T-shirt with black letters that said, "If You Think These Shorts Are Ugly, You Should See The Ones I Left In The Store!"

"Better not go out looking like that, Max. The Fashion Police have orders to shoot you on sight."

Max laughed. "How could they miss me?"

For the second straight day, Fred couldn't focus on his work. Try as he might to finish his editing, the words either swam around the page or congealed into an illegible mass. Frustrated, he gave up temporarily and took a break.

Usually fifteen minutes in the cafeteria with a Diet Dr. Pepper was enough to clear Fred's head of any workday malaise, but this day was different. He lingered an extra ten minutes, mind awhirl with the stresses and revelations of the past week. He wondered if the idea forming in his head was something he should follow up on.

Best to forget all the drama and get some editing done. After all this with Merry, I can't blow a plum opportunity like this.

Merry lay calmly on her blanket, umbrella tilted to just the right angle. She wore a dark blue one-piece bathing suit and sunglasses and read the latest Terry McMillan novel, using the book to ignore the many lecherous stares she got from passersby.

I wish I could see the look on Hemingway's face when he realizes he missed me, she thought. *You'd think the moron would remember bragging to me about all the skills he picked up in "the 'Nam," but no. Men can be so stupid. And predictable. I knew he'd come after me, and I knew he'd get dramatic. Regular stalking isn't enough, and he knows he can't get close enough for me to hurt him again. He could have tried a sniper move on me, but I know him. Shooting me isn't enough; he has to wipe me off the planet before he'll be happy.*

I'll be glad when they identify Karl and Taylor's bodies so I can figure out how soon I can get the money. I'm not exactly in the will, but if I'm his only living relative, how can I not get it? Nobody would be suspicious if my alcoholic mother died in a drunk driving "accident." And Bryan, well, college kids get killed by muggers all the time. And I happen to know a few muggers.

Her thoughts turned to what her life would be if she had all the money she would ever need, and Fred immediately came to mind.

This would be the perfect vacation if he were with me. If nothing else, he could keep the raggedy men from leering at me. Well, once all this is settled I can make it up to him. If he doesn't dump me, I'll take him for a Caribbean vacation. We can get married and move there if that's what it takes.

Just then a portly Hispanic man stared at Merry so long he stumbled over his own feet and nearly landed at hers. Merry shook off her mild depression and laughed out loud.

Fred sat on his couch, absently channel-surfing. He'd gotten a little work done, but not as much as he'd hoped. Now that he was home, he couldn't relax.

He reached for the phone, pulled his hand back and reached for it again.

He punched two numbers this time and hung up.

Get a grip Fred. You must've called fifty million women and now you're scared to call one more? Stop acting like a punk, pick up the phone and just do it!

He grabbed the phone and punched in the number before he could change his mind, referring to the phone book to make sure he had it right. Someone answered on the second ring.

"Hello?"

The voice on the other end was rich, musical and lightly accented, causing Fred to hesitate. "Um, may I speak to Yolanda please?"

"This is Yolanda."

"This is Fred. Fred Bennett. Max's friend?"

"Yes, I remember you."

Silence ensued. *Come on Fred*, he thought. *You're coming off like a high school nerd!*

Yolanda adopted a businesslike tone. "Is there something in particular you called for?"

"Yes. Well, I guess you know about Virginia Beach."

Yolanda relaxed. *Good, he's not calling to hit on me.* "I do. Donna told me what she could. I'm still not a hundred percent sure why they had to go."

"Me too. If it was anybody else I know, I'd think they were just sneaking off on a romantic vacation. But that's not Max's style. Donna's either if she's Max's girl."

Yolanda hesitated. *How much does Fred know? He doesn't seem like he'd understand the whole story. Then again, I've known Donna all her life and I still have a hard time comprehending what she can do.*

"Fred, I think we need to get together and talk."

Fifteen minutes later, Fred's black Saab pulled up in front of the Newark Bennigan's. Yolanda waited by the front door. She wore a University of Delaware T-shirt, blue jeans, hair pulled back in a long ponytail. Once again, Fred couldn't help but admire her athletic grace, her robust figure and her luxurious auburn hair, but he was subtle in his appraisal this time.

"Thanks for coming out on such short notice, Fred."

"No problem. Wasn't doing nothing but sitting around."

That doesn't sound like the Fred I met, she thought. *He seems subdued. It's like something seriously broke him down since the last time I saw him.*

They went inside and were seated within ten minutes. After they ordered, Fred settled back in his seat and smiled.

"So tell me Yolanda, why the sudden desire for my company? I was under the distinct impression you hated my guts."

Yolanda smiled grimly. *Now that's the Fred I remember.*

"Let's get this straight. This is *not* a date. I asked you here because we need to talk about our friends. I'm worried about Donna, and I'm sure you're worried about Max too."

"You think this might be related to what happened on their first date?"

The waitress brought their drinks. Yolanda took a sip of her iced tea.

"Could be. Ever since then, Donna's been acting strange. She usually tells me everything, but she's been secretive lately." Fred looked thoughtful.

"Max been holding out on me too, but I get the impression that he and Donna don't keep secrets from each other. It's like they have this bond since that first date, like a secret that only they know and it's making them closer."

"I get that same feeling. Then again, maybe it's just that they're falling in love and don't need us anymore."

Fred frowned. "Maybe that's part of it, but not all. I don't know why, but I feel like he and Donna are in trouble. Thing is, if we don't know what, how can we help them?"

Yolanda took a deep breath as she pondered her answer. "We can pray."

The waitress arrived with their food, and they paused their conversation long enough to start eating.

"Fred, I think it's in our best interests that you and I tell each other all we know about Max and Donna and this situation. And I mean everything."

Fred sipped at his Dr. Pepper, for once forgetting his preference for diet soda.

"Okay, get us started. I need an idea of what information you think is important."

Yolanda hesitated. *He doesn't seem to know anything about Max having a special ability,* she thought. *Well, I've come this far, and I can't stop now.*

"How long have you known Max?"

"Two years now, ever since he started at the Voice. Why?"

"In that time, have you ever noticed anything strange about him?"

"Depends on what you mean by strange. He's the most uptight guy I know sometimes. He can't lie to save his life and he turns down more chances to get l- -, um to have sex in a month then most guys get in a year. Besides that, I haven't seen anything strange."

Yolanda sipped her iced tea. *This isn't working. I was hoping Fred had seen Max do something. Then I'd have a better chance of convincing him I'm not on drugs.*

"Wait a minute. There *is* something else. He did say he had this dream."

Yolanda's heart leaped for joy. *Now we're getting somewhere,* she thought.

"What was the dream about?"

Fred took a forkful of chicken fingers. "I can't tell you all of it because it's kinda personal for him. But I will tell you this; he said Donna was in the dream with him, and that was before he met her!"

A look of dawning comprehension crossed Fred's face. Yolanda took a bite of her cheeseburger and asked for a refill of her iced tea.

"Fred, that was just what I was looking for. Now it's my turn to talk, about Donna *and* Max. You have to promise me you'll hear me out and keep an open mind, 'cause I guarantee you this will be hard to believe."

Fred smiled wistfully, thinking of Merry. "After the past few days, nothing much could surprise me."

Yolanda explained all she could about the special bond between their friends, about the shared dreams and the gifts that Max and Donna each possessed. Fred sat quietly, not wanting to interrupt until he heard it all.

"Let me get this straight. You're saying that our friends have psychic powers or something, and that they saw in a dream that they have to go to Virginia to prevent some kind of crime."

Yolanda nodded. "Donna wouldn't tell me everything, but she did say that it could be a matter of life or death."

"And not only that, you say my girlfriend- my ex-girlfriend as far as I'm concerned now- is tied up in this."

"Fred, I know how crazy this sounds, but I believe Donna. She can't be around Merry without getting really bad feelings, and she saw Merry in one of the dreams too."

Fred finished his soda. "Come to think of it, Max tried to warn me about her. It sounds crazy, but I don't know a lot about Merry. She could be a drug dealer or an assassin for all I know!"

Yolanda started to say something, but the melancholy look on Fred's face choked the remark off in her throat.

" 'Scuse me, be right back."

Fred quickly walked off in the direction of the restrooms, rubbing his eyes as he went.

I was right. He is hurting. Apparently he was in love with her and she played him somehow. How people can be that cruel, I don't know.

Fred and the check arrived at the table simultaneously. Yolanda dug in her purse for her share.

"That's all right. I got it."

Yolanda started to protest, but thought better of it. "Thanks."

Fred paid the check, held the door for Yolanda as they left, and since it was dark out, walked her to her car. Yolanda was surprised; her initial impression of Fred hadn't included good manners.

"Fred, thanks again for coming. I really appreciate it."

"No problem. I think we both needed to talk about this. Maybe now I'll sleep tonight after all."

Yolanda smiled. "Yeah, it's tough not being able to help them. Like I said, all we can do from here is pray for them."

Fred smiled wistfully. "Pray. It's been a long time since I did that."

He started to walk back to his car, and then turned back with a sudden thought. "Listen, if anything new comes up, give me a call."

Fred passed a business card through her open window. She accepted it, promised to keep him informed and started her car. Fred climbed into his Saab and started the engine, but didn't leave until Yolanda's car cleared the lot.

17

Max and Donna lay peacefully on their beach towel, as if they didn't have a care in the world.

This is what I'm talking about, Max thought. *Lying on a beautiful beach with a beautiful woman. If it wasn't for that bomb threat, I'd really be into this.*

Beside him, Donna was completely relaxed and she felt that Max was too.

That's good. His calmness is helping me keep cool too.

Later that afternoon, Max and Donna walked up and down "The Strip"- one hundred different stores, all within walking range of the beach. They passed Sunsations Beachwear, David's Beach Shop and the Shore Store. They stopped briefly in Curiosities Rock Shop and browsed through Eagle Dancer Native American Arts and Crafts. After that, they went to Whizzo's Game Room, where Donna beat Max three straight games of Centipede while Max dominated her at Ms. Pac-Man.

After about two hours of nonstop walking, they found a shady bench and sat down.

"This place is incredible! I've never seen so many stores all together in my life."

Donna nodded and leaned her head on Max's shoulder. "I haven't been here since my parents brought us here on vacation when I was seven. Most of these stores weren't here then; most of the hotels either."

They chatted and rested until Max finally broke the spell by looking at his watch. "I can't believe it's nearly five o'clock. Where'd the day go?"

Donna smiled. "They say time flies when you're having fun."

"If that's the case, we should be into the next century by now."

Donna smiled at Max's strangely worded compliment. "I'm having a good time too."

"Shall we retire back to the hotel? We could hit the pool."

Donna looked at him and laughed. "There's an entire ocean not thirty feet away and you want to go get in a swimming pool?"

"I don't know about you, but when I swim, and I use that term loosely, I like to know where the sides are. And you can bet there are no waves or sharks in the pool!"

Donna laughed again. "Can't argue with that logic."

Hemingway drove slowly back to the hotel, mind awhirl with plans. He'd seen Merry at the beach, and barely restrained himself from killing her on the spot.

That would've been the second biggest mistake of my life, right behind messing with her stank behind in the first place. Best to stick with the plan.

Hemingway quickly went the other way so Merry wouldn't see him. She was gone when he circled back twenty minutes later.

Her car's not in the hotel lot. She must be out enjoying her vacation. Probably picking up some poor unsuspecting sucker to play and betray.

Hemingway decided not to delay the final phase of his plan any longer and headed upstairs. *If she's in her room now, I'll have to knock her out and leave her in there with it. If she isn't, I can hook it up, set it for two in the morning when I know she'll be there and be gone before anybody knows what happened.*

Hemingway remembered his fugitive status and a thought hit him. *Why go back and face jail time? I can keep right on going, head back to Georgia or to one of the Carolinas.*

The thought of living in the South again warmed him as he reached for his travel bag and the equipment inside.

Max and Donna entered their hotel, awash in the afterglow of an idyllic day.

"How about this? We rest for a few minutes and then we go get in the pool. We get out, we dry off and then go get some dinner."

Donna smiled. "Sounds like a plan to me."

As they headed for the elevator, Donna felt a sudden wave of uncertainty. Max noticed the abrupt disappearance of her smile.

"Donna, what's wrong?"

"I feel strange. I can't put my finger on it, but something just isn't right."

They fell silent as the elevator came. Neither of them wanted to acknowledge that the crisis point they'd dreamed of might be upon them. As Donna absently pushed their floor, Max could tell she was praying for discernment. He joined her, wanting his mind and spirit clear for whatever was to come. The elevator door opened, and Max and Donna stepped out, still praying silently. They walked down the hallway towards their room, deep in concentration.

"Max, look! We got off on the seventh floor instead of the eighth!"

Max looked up to see room 709 staring at them instead of 809, and laughed.

"I can hear Fred now. "Oh, they can see the future but they don't know what floor they room is on!"

Donna laughed too, and they turned back towards the elevator. As she dug in her purse for the room key, Max's attention was drawn down the hall.

"Donna, look!"

Max's whisper carried the force of a shout. Donna followed his gaze and froze. The tall, thin black man wore a blue jumpsuit and carried a raggedy toolbox. As they gaped in astonishment, he did something to the nearest door and ducked into Room 717.

This is it! That's the room, and that's the man we saw!

A chilly burst of fear broke Max's paralysis.

"Donna, go get security. I'm going after him!"

Max moved before Donna could object, sprinting full speed up the hallway towards Room 717. She hesitated briefly and then caught the elevator to the lobby.

Hemingway calmly entered Merry's unused room. *Just one more repairman in to fix stuff. None of the hotel staff so much as looked my way. They just assumed I belong here.*

With practiced ease, Hemingway removed the firebomb from its carrying case. His gaze settled on the TV set. *This should do it. Set the timer for early morning, and I get rid of "Crystal" once and for all.*

He opened his toolbox and looked for the best place to set up.

Max ran hard, trying to get there before it was too late.

Lord, I have no idea what to do when I catch up to this man, but this is why You called us here. Help me stop him from killing all these people.

Max reached the door and stood still for a moment, praying for guidance. Just then, he heard a click. *I have to stop him, right here and right now. Lord, be with me.*

His heart skipped a beat as he took another deep breath and burst through the door.

Hemingway removed the back panel of the TV set to expose the wires and set to work.

If she comes back and turns the set on, the bomb will go off that much sooner. Needless to say, once I finish, I better get out of Dodge in a hurry.

Despite his growing annoyance, he worked meticulously. He knew that impatience could cost him a limb.

"Get away from there!"

Startled, Hemingway nearly dropped everything as the door flew open and a wild-eyed black man charged at him.

Max ducked the toolbox Hemingway threw and barreled into him like a football player, driving him backwards into the wall. Max hoped the impact would knock the wind out of his opponent, but Hemingway merely grunted in pain and fought back. Max ducked a wild punch and struggled to grab Hemingway's arms, hoping to wrestle him to the floor and hold him there until Donna sent help.

"It's Room 717! There's a guy up there and he has a bomb!"

To their credit, the hotel staff reacted immediately. Two of the three security men on duty raced for the stairs while a third dialed 911.

Hold on Max. Lord, help him. Put a hedge of protection around him and give him strength for his task.

Hurry up security! I can't hold this guy all day. What's taking so long?

Hemingway was the better fighter, but age and excessive beer consumption had eroded his skills. After an exchange of punches, Max spun Hemingway around and forced his arms underneath Hemingway's. He locked them behind Hemingway's neck in a full nelson wrestling hold.

In response, Hemingway jerked free of Max's grip, lunging towards the open door. Max closed the distance between them with a flying tackle, driving Hemingway's face into the floor and knocking him cold.

"Freeze!"

Even though one of the two guns was trained on Max, he thought the two armed policemen and the two hotel security men were a beautiful sight. Max raised his hands in surrender, wincing in pain from the effort.

"What's going on here?"

Max indicated Hemingway, who lay motionless on the floor. "He was trying to attach that bomb to the TV set. I stopped him."

The bomb squad arrived and set to work. As Hemingway slowly came to, the police handcuffed him and Max and led them out of the room. As Donna and the hotel manager got off the elevator, she nearly had a fit when she saw Max in custody.

"Let him go!"

She pointed to Max. The officer holding him looked to the manager, who nodded in assent. The officer unlocked the cuffs, freeing Max for a much-needed hug.

The rest of the day was one long interrogation. Once the bomb squad was satisfied that the device was harmless, they took it as evidence and took Max and Donna in for questioning. A grueling three hours later, Max and Donna returned to their hotel room, ducking into the stairwell and running up to their floor to elude the reporters who waited for them in the lobby.

Max flopped onto his bed, exhausted. "Man, I thought they'd never stop questioning us."

Donna sat down on her bed. "I'm surprised they didn't arrest us too."

Max laughed. "They sure tried hard enough."

Donna stretched. "Was it me, or did Officer Unfriendly there seem disappointed when he couldn't find enough evidence to lock us up as that man's disgruntled partners?"

Max laughed. "Hey, it made sense. Obviously I helped him sneak that huge bomb into the room, helped him attach it and then beat the snot out of him just for kicks."

Donna laughed so hard that tears formed. "Max, think about it. All they saw was two black men fighting in the same room with a firebomb capable of blowing up a small country. Wouldn't you be suspicious?"

Max smiled. "Good point."

In her small room at the Virginia Beach Budget Inn, Merry slammed clothes into her travel bag. She saw the news report of Hemingway's arrest, and the results were extremely disappointing.

He was supposed to blow up the hotel and then get arrested! Thanks to his incompetence, my father and his heifer are still alive.

That couple ruined everything. Well, I hope they have fun here, because when we get back to Delaware, it's on.

Still fuming and cursing, Merry grabbed her bag and headed downstairs to check out.

After the best night's sleep either of them enjoyed in weeks, Max and Donna celebrated the success of their mission by spending the next day (a Saturday) at Busch Gardens. They got on every ride, played arcade games and enjoyed themselves with the enthusiasm of small children. After six hours, they returned to the hotel, exhausted.

"We're gonna need a child seat to get this thing home."

Max dragged a stuffed panda roughly the size of a Nissan Sentra into the room. Donna laughed.

"Hey, you're the one who won it for me; deal with it."

Max smiled, plopped the bear down on the floor, and flopped onto his mattress. Donna followed suit, sinking onto her own bed and smiling with relief.

"It feels good to have this over with!"

Max pumped a fist in the air. "Yes, Lord! We've given the police every statement they could possibly need and now we can go home tomorrow."

Donna frowned. "Max, what time do you want to get started?"

"I figured we'd check out first thing in the morning, go to that church we found for the eight o'clock service and hit the road from there. Why?"

She looked towards the phone. "Our parents have surely seen the news by now, and they're going to want to know why we're here instead of in Delaware. I think we should stop on the way home and visit my parents."

Max blinked, and Donna nearly laughed at the quick burst of apprehension she felt surge through him. He recovered quickly, and Donna allowed him to play it off.

"That makes sense. We're going right past Baltimore. If we get on the road from here by eleven, we should hit Baltimore by four thirty or five in the afternoon."

"Great! I'll call and set things up."

Max grabbed his shaving kit and excused himself into the bathroom, giving Donna privacy for her phone call. She smiled at his thoughtfulness as she dialed. *Nobody home*, she thought.

Donna next called the family restaurant her parents operated, which she thought of as her second home.

"Nap Afterwards."

Donna felt a surge of warmth over the phone. "Hi Mom."

"Roland, pick up the extension. Donna's on the phone! Child, why on earth are you in Virginia Beach? And why are you and Max in the news beating up more criminals?"

Donna laughed. "Fine, thanks Mom. How are you?"

Mrs. Randall laughed. "Okay, so sue me for being worried about you. I'm glad to hear from you. I called you Thursday night and got your machine. Now I know why."

"It's a really long story Mom, and I can't wait to tell it to you in person. Max and I are leaving here tomorrow morning around eleven, and we want to stop through on the way home."

Mr. Randall's hearty voice boomed through the phone. "Good! Why don't you bring him here? Sunday afternoons are pretty hectic, and you know we like to work the rush."

"Sounds good to me. We'll be there around four thirty or five, depending on how the traffic treats us."

"Bring your appetites."

As they finished the conversation, Max emerged from the bathroom clad in a T-shirt and sweatpants over his swimming trunks.

"Well?"

"They want us to come to the restaurant."

Max licked his lips in exaggerated fashion. "Oh, so I finally get to taste that Nap Afterwards cooking you've been telling me about all this time!"

Donna laughed. "Yeah, this is your chance. I told them to expect us around four thirty or five in the afternoon."

"That sounds about right. Hey, how about that swim we never took yesterday?"

Donna smiled. "Sounds good to me. Go on ahead, I'll be down in a few minutes."

Max grabbed a towel and headed for the door, and then stopped.

"Hey, your dad never served any time, did he?"

Donna laughed. "No, but he played pro football. I think that's the same thing."

Max groaned, pretending to talk to himself as he left the room. "Oh, great. Her dad's a linebacker. I'm a *dead* man."

Donna laughed harder and pulled a bathing suit from her luggage.

Merry sat on her bed, scowling. She'd chosen to remain in Virginia Beach a bit longer rather then head back to Delaware immediately. With Hemingway arrested, she checked out of the hotel she'd sneaked to and slipped back into the Portsmouth Holiday Inn as if she'd stayed there all along.

I haven't had a vacation in years. Hemingway's locked up; there's no reason I can't spend another day here.

I might as well quit lying to myself. I don't want to go home because I don't want to explain this to Fred. I left him hanging, and I'm not sure what I'll say when I see him.

Frowning, Merry lay down, lost in thoughts of life without Fred. She didn't like what she came up with.

18

"There, Max. The restaurant is at the end of the block."

Donna indicated a building the size of a Denny's bearing a white sign with red letters spelling out NAP AFTERWARDS in the middle of a pillow. Max chuckled. *Nice to know her folks have a sense of humor.*

He pulled into the parking lot and found a space with little effort. Max got out, opened Donna's door for her and took her hand gently as they headed for the door.

We drove five hours without stopping to get here, and I'd rather do five more than walk inside this building.

Donna patted Max's arm. "Relax Max. My dad only keeps a .45 here. His Uzi stays home in the closet."

Max sighed. "Why even try to play it off? With you, I might as well let my knees knock and be done with it."

Donna laughed and squeezed his hand, pleased that Max was so nervous about meeting her family.

Max held the front door open for Donna and followed her in. By unspoken agreement, their first stop was the restrooms.

As Max waited for Donna to emerge, he looked around, impressed with his first view of the place. Donna told him that the Randalls bought the restaurant fifteen years ago, using money Roland Sr. earned during his brief football career with the then Baltimore Colts. The atmosphere was homey; oak tables covered with red and white tablecloths, houseplants placed at strategic locations around the room and pictures on every wall. One particular picture caught Max's eye; a depiction of Jesus in the garb of an African prince. It was the same portrait Donna admired on her first visit to Max's apartment.

"What do you think?"

Max was startled; he hadn't heard Donna come out. He indicated the picture. "I haven't met your folks yet, but I like them already."

Donna laughed. Just then, a dark-skinned Hispanic teenager wearing a red T-shirt with the restaurant's name in white letters ran over to them, smiling broadly.

"Donna! Long time no see, stranger."

They hugged exuberantly while Max looked on, amused.

Donna managed to untangle herself from the girl's embrace. "Max, this is Yolanda's little sister Carmen. Seeta, this is Max."

"I thought you looked familiar."

Carmen smiled and hugged him not quite as hard as she did Donna. "I've heard so much about you I feel like I know you already."

Max smiled. "All good stuff I hope, Carmen, or I'm in for a long night."

Carmen laughed. "You can call me Seeta. It's short for Carmencita, and everyone calls me that. And you're okay. If you weren't, Donna's dad would've met you instead of me."

Max rolled his eyes. "How reassuring."

Carmen reached behind the counter and pushed the intercom button on the phone. "They're here, Uncle Ro. I'm gonna put them in the party room, okay?"

"Okay. We'll be right in."

Carmen led them through the main dining room towards the banquet room normally reserved for special occasions (wedding parties, anniversaries, birthdays, etc.). It afforded the perfect amount of privacy for this family gathering.

"Donna, your mom and dad have been working in the kitchen all day acting like they weren't worrying about when you were getting here. Your brothers too."

Max smiled. "Probably strategically placing sharp knives for the interrogation."

Donna laughed. "You don't know the half of it."

As they waited for the Randalls, Max's mind rolled back to their last night at the hotel. A message from the hotel manager greeted their return from swimming. He thanked them profusely for their heroic actions and insisted that they attend a banquet he had arranged in their honor.

Max and Donna went reluctantly, wearing the dressy outfits they'd each packed without being sure why. Mercifully, the dinner lasted only an hour and a half, long enough for the manager to publicly thank them and for any hotel guests who wanted to do the same to express their gratitude as well.

Out of all the hotel patrons who came, Max remembered the last couple most vividly. Karl Hurzen looked to be in his late forties/early fifties and had the haughty bearing of someone used to being obeyed. His wife Taylor was fashion model thin and easily half Karl's age. Karl explained that he and Taylor were there on the honeymoon they hadn't been able to afford two years ago and thanked Max and Donna for enabling them to live to continue enjoying their Powerball winnings.

Donna felt something about them, but she couldn't tell me exactly what. If it's anything big, God will reveal it to us.

Just then the door swung open and a couple walked in, holding hands and smiling. The man was well over six feet tall and powerfully built; the only sign of age on him was the onset of a potbelly. He was dark brown-skinned with a thick, graying moustache and a twinkle in his eye that diluted his naturally stern expression. The woman was closer to five feet tall than six, about three inches shorter than Donna. She was tan skinned with shoulder length graying hair and a solid build. Max could tell that she must have been a heartbreaker like Donna in her youth because she was attractive now, in her late forties/early fifties. Despite their vast size difference, Donna's parents looked completely natural together.

"Mom, Dad, hi!"

Donna flung herself into a group hug capable of making the Brady Bunch gag. Max smiled at their enthusiastic greeting, even as his stomach jumped at the thought of his impending introduction to the most important people in Donna's life.

"Mom, Dad, this is Max Carson. Max, these are the parents I'm always bragging about. Roland and Antoinette Randall."

Glad that he and Donna had traveled in their church clothes, Max took a deep breath and stood anxiously to shake hands. Mrs. Randall ignored his outstretched hand and gave him a maternal hug instead.

"None of that handshake business. We might have just met, but you saved my daughter's life. That rates a hug in my book."

Embarrassed, Max straightened up from the hug to receive a knuckle-cracking handshake from Mr. Randall. It was all Max could do not to wince at Mr. Randall's powerful grip.

"Pleasure to meet you, Max. Our little girl talks you up every time we talk to her."

Max smiled. "We're even then, because she talks about you two constantly."

Just then, the door opened and two six-foot-tall young men entered. The first was tall and tan-skinned, looked to be around eighteen or so and had the lean, muscular bearing of a basketball player and the overtly handsome features of an actor; he strongly favored his mother. His brother was a stocky, dark brown-skinned mirror image of his father. Donna quickly moved to hug them, but they were too busy failing to intimidate Max to give her more than a perfunctory hug in return.

"Max, these are my younger brothers. That's Roland, Jr. and this is Richard."

Max extended his hand. "Good to meet you, fellas. Donna's told me a lot about you."

They each shook hands, still grim-faced. Richard looked so stony Max thought his face would crack any second.

"We can't say the same. Yet. Let's step over there. We got a couple questions to ask you."

Max suppressed a smile as he followed Roland and the as-yet silent Richard to the small table in the corner of the room.

Their tough guy act is good. If Donna hadn't warned me, I might have actually taken them seriously.

Naaaaaah.

○━━▮━━○

"Think he'll make it?"

Donna smiled. "Yeah Mom, he'll do just fine. I warned him about the Bruise Brothers on the drive here."

"But Donna, they don't have guns. He might not know how to handle them."

"Dad!"

Over in the corner, Max fielded questions from Roland, Jr., under the menacing glare of Richard.

"We heard about all those beat-downs you been handing out. What we don't know is why y'all was in Virginia Beach in the first place."

"And why y'all had to stay in the same hotel room."

Having inserted his two cents, Richard returned to his silent vigil. Max contained his laughter and took a deep breath, as if steadying his nerves. He took a moment to remember the story they had agreed upon. "The police didn't take us seriously when we called them with what we'd learned about that bomber. Donna and I had to move fast to get there ahead of him, and we didn't have enough money to get separate rooms like we wanted."

Roland leaned forward, adjusted his baggy jeans and put his chin in his hand. "You mean to tell me you *wanted* separate rooms when you're so in love with our sister?"

Max smiled. "Part of being in love with somebody is respecting her wishes. Neither of us believes in having sex outside of marriage. If I pressured her to do that, I would be seriously disrespecting her, and worse, I'd be disrespecting God."

Richard raised his eyebrows and broke his silence again.

"Good answer."

"Donna, you meant to tell us that your mood swings aren't just your hormones acting up?"

Donna took a deep breath. "Mom, it's a whole lot more. It always has been."

She started with the first dream and ended with how her shared dreams with Max brought them together and sent them to Virginia Beach.

Mr. Randall shook his head slowly. "This- - -this is hard to take in. I remember you used to tell us about dreams you had when you were a little girl, but I never imagined- -. You're telling us that you're---gifted by God to do these things. That sounds like a wonderful calling, but also a dangerous one."

"I know, Dad. And that scares me. What if we have to go somewhere else dangerous?"

Mrs. Randall smiled. "I think you know the answer to that one. God protected you this time, and I'm sure He'll do it again wherever you go. And I'm sure you'll never have to do anything like this without Max. I assume you two have discussed this thoroughly?"

Donna smiled. "We sure did."

She described how Max took the lead throughout their adventures, including details of the carjacking. The elder Randalls blinked in amazement at Donna's description of the power of God in evidence during Max and Donna's life and death struggle.

Mr. Randall struggled to speak. "This is incredible! The both of you gifted and if I'm hearing this right, called together for some reason."

Mrs. Randall laughed, trying to break the tension. "Donna, I don't suppose you've been bored lately."

Donna cracked up. "No Mom, that hasn't been a problem."

Just then Max and the boys returned to the main table. Mr. Randall took one look at the sour expressions on his sons' faces and laughed. "All done over there? Sure I can't get you boys some thumbscrews? Or better yet, we have some live ants and honey left over from Donna's last boyfriend."

Everybody laughed. Roland and Richard even chuckled a bit, but they were visibly upset that their "bad cop, worse cop" routine had failed so miserably. Max looked at Donna inquisitively. She mouthed the words "I told them." Max understood, smiled and took his seat.

With the initial tension broken, they all sat down to dinner, including Seeta, who took a break on the arrival of two of the Randalls' other evening workers. Donna's mother brought out her famous chicken and dumpling platter for each of them, which included macaroni and cheese, collard greens and Mr. Randall's famous rolls. Donna reveled in the extreme pleasure she felt from Max as he tasted her parents' food for the first time. He could barely stop eating long enough to tell them how good everything was.

Mrs. Randall couldn't stop beaming. "You need to come here more often, Max. I bet we could put some weight on you."

Max laughed. "That's for sure. I could weigh about three hundred pounds if I lived here! I see how you named this place- I could definitely go to sleep right now."

Mr. Randall laughed and patted his stomach. "You see what happened to me. When I was with the Colts, I played at two hundred thirty pounds. Now I'm at two-sixty and climbing!"

Max chuckled politely. "What position did you play?"

"Middle linebacker."

Max shot Donna a sideways glance. She stifled a laugh, hiding her smile behind her napkin.

"Well, this was an exciting trip."

Taylor Tyler-Hurzen laughed as she finished packing her suitcase. "That it was. I don't remember anybody trying to blow me up anyplace else I've ever been."

Karl sat on top of his own stuffed suitcase to close it. "They're still not a hundred percent sure why that psycho wanted to blow up the hotel. He wasn't making a whole lot of sense after that young guy beat his head in."

Taylor chuckled. "Take it from one who knows. Being on the receiving end of a beat-down tends to impair your communication skills."

They laughed dragged their luggage downstairs. Karl checked out and went to get their car while Taylor waited with their bags, reminiscing about the event she'd just alluded to with Karl.

Man, did I ever get my butt kicked. I have to admit, I underestimated Merry by a ton. That witch could fight! One minute I was having the best sex of my life and the next thing I know, Merry was bouncing me off the walls. I was in the infirmary for two days, and missed classes for two weeks.

Considering how she reacted to me "borrowing" Nelson, I'm glad she wasn't around when Karl proposed. She might have blown my brains out!

Just then, Karl pulled up in front of her. Smiling, she helped him pack the car for the long ride home.

Three and a half hours later, Max and Donna insisted they had to get back on the road.

"So soon? Donna, you haven't been to see us in three months and now you have to run off without even staying the night? You know we have room for both of you at the house."

Donna smiled. "Mom, you know why we can't. We both have to go to work in the morning, there's unpacking to do and we also have to go see Max's parents real soon."

"Yeah, right about now they're blowing up my answering machine wanting to know why I was in Virginia with Donna instead of at home where I'm supposed to be."

They all laughed. "Okay, okay. Get on home then. I know how your folks must feel right now, and you two have a lot to tell them, don't you?"

Donna smiled. "We do. They don't know the full story yet."

Half an hour later, Max and Donna were back on the road,

loaded down with all the food Mrs. Randall insisted on sending with them and somewhat recovered from their unexpected vacation time.

Merry pulled up in front of her townhouse. Stretching as she got out of her car, she searched her purse for her keys and opened the door fearlessly, knowing that this time, nobody had broken into her house while she was out.

Her place was just as she left it, with the exception of two missing items; the Virginia Beach brochure and hotel confirmation she'd "accidentally" left on the kitchen table.

I knew he'd find them. The idiot walked right into my trap and now his dumb behind is in jail where it belongs. And I hope there's a big bruiser named Spike in the cell with him asking for a date.

Laughing, she carried her bag upstairs and collapsed into bed.

In the seventeen hours that Max and Donna had been back in Delaware, they found time to unpack, sleep far too little and get up way too soon to return to work. Now they pulled up in front of the Carson home.

"Should we tell them right away Max, or should we save it for dessert?"

Max chuckled. "Why buck tradition? Let's wait until after dinner."

Smiling, Max let them inside. "We're here!"

Footsteps sounded from the hallway ahead of them. As Max closed the door behind Donna, Mrs. Carson hurried in from the kitchen, wiping her hands on a towel.

"Max! You finally made it."

Max laughed as he hugged her. "Darn Mom, you make it sound like I was gone for a year. It hasn't even been a month."

She stared him down. "You live half an hour away. How tough can it be to visit your poor old parents? Then again, you *have* been rather busy lately." Donna laughed at how much Mrs. Carson sounded like her own mother. Mrs. Carson hugged Donna and then stood aside as Mr. Carson padded down the hall in his stocking feet to greet them as well. To Max's amusement, he hugged Donna first.

"It's good to see you again, "daughter." Has my boy been treating you right?"

Donna smiled. "He's never done anything but."

"Long time no see son."

They embraced heartily, and the warmth of their relationship touched Donna again.

Mr. Carson turned to Max and smiled. "Did the paper get it right this time or do you two need to straighten us out?"

Max laughed. "Pretty much, but I'm sure we can fill in a few details the paper missed. We might want to sit down, though- this could take awhile."

Mrs. Carson insisted that they talk over dinner, and they all took their places around the table before starting the conversation. "Mom, Dad, there's something we have to tell you."

Max, Sr. raised a questioning eyebrow.

"No, Donna's not pregnant or anything crazy like that!"

The Carsons laughed nervously while Donna shot Max a "why did you have to go there?" glare. Max took a deep breath and then told them the whole story. Both Carsons listened intently without interruption.

"Son, that's incredible! You and Donna actually saw that bombing in a dream before it happened?"

"Dad, I know it sounds crazy, but we did. We each saw different parts of it first, and then after we compared notes, we had that final dream together that gave us the rest of the details."

Max, Sr. shook his head in disbelief. "And you had to go there yourselves instead of letting the police handle it?"

Max laughed. "Believe me, we wanted to do it that way, but we just didn't have any hard evidence to convince them with. The cops might have thought we were the ones planning the bombing."

Mrs. Carson laughed. "Well Max, I'm glad you did get there. All those people would've been killed if that bomb had gone off. It could have been worse than that Oklahoma City bombing a few years back."

As dinner ended, Mrs. Carson asked Donna to "help with the dishes." Donna smiled, knowing that this was a summons to a round of "woman talk." Max smiled; he'd been hoping for a chance to talk to his father alone before they left.

"Son, I'm impressed. You picked a winner this time."

Max settled into the small chair across from his dad's favorite recliner and smiled. "Well, God picked her for me. I'm just glad I was smart enough to listen to Him."

The elder Max shifted in his seat and leaned forward. "Whether you realize it or not, you love that woman and I bet you're wondering when you should ask her to marry her. Am I right?"

Max burst out laughing. "Never could fool you, could I? Here I was thinking I could blow your mind and you got me figured."

"It's written all over your face. You haven't stopped grinning since you brought her here the first time and realized we like her too!"

Max laughed harder. "That obvious huh? Yeah, I do love her. And I've told her so."

"Did you propose to her yet?"

Max frowned. "No, and that's what I want to ask you about. Dad, when---how did you know when it was time to ask Mom to marry you?"

Max, Sr. sat back and thought for a moment. "It was pretty basic. We were both twenty-three and not too long out of college when we started dating. I remember about a year into our relationship, she turned her ankle. I visited every night; I helped her keep it elevated, got her warm water to soak it, played checkers with her and basically spent as much time with her as her parents allowed. Doing that made me realize that I really loved her, and I wanted to spend the rest of my life taking care of her. I knew I wanted to marry her from the day we met, but it didn't sink in until then."

"When did you propose?"

"She was back on her feet about a week after it hit me. I took her to our favorite restaurant, bought her favorite meal and took a knee for dessert in front of the entire restaurant."

A faint smile crossed Max's lips. "Dad, you're giving me ideas. Let me ask you this: how did you get her ring size without her figuring out why you needed it?"

Max, Sr. smiled. "Let this old dog teach you a few new tricks."

"Where do these go?"

"In that cabinet right over your head."

Donna carefully put a small stack of plates in the cabinet Mrs. Carson indicated and wiped the water from her hands. "That's all of them."

Mrs. Carson smiled. "Thank you for helping me, Donna. I really missed out on having a daughter. Making Max help in the kitchen wasn't the same."

Donna giggled. "Sounds like my brothers. They never refused to do anything my mother asked, but they'd mess it up so badly she'd never ask for their help again."

Mrs. Carson laughed. "Max never had a choice. He had no brothers or sisters to put it off on."

Donna smiled. "He told me he was an only child. Sounds kind of lonely. I would've missed having my two little brothers around to annoy me."

Mrs. Carson laughed. "Well, Max asked for a brother or sister all the time, but the Lord blessed us with Max only. We were never able to have other children."

"I'm sorry."

Mrs. Carson smiled slyly. "Be warned, child. If you marry Max, he's going to want lots of children!"

Donna blushed slightly and smiled. "That makes two of us."

Mrs. Carson raised her eyebrows. "So, you two have discussed marriage, have you?"

Donna blushed even more deeply. "Not formally, but we have used the "L" word."

Mrs. Carson gave Donna a knowing look. "You've already got babies named, don't you?"

Donna looked for more dishes to dry.

The day following her return from Virginia Beach, Merry woke up to an intense bout of nausea. After a protracted period of vomiting, she wasted no time making an appointment with her doctor. Fortunately, there was a cancellation and Merry got one that morning.

What now? I wanted to call Fred and explain what happened, not waste time at the doctor's. Who knows, maybe I can use this. I can tell him I was sick with the flu and had to go to the hospital for a few days and that I was too proud to tell him.

Still queasy, she grabbed her car keys and headed off to see her doctor.

19

"Well Donna, we've almost been blown up, arrested and survived visits to both our parents to explain why we were almost blown up and then arrested.

Now, are you ready for the tough part?"

Donna laughed. "Let's do this."

She pulled out her key and let them into her apartment. A tribunal consisting of Yolanda and Fred awaited them, bursting with questions.

Max leaned over and whispered in Donna's ear. "Last chance to ditch these guys and run off to the islands."

She laughed and pulled Max into the room.

Merry let the doctor's office in a daze. *I can't believe this. After all the garbage I've been through in my life, this happens too?*

Completely unaware of her surroundings, Merry drove home on automatic pilot. Back at her townhouse, she went inside and sat on the couch to think things through.

Fred's a good man. He won't freak out if I tell him what's wrong with me. We're a couple, and couples are supposed to talk when they have problems like this.

Hesitating only slightly, Merry reached for the phone.

"I'd ask you guys what happened, but this pretty much tells it all."

Yolanda held up a copy of the previous Sunday's newspaper,

which contained a front-page story about how Max and Donna "thwarted a plot to blow up the hotel."

"Don't think, Miss Donna, that I don't know you snuck in here Sunday night while I was still asleep to avoid talking to me."

She put her hands around the huge stuffed panda's neck. "Spill it, or the bear dies!"

They all laughed. Max and Donna exchanged a quick glance and then Max took a deep breath.

"Fred, Yolanda, this might shock you guys a little. Promise me you'll keep open minds."

Fred smiled knowingly. "Let me guess. This is where you tell us about your special abilities."

An hour had passed and Merry still sat by the phone, paralyzed with indecision. *Why should I go through this alone? This concerns him too, so I have to tell him.*

Resolved, she dialed Fred's number, holding her breath as the phone rang repeatedly. When his voice mail came on, she quickly hung up without leaving a message.

Just as well he wasn't home. He all but told me he loved me and I blew him off. He has every reason to hate me.

She absently rubbed her stomach as if she were already showing. *Maybe I can't have Fred anymore, but I can and I will have his baby.*

Max's jaw dropped in surprise, and Donna's eyes widened. Fred and Yolanda sat back, enjoying their friends' shock.

"Don't even play the surprised role, Max. Did you really think you could hide it from me forever? You're my boy, Max. Stuff like this gets obvious after awhile."

Donna smiled knowingly. "Okay Fred, how about the truth?"

Max snapped his head around to face Donna. "He's lying?"

"I should have known I couldn't fool you." Fred smiled. "Fact is, Yolanda and I were worried. She called me to talk the night you left, and we had dinner together. She told me everything."

Donna looked horrified. "You and Fred had *dinner* together?"

Yolanda narrowed her eyes. "Hey, it was late, I was hungry and we needed to talk."

Max smiled and put an arm around Yolanda's shoulders. "Yolanda, I know you're not seeing anybody, but I didn't realize you were *that* lonely."

Max laughed and ducked the pillow Fred threw at him. "Okay, that was a cheap shot. Serves you right for trying to trick me!"

The four of them laughed, and then Max and Donna told their story for the third time in three days.

Fred laughed. "Dag! Anybody else just goes on vacation and brings back some pictures. You guys took it to a whole new level!"

Max cracked up. "Guys, unless somebody has another question, it's time for me to get outta here. I still haven't finished unpacking or read all my mail, or slept enough for that matter."

Donna chuckled. "Yeah, it'll take us about a week to get back on track."

Fred stood up. "Well, this has been real informative, but I got to get up outta here too."

He started towards the door, but turned back. "Yolanda, quieres ir al cine conmigo? O podemos ir a comer?"

Yolanda smiled. "Por que no? Voy a llamarte mas tarde."

Fred returned her smile. "Bueno. Hablamos mas tarde."

He picked up his car keys and left. Max exchanged a puzzled glance with Donna and followed Fred out the door.

Merry smiled, thinking of how her baby would remind her of the wonderful times with Fred before Hemingway ruined it.

If nothing else, the baby won't be ugly.

She smiled and put the head cleaning tape in her VCR. As it ran, Merry pondered her future.

Obviously I can't make any new tapes, and there's no guarantee that the current crop will pay forever. And I refuse to be somebody's secretary.

Maybe I can invest what I already have and live off the interest. Maybe I could start a legitimate business of some kind. She rubbed her stomach again.

Whatever I do, it's us against the world. And I choose us.

"Fred, what was all that with Yolanda?"

Fred feigned ignorance. "Can't I practice my Spanish if I feel like it?"

Max narrowed his eyes. "Fred, my own Spanish is rusty, but it sounded to me like you asked Yolanda for a date."

Fred smiled. "What do you think?"

"I think you and Yolanda spent more time together while we were gone then I thought."

"Let's just say we came to an understanding."

Still smiling, Fred got behind the wheel of his Saab and started the engine.

"Fred don't make me drag you out that car. You don't want a *second* beat-down this month."

Fred laughed. "I'll come over your place then. We got a lot to talk about."

"Yolanda, I speak virtually no Spanish, but it sure seemed to me like Fred asked you out. He felt hopeful when he said whatever he said, and you got all warm and fuzzy when you answered. Am I right?"

Yolanda smiled, and Donna caught a "glimpse" of her feelings, enough to confirm her hypothesis.

"Uh huh. Just how much time *did* you spend with him while Max and I were gone?"

Yolanda laughed. "Enough to convince me he's not such a bad guy after all. He called because he was worried about you and Max, and I met with him because I was worried too. That's when I told him the whole deal. You aren't mad at me, are you?"

"No, I'm not mad. Max was going to tell Fred anyway." Donna smiled wistfully. "Besides, like it or not, the four of us are more than likely stuck with each other."

Yolanda laughed. "I have to admit, it was nice to go out at night for once. And Fred acted like a human being. We didn't bust on each other or anything; we just talked. I liked that. I think he and I can be friends."

Donna raised an eyebrow. "Just friends?"

"He broke up with that witch from the club. Whatever happened between them was recent and rough; he almost started crying when we talked about her."

"So in other words, it's too soon to think about dating him."

"That and he's not saved. Maybe when he's had time to process all this, but right now---and I'll tell him this when we go out---I just want to be his friend. Besides, with all the craziness you and Max keep getting into, we need to be like a support group for each other."

They talked for another two hours. Donna filled Yolanda in on details omitted from the group conversation, and Yolanda laughed until she cried when she heard about the towel incident.

Fred put his Cherry Coke down and looked at Max wide-eyed. "Hold up. You mean Donna was *naked*?"

Max took a sip of his own soda. "Nothing but a towel, Fred."

He described the boxer shorts incident. Fred laughed heartlessly about Donna's horse comment, and sighed when Max told him that despite the clear opportunity, they didn't have sex.

"Max, Max, *Max*! Have I taught you nothing over the past two years? Maybe she wasn't ready when the towel thing happened, but clearly she was with it that next time."

He adopted a voice like Yoda from the Star Wars movies. "Failed as your teacher, I have."

Max laughed at the near perfect imitation. "Believe me I wanted her, and I know she wanted me too. We didn't do it because it wouldn't have been right. That's not what God expects from a Christian relationship."

Fred shook his head slowly. "Not having sex when you got two consenting adults in the mix ain't natural."

Max didn't hesitate. "Having sex with someone you're not married to, or even committed to, *shouldn't* be natural."

Fred let Max's rebuttal sink in.

"The Bible is clear on this one; God didn't create sex to use as a toy. Like it or not- and believe me, I sure didn't like it- we had to do things God's way and not ours."

"God must be something else- if it were me and Yolanda in a situation like that, it'd take a whole flock of angels to keep me off her!"

Max laughed. "Fred, what is it with you and Yolanda? You didn't call her Shenaynay Gonzalez or Laquita Maria once while we were together."

"Man, this is wild! I called her to see if she knew anything about your trip and the next thing I know, we're hanging out. She wasn't just a great body I could try to get my hands on, but a person I could talk to. That was nice."

"Seems to me she feels the same way. She did say she'd call you?"

"She did. Crazy, isn't it? Here I was kind of envying what you and Donna have and now I got somebody I can hang with."

"You might want to hold up on that, at least until you're sure Merry out of your life. She might call you tonight and then where would you be?"

Fred pondered that. "Yeah, I know. When we go out, I'm gonna tell her I don't want to get deep in a relationship with her now because of all this drama with Merry. I just want to be friends with her. This is weird though. Sister is FINE, but I can be real with her."

Max nodded. "It can be like that. That's what I've been trying to tell you all this time."

Fred laughed. "Well, now I get it. It was real comfortable, like hanging out with you. Of course Yolanda *does* have a better body."

Max laughed. "So much for my changed man theory."

"Do you understand what I want you to do?"

It took all Merry's willpower to remain in the presence of a man straight out of her nightmares. Oblivious to her discomfort, the big man smiled.

"Yup. You want me to kill them two." He indicated the picture Merry gave him. "And you're gonna give me two thousand bucks. And you're gonna let me *do* it to you."

Leonard "Lundy" Burroughs licked his lips in anticipation. Merry shuddered as she imagined the fantasy that was undoubtedly playing itself out in his mind. She studied him; six foot three, two hundred twenty pounds, black hair, yellow teeth, pale pink skin and a head like a cinderblock. His protruding forehead and squashed nose reminded Merry of the potholes in the street in front of Lundy's house. She looked away so she wouldn't have to keep that face in full view.

He's uglier than I remembered. Not to mention still dumber than a box of rocks.

"That's right Lundy. You do what I asked you and I'll give it to you."

He smiled as the potential double meaning of her words flew over his head. Merry handed him a flower box containing a hunting rifle and a picture of Max and Donna clipped from the newspaper.

She then told him where to find them and where to meet her when he completed his task before leaving. Merry forced herself to walk slowly down the porch stairs, trying to ignore Lundy as he visually groped her.

This is too easy, she thought as she drove away. *Lundy's just a year out of prison from the last woman he tried to rape. He'll kill both of them and then come here. I'll tell him no, he'll try to force me to pay up and I'll shoot him in "self-defense."*

Merry shuddered, remembering her first Lundy encounter. When she and her mother moved into a development called Oakmont following the divorce, they discovered that Lundy and his mother lived three houses down.

At thirteen, Lundy developed a crush on Merry (who was his same age). Lacking the mental capacity to properly express said feelings, he found her alone in a wooded area near their houses and tried to rape her. Merry had the presence of mind to tell him she would do what he wanted, but that she needed to use the bathroom first. When Lundy was dumb enough to let her go, she ran straight home and locked the door. Her mother called the police, and Lundy spent the remainder of his teen years in Ferris School for Boys contemplating the error of his ways.

I'm going to enjoy this. Killing you will be worth every nightmare you ever gave me.

"You ready, Max? The picnic starts at eleven and I said I'd help them set up."

"Yup. Let's go."

Max grabbed his prescription sunglasses and his Wilmington Blue Rocks baseball cap and he and Yolanda followed Donna to her car. The three of them headed for the annual church picnic at Brandywine Picnic Park in Lenape, PA.

As they pulled out of the parking lot bantering lightly, a battered Ford Explorer pulled out and followed them.

Merry lay on her couch, ignoring The Terminator as it played on her VCR and absently rubbing her stomach.

He better not screw this up. All I need is for that idiot to get caught and there could be trouble.

Ignoring the growing scratchiness in her throat, she drank from the glass of ginger ale sitting on the floor beside her; it soothed her throat and calmed her turbulent stomach somewhat.

If he did get caught, who would believe a word he said? After all, this is the same man who celebrated his thirteenth birthday by setting the neighbor's Chihuahua on fire.

As Merry tried to rest, thoughts of Fred blocked her efforts to sleep.

Max, Donna and Yolanda arrived at the picnic at a quarter to eleven and hustled out of the car to see what help they could offer the picnic committee. A minute later, Lundy Burroughs pulled into the parking lot and watched from a distance to see where his prey went. He was dismayed to see them get tickets to go inside, and then wristbands identifying which group they were there with.

How'm I gonna get in there? I ain't got no money to buy a ticket.

As Max, Donna and Yolanda donned their red wristbands, Donna shuddered.

"What's wrong, Donna? I know that twitch."

Donna forced a smile as Max put his arm around her and guided her towards the entrance. Yolanda trailed them at a discreet distance. "Nothing really. I just, well I felt something---strange."

"Strange how?"

Donna frowned. "I'm not sure."

Max looked Donna in the eye. "As soon as you *are* sure, *please* let me know. After all the stuff we've been through, I don't want to take any chances."

Donna laughed. "Listen to yourself. You sound like we're in a spy movie!"

Max shook his head nervously. "The way things have been lately, we might be. But I'll try to cool it. I know you wouldn't hold back anything important."

Just then, Pastor Nathan called Max over to help start a basketball game.

Lundy drove away from the park. *Merry ain't said nothing 'bout needing a ticket. How am I gonna kill them two if I can't get in?*

He passed a shopping center and an idea hit him. Lundy did a fast U-turn into the parking lot. He found a shaded space near the back and pulled in beside a dark green Lexus.

Max took the inbound pass from his teammate and dribbled up the court.

They're whipping us pretty bad out here. We might want to make a basket this time around.

Max dribbled to his right, but his opponent anticipated him and knocked the ball loose. In one fluid motion, the man recovered it and fired a long pass to a teammate, who caught it in full stride and streaked towards the basket. Max groaned. "Oh no, not again!"

With Max in vain pursuit, Pastor Nathan consumed the space between him and the basket with long strides. He leaped from halfway past the foul line, dunked thunderously with one hand and hung from the rim momentarily to keep from falling. As the Nathan family and other onlookers cheered raucously, Max grinned sheepishly.

"I don't know why, but getting dunked on by your pastor makes it twice as embarrassing!"

The crowd laughed as Max inbounded the ball to his teammate Joe. Joe advanced the ball cautiously, looking to throw an "alley oop" pass to Larry Boyd, the only one of their teammates who could dunk.

As Joe raised his arm to pass, Pastor Nathan came out of nowhere and stole the ball. He rocketed towards the basket again, but this time he had a teammate running with him, signaling for the ball. The pastor obliged him with a perfect alley-oop pass; his eight inches shorter teammate vaulted up as though his legs were spring-loaded and executed a gravity-defying two-handed reverse dunk that would have made Michael Jordan smile.

This time Max, Joe and their other teammates stood openmouthed for a long moment.

Max finally broke the silence. "Okay, we *know* Pastor can ball, but why didn't somebody warn us about Brother Skywalker over there?"

The crowd burst out laughing. Lamont Crawford, all of five foot eleven, smiled and bowed. "Four year starter at Howard U, baby. Still got the ups!"

Max turned to five-foot four Crystal Kennedy, the only woman on the court and one of Pastor Nathan's teammates.

"Anything *you* want to share with us before we start back up?"

Everybody laughed out loud and the game continued. The pastor's team showed mercy by quickly reached the agreed upon winning score, taking the game twenty-one to six. The players left the court rubbing their achy legs and laughing about the lopsided score.

"Talk about mounting up on wings like an eagle. Pastor, what kept you out of the NBA?"

Pastor Nathan looked at Max and laughed. "God. I played four years at Temple, but I didn't get drafted. I might've had a shot if I'd hung around all the camps or played overseas, but I knew pro ball wasn't my calling. I miss playing though- this was fun!"

Max rolled his eyes. "Yeah, for you. You're not the one on the receiving end of those "in-your-face disgrace" dunks!"

Pastor Nathan laughed again. "Brother Lancaster suggested we put a team together and play charity games against other churches. We'd divide the money three ways, between a chosen charity and the two churches playing. Our share would go into the sacrificial fund."

Max thought about it. "Not a bad idea, but between Crystal doing her best Magic Johnson impression running the point and you dunking on folks, we'd make enemies out of every church in the state!"

You have to do this. You can't just give up on Fred without trying.

Merry dialed the phone, willing herself not to hang up this time. *Come on, pick it up!*

"Hello?"

Merry exhaled silently, grateful to hear his voice. "Fred?"

Fred nearly leaped off his couch in surprise. "Merry? I've been worried about you! Where have you been all this time?"

Worry drained from Merry's body, and the concern in Fred's voice untied the knots in her stomach instantly.

"It's a long story Fred, and I think you deserve to hear it in person instead of over the phone."

Fred wanted to rush right over to her house, but managed to play it cool. "When do you want to hook up?"

"I have to run some errands this afternoon. How about eight o'clock tonight?"

Fred smiled. "Well, I was going out with Halle Berry, but for you, I can cancel."

Merry laughed; she'd almost forgotten how funny Fred was. "Since you think Halle will understand, how about coming over here?" "That'll work."

An apology and a few exchanged pleasantries later, they hung up.

She's alive and well. Now what?

He got a Diet Dr. Pepper from the refrigerator and returned to the couch. He remembered how alive he felt when he first met, particularly the all-consuming passion that fired their weekends together. He then thought about Yolanda and how they spent hours just talking after the movie they saw together the night before.

That had to be the first time in ten years where I didn't expect to get some after a date. Shoot, I didn't even try! And I had a great time anyhow.

Fred took another long pull of his soda as he pondered the choice he might soon be forced to make, and how surprising the answer might be.

Merry hung up her phone, completely satisfied.

I'm glad he still cares. I might've had a tough time finding another one like him. Now all I have to do is figure out how in the world I'm going to explain everything and tell him about the baby.

"I'm open, Joe!"

Max's teammate shot him a perfect bounce pass; Max caught it, turned, shot and missed in one fluid motion.

"Time out!"

Both teams took a much-needed rest. With both Pastor Nathan and Brother Crawford sitting out this game, Max's team was competitive. The teams were tied at twenty, and both wanted to make the final point and end the game.

"Next point wins. Max, you wanna try and get it in the basket next time I pass it to you? You done put up enough bricks to build a house!"

"Next time?" Max laughed. "The next time you pass will be the first time all day. You need to dish more instead of taking every shot, Sir Miss-A-Lot!"

Both teams cracked up. Donna and Yolanda laughed too as they watched from the sidelines.

"Donna, you got a good man, but he's no Michael Jordan."

Donna laughed. "Really! What's he shooting, one for thirty-seven?"

"I heard that!"

Donna and Yolanda saw Max sticking his tongue out at them, and laughed as the teams took the court.

In the parking lot of the Safeway, the police arrived to take a statement from mugging victim Conrad Callison and the three people who witnessed the incident.

A black eye formed, made clear by Callison's tan complexion. He was animated as he spoke to the officer, speaking as much with his hands as with his mouth.

"He just came out of nowhere, punched me in my face and took my wallet. He was a big white guy, about six three and had over two hundred. He had black hair, yellow teeth and he had on a black T-shirt and blue jeans. And he drove outta here in a raggedy blue Ford Explorer."

One of the bystanders remembered the Explorer's license plate number and added that information to the officer's report. A second bystander remembered which direction the Explorer took when leaving the lot, and the second officer called the information in. A nearby patrol car called in quickly with a report of a vehicle matching that description entering the Brandywine Picnic Park.

Callison rubbed his black eye and blinked in surprise. "That's where I'm going. Our church picnic is there today."

The officers looked at each other and agreed that one of them should accompany Mr. Callison to the park while the other took the squad car to search the area.

Having bought a ticket, Lundy prowled around the park, trying to look casual as he hunted for his targets. *They gotta be around here somewhere. First I gotta find 'em and then I gotta find how to shoot 'em without everybody seeing me do it.*

"I'll be right back. 'Landa. Let me know if Max messes up again so I can laugh at him."

Yolanda laughed as Donna headed in the direction of the restrooms. There had been no further sense of the uneasiness Donna felt earlier, and she hoped that it wouldn't return at all.

Lundy made sure his T-shirt covered the pistol stuffed into the waistband of his jeans and kept walking. He reversed his course through the park and froze at the sight of the gorgeous woman walking past him.

Snapping out of his paralysis, he reversed again and quickened his pace, hoping to intercept her. As he closed the gap between them, she turned and headed towards the restrooms.

I can pretend like I gotta take a leak, he thought, *and go over close enough to see her better.*

The uneasiness Donna felt earlier returned as she washed her hands.

Here we go again, she thought. *Best keep my eyes open for anything strange.*

She dried her hands and left the Ladies Room, squinting as she came out into the sunshine. As her eyes adjusted to the light, her uneasiness intensified.

She looked around and saw a large white man standing about five feet away, blatantly staring.

Oh Jesus help me. I have a pervert on my hands.

Fighting down a surge of fear, Donna forced herself to walk past him, and even said hello as she would to anyone she passed. His silence unnerved her, and she quickened her pace, anxious to get back to Max and the others.

That's the girl in Merry's picture, Lundy thought. *She looks more pretty than I thought. I wish she'd let me do it to her.*

If I get her by herself, maybe she will.

He quickened his pace slightly as he followed Donna towards the basketball courts.

"That's his car! Right there!"

Callison slammed on the brakes and jumped out of his car, pointing to the Explorer. Officer Drew compared the license number to the one the bystander provided, and they matched.

"Sir, please come with me. If this is his car, he's probably inside the park. I'll need you to identify him."

Donna's unease exploded into all-out fear as she felt Lundy's lustful presence closing in. Dropping all pretense of calmness, she sprinted through the crowd towards her fellow church members. Lundy sped up as well, but couldn't cut Donna's lead.

Come on Max. Be where I left you.

"Game!"

Max's final shot banked through the hoop to win for his team. As his teammates congratulated him, he looked around for Donna.

"She went to the bathroom, Max. She'll be right back."

Max feigned disappointment. "Oh, she just *had* to leave right before my moment of glory!"

Yolanda smiled. "I guess she figured if she waited for *you* to make a shot, she might have an accident!"

"Ooh, that's cold."

Donna slowed to avoid a group of children. As she adjusted her path around them, she felt a hand on her shoulder, gripping harder than she thought possible. Without looking back, she rammed her elbow backwards, hitting something that felt as solid as cement. The hand yanked savagely, pulling her behind the log edifice in which they sold and served ice cream. Another hand grabbed her other shoulder and spun her around. Despite her fear, one thought consumed Donna's mind.

This is the ugliest man I've ever seen in my life!

"I wanna talk to you. You're real pretty."

Donna kneed Lundy in the crotch. He roared with pain and loosened his grip, allowing Donna to twist free. Leaving Lundy doubled over, she flew past him towards the basketball courts.

Callison was describing Lundy to his fellow church members when Max looked up and gasped in surprise. Donna ran towards him, crying and out of breath. The right sleeve was torn off of her T-shirt, and her exposed shoulder bore red finger marks.

Rage flooded Max's being. "Donna! Who did that to you? What happened?"

Donna threw herself into Max's arms as the story spilled breathlessly from her.

Callison's eyes lit up. "That's the guy who mugged me! I knew he was here!"

Officer Drew pulled out his service revolver. "Where did the assault happen?"

As Donna watched him head towards the ice cream shack, her eyes widened. Lundy limped towards the group, looking left and right for Donna. He held the ripped sleeve from her church picnic T-shirt in his right hand, and steam practically came out of his ears. He heard Donna scream, and looked up at his worst nightmare; an armed police officer looking his way.

"Police! Freeze!"

Lundy cursed, turned and ran as fast as he could, with Officer Drew in hot pursuit. Max, Callison and three of the younger men of Calvary joined the chase. The crowd parted like the Red Sea. Lundy ran hard, fear pumping him full of adrenaline.

I ain't going to jail no more. If I get away, I can shoot them two later and Merry will still let me do it to her after.

He ducked back behind the ice cream shack and sighed with relief when he heard the pursuing footsteps run past.

Maybe I can get outta here now.

He stepped out from behind the building and walked fast, heading for the exit. He was halfway there when he saw Donna, and his fear turned to red-hot rage.

"You!"

Lundy charged, determined to beat her head in for not cooperating. Donna screamed and turned to run. As Lundy closed in on her, a hard tackle knocked him off his feet. The pistol flew out of his waistband and landed well out of his reach.

"Keep your dirty hands off her!"

Lundy tried to defend himself against the unexpected attack. Max landed on top of him and made a determined assault on Lundy's ribs with both fists.

This man is huge. If I can hurt him bad enough, he won't be able to go after Donna again.

Lundy threw a vicious punch. He lay in an awkward position, but still put enough force behind the blow to send Max sprawling. Before Max could regain his balance, Lundy jumped up and tried to force him to the ground. They grappled furiously, but Max knew he had no chance against Lundy's superior strength and weight. He threw a punch, but it seemed like a mosquito bite compared to the haymakers Lundy threw.

Max tried to block a return punch and winced as the pain of the impact shot up his arm and into his shoulder.

Can't let him pin me. If I go down, he'll beat me to death out here and go after Donna again. Gotta get some space to use a few Tae Kwon Do moves on him.

"Freeze!"

When Lundy saw the policeman's gun aimed at his head, he immediately released Max's hands and raised his own in surrender. Without hesitation, Max stepped forward and threw a devastating right cross. He put everything he had into the punch, taking the bigger man by surprise and sending him sprawling to the ground, nearly unconscious.

Officer Drew smiled. "I didn't see that."

20

"Are you all right?"

Donna smiled and touched the bandage the park's first aid station applied to her shoulder.

"I'm fine, Max. And I was fine the other thirty-seven times you asked too."

Max chuckled at her gentle rebuke. "Excuse me for being concerned!"

They laughed. Donna held an ice pack to Max's own bruised shoulder with her free hand, while he held a second pack to his injured jaw. The entire right side of Max's face swelled.

"Man, that guy could *hit*!"

Donna laughed. "What did you expect? The man's about six foot fourteen, four hundred pounds! You might want to watch who you jump on next time."

Max glared at her. "Next time, try to attract a smaller pervert."

Donna laughed harder. "Max, I appreciate the thought, but admit it; you stepped out from under your anointing."

"Okay, maybe I was a bit out of line in going after him." Max smiled sheepishly. "At least I could have used Tae Kwon Do instead of tackling him."

"You know, God seems to call you to beat people up an awful lot. I'm beginning to think you're just taking out your anger on these poor unsuspecting people you run into."

"Could be." Max laughed. "I'm just an old comic book fan at heart. Batman and Spiderman always made punching guys out look so cool."

"Well, I like it. Thank you for saving me again."

Max blushed and smiled. "That's what I'm here for; to make you laugh and to beat up any really huge guys who harass you."

She leaned into his embrace, drawing strength from his closeness as they sat at an umbrella-covered table in their church's assigned area. Passersby paused now and then to inquire about their condition, but nobody lingered. Everyone sensed that Max and Donna needed uninterrupted time together.

"Okay Burroughs, talk! Why were you at that park today? I *know* you don't belong to that church group!"

Lundy fidgeted; he spent nearly an hour trying to convince the police that he had a good reason to be there with no success.

"I tole you, I was there to go huntin.' My friends tole me there was rabbits and squirrels there, and I wanted to shoot some."

Detective Garrett leaned close enough for Lundy to smell the stale cigarettes on his breath.

"I'll be honest, Burroughs. I don't believe a *word* you're saying! Number one, that's a picnic park and even a moron like you should know they don't allow hunting. Number two, when we arrested you, the only weapon you had was that pistol. There is no way on God's green earth you could hit a rabbit or a squirrel with that thing. What were you gonna hunt, turtles?"

Detective Garrett put his face even closer, so that his nose and Lundy's were almost touching. Lundy nearly wet his pants.

"Tell me the truth or so help me God, I'll have you locked up so far away they'll have to fax you air. You're looking at three to five years for violating parole, three to five for armed robbery and assault, another two to three for the second assault and four to five for attempted rape. I'm sure we can find something else if we try hard enough. You're looking at ten years easy."

Lundy squirmed in his chair. "Okay, if I tell you the truth, can you let me go?"

Detective Garrett glared daggers at him. "If you do, I might not kick your teeth down your throat. Start talking!"

Lundy stumbled and stammered and eventually explained the situation, including the fact that he ditched the rifle Merry gave him because he preferred his pistol. Detective Garrett listened stone-faced and then called his partner. Detective Gonzalez made Lundy retell it, and he didn't change a word of his account.

Detective Gonzalez stared Lundy down. "Now let me get this straight. This old friend "Mary" whose last name you can't even remember hired you to kill this couple. And then, when you saw the woman, you decided to try to rape her first. However, you were so stupid you didn't use the rifle Mary gave you, which blew your hunting lie right out the window. Am I right?"

Lundy swallowed hard. Detective Gonzalez' voluptuous figure distracted Lundy's attention and made it tough for him to answer.

"Yeah, that's right. Merry gave me a rifle and told me where to find those two people she wanted me to kill. When I did it, she was gonna gimme two thousand bucks and she was gonna let me do it to her."

The two detectives exchanged "I don't believe this moron," looks before Detective Garrett continued the investigation.

"We're not gonna get much sense out of him tonight. Maybe after a good night's sleep, he'll be ready to tell the truth."

He turned to the uniformed officers waiting outside the interrogation room and told them to take Lundy to Holding and lock him up.

"Hey, since they sent us this jerk from Pennsylvania, why don't you put him in with the guy they extradited from Virginia? Maybe some time together will make them both ready to talk some sense."

Lundy struggled as they took him away. "I told you the truth! Why don't you believe me?"

The two detectives watched him until he was out of sight. Garrett rolled his eyes. "Pathetic."

Merry turned off her TV with a flourish and threw the remote control as hard as she could. It hit the wall, jarring the battery cover loose and sending the batteries flying.

That moron deserves to be back in prison, Merry thought, *but I wish he'd met me at Brandywine Park like I planned so I could've shot him instead. Trying to grab women in broad daylight; he's lucky the cops didn't shoot him.*

Merry forced herself to sit back down on the couch.

It's not like Lundy knows my last name or where I live. And who would believe him if he did?

A spasm of coughing interrupted her thoughts.

"Okay Hemingway, what's so important? And it better be good or I'll see to it that you room with Brickhead Benton tonight. I hear he wants to ask you out."

Hemingway smiled. "Oh, this is righteous. You'll make it worth my while after I spill it?"

Gonzalez glared at Garrett as he turned on the tape recorder. "We'll see."

"My new friend Lundy and I had a long talk, and I learned some interesting things about a mutual acquaintance of ours." Detective Garrett glared at him. "Such as?"

Hemingway eyes sparkled. "I know who Merry is."

"You sure you don't want to stay with me tonight? Or let me stay on your couch?"

Donna stifled a laugh as Max got out of her car and into his. "Max, I'll be fine. Yolanda will be here to protect me in case Jack The Ripper or somebody decides to break in."

Yolanda smiled and flexed her muscles. "Yeah, she'll be fine. You think *you're* bad? I've seen every Bruce Lee film ever made. If anybody sneaks in here, I'll kick his butt so hard his kids will feel it!"

Max laughed. "Okay, okay. I guess this protector thing is growing on me."

Donna smiled, leaned into Max's window and kissed his non-swollen cheek. "I like it too. It makes me feel safe when I'm with you."

She and Yolanda watched Max drive off before going inside. They sat on the couch, and Yolanda turned to face her friend.

"Donna, are you really okay? This is the second time in two months you've been attacked."

Donna took a deep breath. "I am kinda shaken up 'Landa, but I can't let it paralyze me. To be honest, I almost took Max up on his offer. But Max can't always be here to protect me. I have to trust God to watch over me all the time. That way I can enjoy Max's company without seeing him as some conquering hero."

She smiled wickedly. "I have to admit this though. I like having a man who isn't afraid to do whatever it takes to protect me."

Their laughter filled the apartment.

"Let me get this straight. This "Mary not only hired your boy Lundy to kill a church couple, but she's also a blackmailer. She allegedly makes tapes of herself having sex with married men and then uses them to extort money from the poor suckers. Is that the deal?"

Hemingway smiled. "Detective Garrett, would I lie to you? When I lived in Atlanta, she did that to me, but instead of extorting me, she sent the tape straight to my wife. I lost my marriage and a sizeable portion of my income because I was stupid enough to mess with her. I have the tape at home if you want it."

He told the detectives where in his apartment they would find the tape and threw in the name of his physician friend who introduced him to Merry. Detective Garrett got on the phone to Atlanta while Gonzalez arranged to have the tape picked up. Five hours later, both tapes were in their possession. The police found Hemingway's tape exactly where he said it was, and a gleeful Dr. Chamberlain boarded the first available flight from Atlanta to Philadelphia International Airport to hand-deliver his.

Hemingway smiled when they brought him and Lundy back out of their cell. "I realize that this tape doesn't exactly show my best side, but I believe you'll get the idea."

They watched the tapes in silence. Lundy's eyes grew wider as the scene between Roscoe and Merry unfolded, and the two detectives couldn't miss the glint of recognition in Lundy's eyes. He maintained his look of glazed recognition through their viewing of Thomas Chamberlain's tape as well.

"That was definitely a *short* film. Burroughs, is that Merry in this tape too?"

Unable to speak through his growing excitement, he nodded yes. Detective Garrett turned to Hemingway. "How did this situation come about?"

Hemingway smiled. "Thomas- -Dr. Chamberlain- -and I were best friends. He once confided in me that he had an affair with a lovely young woman and asked if he could introduce her to me to help him break things off with her. You see here the results of my misguided desire to add some spice to my life."

Dr. Chamberlain nodded sadly and Detective Garrett smiled wryly. "Maybe you should've taken up a hobby."

Hemingway chuckled. "Maybe so. I know Thomas wishes he had. He's very protective of his reputation, so naturally he pays through the nose to ensure that his wife never learns about his indiscretion."

Detective Gonzalez stared at Hemingway. "So why did she out you? Your credit card decline or something?"

Hemingway rolled his eyes. "We had a disagreement, and out of revenge, she sent the tape to my wife before I could even think about paying her. She told me her name was Crystal Lawrence, but I've since learned her real name is Merry Lucas."

Hemingway spelled her name and gave them her address as well. They requested a search warrant for Lundy's house to find the rifle while they ran Merry's names through the computer to see if she had a record.

A file clerk handed Detective Gonzalez a folder. She flipped through it and smiled. "Got her! Nothing on Crystal Lawrence, but Merry Lucas was busted for shoplifting when she was eighteen."

She showed Hemingway and Lundy the picture. "This your mystery woman?"

Lundy nodded and Hemingway smiled. "Oh, yes. I could never forget that face. This is the woman you're looking for."

Detective Garrett looked at his partner and smiled. "Let's roll."

Merry jumped, startled awake by a feeling she couldn't yet identify.

Something's wrong, but I can't put my finger on it. Just then she heard the sound of a car passing slowly through the neighborhood.

That punk from around the corner again. I'm tempted to slash his tires so he'll stop cruising the neighborhood at all hours of the night.

The unmarked police cruiser identified the address from the file, noted that the vehicle registered to the owner was parked out front and turned the corner, satisfied that she would be home. Detective Gonzalez called their findings in.

"Roger that. We've got the rifle from the Burroughs house—move in and arrest the suspect."

She turned to Detective Garrett and smiled. "Showtime."

Merry got off the couch, preparing to deal harshly with her teen neighbor this time.

That little snot might be bored of cruising and decide he wants to vandalize my house or my car again. I bet a face full of pepper spray would take the fun out of it for him.
They're coming for you!
She looked out the window and was chilled to the bone. A vehicle that screamed "Unmarked Cop Car" passed her house, circled back and parked on her side of the street.
They know everything- RUN!
A burst of fear propelled Merry upstairs. Although there was absolutely no reason for her to think so, Merry was possessed by the unshakeable belief that the police were coming to arrest her. Realizing she could never hide or destroy all her tapes and equipment in time, she raced into her bedroom, grabbed the carryon bag from her luggage set and packed at warp speed.

She forgot Fred's imminent arrival as she threw all the clean jeans, sweatpants, T-shirts, blouses, socks and underwear she could find into the bag. She added the remaining $9500.00 from her emergency cash stash.

A knock sounded at her front door as she reached for her gun.

Back in their cell, Lundy slept soundly. Judging from the huge smile on his face, Hemingway figured he was replaying the X-rated tapes of Merry in his head. Hemingway couldn't stop smiling himself. *Take that Merry or Crystal or whoever you are. See how you like being arrested like a common criminal.*

Lundy woke up suddenly, and looked at Hemingway, unable to contain his burning question any longer.

"You lucky dog. How was it?"

Hemingway lay back on his cot and laughed himself back to sleep.

Merry fought down panic and tried to ignore the feverish heat she felt welling up inside her.

I don't have time to be sick, she thought. *I have to do something about this situation.*

A voice both familiar and unfamiliar at the same time replied.
You can. This is what to do.
As Merry stepped off the final stair, an idea hit her. She slung

her bag behind the couch, kicked off her sneakers, snatched up a blanket and wrapped up snugly before answering the door, acting for all the world as though she just woke up. "Yes?"

Two plainclothes police officers stood outside, one male and one female. They flashed their badges immediately and held them up until Merry was satisfied with their authenticity.

"Good evening, ma'am. I'm Detective Garrett and this is Detective Gonzalez, New Castle County Police. Are you Merry Lucas?"

Merry took what she hoped wasn't too deep a breath. "That's me. What can I do for you?"

"We have a warrant to search this premises."

Merry's fever intensified. She forced a weak smile and stepped aside to let them in.

"Certainly, go ahead. May I ask for what reason?"

Gonzales started her search in the closet while Garrett pulled out a pair of handcuffs. "You are under arrest. You have the right to remain silent- - -."

I am screwed. I've only got one chance to get out of this. Okay Big Mouth, now would be a great time to hear you tell me how to get out of this mess.

She slowly shifted her hand beneath the blanket, clutching the pepper spray she'd taken from her purse.

I can't believe I'm doing this. Fred tied his sneakers and headed out the door.

Enough is enough. I'm going over there to hear what she has to say, but unless aliens abducted her, it's over between us. I really like her, but I can't live my whole life waiting for her to disappear again.

Fred looked at his watch, realized that he was running late and got up to leave.

"When you take me in, can you please make sure there's a doctor on hand? I don't feel well at all."

The opposite was true- Merry was suddenly bursting with energy as well as the knowledge of what to do with it. Gonzalez backed out of the closet on all fours, dragging a box of videotapes with her. She pulled out a few at random, labeled "Spencer," "Arthur," "Dr. Tom" and "Roscoe" respectively.

"I think we have what we need."

Garrett reached for Merry's hand to cuff her. She pretended to swoon just as he reached, causing him to move closer to grab her hand. Without warning, she threw her blanket off and pepper-sprayed him in the face.

As he recoiled and screamed in surprise and pain, Merry grabbed his arm and threw him clear over the couch. He landed on an equally surprised Gonzalez, knocking her to the floor. Merry ran around the couch and gave Gonzalez her own faceful of spray before she could recover. Drawing her pistol from her bag, she briefly considered shooting them both before settling for a pistol-whipping apiece. Without stopping for breath, Merry stepped into her sneakers, grabbed her bag and ran out the back door as if the devil himself was on her heels. She thanked the voice for suggesting her course of action as she ran.

Fifteen minutes later, Fred turned into Merry's development, whistling a tune as he approached her townhouse

Hope she takes it well, he thought. *I don't want her getting hysterical; she has a gun!*

Just then, flashing red lights caught Fred's eye. Three police cars sat in front of Merry's house, and the area was cordoned off. Fear stabbed at his heart as he pulled over and jumped out of the car, joining the crowd that milled around as close to Merry's lawn as the police would allow.

"What happened?"

A stocky middle-aged black woman eyed him suspiciously. "The girl living there must be into something shady. The cops come to get her and I hear she shot both of them and run like an escaped slave!"

A few bystanders later, Fred had a more accurate picture of what happened. Stunned, he got in his car and drove off, wondering just what it was he did that made God so angry as to throw this on him.

Detective Garrett rubbed his irritated eyes and looked at the nosy throng. "All these people out here and none of them saw anything?"

Detective Gonzalez glared at him. "Guess not. But we got the rifle, we got her tapes and her recording equipment with her prints all over it. That's enough to put her away."

Garrett flexed his shoulder, which ached from having landed awkwardly on top of Gonzalez. "Yeah, but we have to catch her first!"

Merry stifled a cough as she waited in the Washington, DC bus station for her next bus to be announced. A quick glance at her reflection in a window reassured her that she'd eluded pursuit. She had on the baggy gray sweat suit she'd worn all day and her overnight bag sat on the floor between her feet. With her long hair concealed under a hastily purchased Wilmington Blue Rocks baseball cap, she looked like any other weary traveler as opposed to an escaped felon.

Along with the things she'd packed, she also had three envelopes in her purse that she'd retrieved from one of her P.O. Boxes on the way to the doctor's office. They contained $1000.00 each, bringing her current net worth to $12,500.00.

That's enough to vanish on.

After fleeing her house, she'd forced herself to slow to a brisk walk until she reached the bus station, four blocks from her house, where she bought a ticket on the first thing heading south. Her bus pulled out at nine P.M., just ahead of a pair of police officers who came to see if she'd been there. Merry slid down in her seat as though asleep, and no one paid her any special attention. Now it was midnight and Merry was more than ready to board her next bus.

It goes to Richmond, VA next and then Fayetteville, North Carolina. I haven't lived in either of those states yet, but Fayetteville sounds interesting. Might be a good place to raise my baby in peace.

She slumped in her seat, clutching her bag and ignoring the subtle pain in her lower abdomen. The unexpected burst of energy had worn off hours ago, and her fever had returned with a vengeance, bringing its cousin pain along for the ride.

This is war, and I don't intend to lose. Hemingway, that moron Lundy and that church couple ruined my plans and now I have to run like a crook. Once it's safe to come back, they'll get theirs.

As she drifted off to sleep, a second cramp shot through her stomach, causing her to wince.

21

D r. Randolph Errell lived for his work.

In the six months since he opened his clinic, he customarily worked long days to accommodate patients who couldn't make it during traditional hours, and accepted all patients, regardless of their ability to pay for treatment.

His father Joseph owned a multi-million dollar corporation and was the richest man in Virginia and the twentieth richest man in the entire country. With the exception of Randy's oldest brother (Joseph's chosen successor), each Errell sibling received ten million dollars at age twenty-one to establish themselves. Randy's older sister moved to New York after graduating law school and opened a law firm, while his younger sister opened a clothing store in nearby Alexandria.

Randy stayed in Richmond. He grew up wanting to be a doctor, and his trust fund made no dream impossible. Within a year of his graduation from medical school, his clinic was up and running.

On this particular Sunday, his cousin Theresa was due in at the bus station from her home in Upper Darby, Pennsylvania. She'd recently received her degree, and after months of unsuccessful job hunting, agreed to work for her cousin as head nurse.

"Theresa! Over here!"

The petite young redhead turned towards the familiar voice, grabbed her suitcase and went to greet her cousin.

"It's been awhile, Randy."

He smiled. "Sure has. When did you grow up on me?"

She grinned. "You must've blinked five years ago. And I hope you meant it on the phone when you said you'd treat me like a head nurse and not a little cousin!"

He took her suitcase and they headed towards his car, talking old times en route.

Merry descended the bus stairs slowly. She burned with a fever that started soon after the bus left Washington, DC, and now the fiery spike of pain in her abdomen worsened by the minute.

Somewhere beyond human sight, a dark hand reached out for Merry. It whispered its fingers gently across her abdomen, leeching strength this time as opposed to imparting it.

In response, pain sang out, reaching a crescendo within seconds. Merry barely felt the bleeding start before the room started spinning.

I'm tired. Feels like I need a nap. Yeah, sleep would be good. Merry passed out.

Randy and Theresa were laughing and talking animatedly when they both noticed the young woman hunched over in obvious pain. Randy shifted into Dr. Errell mode, but before he could take a step in her direction, her already pale complexion went ashy white and clutching her stomach, she crumpled off the final bus steps to the floor.

Randy was at her side instantly.

"Theresa, take this card and call my ambulance service. Hurry!"

Theresa pulled out a cellular phone and punched in the numbers at warp speed. Randy knelt beside the stricken woman. Her pulse was erratic, and a dark liquid ominously stained the floor around her.

"Oh no, she's hemorrhaging!"

Randy spoke more to himself than anyone else as he went for his medical bag and set to work.

"Max, I told you a million times. Never tell your woman an outfit makes her look fat!"

Max cracked up. His face was no longer swollen, but it was clear that he'd been in a fight. He arrived at work to find a host of coworkers determined to tease him to within an inch of his life.

"That first fight musta got good to him. Now he's out there diving on linebackers!"

Fred chose this moment to take his first shot. "Hey Max, why didn't you just turn the other cheek? Oh wait a minute- -you did and he kicked you in that one too!"

The assembled crowd howled with laughter as Fred pressed his point. "Next time, make sure you pick on somebody your own size."

Max chuckled and rubbed his tender jaw. "Maybe you're right. Your mother was tougher than I thought."

Laughter exploded as the crowd gave Max high fives for his unexpected rejoinder. Fred did his best karate sensei imitation, pressing his hands together and bowing Japanese style.

"I taught you well, my son. I am proud."

Donna cracked up as Max finished his story. "No you *didn't* talk about Fred's momma like that! You got him good!"

Max smiled. "Yeah, that tends to happen about once a year. He'll probably tear me up next time he sees me."

Having returned from a movie, they entered Donna's apartment laughing and talking, but Max quieted down quickly.

"Oops, we might wake up Yolanda."

Donna concentrated. "No chance of that- she's not here."

"How did you- -never mind. Dumb question. But where is she? Don't tell me she has a date!"

Donna laughed. "Why'd you say it like she's Quasimodo? It's conceivable that somebody would want to take her out."

Max smiled. "Yeah, but he usually has three teeth and a Jheri curl."

Donna cracked up. "Max!"

As they flopped down on the couch, they heard a key in the lock. They looked up and backwards in unison in time to see Yolanda come in, humming a tune.

"And where have you been, young lady? It is *past* your curfew."

Yolanda laughed. "If you'd said that in Spanish, I would have thought my mother was here. To answer your question, the Young Adult Fellowship went to the Monday Night Gospel Skate at the Elsmere rink. It was either that or stay home and listen to the Owens Love Marathon all night, so I went."

Max and Donna laughed. Everybody in the whole building knew about the Owens' reputation.

"Did you have fun? I thought you couldn't skate."

Yolanda laughed and rubbed her left leg. "I can't. I probably spent more time picking myself up off the floor then I did actually skating."

Max laughed. "Perhaps you should stick to bowling."

Yolanda snapped her fingers. "You just reminded me of something. The Fellowship went bowling on

Saturday, and guess what? We saw Fred there!"

Max's eyebrows went up. "You did?"

"He was there by himself. His lane was next to mine, which gave him a perfect view of me throwing about seventy-five straight gutter balls."

Max laughed. "You know you're going to hear about it for the rest of your life."

Yolanda smiled. "He was sort of nice about it. After he stopped laughing, he showed me how to throw it better. I only had three gutter balls after that."

"Yeah, Fred's pretty good. He pretty much kicks my butt when we bowl."

Donna looked at Max and smiled knowingly. "The four of us should go sometime. Max, I bet you and I could take Fred and Laquita there."

Yolanda laughed. "See, there you go! Now we're gonna have to hurt you."

"How do you feel?"

Merry awoke suddenly, completely disoriented. The mattress beneath her was firm, and the blankets covering her, warm and comfortable. She looked around in panic.

"What- -? My bag. Where- -?"

A tall brown haired white man stood over her bed. She'd seen him through a haze of pain when she collapsed, but this was her first clear look at him. A short redhead stood beside him, looking concerned.

"Your bag is in that closet. Relax, we didn't steal anything."

Merry tried unsuccessfully to smile. "You brought me here?"

Randy nodded. "Yes. We saw you collapse in the bus station, and we figured we'd better get to you before the muggers did."

Merry noticed for the first time that there was an IV in her left arm. "Where am I? And who are you?"

"You're in the Errell Clinic, in Richmond, Virginia. We brought you here to take care of you. I'm Dr. Randolph Errell, but hardly anybody calls me that. Call me Doc or Randy. This is my cousin Theresa, who as of Monday officially starts as my head nurse."

He checked to make sure her IV was attached properly. "Now then, I like to know the people whose lives I save. What's your name?"

Merry hesitated slightly, hoping that this doctor wouldn't notice and become suspicious. "Jennifer Bannon."

Merry remembered how fast everything happened at her house. Knowing that her Jennifer Bannon license was in her purse, she made a snap decision. As she fled her house, she left the license she had under her real name in her mailbox. By becoming Jennifer for the foreseeable future, she hoped to throw off anyone who might be looking for her.

A pain in her stomach cut off a faint smile before it could start. "What happened to me? Why did I pass out?"

Randy's expression darkened slightly, causing Merry to panic and sit straight up in bed, dreading what he might say. Theresa gently guided her to lie back down.

"You've clearly been under a lot of stress lately, and you picked up a nasty sinus infection to boot. In short, you couldn't breathe properly and your blood pressure shot through the roof. The combination nearly killed you."

"Doctor, my baby. How is--?"

Randy's smile faded. "I'm sorry Miss Bannon. We were able to stabilize you, but we couldn't save your baby."

Merry collapsed back into her pillow, feeling as though her will to live had just been siphoned from her body. Tears welled up and she made no effort to stop them.

"I'm sorry."

Randy's strong hand on Merry's shoulder was more than she could bear, and she wailed like a lost soul. Theresa started to say something, but instead hugged Merry, holding her while the emotional storm raged. Randy quickly left the room so that his patient wouldn't think him unprofessional for weeping as well.

Fred hesitated with his hand on the phone.

Come on, he thought, *Max won't laugh. He'll probably bust out in a holy dance.*

He rubbed his shoulder, still sore from having bowled three consecutive games last Saturday. Resolved, he dialed, waiting while the phone rang once, then twice, again, a fourth time.

Come on Max. I know you got a woman, but she gotta let you rest sometime.

The answering machine came on, and Fred hung up.

Naw my brother, I need to ask you this in person. Hope you're carrying.

Max felt the buzzing at his waist almost immediately and checked his pager.

"Excuse me a second- I need to return this call."

Donna smiled impishly. "Sure, go ahead. I'll even leave the room so you can talk to your other woman in peace."

She laughed and disappeared into the bathroom. Max chuckled as he grabbed the phone. "Hey Fred."

"Max! So she does let you off the leash once in awhile. I was wondering about that."

Max laughed. "Yeah, she gives me a free hour every week whether I need it or not. What's up?"

"Nothing much. Hey, I ran into your girl last Saturday. Well, your girl's roommate. You know, Laquita."

Max cracked up at the familiar nickname. "I'm at Donna's now. Yolanda came in right after we got here, and she told us you showed her how to bowl."

"I had to. Sister had no skills. I couldn't let her continue to embarrass herself like that."

"Donna suggested that the four of us bowl sometime, us against you and Yolanda."

Fred laughed. "Obviously she's never seen you bowl!"

"Very funny. If you're down, maybe we can do that next weekend."

Fred felt warm inside at the prospect of spending more time with Yolanda. "Yeah, that'd be cool. Hook that up and let me know when."

"No problem. Listen, let me get off here now and go home. It's my turn to drive the women to church tomorrow, and if I'm late, I'll never hear the end of it!"

Fred laughed and marshaled his courage to ask the toughest question of his life.

"Listen, what time does service start at your church? I was thinking of going."

Max could barely restrain a shout of joy. "There's two services, one at eight and the second at eleven. We're going to the eleven- if you want, I can pick you up after I get the women. Parking can be hard to come by around there."

Fred smiled. "Uh huh. You just want to make sure I get there!"

They cracked up. "Seriously though, what time you want me to be ready?"

"I told Donna and Yolanda I'd pick them up at ten thirty. If you can be ready around ten fifteen, that would work."

"Cool. Seeya tomorrow then."

Fred hung up, feeling like a hundred pound barbell had been removed from his chest.

Well, I can't back out now, he thought. *Shoot, all this craziness happening, I need to be there. Bowling isn't going to help me resolve this.*

Wonder if church women still wear those big giant hats?

He cracked up and went to his closet to pick an outfit.

Randy looked at the Sunday paper. Shaking his head at one of the headlines, he put it down and went to check on his sole current inpatient.

Merry seemed to hear him when he came in and awakened as he checked her vital signs and her IV.

"You're doing a lot better, Miss Bannon. I wouldn't be surprised if you weren't up and around by the end of next week."

Merry made a face. "That long? And I told you to call me Jennifer. Considering the fact that you've seen me naked, why be formal?"

Randy laughed. "Okay Jennifer. You have to realize that the human body is a complex machine, and when part of it breaks down, it's not easily fixed all the time. Rest and the antibiotic I've got you on for the sinus infection should fix you up soon, but I don't want you pushing it. If you take it real easy the next few days, it'll be better for you later on. You could even be out of here by the middle of next week and then you could do the rest of your recovering at home."

Merry/Jennifer smiled. "Uh huh. You just want to make sure I stay long enough to pay you."

He laughed again. "That's the spirit! They say laughter promotes healing. If you can make jokes, you're halfway down the road to recovery; the emotional half. Just keep your physical half in bed where it belongs and you can leave here sooner rather than later."

She smiled and grudgingly settled back into the warm sheets, giving a mock Nazi salute. "Sieg Heil, Herr Doktor."

Randy laughed and left the room as she drifted back to sleep. He marveled at "Jennifer's" resilience and wondered how such a beautiful, gentle woman could possibly do what the newspaper article said she did.

"Come on up. We're almost ready."

Donna released the door so that her guests could get in. Max smiled as he went upstairs, wanting to savor the look on the women's faces when he revealed his surprise.

"Max? I thought two people came in just now. Did somebody come in behind you?"

Max laughed. "I really can't fool you, can I?"

He came in and motioned behind him. Donna and Yolanda both gasped in surprise to see Fred come in behind Max.

Yolanda found her voice first. "Fred! You're coming with us?"

He smiled. "Yeah, I twisted Max's arm until he allowed me to come along. Figured I couldn't be a heathen all my life."

Yolanda hugged him, sending welcome shivers up his spine. "We won't embarrass you by asking when the last time you went to church was, but I can't guarantee that for all of our fellow church members."

Fred laughed. "Tell you what. You don't ask about the last time I went to church and I won't ask about the last time you went bowling!"

They all cracked up and headed for Max's car.

Merry sat upright in bed. Her heart raced, the aftereffect of the first night terror she'd had in over a month.

I didn't have so many of those when I was with Fred, she thought. *Guess having a man around made me feel safer.*

She drifted back to sleep. She didn't dream this time.

Fred sat stiffly in the pew beside Yolanda and tried to relax and enjoy himself. Despite not having attended a church service in fifteen years, he felt almost at home.

All I really have is club clothes. Hope this suit's okay.

Fred had on a royal blue suit with a black banded-collar shirt, one of his quieter club ensembles. Looking around, he noticed several other men close to his age wearing similarly bright colors.

I'm here. Now maybe I can find out why Max spends half his life in church and what it has to do with him being such an all-around great guy. Maybe this will help me understand Yolanda a little better.

Maybe I can finally get some peace of mind.

Awake after a three-hour rest, Merry/Jennifer picked up the Sunday paper Randy had left for her. The headline sent her stomach into spasms all over again.

'NEWARK WOMAN INVOLVED IN SEX BLACKMAIL SCHEME STILL AT LARGE'.

At the bottom of the page was a write-up about her and a small picture. It detailed how the police got information from Hemingway and Lundy that led them to search her house, how they found evidence that corroborated the men's stories and how she evaded capture when the police came to arrest her. The story also mentioned that she was armed and dangerous and had probably fled Delaware.

I can never go back to Delaware now. They're looking high and low for me. And what if Doctor- - -Randy- - recognizes me from this picture? He might turn me in!

Merry/Jennifer lay back and tried to relax. *No it won't happen. That's an old picture, and I look like crap now. No way he'll recognize me. Glad I have the Jennifer ID on me though. If I'd given my real name- -.*

She drifted off to sleep, still worrying slightly.

As the service continued, Fred relaxed and got into the spirit of things. The atmosphere was warm and inviting, the people were friendly and the music was as compelling as Fred remembered from his youth. Fred even recognized one of the hymns and was able to sing along. Max blinked in surprise at Fred's better-than-average singing voice.

The hymn ended, and Reverend Travis Nathan stood to preach the Word. Towering over his pulpit at six foot seven, the slender brown man smiled as he opened his Bible.

"This morning's message will be taken from the book of Acts, the ninth chapter, verses three to six and then skip down to verses seventeen through twenty. This is one of my favorite portions of Scripture, the conversion of Saul, persecutor of Christians, into Paul, greatest of apostles."

Yolanda leaned slightly in Fred's direction so that he could follow along in her Bible as Pastor Nathan read.

"As he neared Damascus in his journey, suddenly a light from heaven flashed around him. He fell to the ground and heard a voice saying "Saul, Saul, why do you persecute me? Who are you, Lord?" Saul asked. "I am Jesus whom you are persecuting, he replied. Now get up and go into the city and you will be told what you must do. Now skip down to the seventeenth verse. Then Ananias went to the house and entered it. Placing his hands on Saul, he said, "Brother Saul, the Lord- -Jesus who appeared to you on the road as you were coming here- -has sent me so that you may see again and be filled with the Holy Spirit." Immediately something like scales fell from Saul's eyes and he could see again. He got up and was baptized, and after taking some food, he regained his strength. Saul spent several days with the disciples in Damascus. At once, he began to preach in the synagogues that Jesus is the Son of God."

Pastor Nathan closed his Bible. "The topic I want to use this morning is "Quit Horsing Around And Get To Work!"

The congregation chuckled as their pastor began to preach. Fred was enthralled. As a child, he had been exposed to the more well-known Bible stories (Adam and Eve, David and Goliath, Noah and the ark and of course Jesus' birth, crucifixion and resurrection). They hadn't taught about the apostle Paul in his early Sunday School days, and since he'd avoided church from the age of thirteen on, he'd never learned any more. He suddenly regretted that.

"Saul wasn't just your ordinary backslider who stayed home on Sundays. He actively assaulted the church. He went out looking for Christians and when he found them, he had them beaten and thrown in prison, and even had some of them killed. He was doing everything he could to destroy "the Way," as Christianity was called back then."

As the pastor preached, Fred borrowed Yolanda's Bible and, using the same techniques he used to edit articles, speed-read the entire ninth chapter of Acts in a minute flat.

Whoa, that's powerful stuff. Saul never saw it coming.

"Saul was hardheaded! God could've easily just sent Ananias to talk to him, but He knew Saul wasn't gonna listen to anybody less than Jesus Himself, so that's who had to approach him. And notice how it happened. He was not gentle; when Jesus revealed Himself to Saul, he manifested so forcefully it knocked Saul right off his horse."

He paused for effect. "Well, He had to get the man's attention!"

The congregation laughed. "Sometimes it takes a major thing to get us to notice God. You might get sick unto death, or almost get hit by a bus or have your best friend backstab you before you realize that people might betray you, but God is with you always!"

Fred stiffened as he thought of Merry. Her latest abrupt exit from his life had indeed cut Fred to the core of his being, and made him realize that all the things he thought were important (women, nice clothes, etc.) weren't the answer; without real love, his life would remain empty.

Donna sensed Fred's moment of dawning comprehension and smiled, squeezing Max's hand. Max smiled too, knowing that Donna would share whatever revelation she just had later.

"Sometimes God has to knock us off our spiritual high horses to get our attention. I ran from the call to preach for years. God called me to preach at seventeen and I ran until I turned thirty and couldn't run any more. Now all of us aren't called to the pulpit, but we can run from Jesus in other ways. We run by not coming to church, we run by coming but just sitting here every Sunday and refusing God's call to serve on that committee or join that choir. We run by coming to church, but not accepting Jesus as Lord and Savior of our lives. Stop running! Get off your horse and come to Jesus today!"

All around Fred, people (Max Donna and Yolanda included) jumped to their feet, clapping, shouting praises and generally acting up for the Lord. They shouted Amen! and Hallelujah! and worshipped God like there was no tomorrow. Noting that it seemed appropriate to do so, Fred joined in the applause, but remained in his seat.

Pastor Nathan concluded his sermon and came down from the pulpit, cordless microphone in hand. "Saul had to be knocked off his horse and blinded before he could see the Light. The prophet Jonah ran from his calling and spent three days in the belly of a huge fish. I ran from my call for thirteen years; my son almost died of a rare disease before I stopped running."

He paused, reaching out to the congregation with his right hand. "It doesn't have to be that hard. If Jesus is calling your name today, come. Take my hand, but give Jesus your heart. Don't wait for Him to get tough. If He's calling you today, then today is a good day to be saved. Won't you come?"

The organist began playing softly as people rose from their seats and approached the altar. Fred felt a stirring in his heart. He felt an urge to get up, to go forward and find out what it was that this minister was talking about.

I can't, Fred thought, *not today. But I do want to go home and read more about this Paul guy while I think it over.*

Donna smiled again as she sensed Fred's inner struggle and its peaceful resolution.

"The altar is open for those who seek prayer as well."

Without hesitation, Max and Yolanda rose from their seats, and Fred and Donna made way for them to get out of the row. Fred felt like he should pray too, but didn't feel comfortable doing so at the altar.

God will hear me if I'm at the altar or not, he thought. *At least that's what I learned as a kid.*

He bowed his head.

God, help me out here. I think You're trying to tell me something. I think You want me to get saved. Trouble is, I'm not sure what that means and I need to before I can do it. Whatever it takes, please tell me. I can't take living like this anymore.

Fred came of out prayer and was startled to notice Donna still next to him instead of at the altar with Max and Yolanda. She had a hand on his shoulder and prayed along with him. She came out of it as he did, winked at him and squeezed his hand reassuringly as if to say, "It's all right, Fred. I got your back."

Just then, Max and Yolanda squeezed back into the row and sat down. As Yolanda brushed past, Fred again felt a quickening in his heart. This time it was physical, and instead of the Holy Spirit, Yolanda's perfume was the catalyst.

Great, get all excited in church. Why not just hold up a lightning rod while I'm at it?

22

The four of them rode home in good moods, discussing the service.

"So, did we scare you off or did you enjoy yourself?"

Fred laughed. "I liked it, Max. It wasn't what I been telling myself. You know, church is boring and nobody there knows how to have fun, all like that."

Max smiled. "I thought the same thing about church when I was a teenager. The second I went off to college, I stopped going, and I only went during the summer when I was home to keep my parents happy. But after I graduated, I started going because I wanted to, and before I knew it, I was learning stuff and understanding why I needed to be there."

Fred chuckled. "Pretty much sums up my day."

He looked at Yolanda. "It helped seeing your group out having fun. Nobody I saw at that bowling alley was acting like boring church people. 'Course nobody cussed when they threw gutter balls, but- - -."

They all laughed. Donna reached up to the front seat and patted Fred's arm.

"I'm glad you came. It takes a brave man to do what you did today." He smiled, and Donna sensed his mild embarrassment.

"A man's gotta do what a man's gotta do. Besides, Sunday morning TV stinks!"

They cracked up. Sensing that Fred was uncomfortable with the conversation, Donna changed the subject and they laughed and talked until first Fred and then Donna and Yolanda were dropped off at their respective homes.

After exchanging his suit for sweats, Fred rummaged through

his closet and pulled out a box containing his Grandmother Bennett's things, left to him on her passing. A few minutes' search revealed the one item he was looking for; her well-used Bible.

Merry enjoyed being the only current inpatient, as Randy and Theresa waited on her hand and foot. Theresa was responsible for Merry's intimate personal needs (sponge baths, bedpans, etc.) but the bulk of her care fell to Randy. Aside from a slew of outpatients who came on Saturday night following a bar brawl, his time was free and he spent most of it talking with Merry/Jennifer.

On the third day of Merry/Jennifer's bed rest, they shared confidences, or so she wanted Randy to believe. She spun a convincing tale of having lived with a wealthy and abusive man for the past year. Not wanting to expose a baby to his violent temper and afraid for her life, she waited until he fell asleep, stole his gun and all the cash she could lay hands on and left.

Randy told Merry/Jennifer about his family and how he started the clinic. He then told her about his last relationship. He and Lysia started dating as teenagers and were engaged until she took exception to his future plans. She became furious as he spurned offer after offer from prestigious medical practices and instead opened his clinic. Not wanting to be shackled to a man who planned to "waste our time and money on welfare patients and homeless beggars," she left him to marry one of his closest friends. Ironically, this man took one of the positions Randy declined.

"That's awful!"

Randy smiled wistfully. "It took me awhile to get over her, but life goes on. Things don't always go the way we plan them."

Merry rubbed her abdomen. "Tell me about it."

Having skimmed through the book of Acts, Fred put the Bible down and sifted through the rest of the box. There was a picture of his grandparents that Fred had never seen before. Both of them were dressed for church. His grandfather wore the ministerial robe that Fred remembered seeing him in more often than regular clothing, and his grandmother wore her favorite dress, the dark blue one she made herself and was often mistaken for store bought.

You'd think Granddad built New Gethsemane Baptist Church with his bare hands, sticks and spit the way they fawned over him. They let him stay on as pastor even when they knew he was getting too old. Matter of fact, he didn't step down until about a month before he died.

Fred shook his head, marveling at his grandmother's foresight.

She straight up told me every time she saw me that she was praying for me to come back to God. And she was so sure it would happen that she left me her Bible.

Fred's gaze fell on an orange wrapped item on his kitchen, and he realized that he'd gotten so caught up in the box that he forgot all about the Sunday paper.

A familiar face on the front page caught Fred's attention. He scarcely breathed, and the blood drained from his face as he read the full story about the woman he once thought he loved.

Randy sat in his office, head in his hands, pondering his prize patient.

What do I do? I didn't turn her in at first because she was so weak, but she's recovering nicely.

He shook his head as he pondered his options: call the police to come get her now or let her finish her recovery and then call them.

Or I could just sit here and figure out why I can't stop thinking about her.

The phone rang around seven that night. Fred wasn't surprised; he'd been expecting to hear from Max sooner or later.

He's too good a friend to let this go. If this ain't him, I'll be real shocked.

"Hello?"

"Hey Fred. You busy?"

Fred smiled. "Naw, not right now. Just sitting here watching SportsCenter."

Max fell silent as he collected his thoughts. "Fred, you see the paper today?"

Fred swallowed hard and fought to keep his emotions at bay before answering. "Yeah. Yeah, I did."

"Fred, I, well- -you okay?"

Fred took a deep breath. "Yeah I will be. I mean, it was a shock, but I guess I'm not totally surprised. Whenever we talked about work, she changed the subject. And then I got that tape and that note from whoever. It all makes sense."

"Donna and I saw her in our dreams a couple of times, but we never did figure out why."

"I don't know what she had to do with your Virginia situation, but she's definitely bad news. Guess it's a good thing she left me when she did; my naked butt could have ended up on the Spice Channel!"

Max chuckled, but he didn't need Donna's gift to know that Fred was hurting and just didn't want to talk about it anymore for now.

"I won't keep you. I just wanted to see if you were okay."

"Well, thanks. I appreciate that. Oh yeah, thanks again for that ride to church today. Service was all right."

Max smiled. "You can ride with us anytime. Just let us know."

Fred smiled faintly. "Yeah. I just might do that."

They chatted briefly before hanging up. To his surprise, Fred found himself diverting from the pity party he'd planned to throw himself and humming one of the hymns from church instead.

On the fourth day, Merry/Jennifer was allowed to walk to the bathroom and back. After three days in bed, the short trips were pure pleasure, and the stiffness eased from her legs each time she got up. The next day, Randy encouraged her to take a longer walk around the recovery area.

"Come on, Jennifer. You were the one who wanted to get up; now's your chance. This is important for your recovery."

Merry/Jennifer grimaced. "I should have known you were too good to be true. Underneath that nice exterior, you're a slave-driver."

Randy laughed. "If you've got enough breath to talk about me, you've got enough to go all the way around and back."

Merry/Jennifer did well until they were halfway back to her room. Seeing her genuine exhaustion, Randy scooped her up and carried her the rest of the way, ignoring Theresa's raised eyebrows when they passed her.

"That wasn't so bad, was it?"

Merry/Jennifer chuckled weakly. "The carrying part wasn't. The forced march however- - -."

Randy laughed. "A bit tougher than just walking to the bathroom and back, huh?"

She tried to smile. "Just a bit."

Randy lowered Merry/Jennifer gently onto the mattress, and arranged the covers over her as if he were tucking his daughter in for the night. She thanked him and was about to drift off to sleep when a question slipped out of her mouth before she could choke it back.

"Randy, have you ever made a mistake so huge you'd give anything to go back in time and change it?"

The sorrow in her voice cut him to the heart. "Yes, I have. But since I can't, I just do my best not to dwell on it and to never mess up that bad again."

He quickly turned to leave before she could see the tears threatening to escape his eyes like water from a ruptured dam.

"Okay Donna, I know you wanted to tell me something earlier. What was it?"

Donna smiled, shifting the phone to her left hand as she finished washing dishes with her right. "It's Fred. Judging by what I sensed from him during service, not only will he come with us again, but he's ready to give his life to Christ."

Max raised his eyebrows. "You discerned all that?"

She smiled. "The sermon really got to him, and when they gave the altar call, he almost answered. I'm sure he will next time he gets the chance." Max smiled and pumped his fist.

"I did see him following the text while he was preaching. I should have seen how it affected him myself."

"And you didn't even have to nag him about coming to church. Fred got this far on his own."

"Got me. Score one for the laid back approach."

Donna smiled. "Works every time."

Max's face grew somber. "Well, he'll need Jesus now. You see today's paper?"

Donna's face matched Max's. "Yes, I saw it. Poor Fred. He must be devastated that his girlfriend kept such huge secrets from him."

Max was silent for a moment as he collected his thoughts. "I just talked to him a few minutes ago. He's putting a good face on it, but I could tell he's really going through. Can't blame him either."

"All we can do is pray for him. The rest is between him and God."

"Karl, look at this!"

Karl looked up from the baseball game he was watching. "What?"

Taylor raced into the room holding the Sunday News Journal. "The lazy newspaper guy *finally* showed up."

Karl laughed. "The morning paper at five PM."

"Anyway, check this out!"

Karl's eyes widened to see Merry's name at the bottom of the front page. He read it all the way through and shook his head.

"Your daughter has lost her *mind*! No wonder she called her asking for money- she was probably sick of prostituting herself and wanted to retire."

Karl winced inwardly at the harshness of Taylor's tone. *Merry must be insane, and if she is, I'm sure she blames me for driving her there.*

Taylor leaned over Karl's shoulder as he finished reading. "I hope they find her soon. She needs to be locked up."

Taylor walked out of the room, leaving Karl alone with his thoughts. To his surprise, Karl felt sorrow at the thought of his daughter spending the rest of her life looking over her shoulder for the police.

I might not want her in my life, but I wish she could somehow find peace.

Merry fell asleep almost as soon as Randy put her back into bed. She awoke five hours later, feeling sore but refreshed. A gimpy trip to the bathroom worked the kinks out of her legs, and she settled back under the covers.

Randy really is too good to be true. He genuinely cares about people, even after that witch of an ex-fiancée hurt him so badly. He doesn't know who I really am. And he's great to talk to. Just like Fred.

Tears stung her eyes as memories flashed through her mind. Her first night with Fred, long talks in his apartment or in her house, walking through the zoo holding his hand, Fred cooking for her and holding her while she cried, her nursing him back to health after Hemingway beat him so savagely.

Merry fought back more tears as she drifted back to sleep.

Randy sat in his office with his hand over the phone. More than anything in the world, he wanted to dial and be done with it, but his hand was rigid as stone.

He couldn't make a call now if his life depended on it.

Why did she ask me that now?

After a lot of soul-searching, Randy had decided to call the police, but Merry/Jennifer's soulful eyes and heart-wrenching question obliterated his resolve.

She's not just some random criminal I came across. She's a real person, a wonderful person in fact. And I have to turn her in.

Randy fell asleep with his hand on the phone.

Merry lay back in bed, trying to get comfortable. The pain in her abdomen was almost gone, and her fever from the sinus infection was gone as well. Theresa had removed the IV yesterday; the only thing left to her recovery was rest.

I could live here. I obviously can't go back to Delaware now, and I haven't lived in Virginia yet. Besides, Randy has made it clear he's interested, and if he recognized me, he would have said so by now.

She smiled, his gentle face clear in her thoughts.

He's nice, he's not ugly at all, and he has plenty of money. Lysia was a fool to leave him.

Merry rolled over, and her gaze fell on her nearby bag, lying next to her bed. She turned on the light and reached for her Terry McMillan novel, but her fingers brushed cold steel instead. Against her will, she withdrew the gun and stared at it almost lovingly.

This could solve a lot of problems. Killing that interfering couple would be a good start. One shot for each of them and that's that.

The voice whispered its insidious suggestions directly into Merry/Jennifer's soul. Suddenly afraid of contaminating the pleasant atmosphere, she shoved the unloaded gun deep inside her bag, turned off the lamp and tried harder to return to sleep. Thoughts of rewarding Randy's kindness romantically after she recovered sent her to sleep with a smile.

Yolanda lay in bed, tired but unable to sleep. She channel surfed for a few minutes before she turned it back off.

I can't stay up all night, she thought. *Those students of mine can smell weakness. I go in there tired and they'll walk all over me.*

Her thoughts turned to Fred for about the tenth time that day. *I still can't believe it. Fred came to church with us, acted like he was into the service, borrowed my Bible to follow the text and then told us he enjoyed himself! I guess miracles do happen.*

I can't believe that woman of his though. I knew she was no good, but I wish she hadn't put Fred through so much grief to prove it. Fred must be devastated, and probably worried that she taped him too.

Yolanda turned over, beat her pillow into submission and tried to get comfortable. *The longer I know Fred, the nicer he gets. This is not the same guy who drooled all over me when I met him. This is somebody you want to get to know better.*

That unexpected thought accompanied Yolanda's descent into slumber.

"Think you can handle this or should we go with the sponge bath one more time?"

Merry/Jennifer opened her eyes and smiled at Theresa. "No offense to your skills, but I'd rather shower."

Theresa laughed. "None taken. Let me get you some stuff."

She brought Merry/Jennifer a complete bath kit, including soap, shampoo, toothpaste and lotion, a towel and a washcloth. Merry/Jennifer accepted it and disappeared into the bathroom.

This has to be the only clinic where every room has a private bath and shower. Then again, most clinics don't have a massive trust fund behind them.

A long, steaming shower made Merry feel like herself again for the first time since she fled Delaware.

I didn't realize how grungy I'd gotten. I bet my bed stinks to high heaven!

Laughing, she dried off, brushed her teeth and left the bathroom wrapped in her towel. She smiled to see that Theresa changed her sheets while she was up, and hummed a tune as she searched her bag.

I'm sick of hospital gowns. Where's my other sweat suit?

Merry found it and put it on, still humming the mystery tune.

I know I heard this song somewhere recently, but I can't remember where to save my life.

Someone knocked on the door. "Are you decent?"

Merry/Jennifer smiled to hear Randy's voice.

"Like you haven't already seen me naked. Come in."

Randy chuckled and walked in carrying a breakfast tray and a newspaper. They both sat down on her freshly made bed.

"My drafty bed gowns aren't good enough for you anymore?"

Merry/Jennifer tried to look serious. "I'm tired of mooning you every time I get up."

They both laughed. "Actually I feel less sick wearing real clothes, and I sleep in sweats a lot; when I'm alone anyway."

Randy looked thoughtful. "Your boyfriend was away a lot?"

Merry/Jennifer thought carefully, not wanting to unravel the elaborate web of lies she'd spun for Randy.

"Yes. Sometimes he'd be on the road four days out of seven trying to expand his shipping business."

"Hardly the way to sustain a relationship."

"Tell me about it. Then again, when he started hitting me, I was *glad* to see him leave town."

They ate breakfast together, talking about whatever came to mind. Theresa stopped by to see how Merry/Jennifer made out with her shower; when she saw Randy there, she smiled and didn't linger.

"My compliments to your chef. This is very good."

Randy smiled. "Actually, since you're the only inpatient, I gave the cook a long weekend off. I've got the duty until she gets back."

Merry/Jennifer's eyes widened. "You cooked this? It's excellent!"

"Glad you approve."

They finished the egg white omelets, whole-wheat toast and fruit before Merry/Jennifer posed her next question.

"When do you think I'll be able to leave here?"

"Maybe another day or two. You're making wonderful progress; ahead of schedule in fact."

"Good genes."

Randy took the tray and their empty plates and left to do some paperwork, leaving Merry alone with her thoughts and the newspaper.

He's single, he's handsome, he's rich and he can cook healthy food. Forget waiting for him to make a move- I need to ask him out!

Just then it hit her. *He Touched Me! I heard that song in that little* church. Maybe if and when Randy and I get together, we should go to church now and then, and try to do things right.

Merry remembered her spiritual close call and shuddered. The voice from the other night's gun experience returned with a vengeance.

You don't need to get religious to keep a man. You know how to do that without God's help!

Yeah, I've got this. I don't have to try to be somebody I'm not to keep a man.

She scanned the newspaper cautiously. *Politics*, she thought. *More politics, more famine in Africa, arrests.*

Merry's blood ran cold at the sight of a familiar name in the paper: Roscoe Hemingway. She quickly looked back to the page where she saw it, and the headline shocked her.

'VIRGINIA BEACH BOMBING SUSPECT ATTEMPTS TO CUT A DEAL'.

I don't believe it! That lizard wants a lighter sentence for selling me out!

Halfway through the story, her eyes caught a second familiar name and she sucked in her breath.

Leonard "Lundy" Burroughs was released on $10,000 bail to the custody of his mother pending his trial on charges of robbery, assault and battery and attempted rape. His testimony corroborated evidence offered by Hemingway and led to the discovery of a sex blackmail ring operating out of Newark. Merry Lucas, the woman who allegedly ran the ring, eluded capture by the police and is being sought for questioning."

A pain lanced through Merry's stomach; she forced herself to relax until it subsided.

This can't be happening, she thought. *This can't be real.*

You can do something about it.

Merry blanked out for a moment. When she came to herself, she had the gun in her hand and she was looking in her bag for a clip to load it with.

Horrified, she threw the gun back into the bag and shoved the bag under her bed. Before she realized it, she was out of bed and heading towards Randy's office, hoping somehow that he could make things right.

Randy cursed under his breath and slammed the phone down yet again. He'd wrestled with his conscience all day and all night, and found himself trying again to call the authorities.

It doesn't matter how I feel about her. She's been lying to me since she got here, and she's wanted for questioning. I can't break the law, even for her. "How do you feel about her? Don't you deserve to be happy too?"

Randy shook off the temptation to just forget what he'd figured out and reached for the phone again. He cursed again and put the receiver down for the fifth time that night. He buried his head in his hands, not hearing the light footfalls outside his partially open door as they faded down the hallway.

"Dr. Errell, we have a situation."

First thing in the morning, and we have trouble already. I thought Mondays were supposed to be no good; this should have happened yesterday.

Randy followed the duty nurse down the hall, and his heart sank when he realized where she was heading.

"Isn't this where you put the patient from last week? Bannon?"

Randy nodded, unable to speak. He was crushed, but not totally surprised to find Merry/Jennifer gone. Her impatience to leave was obvious, but he thought the spark between them might have been enough to keep her there.

Then again, if it had, she'd be under arrest right now. I was going to make that call as soon as I checked on her this morning.

The nurse pointed to the bed. "Apparently she was quite satisfied with our services."

Randy blinked in surprise to see a neat stack of money sitting on the bed.

A closer look revealed that every bill in the stack was a hundred dollar bill.

"Ooh, is that the raise you promised me?"

Startled, Randy whirled around to see Theresa standing in the doorway. He'd been so lost in thought he didn't hear her coming.

"What? Oh, good morning Theresa."

"Come on, the joke wasn't that bad. And what's with all that money anyway?"

"Jennifer's gone."

Theresa's eyes widened. "Gone? You mean- - -?"

"Gone as in sneaked out of here between ten P.M., when I last checked on her and seven this morning. Nurse Jackson alerted me."

Sensing the tension level in the room, Nurse Jackson looked to Theresa for guidance. Theresa indicated that she could leave, and Nurse Jackson gratefully slipped away.

"Did Jennifer leave that?"

Randy finished counting. "Yes she did. This is two thousand dollars, about a fifth of what she was carrying."

Teresa smiled wryly. "So much for patient privacy, huh?"

Randy saw a piece of paper that had been under the bills and picked it up." I found it the first night. I was looking through her bag to see if she had a nightgown with her and found a lot of money and a pistol. It was unloaded, but there were full clips in the bag under the money."

Theresa looked her cousin in the eye. "And you didn't think this was cause for alarm?"

"At first I wanted to be sure she was going to live. Then she told me she left a rich and abusive boyfriend- she said she took the gun and a lot of money and hit the road."

Theresa touched his arm. "I see. You wanted to make sure she healed and then you were going to do what you could to get her back on her feet."

Randy shrugged. "It wouldn't have been the first time."

"No, you always help patients in trouble, beyond just medical help. But unless I miss my guess, this is your first time falling in love with one."

Randy stared at her openmouthed. "It was that obvious?"

"Every time you came out from talking with her, your eyes lit up. And to be honest, hers looked pretty shiny too."

Theresa turned to leave, but turned back with a final thought.

"By the way, Randy, I saw that article."

Theresa left the room to check on a new patient, leaving Randy with his thoughts and the note. He looked down at the note. His heart beat faster as he scanned the page.

Randy,

My being here forces you to make a choice no man should ever face, and I won't put you through that any longer. Thank you for giving me the opportunity to make one of the toughest decisions I've ever had to make. I've made horrible mistakes lately, and I need to do what I can to set things right.

Maybe we'll see each other again someday, but if we don't, thank you for saving my life. Remember me.

Merry "Jennifer Bannon" Lucas

She must have seen me wrestling with making the call. Why else would she have left?

He reread the note and a sudden thought furrowed his brow.

She probably went back to Delaware to resolve her situation. And considering the fact that she has a gun and a lot to be angry about, things could get ugly.

God, if You're really up there, watch out for her. She needs all the help she can get, and I get the feeling I'll never see her again.

He rushed to his office to make the phone call he should have made days ago.

Merry sat in the back seat of the bus, lost in thought. A familiar voice thundered within her and force-fed opinions into her heart and soul.

You just lost another chance to be happy. There are a whole lot of people out there who contributed to ruining your life, and you need to do something about them.

Every time I try to avoid the issue, I lose something precious. Well, I've taken all I'm going to now. I'll take care of all the loose ends in my old life and then I'll find a new one somewhere.

She reclined her seat and counted the hours until she reached Delaware- and her destiny.

23

The sun set as Merry drove into Oakmont.

Nothing's changed. It's still the same families living in the same houses and doing the same things.

She marveled over how easy it had been to sneak back into Newark, grab a few things from her house and reclaim her car.

Apparently the police gave up on me ever coming back here. If they do think to look for me, I hope they don't start in New Castle.

As she approached Lundy's house, she heard the sounds of a struggle coming from the backyard.

Out of prison two days and he's already up to his old tricks.

"Get off me! Help!"

"You said you liked me! You said!"

Merry drew her gun from her purse and walked around the house to the backyard, where Lundy struggled unsuccessfully to undress a tall red-haired girl. Merry recognized her as her former neighbor's daughter Kathy, a star high school basketball player.

Merry cleared her throat. "Lundy!"

Lundy stopped pawing at the girl's sweat suit and stared openmouthed.

"Merry?"

"I came to give it to you, Lundy."

Lundy quickly released Kathy and started towards Merry. She calmly raised the gun and shot him twice through the heart. Lundy died before he hit the ground.

"Hope you liked it."

Kathy gaped at Lundy's corpse for a moment and then her tongue loosened. "Thank you! I was out here watching the sunset and he came out and asked me if I liked him- - -."

She moved to hug her unexpected benefactor. Merry warded off Kathy's display of affection by raising the gun again.

"Leave now or be next."

Kathy turned and ran into her house as fast as she could without looking back.

"You'd better get out of here. She'll call the police, and you're not finished yet."

I'd better get out of here. She'll call the police, and I'm not finished yet.

"Okay Hemingway, move it! Today's your big day."

Two guards handcuffed Hemingway and took him out of his cell. He sucked on a peppermint drop, exuding a sense of calmness that he really didn't feel. The guards led him towards the car that was to take him to his trial.

There's no way I'm getting off this time, and if they lock me up for eight million years, I'll never get a chance to nail "Crystal's" hide to the wall. I gotta do something.

Unseen by either Hemingway or the guards, a spectral hand snaked out and slapped Hemingway across the throat. He coughed violently as he accidentally swallowed his peppermint; his face turned beet red and he clutched his throat frantically. The guards sighed noisily and looked at each other. One of them nonchalantly stepped behind Hemingway and applied the Heimlich Maneuver, dislodging the candy on the first try. Hemingway hunched over gratefully, breathing heavily as his face returned to its normal color.

"You gonna live?"

Hemingway swallowed painfully. "Think so."

"Too bad. You could have saved the state the trouble."

The guards turned him over to the two police officers and, with the transfer complete, returned to their duties inside. One officer opened the car door while the second grabbed Hemingway's arm to shove him inside.

The same hand that slapped his throat now touched his shoulder, flooding his system with adrenaline.

Now!

It's now or never, Hemingway thought.

Hemingway suddenly spun and head-butted the guard solidly

on the jaw. Stunned, the man stumbled backwards and fell to the pavement, hitting his head. "What the- -?"

The second officer reached for his gun. Hemingway lunged towards him, and as a bullet whizzed over his head, Hemingway shouldered him in the stomach and drove him into the car door. He balanced on one leg and kicked the second man in the crotch with the other. The second officer slumped to the ground, stunned.

Amazed that he'd actually disabled both men, Hemingway quickly found the key to his handcuffs and freed his hands. He disarmed both officers and struck them each a powerful blow to the head with one of the nightsticks before jumping into the police car and speeding off, leaving both men unconscious.

The fraternity house sat directly in the middle of Amstel Avenue. From across the street in front of Smith Hall, Merry heard the sounds of a full-fledged blowout.

I can't believe they're partying this hard in the middle of the week. It works for me though- the more confusion there is, the better my chances of pulling this off.

As Merry got out of her car, the door to the house opened and a group of men in Lambda Beta T-shirts staggered out, laughing and holding on to each other for support. Merry quickly found the one she came for in the middle of the group.

Now is your time! Those fools are all drunk- they can't even see you, much less identify you!

They're all drunk. Hopefully none of them will be able to identify me.

She avoided the streetlights, using the shadows to conceal her features. "Bryan!"

Bryan Hurzen looked up through alcohol-glazed eyes, startled and hopeful at the same time at hearing a woman call his name.

"Who'zat? You soun' fine."

The group laughed. Bryan and one other man moved in the direction of the seductive voice. Merry raised her pistol and shot twice. The first shot knocked Bryan's nosy frat brother out of the way and the second hit her brother in the chest, dropping him in his tracks. When the rest of the group turned her way, she fired two shots over their heads. As Lambda Betas dove for cover in every direction, Merry calmly retraced her steps to her car, climbed in and drove off the campus, leaving chaos in her wake.

Fred had a hard time sleeping. He was off tomorrow, but try as he might, he couldn't relax. His goal was to sleep in, work out a little, eat and then lie around the rest of the day unless he decided to go out to a movie or bowl or something.

I'm nervous for no good reason and it's killing my chance to get some sleep.

Well, actually I do have a reason. My HIV test result isn't in yet. I mean, I use condoms all the time, but you just never know.

And why am I thinking about Merry? I still kinda miss her, but I didn't really think about her all last week. Now suddenly she's on my mind. I don't get it.

Maybe God's trying to tell me something.

Karl Hurzen hugged his wife and laughed out loud, trying to dispel his earlier melancholy mood.

"I still can't believe you had me send Merry five dollars! And then that note was a great touch!"

Taylor smiled impishly. "Serves her right. She's always been too high and mighty for my tastes. I knew she had some man- excuse me, men- taking care of her."

Taylor flipped through the articles they'd cut out of the paper earlier. "Honestly, I didn't think she had all that in her. She was a goody two-shoes when we roomed together. She had a hot boyfriend for the last two years we were in school and she never had sex with him before she dumped him. Guess she's making up for lost time."

Karl laughed halfheartedly. *She's out there*, he thought, *and in her shoes, I would be real mad at Taylor and me.*

He kissed his wife and went downstairs to double-check the locks on the doors and windows.

From her vantage point behind the house, Merry saw the light in what she assumed was a bedroom window.

They must be settled in for the night. Hope they're having a good time, because this will be their last.

This time, Merry felt two voices in her heart and soul, one demanding and insistent, one still and silent.

This is your chance! Kill them both. They deserve that and more for all they've done to you!

"Killing them won't solve your problems. It will only increase them."

I've already got a murder to my name, Merry thought, *and they'll execute me no matter how many more I kill. I've waited years for this, and this is my time.*

Ten minutes later, the light went out. Merry crept up to the house and tried window after window. She thought she saw shadows move in her peripheral vision, but when she turned to look, nothing was there. She completely missed the ephemeral hand as it disengaged an aging window latch.

Try this window.

To her surprise, the basement window was unlocked. It was old and clearly not used often, but Merry got it open with a minimum of noise. She let her eyes adjust to the darkness and then moved towards the stairs, gun ready.

It was completely dark when she emerged on the first floor, but Merry moved as though the house were lighted. Her senses felt supernaturally strong as she ascended cat-quiet to the second floor. Karl and Taylor's bedroom was the first room she encountered. She slipped in as quietly as a phantom.

Karl was alone in bed; Taylor was apparently up getting a drink or using the bathroom or something. Merry pulled a pair of handcuffs from her pocket and swiftly cuffed Karl's right hand. He woke up from his light dozing to see a gun in his face.

"One word and I'll kill you."

She made him put his left hand through the space in the headboard and handcuffed it too, using the headboard to hold him in place. With his hands secured, she stuffed one of his socks in his mouth. "I really don't want to hear your lies now."

Just then a toilet flushed and water ran in the sink. Merry barely had time to step back into the shadows before Taylor came out of the bathroom. Merry eased around the bed, stalking her prey. Taylor had no clue anything was wrong until she felt the gun barrel at her temple.

"Turn the lights on, witch. I want you to see what's coming."

Terrified, Taylor groped for the lamp. The look on her face was balm to Merry's soul; both she and Karl looked like they'd seen a ghost.

"I've waited a long time for this."

She threw Taylor forcefully onto the bed. Taylor lay where she fell, whimpering and begging for her life. Merry's gaze fell on the articles about her, lying on the bed next to Karl.

"I see you've been enjoying some light reading. Having a good laugh at my expense? Why aren't you laughing now?"

Taylor switched from whimpering to praying incoherently to a God she'd never believed in to save her. Merry wasn't impressed.

"By the way, thanks for the five dollar bill. It just so happens I was on my way to the grocery store. That came in handy."

Merry paced the room, but her gun stayed trained on Taylor's chest. "That had to be your idea. Karl's just not bright enough to come up with something like that."

She shifted her aim to Taylor's head. "I should shoot you here. You've proven over and over that you don't have a heart."

Taylor was too frightened to speak; she begged Merry with her eyes not to shoot. The windows to Merry's soul were cold and unforgiving. Anger had been her constant companion since Taylor betrayed her trust in college, and Merry turned over complete control to the rage that was now second nature.

Reveal her sins to her husband! Twist the knife before you finish her!

"Karl, you know why I can't stand the sight of you, but do you know why I hate Taylor so much?"

He shook his head no. The look on Taylor's face told Merry that she'd never told him the truth about the end of their once strong friendship.

"When we were roommates at Rutgers, your loving wife backstabbed me. I was engaged to Nelson Young."

Karl's eyes widened. As an avid sports fan, he recognized the name instantly.

"Yes, *that* Nelson Young. The star point guard for the Milwaukee Bucks, currently averaging 20 points and 13 assists a game and who just signed a $120,000,000 contract extension. Back then, I loved him, and he loved me. And I caught him loving your wife as soon as my back was turned."

Karl looked at Taylor, pleading silently for answers.

"It's true, Karl. I came into our room one day and caught them going at it like dogs in heat. And I *know* who seduced who."

Merry glared daggers at Taylor. "Say it! Who was the aggressor that day?"

Taylor cried, knowing that her words would sign her own death warrant. "I was."

Merry nodded grimly. "Oh yes, Karl. Your wife is a ho. And I see she still has one of the scars I gave her that day. Taylor, I do hope your broken arm and ribs healed properly."

Tell him the rest!

"Karl, a leopard never changes its spots, and a ho never changes her ways. Taylor, do you want to tell him who you've been doing on the side or should I?"

Karl whipped his head around and glared at Taylor.

Merry smiled. "Ah, you must have suspected something. Does the name Bob Coleman mean anything to you?"

The withering glare Karl directed at Taylor spoke volumes. "I followed your wife around so I could find your house. I followed her from the grocery store yesterday, but she took a detour past Motel Six before leading me here. It didn't take much snooping to find out who she was there with. Taylor's pretty good with best friends, isn't she? Yours sure wasn't complaining."

Karl didn't know whether to scream, cry, beg Merry for his life or slap Taylor. His discomfort was balm to Merry's soul.

"Clearly you care about nobody but yourself, Taylor. After you ruined my chance to be happy with Nelson, you just had to twist the knife, didn't you?

You married the man I hate the most just to *piss me off*!"

Taylor finally found her voice and sat up. "N-no. I m-married Karl be-because I love him!"

Merry backhanded Taylor across the face. "Witch, please! You're sleeping with his best friend! You don't know what love is, but you're about to see hate up close and personal."

She raised her gun and aimed at the center of Taylor's forehead. Taylor closed her eyes, still whimpering. Karl struggled valiantly against his bonds, trying to get free and protect his wife at all costs.

Merry smirked. "Amazing. You really do love her. Looks to me like you're trying to take her bullet, even though the witch is cheating on you. And I thought you couldn't love anyone but yourself."

She swung the gun over towards Karl. "How about you, Taylor? Would you take his bullet? I'm feeling generous. Beg me for your life and I'll only kill *him*. How does that sound?"

Taylor slowly moved towards Karl, either to shield him or to die with him.

"Now I'm really impressed. You might be screwing his best friend, but you really do love him. How touching."

Merry pretended she was about to leave, but turned back casually.

"Oh Karl, one more thing. I killed your son."

All the vitality drained out of Karl. Tears flowed unabated; Karl knew without having to ask that Merry was dead serious.

"I shot him about two hours ago, but I didn't enjoy it. He was annoying, but he never did anything to me except be born and earn your favor. I only killed him because if I didn't, he would inherit your money. I intend to have that for myself."

Merry lowered her gun and turned again as if to leave. Taylor tensed, ready to pounce.

"Don't even try it. This is for all the pain you've both caused me."

Merry spun and fired three shots. The first thudded into the wall above the headboard. The second caught Taylor in mid-leap and in mid-chest, and threw her back onto the bed. The third ceased Karl's struggles.

Merry looked down at their prone, bleeding bodies for a long moment. She then used a tissue to dial 911. Leaving the receiver off the hook, she uncuffed Karl and removed the sock with her fingerprints on it from his mouth.

She then turned on her heel and left without looking back.

Only three remain.

Three down, three to go. Hemingway's going to prison for the rest of his life, but that church couple's got something coming. And I won't get Karl's money if any possible heirs are around. That means my dear mother has to go too.

Hemingway ran as silently as he could, using the shrubbery for cover. Having abandoned the stolen police car five miles ago, he sought shelter wherever he could find it.

Figures. All my planning and then I choke for real and set up my chance to break camp. Now I need to hide. I beat down two cops; that won't exactly get me invited to the Policeman's Ball.

He patted the police revolvers tucked into his waistband and smiled. *I got something for anyone who finds me. The cops will probably find me, but they won't take me in.*

Merry cursed like a Marine drill sergeant with Tourette's Syndrome as she read the front page of the next day's paper. She'd slept in her car in the parking lot of a supermarket, and she wasn't in a good mood. Reading about Lundy's death was satisfying, but the top story wasn't.

'BOMBING SUSPECT ESCAPES CUSTODY'.

Merry read the details and seethed with anger.

He's back out there, but if I find him before the police do, they'll have an easier time bringing him in. Corpses don't resist arrest.

A related story caught her eye, and she launched more profane missiles into the atmosphere.

TWO WOUNDED IN UD FRAT HOUSE SHOOTING.

Newark- An unknown assailant shot two students outside the Lambda Beta fraternity house on the University Of Delaware campus late last night. Eyewitness said that six or seven fraternity brothers were gathered on the front lawn when an unidentified woman approached them and opened fire, hitting two of them. Bryan Hurzen, 19, of Bear was listed in critical condition with a gunshot wound to the chest. Perry Carpenter of New Castle, also 19, was treated for a shoulder wound and released. While witnesses believe that Hurzen was the target, the motive for the shooting is unknown.

A third story made Merry curse even harder. Her father and stepmother (how she hated having a stepmother her own age!) survived her attack. Paramedics found them and saved their lives, at least for now. They were both in critical condition.

Merry threw her newspaper down in disgust. *I didn't kill any of them but Lundy. Bryan knows my voice- he could identify me if he put his mind to it. And how could I miss killing Karl and Taylor? I figured they'd be dead before help could get there.*

Finish this and get out of here before you're captured.

I'd better take care of the rest of my business ASAP and get out of Dodge.

She reloaded her gun and set out to find the next two people on her hate list.

Nice to see there's plenty of work this week, Donna thought as she took another letter from an overflowing bin. Customer Service Correspondence is only a plush job when the letters are coming in. *I need the money more than I need them to send me home early- well, more than once a week anyway!*

The harsh ring of her phone startled her out of her reverie. "Statebank Correspondence, Donna speaking, how may I help you?"

"Ooh, you sound so official. You never do that when I call you at home."

Donna laughed and lowered her voice. "Funny. If I'd known it was you, I wouldn't have gone through all that. I could've just been like, "What you want?""

Max laughed. "Ready for lunch?"

She smiled, savoring the essence of Max, to her, he felt wonderful even over the phone. "Sure am. Your bench or mine?"

He cracked up. "The usual bench. I'll be waiting."

They hung up. Donna laughed as she shut down her computer. Without warning, a wave of concern washed over her. For a second, Donna felt like she was adrift in a sea of troubles with a storm on the horizon. And as fast as it came, the feeling left.

Donna frowned. *What was that all about?*

She shrugged, picked up her purse and went to meet Max.

Max turned off his computer and prepared for lunch.

This isn't the right time or place, he thought. *I should take her to a nice restaurant or something. Then again, where else is more special than "our" bench?*

Merry crept through the trees, intent on her prey. *There's "Ken" now,* she thought. *Once "Barbie" joins him, I can get them both and be out of here in no time flat.*

She drew the gun from her bag, reflecting on how easy it was to find her targets. Fred casually mentioned his workplace once, and how cute he thought it was that Donna worked nearby and that she and Max met outside for lunch almost every day.

I'll shoot her first, and then I'll get him while he's standing there shocked. Once people start running and screaming, I can escape before anyone identifies me.

Merry fought off a wave of dizziness. *Randy was right. I needed another day or two to recover. Wonder if I can risk going back? If I'm still sick, he's the only doctor I know of who might not turn me in. Maybe if I give him a night to remember- -.*

She smiled, checked her gun to be sure it was fully loaded and settled into a comfortable position directly across from the first group of benches.

"Been waiting long?"

Max looked up from his Bible. "Hey, you!"

He stood to greet her, kissed her gently on the lips and then sat down beside her on their favorite bench. "How's your day been?"

Donna smiled. "I had a weird one today. This guy sent in legal papers to change the name on his credit card, and it was the medical records of his sex change!"

Max's eyes widened. "You serious?"

"Dead serious. This guy went from something tough like Rocky Montana to something like Gloria Sunrise."

Max laughed. "Guess he couldn't find the woman of his dreams, so he *became* the woman of his dreams!"

Hemingway lay snake-flat, watching Max and Donna laugh and talk. He'd made it as far as Basin Road before the sun came up. Unfortunately, the small park in the corporate center was the only place where he could find any significant cover.

If I stay still, nobody should find me here. I can get some rest and figure out how to find Crystal's stank behind before the cops find me.

Hold up. What's going on down there?"

Max stopped laughing, and wiped his suddenly sweaty brow.

Donna felt his abrupt emotional shift. "You okay, Max?"

"I'm fine. It's just, well, I need to ask you something."

He took Donna's hand. "Donna, these past few months have been almost unreal to me, and I don't want this to end."

He pulled a small jewelry box from his pants pocket. Max used his share of the reward money to buy it, and guessed at the size by holding Donna's hand at every opportunity. Donna's eyes widened as Max got off the bench and knelt in front of her. She fought back tears; a few passersby stopped to look, smiling with anticipation.

"Donna, you're everything I ever dreamed of, and more than I ever hoped for. I love you, and I want to spend the rest of my life with you. Will you marry me?"

Max opened the box, revealing the ring. Donna couldn't speak to save her life.

Why should they be happy when they've ruined your life? Do it now!

Merry's finger tightened on the trigger. *Time to put them out of my misery.*

To Merry's surprise, she couldn't shoot. A sudden wave of guilt raced through her, and she lowered the gun.

"They're not the ones who ruined your life Merry."

Merry jumped and nearly revealed her hiding place at the reemergence of the soft, silent voice. It rang out in her spirit as clearly as when she first heard it at the small church she stumbled into not long ago.

If they hadn't stepped in, Hemingway would've been caught red-handed and my father would be dead now like he deserves. I wouldn't be on the run like a common criminal!

Search your heart, Merry. That's where the problem is.

She tried harder to ignore the gentle voice and focus on why she was there.

"Max, I- -oh no!"

Donna stopped in mid-sentence. A strange look settled over her face as she struggled to process the eerie coldness that dropped on her for the second time in the last twenty minutes.

"Donna? You okay? I know I caught you by surprise, but- - -."

Donna shook her head. "No, it's not you. You've heard the expression, "Somebody walked over my grave?" Well, that's what I felt. It was cold, eerie."

Max was on his guard instantly. "You think there's danger coming?"

"I don't kn- - yes! That's it! I'm in danger. *We're* in danger!"

Donna glanced nervously from side to side. "There's somebody here, somebody close by, violent, angry about to explode!"

Now!

Merry stepped into the open and fired.

24

"Look out!"

Donna pushed Max off the bench. As she landed hard on top him, bullets struck the bench exactly where Max's face had been. One grazed Max's right arm; he cried out involuntarily, grabbed Donna and rolled them beneath the bench for protection. The other two shots hit the spot they vacated.

"Thanks, Donna."

She frowned. "Don't thank me yet. Merry's out there, and she's trying to kill us."

"Fred's Merry? Oh, man! How are we gonna tell him about this?"

Donna glared at Max. "You're assuming we'll live long enough to call him. What do we do now?"

In response, Max prayed, ignoring the burning wound on his arm, seeking guidance and hoping for a repeat of the authority he felt in that parking lot about a hundred years ago. Donna followed his lead, seeking calmness. As it filled her being, she let it flow outwards, doing her best to enfold Merry in a blanket of tranquility.

Merry felt a bit more clear-headed, but also a bit tired.

Accept My peace, Merry. Rest in Me.

This is no time to rest! Your enemies are within your grasp. Kill them!

Merry shrugged off her lethargy and squeezed off her final two shots. Without hesitating, she ejected the spent clip and pulled a new one from her bag.

Hemingway used the gunfire to cover the sounds of his movements as he inched closer to the conflict.

Talk about Mohammed coming to the mountain. Not only is she right where I can get her, she's lost her mind! There's no way she's getting out of here without getting arrested.

Hemingway crept to within fifteen feet of Merry and resumed his snake position.

I'll just lay here in the cut and see how this plays out.

"It's not working, Donna. I'm not feeling it like I did in the parking lot."

Donna looked worried. "I feel the same way. What do we do now?"

Just then, Max heard a familiar click, reminiscent of many of the action movies he enjoyed.

"She's reloading- now's our chance!"

Max pulled Donna to her feet and guided her towards the cover of nearby trees. Merry slapped the fresh clip into her gun and fired, but her targets were too far away. Determined not to let them escape, Merry cursed under her breath and raced after them.

Max and Donna ran full tilt through the trees, not caring how much noise they made. A bullet passed so close between their heads that the bullet burned the tips of each of their ears.

Donna flinched and prayed for deliverance. "This way!"

Max pulled Donna to the left, onto a seldom-used pathway. As they burst into the open, Max looked for a hiding place, but stopped abruptly. Donna sucked in her breath at the view.

Tall pine trees surrounded them. A pond of blue water sat in the exact center of the grove, with goldfish slipping through its clear depths. A large monarch butterfly swished past, and squirrels ran in all directions, startled. The scene before them was achingly beautiful, and hauntingly familiar.

"Jesus keep me near the Cross."

Donna started to respond to Max's odd sounding prayer, but the words stuck dry in her throat. Suddenly, an overwhelming sense of dread overpowered her.

"Max, duck!"

She pushed him aside with all her strength just as Merry burst into the clearing from a side path and fired again. The first two shots missed, but the third struck Donna solidly. She screamed once and toppled into the pond.

"Donna! No!"

Leaving his back exposed to Merry's gun, Max waded in and pulled Donna out of the pond. He laid her on the grass as gently as he could, and, ignoring his own shallow wound, he used his tie to make a tourniquet. He stripped off his bloodstained white shirt and pillowed her head with it. Donna neither moved nor breathed, causing Max to feverishly begin mouth-to-mouth resuscitation, praying silently and constantly as Merry drew near. Merry made sure she had enough shots left and moved purposefully towards her prey.

"You're wasting your time. I'm going to kill you both anyway."

Max looked up, tears streaming down his face.

"No matter. If she dies, part of me dies with her."

Merry blinked back unexpected tears as Max gave Donna another "kiss of life." She aimed her gun at Max's head.

"Stop it. *Now!*"

Max slowly raised his head, tears flowing freely. He tried desperately to resist, to rebuke some demons, to do something, anything but just kneel there and let her kill them both.

Stand still.

Lord, I've got to do something!

This battle is not yours.

Max started to resist further, but stopped.

Okay, I trust You. If You allow me to save her, I will. But if you say no, I'll accept it. Your will be done.

He rocked Donna gently in his arms and prayed that some passerby would call the police. To Merry's surprise, she felt empathy for him. Unconscious, Donna involuntarily poured out the love she shared with Max and drenched Merry with it. It was almost more than Merry could bear; it reminded her of Karl and Taylor's final display of love.

Why can't I have that? I lost Nelson and now Fred. Nobody else could love me like that.

I do, Merry.

The familiar voice was more insistent now, and louder than the harsh, grating voice that normally goaded her into action. Her resolve weakened in the face of the Truth.

"It's not too late, you know."

Merry nearly shot Max out of pure surprise. "What?"

Max felt the presence of the Holy Spirit guiding his speech and thoughts. "You don't have to do this. You don't have to live like this. There's a better way."

He briefly told her about Christ's birth to the virgin Mary, His three-year ministry, His crucifixion and His resurrection, concluding with the first scripture that came into his spirit, John 3:16-17.

"For God so loved the world that He gave His only begotten Son, that whosoever believeth in Him, should not perish, but have everlasting life. God sent not His Son into the world to condemn the world, but that the world through Him might be saved."

Merry looked stunned. She wanted to shoot Max dead, but she couldn't. In the back of her mind, she heard a harsh voice screaming for her attention, but she found herself uninterested in its rantings and ravings any longer. In frustration, it left.

Words of Scripture Max never memorized flowed into his spirit. "When Jesus hung on the Cross at Calvary, there were two thieves hanging next to Him on either side. One of them called out to Jesus, *"When thou comest into Thy kingdom, remember me!"* Jesus ignored His own suffering to have mercy on a thief. *"Today, thou shalt be with me in Paradise."*

Merry felt like she'd been slapped upside the head with the Word, twice over. As she remembered the minister of the small church quoting those same verses, her hand wavered, and she lowered her pistol slightly.

"Merry, Jesus is real. I know Him for myself. He'll love you like no person can, and the reward is eternal."

Merry couldn't stop her tears. *I need that kind of love, and I'm about to kill someone who can help me get it.*

Just then, Donna coughed violently, forcing water out of her lungs and spewing it from her mouth.

Max couldn't contain his joy. "Thank You, God- she's alive!"

Leave them in peace.

Merry lowered her pistol. "You're safe. I can't do this. Not now."

"Good!"

Merry felt the air nearly crushed from her lungs as a strong arm wrapped itself around her windpipe.

Goaded on by the same murderous spirit that had guided Merry until just a few minutes ago, Hemingway slipped into the clearing behind Merry and held a stolen police revolver to her temple as he glared at Max.

"Don't even *think* about playing hero this time, "brother." I'll kill her, you and your woman before you can blink."

Having been forced to drop her gun, Merry shifted her feet slightly to use her self-defense training. Hemingway moved his feet to match hers and pressed the gun harder into her head.

"Try that again and you're first instead of last."

Merry didn't flinch. "You need me to get out of here alive, *Roscoe*. Kill me now and you lose your protection."

Hemingway thought for a moment. "True. Brother, this is your lucky day. I'm gonna let you live, but this one's coming with me. We got unfinished business. First stop- those bushes over there."

Merry snickered. "Negro, please. You think you have time for that with the cops coming?"

He snapped his head around, startled to hear sirens approaching.

"Maybe you do. As I remember you, thirty seconds is enough."

Hemingway nearly blew her brains out, but remembered he needed her as a shield.

"Okay hero, listen up. Crystal or Merry or whoever she is comes with me. Your woman can lay there and bleed to death for all I care. And as for you--."

He aimed at Max's head. "I changed my mind. Think you can whup this bullet, punk?"

Even as Max prayed for deliverance, Merry reached across her body with her left hand and slapped the gun out of Hemingway's hand with her right. She then bit his left forearm hard enough to draw blood, eliciting a howl of pain. As he loosened his grip, she elbowed him in the stomach, and when he let go of her, she spun around and punched him in the face.

Max rolled away from Hemingway, hoping to circle behind Hemingway and take his legs out from under him while he focused on Merry. Not seeing Max, Hemingway reached for the gun he'd dropped.

"Don't."

He looked up into the barrel of Merry's retrieved gun. He backed away and slowly stood, hands raised defensively in front of him.

"Police! Drop your gun, NOW!"

Merry took a step back from Hemingway and complied. Hemingway quickly drew the second stolen police revolver from the back of his pants and shot Merry twice in the chest at pointblank range. As Max hugged the ground, the officers opened fire, dismissing Hemingway from this world.

Thank you. Now come with me- you are mine!

Hemingway's final awareness was of a harsh voice sounding in his spirit as its owner ushered him to his final destination.

Merry groaned in pain. Max crawled over and took her hand.

"Hang on, Merry. Help is coming. Be still; don't exert yourself."

"Couldn't let- -any more- -get hurt- -'cause of me."

One of the police officers came over to see about Merry. Her breathing was shallow and uneven; she could barely speak and when she did, her words ran together.

"Jesushelpmeldon'twannadie."

The youngest of the four police officers was at her side in an instant. "An ambulance is coming. Hang on, miss."

"don'twannadie."

The world around Merry vanished. She saw Randy, tall and handsome as he tended to her at his clinic; Fred, smooth and suave as he approached her in the club to buy her a drink; Taylor in their college days when they were still friends. She saw her mother; despite the fact that she had planned to kill Lorraine after Max and Donna, Merry really wanted to see her just now. Inexplicably, a wave of regret moved Merry to tears; she knew she would never see any of them again.

The scene shifted; she saw the pastor of the small church. As she relived his sermon, his image and words blurred with Max's.

What did that thief say, she thought. "R-remember."

"Don't try to talk, miss. Help is coming."

"Remember- - me."

In response, the entire area shone with an impossible brilliance. An endless host of luminous beings hovered over Merry, quivering in anticipation. Suddenly, as one, they bowed in supplication. Merry looked up and saw a figure in the center of the host. He drew near, and offered her a scarred hand as if to help her up. Without hesitation, she reached out to Him in acceptance. Amid victory shouts and songs of praise from the celestial chorus (and a hiss of disappointment from a displaced shadow as it fled the scene), Jesus took her hand, forgave her sins and welcomed her home.

The young officer blinked back tears. Max sat beside him on the ground, cradling Donna in his arms. Their spiritual eyes were opened and they witnessed the incredible transaction that unfolded before them. Unable to speak, the young officer crossed himself, mumbling long forgotten Hail Marys.

Bleeding profusely and barely conscious, Donna shook violently and spoke in tongues. Fearful that she was going into shock, the other three officers rushed to stabilize her and frantically signaled the approaching ambulance to hurry up. Max held Donna carefully, favoring her injury and ignoring the tears that ran down his cheeks.

"Donna, it's all right. The ambulance is here. Don't try to talk. Save your strength."

"She- -made it. Max, she-- -made it!"

Donna passed out just as the ambulance arrived.

25

Fred was channel surfing when the phone rang. Unwilling to break his comfortable laziness, he switched the remote to his left hand and grabbed the phone with his right. "Hello."

"Fred, it's Max."

"Hey, Max! Couldn't survive a day at work without me, huh?"

"Fred, Donna's been shot. We're at Christiana Hospital."

Fred sat up straight. "You serious?"

"Serious. Listen, I need a favor."

"Name it."

"Pick Yolanda up at her school and bring her here. Her car broke down this morning, and Donna drove her to work. She'll be waiting out front."

Fred looked around for his car keys. "Brookshire, right? No problem. Hey, who shot Donna?"

Max hesitated. "That's a long story. We'll explain it when you get here." "Gotcha. On my way."

Fred found the keys and was about to turn off the TV when a news bulletin caught his attention.

"- - -would-be assassin was shot and killed by an as-yet unidentified assailant after she had surrendered to the police. She has been identified as Merry Lucas of Newark, Delaware. Lucas escaped capture nearly two weeks ago when the police came to arrest her on charges of conspiracy and blackmail. Lucas may also be connected to the recent shootings of her father, stepmother and brother.

More on this story as it breaks."

The immaculately coifed newsman droned on, but Fred heard

nothing. His finger froze on the remote as the image of Merry's body covered with a white sheet burned itself onto his brain.

"Oh, Jesus! Jesus help me!"

Fred slumped back into his chair. He tried to look away, but the gruesome image held him until tears blocked his vision.

Max looked like a butcher after a hard day's work. His suit jacket, shirt and tie lay where he'd left them in the park in a pool of blood, and his undershirt and suit pants were covered in the same gore. He stood tensely in the waiting room as Fred and Yolanda arrived. Yolanda's face was a mask of concern, but Fred's features had turned to stone.

"Max, que paso? What happened?"

Max took a deep breath and fought back tears. "The bullet went through her left arm. She lost a lot of blood, but it missed all her bones. She'll be fine."

Yolanda exhaled. "Thank God! What happened though? Who shot her? Why?"

Max looked at Fred uneasily. "Fred, you might want to sit down for this."

Fred's blank expression didn't change. "I saw a news report when I was leaving to get Yolanda."

Max's eyes widened. "Oh."

"I'll get the rest of the details later."

Without another word, he turned and headed for the waiting area. He slumped into a seat and put his head in his hands while Max explained things to Yolanda.

"Oh my God. Poor Fred- this must be killing him."

"Yeah, it is. I can see it in his eyes. He just- -shut down."

Yolanda reached into her purse and pulled out her calling card. "Listen, I'm going to call Donna's folks. They should hear this from me instead of from some doctor."

"Good idea. I'll find out when we can see her."

Max found a nurse, who assured him that it would be okay for each of them to visit Donna for a short time, and that she'd let him know when. She also found him a hospital sweatshirt and pants, for which Max was grateful. He changed quickly in the nearest restroom, discarded his bloody T-shirt, and looked around for his friends. Noticing that Yolanda was still on the phone, he folded the pants to be cleaned later and went to sit with Fred, who barely acknowledged his presence. Fred stared vacantly in the direction of the TV set without really seeing it.

"You okay, Fred?"

Fred greeted Max with a faint smile. "Shouldn't I be asking you that?"

"Nah. Donna's doing okay and I only got grazed. You're the one I'm worried about now. Talk to me."

Fred's voice was thick with the emotion he had been trying unsuccessfully to suppress.

"No need for me to say a word- *they* got it all covered."

He pointed to the news telecast, where they updated the shooting story every few minutes with whatever new tidbit of information they could get. Pictures of Merry, Donna, Max, Karl, Taylor, Bryan and now Hemingway flashed across the screen. Only the police officers outside kept the reporters from badgering Max and friends inside the hospital.

Fred gestured out the window at the media throng in the parking lot and cursed. "Look at them, Max. A bunch of vultures picking off her corpse, and she's hardly been dead two hours."

The latest information was that Merry might be connected to both the recent bombing attempt at the Holiday Inn of Portsmouth, VA, and that she'd gotten as far as Richmond, Virginia where she'd had medical treatment before returning to Delaware to finish what she started.

"She never would've told me."

Max turned, startled by Fred's off the wall comment. "She never would've told you what?"

Fred's eyes were empty. "Didn't you hear? She turned up at a clinic in Richmond, where they treated her for a miscarriage. She was *pregnant*, Max. Wanna guess who the father was?"

Max felt like a cold hand grabbed his heart. He started to say something, but the words died in his throat. The look on Fred's face could scare a demon.

"I would've had a kid out there and never even known it. So much for safe sex, huh?"

Tears formed in Fred's eyes. Max put a supportive arm around Fred's shoulder. "Fred, I- -I don't know what to say."

"What is there to say? Merry was a cold, manipulating witch and I fell in love with her. And now she's dead."

A tear rolled down Fred's cheek, closely followed by another. He quickly blotted his eyes, and turned his head.

"Can you beat this? She played me like a saxophone and I'm *crying* over her!"

Max blotted a tear of his own. "There's never any shame in crying for one of God's children."

Just then the nurse came over to Max and let him know that Donna was being moved into a room, and that they could see her soon. Max thanked her and told the others the good news. They took the elevator to the second floor. Yolanda found a seat in the waiting room. Max started to join her, but Fred motioned him in the other direction. Curious, he followed Fred down the hall and into the chapel.

"Okay Max, you've been wanting to do this for years and now you get your chance. Tell me about Jesus."

Max's eyes widened.

"When we talked about Merry just now, you called her one of God's children. Matter of fact, you slip God into every conversation we have. I just started going to church again- I don't get this. Tell me what God can do for me now. And where does Jesus fit into all this?"

Max took a deep breath. "Fred, it says in the book of Revelation that Jesus is the Alpha and the Omega, the Beginning and the End, the First and the Last. He can do anything."

"Oh really? Can He stop me from being all depressed about this? Can He make the pain go away?"

Fred's voice was heavy with pain, and his question, laced with expletives. Nevertheless, his eyes showed more hurt than anger.

"He can, Fred. You just have to let Him."

Fred fixed a steady gaze on Max. "Tell me how."

Max prayed briefly and started talking. Fred listened, interjecting a question here and there.

"So basically you're saying that Jesus is a go-between?"

Max smiled. "That's it. God sent Him to die for us and give us back what we lost when Adam and Eve messed up in the Garden of Eden. He hadn't been revealed on Earth yet, but Jesus was there when it happened."

Max pulled out a small New Testament from his pocket, thanking God he'd grabbed it when he left for work in the morning and then transferred it when he changed clothes.

"This is from John 1:1. *"In the beginning was the Word, and the Word was with God, and the Word was God. He was with God in the beginning. Through Him all things were made; without Him, nothing was made that has been made. In Him was life, and that life was the light of men. The light shines in the darkness, but the darkness has not understood it."*

He closed the Bible. "Jesus is also called the Light of the world, Fred. He came to dispel the darkness of sin and to give us a chance for redemption."

Fred nodded slowly. He felt as though a light bulb was turned on inside of him, allowing him to see things he'd never seen- or wanted to see- before.

Max quoted John 3:16 and 17 from memory for Fred, causing him to laugh.

"That's what's on those signs them jokers at football games keep holding up when they get on camera? I was wondering what that was about."

Max laughed. "They're trying to spread the Word. If one person sees that sign and looks up the verse in the Bible, they just might get a blessing from it."

Fred chuckled. "It sure made me curious, but I was too lazy to find my grandmother's old Bible and look for it."

"If you still have it, dig it out. The Bible is the rulebook for life. Everything we need is in there; all we have to do is learn how to read it and understand it. Donna and I started going to Bible Study on Wednesday nights because some of it is confusing to us."

"Seems like you got it down pat to me."

Max laughed. "I'm glad, because I wouldn't want to mess you up. I can't have you going around believing stuff like, "And Jesus said you have to give Max money for the rest of your life because he's your best friend and he told you how to be saved."

Fred chuckled. "You know, I'm still shaky on just what "getting saved" means. My granddad was a Baptist preacher and he hollered about folks needing to get saved every Sunday, but I never asked just what that means."

Max thought for a moment. "The best way I can describe it is this way; "- - -*if you confess with your mouth "Jesus is Lord," and believe in your heart that God raised Him from the dead, you will be saved."* That's Romans 10:9. Getting saved means accepting Jesus into your heart as your personal Savior."

Fred ingested this latest morsel. "All you have to do is believe.

It's that simple?"

"It's that simple. Jesus acts like a lawyer for us. He's there talking to God like "Remember, I've been there, done that. I know what they go through and it's not easy. You know, I died for them! Cut them some slack." There's nothing we can do that's so bad Jesus won't forgive us if we sincerely ask."

Fred mentally digested all that Max had told him. "Do a lot of Christians come with baggage like mine?"

Max smiled. "Most of us have more. Nobody's born saved, and we lived a good long time before we found out who Jesus is."

"You mean it's ex-junkies and pimps and hoes all up in church?"

"And ex-gang-bangers and drug dealers and alcoholics too. Jesus saved us all just the same."

Fred thought some more. "So, even after all that mess Merry pulled, if she asked Jesus to save her, He would have done it?"

Max smiled. "Definitely."

He did his best to describe the spiritual vision of Merry's salvation that he and Donna and the young policeman saw, and Fred was awed at the sound of it.

"Dag, you were right- anybody *can* get saved." Max smiled. "God doesn't play favorites."

Fred sighed. "This is a lot to think about. Nobody ever broke it down for me like this. If somebody had, maybe I wouldn't have been so hardheaded."

Max chuckled. "Sometimes it takes a lot for God to get your attention."

Fred smiled. "Well, He's got mine now, although a simple "Yo, Fred!" would have done the trick."

"Now that He has your attention, are you ready to take this all the way?"

Fred nodded his head yes. Max grabbed Fred's hands and prayed with him, asking God to consecrate this spiritual transaction. "Do you believe that Jesus is the Son Of God and that He died for our sins and was resurrected from the dead three days later? Do you believe that He sits at God's right hand interceding for us until He comes back for His children?"

Fred nodded yes.

"Then tell Him so. If you want to be saved, ask Jesus to come into your heart, and welcome Him when he does."

Fred did as Max bade him, and without any witnesses but God, Max and a host of angels, Jesus accepted Fred's invitation.

Fred wiped a tear from his eye. "Hey Max, do you think God'll be upset 'cause I cursed earlier?"

Max looked skyward and backed slowly away as if seeing a lightning bolt forming. "No Fred, I don't think so. Hey, stay over there, will you?"

Fred laughed. "Funny."

He walked back towards the waiting area, still sad but a lot lighter in spirit. Max watched him go, feeling good about what had just occurred.

God, You wanted me to tell Fred about You and Jesus, and I did it. Two chances to witness in the same day, and I was able to do it both times.

Just then, a police officer approached, the one who was with him and Donna at Merry's passing.

"Max Carson? I'm Officer Flanagan. Jason Flanagan. Look, uh, I'd like to talk to you. About what I saw--what we saw. I need some help understanding this."

Max smiled. Okay Lord, I hear You. Strike while the iron is hot.

"Sure. There's a lot to talk about."

Officer Flanagan smiled. "Great! By the way, I think these are yours."

He handed Max two boxes. One held a bloodstained white dress shirt, tie and suit jacket. The second was a jewelry box.

The TV news saturated the airwaves with information about Merry and those connected to her. She was now identified at the scene of Lundy Burroughs' murder on top of everything else. Karl and Taylor Tyler-Hurzen remained in critical condition. Bryan Hurzen was now listed as stable, and his fraternity brother Perry Carpenter recuperated at home. The latest news commentary blamed police negligence for letting Merry and Hemingway escape to do their damage.

Merry is dead! Hemingway is dead. Let it rest!

"Mr. Carson? You can go in now."

Max leaped to his feet and barely restrained himself from running into Donna's room. He entered slowly, heart pounding with anticipation. Despite the doctor's report, he needed to see Donna for himself in order to relax.

"Hi."

Hearing her speak that one word made him grin like a child being paid a compliment. "Hi yourself. How you feeling?"

She smiled weakly. Her voice was a ragged whisper, but to Max, it sounded like music. "Tired, sore and glad to be alive."

Max took her uninjured right hand in his and kissed it.

Donna coughed. "Max, every time I look up, I'm thanking you for saving my life."

Max smiled. "God saved you, but I'm glad He used me to do it."

Donna patted his arm. "So modest."

She tried to get comfortable. "Max, do you realize what happened?"

"You mean besides being shot by a crazy woman who used to date Fred?"

Donna chuckled. "Yes, besides that. At the pond."

Max laughed. "We finally found out what that dream was about."

Donna smiled weakly. "Wish I'd been in better shape to enjoy it."

Max laid his hand on top of hers, and they reveled in the fireworks their touch engendered.

Donna thought for a moment before speaking again. "You know, you were- -in the middle of something- - when all the -craziness started."

Max feigned surprise. "We were?"

"We were. And the answer- -is yes."

Max smiled broadly. "What? You mean you still want to marry me?"

"More than ever. I want- -to see what happens next."

Max pulled the ring box out of his pocket.

Ten minutes later, Fred and Yolanda joined them. Donna complained in a hoarse voice.

"I keep telling you guys, I'm fine. My arm hurts and my throat is sore from choking, but this is overkill."

Max gingerly patted her left hand, near the ring Donna insisted he put on her finger.

"I know I can be overprotective at times, but you almost died today. I don't think staying a day or two for observation is "overkill.""

"All I'm gonna do here is rest. I could do that at home!"

Yolanda laughed. "Yeah, but I'm not gonna save you if you choke. Max might love you enough to give you mouth-to-mouth, but you sure won't get that from me!"

They all laughed, but Donna's quickly degenerated into a raspy cough.

Max looked at her. "See? You need to stop complaining and let the doctor pamper you."

Donna rolled her eyes. "Clearly you've never been in the hospital before."

They talked for ten minutes before one of the nurses told them to leave so that Donna could rest. Max immediately went into beg mode.

"Could I have just another minute with her alone, please?"

Nurse Fretter regarded Max warily. "All right, but only because you're her fiancée. She lost a lot of blood and needs to rest."

Donna crossed her eyes behind the nurse's back. Laughing, Fred and Yolanda followed the nurse out of the room, closing the door behind them. The nurse went to see about a different patient while Fred and Yolanda returned to the waiting room.

The latest update was that the police had confirmed Hemingway as one of Merry's blackmail victims, and speculated that he didn't try to kidnap her just to escape, but out of revenge.

"You okay, Fred? You look pale."

Fred worked up a weak grin. "Hey, my grandma was white. I'm supposed to look pale!"

Yolanda laughed, and Fred surprised himself by joining her.

"Seriously though, I'm okay. Well, not really, but I'm getting there. All this hit me at once. It's kind of tough, you know?"

"Yeah, I guess so."

They sat on the generic blue hospital couch to wait for Max. Yolanda looked at Fred, smiled reassuringly and rubbed his back gently. Fred tensed at first and then relaxed in spite of himself.

Fred forced himself to clear his throat and to look Yolanda in the eye. "Yolanda?"

"Yes?"

"Thanks."

She smiled and wrapped him in a warm, friendly hug. They held each other in silent communion while they waited for their mutual friend.

The rest of the day was an exhausting blur. The Carsons arrived first, and the Randall entourage (including Carmen Mason) arrived soon after. After they each had brief visits, Max told them the full story.

Max, Sr. smiled. "You certainly did this the exciting way, son. When I proposed to your mother, all I did was take her to dinner. I don't recall any gunfire."

Corrine Carson smiled. "That's because my father wasn't there."

They all laughed; in the short time they'd known one another, the two families had become one.

Mr. Randall spoke up. "They're keeping Donna overnight for observation. We mean to stay until they release her. Can someone name us a good hotel?"

Max and Yolanda immediately volunteered their apartments, but a withering look from Mrs. Carson stopped them cold.

"You children know good and well we have the most room."

She turned to the group. "We can make you comfortable in our spare rooms. No sense wasting good money on a hotel."

After a slight negotiation, it was agreed that the Carsons would take in the elder Randalls, Max would take Donna's brothers and Yolanda would have her little sister stay with her.

Corrine Carson smiled. "Okay, that's settled. Now, how do we get past all those reporters?"

After a brief conference, they reluctantly stepped outside. An exhausted Max gave a brief statement to the media hordes and stepped away. A group of police officers led by Officer Flanagan formed a cordon and ushered Max, Fred, Yolanda and their families safely through the mass of reporters and cameramen to their cars.

"So, what do you think about a spring wedding?"

Mrs. Randall smiled. They'd all assembled at the Carson house to bond over buckets of KFC chicken, and the engagement was the hot topic of conversation.

"I like it fine Corrine, but it's not my wedding. Donna's hardheaded- if I say it's night, she'll say it's day even with the moon shining in her face!"

Mrs. Carson chuckled and pulled out the small notebook she

always carried. "We have plenty of time to help them make arrangements."

We've been engaged about three hours, Max thought, *and Mom's already trying to hijack the wedding plans.*

As the two families interacted, Fred sneaked looks at Yolanda. Completely at ease with Donna's family, she was laughing at something Roland, Jr. said between bites of a chicken wing.

She didn't laugh or anything when she saw me all tore up. She didn't act like I'm a punk for showing my feelings, and she even did what she could to make me feel better. Didn't think women like that existed.

Fred caught himself staring at her, and quickly looked away and reached for a drumstick before she noticed.

We hang out as friends and all, but I wonder if she'd ever seriously consider going out with a guy like me?

As quickly as the thought entered Fred's mind, he brushed it aside. *Nah. She's been saved a lot longer than I have. She needs a guy more on her level spiritually.*

Unconvinced, he turned his attention back to his food.

Max and the Randall boys didn't get to his apartment until after eleven PM, and it took an hour and a half for them to stop peppering him with questions.

Once the boys finally fell asleep, it didn't take Max long to follow. Max fell through the kaleidoscopic darkness yet again as he searched for the place he'd first dreamed of a lifetime ago.

As it had many times before, the darkness broke, revealing an idyllic glen. Again he smelled pine, heard squirrels and saw butterflies float past. *Found it on the first try,* he thought.

And then he saw her.

Comfortable in her hospital bed, Donna smiled in her sleep as Max strode across the grass to meet her. For whatever reason, they wore the clothes they'd worn to work that day, and both of Donna's arms were whole. She stood up from the park bench to greet his arrival. Max came to her, and their lips met in an ethereal kiss.

BEEEEEEEEEEEEEEEEEEEEEEP!

Max jerked awake suddenly, angry at himself for not turning the alarm clock off before going to sleep last night. He tried to regain the dream, but couldn't go back to sleep.

Donna's probably awake by now too. The vampires have surely been by to draw blood and all.

Oh well, it doesn't matter where she is anymore. I know just where to find her now.

26

Nine Months Later

"And next we have the best man and maid of honor, Fred Bennett and Yolanda Mason!"

Yolanda took a deep breath and linked arms with Fred. *Here we go. Hope I don't trip.*

Despite her nerves, she felt radiant as she and Fred entered the reception hall together and strode to the head table in perfect rhythm, arriving without incident.

"And now, for the first time anywhere, Mr. and Mrs. Max Carson, Jr.!"

The bride and groom entered to thunderous applause.

Fred nudged Yolanda and laughed. "Look at them big Kool-Aid smiles."

Yolanda cracked up as Fred whispered in her ear.

He's right. If they smiled any harder, they'd lock their jaws.

The wedding ceremony went off without a hitch, and as Max and Donna shared their first married kiss, Donna's emotional gift released outward, sharing the love she felt for Max with the entire congregation. Those who had somehow managed to remain dry-eyed during the service groped in pockets and purses for Kleenex.

The whole day has been so beautiful, Yolanda thought. *After all Donna's been through, she deserves this. When I meet my Mr. Right, I hope my day is half as blessed as this.*

Max was pretty much immune to Donna's gift, but it didn't take her emotional prodding to have him near tears from the sheer beauty of the day. Both he and Donna looked like they could burst into tears at any second.

Fred leaned over to whisper in Max's ear. "Don't worry about it, Max. Her family's paying for this!"

Max cracked up. "Thanks Fred. I needed that."

As they enjoyed the meal, Yolanda looked over at Fred, who abused Max as usual. Max laughed as though Bill Cosby, Richard Pryor, and Eddie Murphy were telling him jokes at the same time.

Yolanda smiled. *Fred's a funny man. Nice to know he can still laugh after all he's been through.*

Wonder if he can still date?

The afternoon flew past, and before they knew it, the MC had returned to her post at the microphone.

"Bride and groom, report to the dance floor. It's that time!"

Max laughed and led Donna onto the dance floor for the ceremonial first dance. As the guests aimed their cameras, the DJ played the requested song: Always And Forever.

A perfect choice, Max thought. *That's how long I intend to love Donna.*

"Parents of the bride and groom, join your children!"

The Carsons and the Randalls smiled brightly and did as they were told.

"Okay wedding party, your turn."

Fred made an exaggerated bow to his escort. "Ready to get down, Laquita?"

Yolanda laughed. Fred still loved calling her by any creation he could think of to tease her about her biracial heritage.

"Careful now, don't make me "accidentally" step on your foot. Sharp as these heels are, I might nail your feet to the floor!"

Fred and Yolanda headed for the dance floor, smiling at how eager each of them was for this portion of the reception. Their relationship was an enigma to both of them. For the time being, they'd come to an unspoken friendship agreement.

"Hey Donna, don't trip on your gown! I'd hate to have to laugh at you on your wedding day."

Fred and Max snickered as Donna stuck her tongue out at Yolanda. "Thanks for your underwhelming show of support."

Yolanda laughed and got into the song and her dance partner. His strong hands guided her gently as they danced, sliding slightly downward on her waist in the process.

Uh oh, she thought. *That feels entirely too good.*

"Cuidado con sus manos, si no quieres perder los."

Max overheard and cracked up. Donna looked at him quizzically.

"What did she say?"

Max kept laughing. "Basically, "Move 'em or lose 'em!"

As Fred sheepishly obeyed, the song changed to Luther Vandross' If This World Were Mine. He looked at Yolanda and smiled. "Quieres continuar bailando conmigo?"

Yolanda smiled back. "Por seguro. Of course I want to keep dancing with you."

And they did. They didn't worry about where their relationship might go, but just enjoyed the moment while they had it.

Nearby, Max and Donna swayed contentedly to the music, lost in each other.

"I wish this could last forever. This dance I mean."

Donna looked up into her husband's eyes and sighed contentedly. "I know what you mean. It's like here and now is Heaven right here on Earth."

Max started to reply, but fell silent, awed by the way Donna just put his innermost thoughts into words.

"I love you, Mrs. Carson."

"I love you more, Mr. Carson."

They danced, oblivious to everything around them. They basked in the glow of family and friends, and the joy of knowing that they were together forever.

Epilogue

"I can't believe we're here!"

Max Carson smiled as he came out of the bathroom dressed in a hotel issue robe- his wife of less than twelve hours said just what he thought.

"Considering the fact that we almost got killed twice before you accepted my proposal, I'm with you on that one."

Donna Randall Carson laughed, and the sound was sweet music to Max's ears.

"There's that too. I just can't believe we made it. I half expected something to go wrong; our flight canceled, our hotel reservation revoked- -."

"- - -one of us dream prophetically that we can't take a honeymoon trip after all---."

More mirthful music, followed by a light punch to Max's arm. "Exactly!"

Max devoured Donna with his eyes. In the short time they'd been on Sint Maarten, her caramel skin had absorbed some sun. He smiled as a pleasant thought occurred to him; he no longer had to check himself when admiring her healthy figure.

"I left you plenty of hot water."

Donna winked at him seductively. "I hope that's not the only thing you saved for me."

She disappeared into the bathroom, leaving Max temporarily alone, and awash in anticipation. After their wedding reception yesterday afternoon, they were so exhausted they retired to a hotel near the Philadelphia International Airport and passed out in separate beds, just as they'd discussed. They were up early to catch a flight to Sint Maarten, their home away from home for the next two weeks. Both the commercial flight and the puddle jumper plane to the island were uneventful, and they found themselves settled in their hotel without incident. They'd agreed to not rush to their wedding bed, but to explore the island a bit, to let the day flow naturally and get there when they got there.

We're there now, Max thought, *and I'm so glad we waited. If we'd tried to do anything last night, it would've been a disaster.*

Max put on the red silk pajamas Donna bought for him and waited for his wife. When she emerged from the bathroom wearing the matching teddy, he wasn't disappointed.

"You are beautiful."

Donna ogled her husband; five feet, eight inches of slender chocolate draped in red never looked so good to her.

"Funny- I was about to say that to you."

He chuckled, closed the distance between them, and kissed her tenderly. The kiss deepened and matured; it reminded Max of a similar hotel room experience with Donna what felt like a hundred years ago. As if reading Max's mind, Donna looked up into his eyes.

"This time you don't have to stop."

As Max gently lifted Donna onto the bed, words flowed into his spirit. "It is not good for the man to be alone. I will make a helper suitable for him."(Gen 2:18)

With whispers of love on his lips, Max joined Donna in bed.

He was not alone.

And it was good.

END

Afterword: Writing the Vision

It's hard to believe that this book has been out this long! The first printing was in October of 2000, after a ten-year journey from idea to completion. I thought that initial journey was something, but the one that began with the publication of this book put that one to shame.

When I first started writing this book, I was not saved. I went to church because that's how I was raised, and as such, the first draft of this book was drastically different. It was a love story from the beginning, specifically Max and Donna's love story, and that never changed. When I got this idea, I meant it to be a short story. The phrase "the woman of my dreams" stuck in my mind and then inverted itself to "the dreams of my woman." At that time, I was fascinated by the so-called "mysteries of the mind" and to a small extent, to the occult. In the first draft, Max and Donna were drawn together by a mysterious power, but that power was not of God. I had it where they each found themselves able to draw on more of the potential of their brains than most folks, hence the "psychic" dreams that brought them together. When they saw each other for the first time, they each thought the other looked familiar, which gave me the original title: Familiar. After three years, I had a nice storyline put together and I figured it would sell. And then I got saved.

At some point after I returned home from college in 1990, going to church became less an obligation and more of a pleasure. As this change gradually happened, my way of thinking changed with it. I got rid of all my books that dealt with psychic abilities and all that, but then I had a problem. If I no longer believed in the mysteries of the human mind, then my book had nothing to hold it together.

Reading the Word put me back on track. I Corinthians 12 discusses the gifts of the Holy Spirit, and it didn't take me long to figure out that such gifts weren't ended during biblical times, but that God still blesses folks with these gifts to this day and will until He comes back. I realized that all these so-called psychics and those others who claim to have power are basically trying to be like God without having to deal with Jesus. In Paul's second letter to Timothy, Paul touches on this ongoing effort to make an end run around God, referring in Chapter 2 verse 4 to those who do so as "Having a form of godliness, but denying the power thereof."

Armed with this revelation, I had to literally rewrite my manuscript. That actually wasn't such a bad thing- I'd had it reviewed by professionals and to a man, they told me it stunk! They were right- at the time, I didn't have the writing skills to do more than tell a one-dimensional story. There was no diversity of plot: Merry, Fred, Karl, Taylor and Roscoe Hemingway were not in Familiar and Yolanda was all but nonexistent. I learned that I had a good story, but I needed more in order to transform it into a novel.

Starting in 1994, I took the criticism and went back to work. By 1997, I had completed the revised version with a new title, The Mystery Of These Blessings. I thought I had it this time, but I was wrong. Publishers still didn't want it, and upon closer review of their criticisms, I was still off track. You can't write Christian fiction from a worldly perspective, and despite having accepted Christ as my Savior, I was still not writing like I had. At that point I did what I should have done all along and asked God to show me what was missing.

I attended the Sandy Cove Christian Writers Conference in North East, MD in the fall of 1998, and again in 1999. At those conferences, I learned a lot about how to write more effectively, how to spot the flaws in my work and many other lessons that I desperately needed to learn. I was almost there, but there was a final piece to the puzzle still missing, and I asked God to show me what it was.

Not long afterwards, I got the answer in my church's Bible Study (Bethel African Methodist Episcopal Church, Wilmington, DE). We were studying Luke, and near the end of Chapter 12, I got the revelation I was looking for, in verses 47 and 48. "And that servant which knew his lord's will, and prepared not himself, neither did according to his will, shall be beaten with many stripes. But he that knew not, and did commit things worthy of stripes, shall be beaten with few stripes. For unto whomsoever much is given, of him shall be much required: and to whom men have committed much of him they will ask the more."

In the NIV version of the Bible, the aforementioned passage reads "- - -To whom much is given, much is required." That gave me the right title for this book, To Whom Much Is Given. When I considered the notion of the responsibility that God gives us in various ways, then I had the missing piece to get the book to where God wanted it. At first I was hesitant to take the book there. I was thinking of the concept of Christians having dreams and visions sent by God as something that didn't happen any more. Ironically enough, a pair of Old Testament scriptures helped me see clearly the direction for a modern day story. The prophet Joel (Joel 2:28-29) spoke of times he would never see, but that he knew would come. "And it shall come to pass afterward, that I will pour out my spirit upon all flesh; and your sons and your daughters shall prophesy, your old men shall dream dreams and your young men shall see visions. And also upon the servants and upon the handmaids in those days will I pour out my spirit."

Finally, I was introduced to the prophet Habakkuk through a song I learned as a member of the Bethel Voices Of Light gospel choir. The song, Write The Vision, was based on Habakkuk Chapter 2 verses 1-3.

"I will stand upon my watch, and set me upon the tower, and will watch to see what he will say unto me, and what I shall answer when I am reproved. And the Lord answered me and said "Write the vision, and make it plain upon tables, that he may run that readeth it. For the vision is yet for an appointed time, but at the end it shall speak, and not lie: though it tarry, wait for it; because it will surely come, it will not tarry."

That's all I needed to read. I was wondering if all the sweeping changes I was considering for the book were necessary, but God gave them to me, and my job is indeed to "write the vision." I did what I was told, and the result is this book which you just finished reading (unless of course you cheated and skipped to the back!). If you enjoyed it, let me know. If you didn't enjoy it, let me know that too!

Maurice M. Gray, Jr.
Box 13083
Wilmington, DE 19850

writevision2000@yahoo.com
www.writethevision.biz

To Whom Much Is Given Discussion Questions

1) Max and Donna each have to balance their desire for "normal" lives with the responsibilities their spiritual gifts bring. How does this help or hinder them as the story progresses?

2) Merry harbors lots of anger from her childhood and uses it to justify her present goals. Do you think she has legitimate reasons to be angry?

3) Max's best friend Fred isn't saved, yet he and Max get along well. Do you think the scripture that urges us to not be unevenly yoked with unbelievers should preclude such friendships?

4) Yolanda has been Donna's best friend and support system for years. How important is this level of friendship with a fellow believer for us as Christians?

5) Max is really nervous about his first date with Donna, whereas Fred is supremely confident at meeting Merry. How do their relationships compare and/or contrast?

6) When Max and Donna faced the gunmen in the Bennigan's parking lot, could they have handled the situation any differently? Should they have?

7) Roscoe Hemingway's obsession with Merry ultimately became his downfall. Who is more to blame for his becoming her stalker- him or her?

8) Neither Fred nor Merry ever had a real relationship before they got together. What could they have done differently in order to make it work? Could Fred have remained in the relationship after learning Merry's secrets if given the chance?

9) Yolanda and Fred had a volatile introduction. Their becoming friends helped both of them grow spiritually. Did it make sense for them to become friends or did it seem contrived?

10) When Max and Donna felt led to go to Virginia to stop Merry's plan, they had to share a hotel room due to financial constraints. Given their strong mutual attraction, should they have tried harder to find a way to afford separate rooms? How well do you think they handled it when temptation came their way?

11) Merry was ready to kill Hemingway in cold blood when he broke into her house and attacked her. Should she have done so or did she handle things the right way?

12) Merry's lack of relationship with her father Karl was a major reason why she was so angry and bitter. Do you think her former friend Taylor married him for love, to get revenge on Merry for thrashing her in college or a combination of the two?

13) Hemingway forced Merry's hand by revealing some of her secrets at just the right time. If he'd not done so, would she and Fred have stayed together?

14) Max was petrified at the prospect of meeting Donna's family. How did their reaction to meeting him help or hinder the progression of their relationship?

15) Merry used "Lundy" Burroughs' obsession with her to get him to go after Max and Donna on her behalf. If she'd left them alone, would she have been able to avoid any of the trouble that ultimately befell her?

16) Max resorted to violence on three different occasions (the robbery attempt, Hemingway in the hotel room and Lundy at the picnic park). Was it justified each time or were there other options available to him?

17) Merry was forced to go on the run after Hemingway cooperated with the police, and suffered a miscarriage as a result. Did this push Merry over the edge or was she already there?

18) What, if any, effect did Dr. Errell's obvious affection for Merry have on her recovery?

19) Merry's final rampage led to her death. How could the rampage and/or her death have been avoided? Did you expect that Merry would in fact die or expect her to survive?

20) Both Merry and Fred gave their lives to Christ as a result of her actions. Were their salvation experiences believable or did they seem contrived or rushed?

BLESSED ASSURANCE

This anthology features six diverse authors bringing the Bible to life in a unique way. Each author took an account from the Bible and brought it to life in a modern context.

Maurice M. Gray, Jr. (parable of the Good Samaritan)- Traveling Mercies

Patricia Haley (Abraham and Sarah)- Baby Blues
Terrance Johnson- (Jepthah)- Sword Of The Lord

Victoria Christopher Murray (Hannah)- The Best Of Everything

Jacquelin Thomas (Tamar, daughter of David)- A Sprig Of Hope

S. James Guitard (Samson And Delilah)- Lust And Lies
There are no copies of this book currently in stock at Write The Vision. You may purchase this book at www.amazon.com or www.bn.com

ALL THINGS WORK TOGETHER

Sequel to To Whom Much Is Given

As Fred Bennett transitions from player to prayer, his heart leans towards his friend Yolanda. Unfortunately, so does that of Child Recovery Specialist Raoul Carizales. He is determined to win Yolanda's heart, especially if it means humiliating Fred in the process.

Fred, Yolanda, their newlywed best friends Max and Donna Carson, Raoul and Dr. Randy Errell are confronted with trials that seem beyond their ability to cope. God's presence in their lives or the lack thereof will make or break their situations.

THE SOUL OF A MAN

Short story: Long Term by Maurice Gray

After a season of sowing his wild oats, Nate Carter is a changed man. He's turned his life over to God, but that doesn't exempt him from the consequences of his past. Nate is challenged when a former conquest comes to work for him and wants to pick up where they left off. The man he is now struggles with the man he was. Who will win? God knows.

HOME AGAIN

"Home Again is a compelling journey into the relationships that matter most: family, friends and self. Each story is founded on natural love, but will require the Father's love to heal the brokenness. Travel with husbands and wives, brothers, sisters, friends and families as they maneuver through life's hurts and betrayals while leaning on a power greater than themselves."

Wanda' Campbell's "friends" include Dr. Linda F. Beed, Pastor Bernard Boulton, Tavares Carney, Shenette Jones, Tyora Moody, Dijorn Moss, Trinea Moss and Maurice M. Gray, Jr.. You can learn more at www.writethevision.biz or at www.micah68books.com. Home Again is now available at a bookstore near you.

Family Matters by Maurice M. Gray, Jr.

Erik Dawson and his mother Charlotte "CC" Dawson are barely on speaking terms after an argument, but when tragedy strikes, both of them must do some soul-searching to get to the root of their estrangement.

SOLDIERS OF THE CROSS

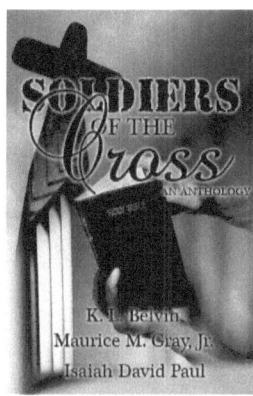

In this groundbreaking anthology, three ministers take three nontraditional ways to convert sinners into believers.

In "Lukewarm Saint" by K. L. Belvin, an educator battles two loves only to find he can't serve two masters and must choose between the Lord or lust. Next in "Called Outside The Lines" by Maurice M. Gray, Jr., a pastor who can ball on the court at an NBA level must decide whether taking a high office truly is his calling or just a temptation to elevate himself for personal gain. Finally in "Follow the Leader" by Isaiah David Paul, a minister who used to lead a life of crime must help two new converts stay on the path of righteousness before all three of them stray by the wayside.

There are many ways to the cross, and these Soldiers of the Cross are leading the way

BUSINESS UNUSUAL / HER GIFTS

By Dr. Linda Beed

Business Unusual
Bernadette Lewis' journey towards fulfilling her purpose faces several obstacles that she must overcome. Determined to have what she believes is rightfully hers, Bernadette sets off on a path of destruction. Shrapnel from the explosive decisions she entertains has the potential to block, detour and/or destroy not only her purpose but also that of future generations.

Her Gifts
Treva Scott has dealt with the demons of her past and is ready to move ahead with plans that will transition her from employee to business owner. If everything goes as she hopes, she'll soon receive the gift she's prayed for.

Brian Chin can't envision his future without Treva in it. Believing her to be his soul-mate, he has dedicated himself to praying for her and loving her the way she deserves in order to help her overcome the insecurities of her past. Looking toward the future, he feels that there's nothing that can take them backwards—or is there? When current circumstances become painfully reminiscent of the past,

Treva is forced to answer her own hard question—Can I live without him?

Business Unusual and Her Gifts are available wherever books are sold. For more information, go to www.lindabeed.com.

COMING SOON

Jeremiah McAllister lost his entire family before he turned eighteen, but was blessed with another one. As the oldest of more than a dozen young adults mentored by CC and Thurman Dawson, Jeremiah takes his role as leader within their chosen family seriously. To his siblings, he is confidante, emergency contact, babysitter and family ATM. However, some among them push his largesse to its limits.

Jenisse Anderson is perhaps the worst offender. Despite Jeremiah's consistently being there for her, she will neither reciprocate nor discuss his feelings for her, or even deal with the issues of her past.

Erik Dawson (CC and Thurman's only biological child) is currently estranged from his parents, and uses Jeremiah as a go-between for indirect communication. Jeremiah's repeated pleas for Erik to reconcile with his parents fall on deaf ears. Between Jenisse and Erik and the constant demands of the others, Jeremiah is pulled in too many different directions all at once.

As he reaches his breaking point, Jeremiah finds himself at a crossroads in his life. How can he break out of an emotional prison he didn't even realize he was in until recently? Can he face his own history in order to embrace a better future?

www.ingramcontent.com/pod-product-compliance
Lightning Source LLC
LaVergne TN
LVHW091532060526
838200LV00036B/575